Ride the Wind

By

Janelle Clawson

Fablespinner
Books

U.S.A.

Ride the Wind

ISBN: 13:978-0692231326

ISBN: 10:0692231323

Fablespinner
Books

For information visit
Fablespinnerbooks.blogspot.com

Printed by CreateSpace in the U.S.A.

Acknowledgements

RIDE THE WIND was edited and proofread by: Cherri Williams, Terry Ward, and Robin Wilson.

Thank you so much for your time and input. Each of you has added to the quality of this book.

For my sister, Cherri Williams
Thank you for your help, enthusiasm, constant encouragement,
and especially for wanting another story.

Ride

the

Wind

Prologue

August, 1937

JESSIE GARRISON WIPED HER HANDS on the front of her damp apron, exhaling relief. The mounds of dinner dishes were finally finished. She searched for a dry spot on her apron, found one on the lower edge, and used it to mop the perspiration from her brow.

"Don't expect me at the campfire tonight," she said to her sister-in-law, Hadlee, and slipped out of the tent through a side-flap before Hadlee could reply. Then as inconspicuously as she could, she skirted the side of the long tent and slipped behind it.

Her romance with Sky Brannigan had incurred a lot of good-natured teasing and too much speculation. The eyes and tongues that ceaselessly followed them had become especially intrusive over the past week. *I've got to find a way to avoid all the busybodies tonight.*

She glanced over her shoulder and reflected that her summer job as a cook in her brother, Ryder's, construction camp was almost over. In less than two weeks she would be free of the camp's wagging tongues. School was about to start again, and although she was looking forward to continuing her education, she groaned. *Being separated from Sky is going to be so hard.*

Massaging her aching shoulders and stretching her neck, Jessie crept through the dense shadows behind the construction crew's tents in the meadow where B. Robert Tulliver, a Texas oil tycoon, would soon start to build his newest mansion.

Ryder and his crew had finished the bridge over the Lake Fork of the Gunnison River—giving the Black Gold Ranch access to the county road—ahead of schedule. The road leading into the meadow was almost finished too. *The Tulliver's now have easy access to Lake City. One of the prettiest little towns in Colorado,* Jessie mused as she reached the edge of the camp and stopped.

The sun had already disappeared behind the mountains. Twilight was only a few minutes away. She frowned at the sky as though she could hold off the coming darkness and pushed back the stray curls that had escaped her ponytail. *Where are you Sky? I didn't think you were so angry with me that you would skip breakfast and dinner just to avoid me.*

Her relationship with Sky had gotten off to a rocky start, and for a few months after they met she hadn't been sure she wanted to give him the chance to court her. But then Sky surprised her and signed on as a member of Ryder's crew, although construction wasn't Sky's kind of work. He'd given up his usual summer job, as a pilot with his father's airfreight company in Utah, to haul and dig, toil and sweat. His willingness to sacrifice an easy job just to be near her had softened her heart, and their relationship had grown. All through the late spring and summer it blossomed—until a few days ago.

Jessie scanned the meadow for any sign of Sky. Guilt punished her with the hurt she knew he felt over her refusal to marry him before the school year started. Still, her guilt couldn't diminish her certainty. She knew if they married so soon, she would lose the opportunity to complete her education and become a teacher—something her heart kept telling her she needed to do.

Sky honestly didn't understand that she could love him and still not want to marry him right away. Or that she wanted him to finish school at Brigham Young University, in Utah, where he'd started, while she attended Mesa State College in Colorado, where she'd started. She needed another year there to get her Associate's degree. Then she intended to finish her Bachelor's degree at the University of Colorado. *I can't give in on this Sky. I have to take things slow. I need to know you see me, not the Amazon.*

She'd gone by the name "Amazon" during the year she lived in New York and worked as a model. The Amazon had taken the world of high fashion modeling by storm. That year taught her she could melt men's hearts with just her smile. It also taught her that all men saw in the Amazon, and were interested in, was what was on the outside. It didn't take her long to realize that the Amazon wasn't who she was or how she wanted to be seen.

She left the Amazon's life behind, but couldn't leave behind the way men looked at her. That never seemed to change. Whether she was wearing an evening gown and drenched in diamonds for a photo shoot or standing in her ranch boots ankle deep in manure. All men seemed to see in her was the Amazon.

Occasionally, Sky looked at her as if she was still the Amazon too, and that troubled her. *I have to be sure the love you feel is for me, Sky, not for the Amazon. Until I know you truly see me, I can't be sure your love is deep enough and strong enough to weather the mistake the Amazon made. I can't tell you what she did until I'm sure it's only me you see, me you love, and we can't marry until you know what she did.*

The last glimmer of daylight was fading when she finally saw him coming across the alpine meadow. She looked back at the center of the camp where the men were already piling logs into the fire pit for the nightly campfire, tugged off her apron, tossed it onto a workbench, and went to meet Sky in the growing twilight. She stopped beside the only cluster of trees the meadow held and waited.

He came to her with a dirty face, his clothes stained with the sweat and labor of the day. In his hand he held a delicate bouquet of wildflowers.

They stood still for a long moment just gazing at each other. His pained expression tore at her. She looked away and broke the uneasy silence. "You didn't come for breakfast or dinner. Did you eat the lunch we sent out for the crew?"

He looked down at the flowers and then back at her. "No. I was fasting."

She took a step toward him. "About?"

"Everything we have been arguing over."

He extended a dirty hand, she put her dishpan one into his, and he led her into the privacy of the trees.

When they were hidden from the camp, he lifted their clasped hands and kissed her fingers. "Jess, I know you love me and want a life with me. I love you too and want the same thing. So I don't understand why we can't just get married now or why you think we need to finish our degrees in different states."

"Sky I—"

He dropped her hand and pressed a grimy finger to her lips. "But that doesn't matter. If what you need is more time to be sure of me—of us—then you've got it."

He handed her the bouquet. She buried her nose in the flowers that smelled of sunshine and watered them with a tear. "Thank you for trying to understand how important getting my teaching degree is to me, and for these beautiful flowers."

"They're meant to tell you that I'm sorry for getting angry, and—although I don't understand why we have to be apart while we finish school—I'm willing to do what you want."

She ran gentle fingers down his sweat-streaked face, looking earnestly into his eyes. "Do you have any idea how distracting you are to me? When you're near me, I can hardly think. So how will I ever be able to study? You have a head start on me in school, and since I intend to graduate at the same time you do, I need all my attention to be on my studies. The course load I'll have to take every semester is going to be enormous. My chances of graduating at the same time you do will be much better if you aren't a constant distraction."

"But that's not the only reason, is it?"

"No," she whispered, hugging her flowers.

"You still think I see you as the Amazon. Well—at times—maybe I do. But more and more, I just see a cowgirl I'm out of my mind in love with." His arms came around her, crushing the bouquet between them as he leaned down and kissed her, expressing all the frustration and longing he felt.

She looped an arm around his neck and kissed him back; trying to reassure him of her feelings and tell him how grateful she was for his patience with something he didn't understand.

When he lifted his head, she tried one more time to explain how she felt. "I know it's hard for you to appreciate, but I really believe that if you're ever going to truly *see* me, then you need to be detached from *seeing* me."

He groaned his frustration. "You're right. It's hard, and you can't expect me to appreciate being kept at a distance. But I want happily ever after with you so badly that I'm willing to do whatever it takes to convince you that it's *you* I adore, not the Amazon. I'm going to prove to you that my love for you is patient, enduring, and everlasting."

Jessie pressed her lips together and took a shaky breath. "Thank you for giving me this time. I can't tell you what it means to me."

"I'm not exactly giving it *willingly*, honey, and I'd be less than honest if I didn't tell you—I'm scared."

"Of what?"

"Losing you to some other guy who can sit beside you in class and pass love notes to you. Or stop by your apartment whenever he takes a notion to and shower you with gifts and sweet talk, while I'm hundreds of miles away—unable to protect my interests."

"I won't have the time, and certainly not the interest, for anyone or anything but my studies. Besides, I intend to write you every day."

"You'd better." He pulled her against him. "I expect lots of phone calls, and there are going to be visits too."

"I'm sure we can arrange to see each other during the holidays and in the summer. I'll come to Salt Lake after Christmas for a couple of weeks, and you can come to the ranch during the summer. Cliff Springs always has an extra bed. And I promise, even being at different colleges, in different states, won't hurt us. It will only strengthen the love that's growing between us, because through our letters we'll be able to really see each other without any physical infatuation to muddy the waters."

"I like the water muddy," he said, and kissed her.

THE UNIVERSITY OF COLORADO'S CLASS OF 1940 threw their caps into the air, hugged each other, and shouted their triumph.

Their families hurried to embrace the new graduates. Sky was the first one to reach Jessie. He picked her up, twirled her around, and kissed her soundly, before they were overwhelmed by her family.

Hours later, Sky looked at his watch. *How much longer will it be before they all leave?* The family celebration following Jessie's graduation seemed endless. *Haven't I endured patiently for long enough? And didn't she promise me we would start planning our future as soon as she graduated? She did, and she accomplished that goal five hours ago!*

The red velvet box in his pocket felt like a paperweight, then an anvil, and finally an anchor—one he wanted to secure Jessie with, without any further delay.

Another hour crawled by before Jessie finally shut the door to her apartment behind the last of her family and leaned back against it. "It's been such a wonderful day. Hasn't it?"

"Uh-huh, and it's about to get even better." Sky walked into her kitchen, opened the icebox, took out a bouquet of the first spring wildflowers, and brought them to her.

She buried her nose in them and inhaled deeply. "Where did you get these? And how did you manage to smuggle them into my icebox?"

"I nearly had to mortgage my soul to the devil to do it, and the last time I gave you a bouquet of these—if you will remember—I made all the concessions." He favored her with a long-suffering look. "This time *you* are going to make the concessions," he said and kissed her, crushing the bouquet between them.

"This day did just get better." She put her hand on his chest and pushed him back a little. "But don't you dare hurt my flowers. They are the best gift I've received today."

"Not quite." His periwinkle eyes locked with her emerald ones. He took her hand and led her to the sofa. "Sit," he said. "I've been patient for three, miserable, frustrating years, and I'm not willing to be miserable for even one more instant."

Jessie sat on the couch and looked up at him, a small crease growing between her brows.

He dropped to his knees in front of her, tugged the velvet box from his pocket, took the bouquet from her hand and tossed it carelessly onto the lamp table. "It's time for us to stop loving each other only through letters, phone calls, and all too infrequent—and heavily chaperoned—visits. It time for us to stop living apart my adorable Amazon."

She winced on the word.

His brows contracted. "After all this time you know I see so much more in you than the Amazon, but that part of you is *very* enticing." He intentionally looked at her with the soulful appreciation of her beauty that had at first put her off. "I want the right to look at you, be with you, love you, protect you, and make you happy. I want my kids to have your eyes, your hair, your determination, and your spirit. I won't even complain if they get your stubborn, opinionated ways. I love you and want you to be mine forever. Will you?"

"Sky, I don't know if I will ever be able to tell you, or show you, how much I love you." She put her hands on his cheeks, leaned forward, and kissed him.

His bones felt like they were on fire. She'd never kissed him quite like that before, and he immediately felt bereaved when she pulled back.

"With all my heart, I want to be your wife," she whispered.

"Is that a yes?"

"Al—most."

His hand stopped short of opening the velvet box. "What do you mean—almost?"

She took the box from his hand, put it on the table, and took a breath. "Before you put your ring on my finger there is something you need to know."

Unexpected dread crawled along Sky's spine. He gave her a crooked smile, thrusting the feeling away. "So what terrible secret have you been keeping that you need to confess before you accept my ring?"

The dread he tried to rid himself of grew with her solemn expression.

"That's just it. I do have a secret I've been keeping from you. One I couldn't share with you until I was sure of your feelings—and sure of mine. I wanted you to see *me*"—she put her hand on her heart—"and know *me*," she said, striking her hand against her heart, "before I told you my secret. You need to understand that I left the Amazon in New York when I quit modeling. She was someone you've never *met*."

"I know that, honey. I know the Amazon was just a part you played because of your job." He smiled adoringly at her, pulling on one of the long auburn curls that danced over her shoulder.

"Yes, and I want you to understand that *I* could never do the things *she* did."

"Just what did the Amazon do that I should know about?" he asked with mounting apprehension.

Jessie tugged on his hand. He rose from his knees and sat beside her. "I've told you how fast I skyrocketed to the top as a model and the success I had."

"I know, and your success taught you that most men just saw you as a prize to dress up their arms. An easy mark because of the way you were portrayed in magazines."

"That's true, but . . . I also ran with a fast and famous crowd of people. People whose lives didn't reflect the gospel values I was taught. I found it hard to always ward off the temptations they plied me with."

"Just what temptations did they *ply* you with?"

"The usual things, you know, alcohol, tobacco, drugs, and—sex."

"Are you telling me you gave into those temptations?"

"Not all of them," she said quickly.

"Just which ones did you give in to?"

Jessie looked out the window, drawing Sky's attention to the quiet spring evening full of budding new life.

"I—I met a man about nine months into my modeling contract." Jessie's voice wavered like the gentle breeze ruffling the leaves on the trees.

The dread Sky felt became cold premonition, and he suddenly didn't want her to continue, but he heard himself ask, "Who was he?"

"That doesn't matter." She waved away his question. "What I need to tell you is, he—he was always trying to get me to lower my standards, especially about alcohol. She gazed down at their hands, clasped in her lap. "I resisted, but eventually I gave in and tried a little wine. I didn't like it and, most of the time, when we went to parties I just held a glass of it and didn't ever drink it."

"All right, so you drank a little alcohol. I can understand how that might happen." Sky felt a little surge of relief.

"That's not all of it." Her fingers tightened around his. "I finally saw that this man I thought I admired, and had been dating, was just using me to build up his ego and dress up his arm. I decided to break up with him. He invited me to a party at his apartment. I went with the intention of ending our relationship after the party was over."

"Good!"

"Yes, but I was afraid of doing it because he was a bit of a hot head. So, when I got to the party and he handed me a drink, I—I downed it before I even took a sip. It wasn't wine. It was hard liquor."

Sky's hand reflectively gripped hers harder. "So you had one glass of liquor."

"I thought that was all I had . . . but I"—she flushed— "must have had more."

"You got drunk?" Sky abruptly let go of her hand.

"I—I must have, because I woke up . . . the next morning—" She swallowed and whispered, "In his . . . bed."

Sky jumped up and stared down at her, talons of disillusion tearing into him. "Tell me he put you there to let you sleep off the booze, and that he wasn't in that bed with you!"

Jessie hung her head and bit her lip.

"Look at me, and tell me you didn't let him *use* you."

Her eyes came up, slowly. The guilt in them, hit him like a sledgehammer, shattering a dream he'd nurtured since he was a child.

"I don't remember *anything* about that night or . . . or being with him."

"Oh, that makes me feel so much better!" He raked his hand through his pale blond hair. "For three years you've led me to believe that all the men who ogled you, during your modeling career, misjudged you. Now you're telling me you're every bit the Amazon they thought you were."

"No!" She jumped up. "I am not the Amazon, and I haven't been, for longer than you've known me! I repented of what I did, and I am just as worthy as you are!"

"Just not innocent anymore!"

Her chin trembled. "No . . . not . . . innocent."

He glared down at her. "All my life I've believed there was a one and only for me. I believed when I found her she would be someone who had waited for me and prayed to find me—just as I had prayed to find her. Someone who had kept herself clean for me." He clenched his fists as the painful claws of disillusion ripped apart his dream and tore into his heart. "The day I met you, I truly believed I'd finally found my dream."

"I'm sorry . . . I'm so sorry for what I did. But surely the past three years of letting our hearts grow together until we're now a part of each other means more to you than a childhood expectation? I know you *love* me. Please—don't let something that happened before we ever met come between us. What the Amazon did doesn't have anything to do with us."

"Then why did you feel the need to tell me about it?"

"Because I wanted to be completely honest with you and because. . . I didn't want you to find out—"

"On our wedding night. How very considerate of you," he said, sarcasm dripping from each word.

"Sky—" She took hold of his hand, shaking and struggling to stem her tears. "I know what I did doesn't fit into your ideal, but I can't believe this one mistake has the power to destroy everything we feel for each other. You've told me, over and over, that I'm everything you hoped to find. And you are everything I hoped to find. I love you so deeply. You *are* my one and only."

"Oh that's rich, considering you've already been with another guy." He shook off her hand and backed away. "I need time to think about this," he said, turned, and slammed out the door.

He walked the streets until dawn, consumed by her betrayal, letting anger grow into disgust, and then loathing. *She deceived me. Right from the very start, she deceived me.* He wouldn't even have considered courting her if she'd told him the truth right up front, but she hadn't. Instead, she'd counted on his love to make him compromise on his ideal, let go of what he had a right to expect—that the woman he married would be as clean as he was, as innocent.

Too disgusted by her deceit to ever want to see her again, he went to his hotel, packed his things, and boarded a train.

He was in Kansas City before he realized he was headed east instead of west. He decided it was a fortunate mistake.

The island

of

Toolowa

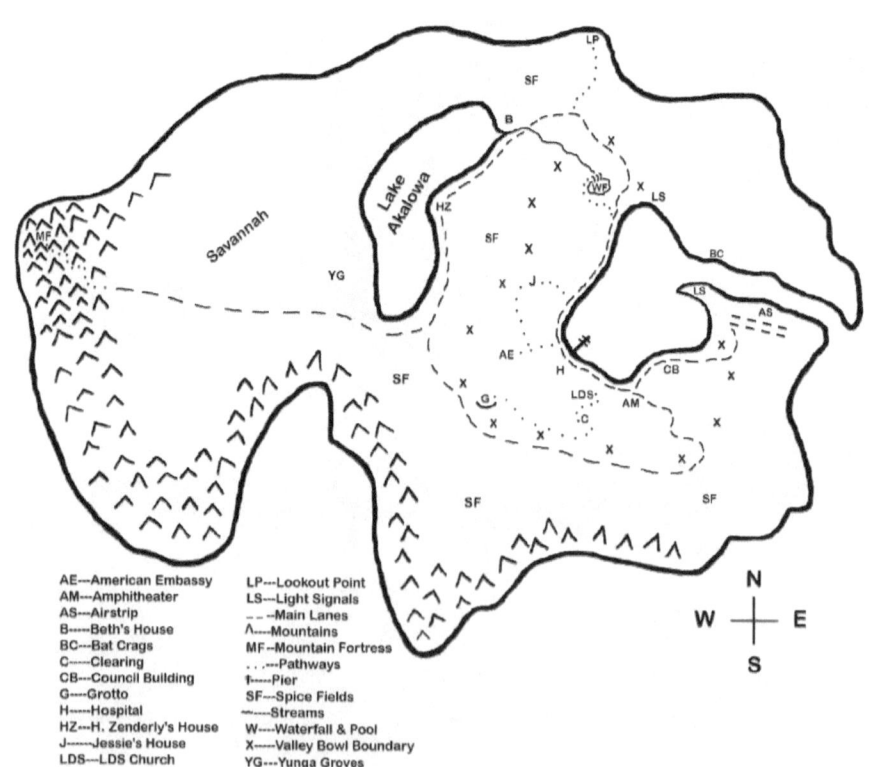

AE---American Embassy
AM---Amphitheater
AS---Airstrip
B-----Beth's House
BC---Bat Crags
C-----Clearing
CB----Council Building
G-----Grotto
H-----Hospital
HZ----H. Zenderly's House
J------Jessie's House
LDS---LDS Church

LP---Lookout Point
LS---Light Signals
-- - --Main Lanes
∧-----Mountains
MF--Mountain Fortress
. . .---Pathways
†-----Pier
SF--Spice Fields
~----Streams
W----Waterfall & Pool
X-----Valley Bowl Boundary
YG---Yunga Groves

1

December, 1944

A DISTANT DRONING WOKE JESSIE. Her brow wrinkled. She was sure she hadn't been asleep for more than a few minutes, and she was reluctant to relinquish that lovely state so soon. With a murmur of annoyance, she adjusted the palm frond hat that covered her face and focused on the gentle swaying of the small canoe, trying to let it rock her back to sleep.

It felt heavenly to be out on the bay away from everything, and everyone. After a refreshing swim, and a little snorkeling, she'd stretched out in the bottom of her canoe and let herself float on a current of utter relaxation. With the sun to dry her and the breeze to keep her from overheating, she'd wrapped herself in contentment and gone to sleep. She was at peace with herself, and the world—even if *it* wasn't at peace.

There had been a time when she'd thought peace was a feeling she would never know. That longed for condition hadn't come easily. It hadn't even come from the direction she'd thought it would—something that still surprised her—but it had come. In slow, small, hard won increments, it had grown from an impossible dream into a yearning hope and finally a satisfying reality.

She sighed and repositioned herself in the bottom of the canoe. The thunderstorm that had rolled in just before noon had almost spoiled her well-deserved afternoon of self-indulgence. One she certainly deserved, now that the school year was finished.

Her lips curved up. She was almost as excited about the annual planting and Christmas break as her students were. They were all free for two glorious months. Well, that wasn't quite true in her case. Her list of things that simply had to be accomplished during this vacation seemed endless, but today she wasn't going to think about a single item on that list.

The droning she was trying to ignore grew louder, the sound more obnoxious. It pulled her mouth into a frown under her hat, and it occurred to her that there was something wrong with it. Not only shouldn't it have been there at all, because no supply plane was due, but it also shouldn't have that growling, uneven tone. She pulled off her hat, squinted up at the cloudless sky, and saw— nothing.

The sound grew louder, more uneven, almost sputtering now. She sat up, put the hat on the back of her head and peered out from under its broad brim, searching the sky in earnest.

A dark blotch, followed by a white tail, was making its way down the channel, heading for the mouth of the bay.

Her heart did a hard once over and stalled as the plane came into focus. *It's too low, and dropping!* She knew with chilling certainty, the plane wasn't going to make it to the landing strip that sat on the plateau above the south side of the bay. *Is that why it's coming down the channel?*

It was close enough now for her to just make out the white star of an American plane emblazoned on its body and wing. That brought her a moment of relief. *At least it isn't a Japanese plane. But what is it doing here?*

The war that raged throughout the South Pacific and Southeast Asia had moved closer, consuming the Dutch East Indies. Java and Sumatra were now held by the enemy. Like everyone on Toolowa, she listened to the war news on the one shortwave radio the island possessed, but felt in no danger. Sitting a thousand miles off the western coast of Australia, on the tropic of Capricorn, in the southern Indian Ocean, Toolowa was too remote to be of any value to the Japanese.

As it came closer, the plane seemed to fill the width of the narrow channel that led into the bay. She decided its wingspan was definitely wider than a fighter plane's. Its body was much bigger too. It began to lurch, as though it would stall out.

She gasped as the western sun illuminated the reason for the planes lurching progress. The white tail following the plane wasn't vapor—it was smoke. It billowed out of one of the propellers. Her attention flew to the other propeller. That one wasn't turning at all. In fact, it was blackened as though it had been on fire. Nevertheless, on that one smoking propeller the plane continued its sputtering advanced.

Intent on watching the plane's progress, she sat motionless in the canoe, coaching it. "Come on, come on." She willed it on until the abrupt realization hit her, and the bottom dropped out of her stomach.

It was coming straight at her.

She glanced back, shocked to find her canoe had drifted out of the mouth of the bay on the tide and into the throat of the long, narrow channel that led to the open sea. *Obviously, I slept longer than I thought.*

The plane was within seventy yards of her, and dropping fast. She couldn't out run it and escape back into the bay. All she could do was try to get out of its path. Four years on the tropical island of Toolowa had taught her how to handle a canoe. She grabbed her paddle, plunged it into the water and dug deep.

Adrenaline powered each stroke, but she was still doubtful of escaping. The thought of being underneath that monster when it hit the water spurred her on. Without a doubt, she knew it was going to crash into the sea. The only question left was whether it would go down into the four hundred foot depths of the channel or make it into the bay and go down onto the much shallower bay shelf.

Even as she paddled for her life, heading for the sheer wall of the channel, she admired the pilot's skill. He was holding the plane's nose up. If he could set it down on the water without it plunging in nose first, he might escape with his life. At least he would have a better chance.

The plane's wing overshadowed her. She dove into the bottom of the canoe and covered her head. The coughing engine blasted her ears. The canoe bounced on a wake of water kicked up by the turbulent air beneath the plane's wing. With a shrieking fury that whipped her long auburn braid into the air, it hurdled passed her. She jerked upright, thrust her paddle into the sea, and made her light canoe fly toward the mouth of the bay.

She cheered when the plane made it past the deep, dark blue water of the channel and into the shallower aqua water of the bay. The smoking engine burst into flames. Even from behind, she could see them. Abruptly the plane nose-dived. It hit the water with a groaning crash, as though hitting solid ground instead of water, and flipped over.

Huge waves caused by the plane's impact barreled toward her as she reached the mouth of the bay. They hit her like the bucking of a bronco. She rode them out like the experienced broncobuster she was, watching in horror as the sea opened its mouth and started swallowing the plane.

Paddling hard for the sinking plane, she thought about how deep the water was. Most of the bay was between thirty and forty feet deep. However, there was an extensive coral reef that jutted upward just inside the mouth of the bay. It ran from one side of the channel to the other, preventing large ships from entering the bay. If the plane went down on top the reef, the water would only be about twenty feet deep. With the tide going out, it would be even less.

She paddled hard, and prayed.

The bay finished swallowing the plane.

A bell began to ring, wildly. It was the bay's alarm signal.

Jessie looked at the shoreline. Half a dozen big outriggers were being shoved into the water.

She reached the spot where the plane had gone under, jumped to her feet, balanced herself in the center of the canoe, set her snorkeling mask in place, took a tremendous breath, and dove into the sea.

The water was as cool as satin sheets and just as smooth. Her body slid through it even as she was hit by a blast of air bubbles. They momentarily obstructed her view of the bottom, but not her progress. She streaked through them, moving downward.

The sun was still high enough in the western sky to send slanting beams through the pristine water. She had no trouble locating the sinking plane. Just as she'd hoped, the plane collided with the reef, slid down it for a few feet, and stopped before plunging off the reef's lip. It looked like a dead dragonfly laying there on its back, but the plane only held her attention for a few moments.

From beneath the plane, something large and grayish moved up from the bottom, straight at her.

Shark! She pulled up, back peddled, and stopped. Suspended in the water, she peered intently through her mask. If she hadn't been under the water, she would have heaved a breath of relief. *No, not a shark.*

The black haired man was only using one arm, but he was pulling steadily upward, while looking down at the plane. When he was just a few feet beneath her, he looked up, spotted her, and stopped. The burst of bubbles that escape his mouth obscured his face. He went limp. His head sagged onto his chest.

Jessie thrust herself downward, and snagged his arm. Wisps of red colored the water around the arm he hadn't been using.

He's bleeding—not good! He hadn't been a shark, but his blood would attract them.

He was a big man and it took all the strength Jessie could muster to haul him to the surface. His gasping breath as they broke into the air sent elation tingling through her. She pulled him across her body, keeping his back to her in case he panicked, tried to grab her, and took them both under again.

He started to thrash.

"Don't fight me," she said into his ear. "Just relax and I'll get you to the canoe. He went limp again, and she swam the few yards to the canoe, while he took in gulping breaths. When they came along side, she asked; "Can you grab the side of the canoe and hang on?"

"Yes." He latched onto the side with one hand and leaned his head against it, breathing hard. "But . . . have to go . . . back down . . . Major . . . still down."

Behind her, Jessie heard the shouts of the men in the outriggers. A glance told her they were almost there. She didn't wait for them. "Stay put, I'll go after him. And don't worry, help is almost here."

After inhaling and exhaling a few times, she dove back under the water. She propelled herself downward with the grace and confidence of a dolphin, but without much hope. *How long has it been since the plane went under? Too long,* she feared.

Then she saw him, struggling upward in a cloud of red. Outside the cloud, not thirty feet from him a tiger shark was closing in.

She cut through the water with grim determination. If she could make it to him before the shark reached him, the two of them might be enough to make the shark back off, but she couldn't match the speed and agility of the shark.

The man didn't see the tiger shark that was coming at him from behind. He looked up at her through the haze of red that swirled around his head, and like the first man, he just stopped, bubbles escaping his mouth.

No! She sliced through the water, using every ounce of power the muscles in her arms and legs could command.

The shark was almost on him when a dozen bodies, followed by shafts of light, streaked through the water.

The shark veered away.

Two hefty Toolowans grabbed the man by the arms and shot to the surface.

Jessie did the same.

She broke into the air and pushed her mask onto the back of her head, hearing the gagging coughs of the man the Toolowans had pulled to the surface. *At least he's alive. They both are.* "Thank you!" she said to the sky.

Half a dozen hands hauled the man into one of the outriggers. He fell out of sight, into the bottom. Jessie looked at her canoe. It appeared to be empty. *Maybe they got the other man into one of the outriggers too.*

Taking a relieved breath, she swam to her canoe, took hold of the side, pulled herself up, and locked her elbows. The black haired man looked up at her from the bottom of the canoe out of a pair of wide grey eyes. With an involuntary gasp, she recoiled. Her elbows buckled, and she fell back into the sea.

Sure hands and muscled arms pulled her to the surface again. "You've done enough, Jayling," Takoa Zenderly said, his bulky arm encircling her waist.

"Yes." Takoa's younger brother, Lowa agreed, swimming up beside them.

"We will bring the canoe in." Takoa waved at the nearest outrigger.

It pulled alongside. Hands reached out and drew her up. She went without protest, noting the outrigger with the other man was already heading for the shore. She glanced back at the canoe, but the black haired man didn't raise himself above the side.

Takoa and Lowa climbed into the canoe on opposite ends, keeping it balanced. An additional paddle was tossed to Takoa, and he and Lowa began to stroke through the water.

Jessie turned away. Kneeling in the middle of the outrigger, she focused on the shoreline as her mind tried to reject what her eyes insisted she'd seen in the bottom of her canoe.

A cold shiver quaked through her.

It was the first time she could remember shivering since she'd come to live in this tropical climate. As she tried to rub the goose bumps prickling along her arms away, she realized the chill trembling through her didn't come from the breeze that made her braid dance. No, it came straight from her heart.

She felt a dizzying disorientation as though the plane's wing had clipped her head. With shaky fingers, she massaged her temples. *It couldn't be him. What are the odds? It just isn't possible—it just isn't!*

2

JESSIE WAS OUT OF THE OUTRIGGER as soon as the men jumped out to beach it. Already the outrigger that carried the second flyer ashore was surrounded by curious Toolowans. She noticed the crowd included Dr. Snyder, Ambassador and Mrs. Hamilton, and Edmund Zenderly—the chief judge.

Normally she would have been one of the gawkers. Just as eager to learn what had brought these men so unexpectedly to Toolowa, and just as curious about the misfortune that had caused them to crash into the bay. However, after what she'd just seen, the only thing she wanted to do was escape before her own canoe landed.

She needed time to think. If the man in her canoe was who she thought he was, then she didn't want to see him again until she'd decided on how to handle it. Veering away from the growing crowd, she ran up the beach and into the jungle.

Her feet followed the broad bay lane, moving north. At the narrow path that broke off to her home, she stopped. *If I go home, Triny will want to know about everything that's happened, and I don't want to deal with that yet, not until I figure out what I really saw.*

She looked down at herself. Normally she never ran around the island with only her swimsuit on, but her sarong, along with her hat and sandals were still in her canoe. *If I stop—even for a moment to change—I won't be able to get away.*

She didn't really need the sandals. Island life had toughened her feet until she could move across any terrain on the island with ease. She could do without the sun hat too. Staying under the shelter of the bay's canopy of trees would solve that problem. It was the sarong she really missed, but as long as she was alone that didn't matter either—and alone was what she was determined to be.

Trotting by the path to her house, she took the trail that led to the plateau on the north side of the island. The trail climbed sharply up through lush vegetation humming with insects. Her body was brushed by ferns and trailing vines that hung from the jungle's exotic trees and swung over the trail. She ducked, and wove in and out, over and through the vines, ferns, and undergrowth that clogged the trail. Four times a year the trail was cleared, but it never stayed that way for very long, not in Toolowa's tropical climate.

As her feet pressed forward, her mind reached backward, and for a moment, she wished she had a mind like her mother or her brother, Ryder, who possessed perfect recall. There wouldn't be any doubt in her mind if she could remember details like they did. Then again, her brother's memory had been the cause of so much pain and grief in his life that she was thankful her memory wasn't like his. She didn't need any more grief than what was nagging at her right now.

The heat, and her physical exertion, dried her swimsuit before she covered a mile. Her skin prickled with the itch of dried sea salt as she took the path to a small waterfall that fell into a fresh water pool. She pushed on, listening for the sound of the falls over the constant hum of cicadas, bees, dragonflies, and birds.

The melody of water tumbling over rocks reached her. Sure footed as any mountain goat on the island, she hurried toward the sound. Rounding a bend in the path, the falls came into sight. Itchy and hot, she pushed aside the ferns that blocked her path. Climbing the rocks along the edges of pool, she pulled herself upward until she could wade across the top of falls. When she reached the center of the falls, she dove into the ten-foot deep pool, swam beneath the water to the other end and then back to the falls. She rose to the surface and climbed onto a shallow ledge that stuck out a foot beyond the falls, before it dropped into the pool.

Sitting beneath the gentle downpour of the falls, she emptied her mind and let the water wash over her. Its crystal purity cleansed the salt from her body, swimsuit, and hair. Pursing her lips, she drank deeply. After a few minutes, she pulled herself out of nature's shower, clean, refreshed, and calmer. She swam over to the one shallow place in the pool, leaned her head back against a rock, and drew the humid air—she'd become so accustomed to—into her lungs.

So, what did I really see? Well, a very large man sprawled from end to end in the bottom of my seven-foot canoe. "That means he is definitely big enough." She groaned. *And if I add his size to his jet-black hair and gray eyes, what other conclusion is there?*

She smacked the water with her hand, not willing to accept that answer so readily. She ripped a frond from a fern that overhung the pond and shooed away the insects buzzing around her as she tried to wiggle out of her conclusion. *After all, how good a look did I really get of his face in that half a second before my arms gave way and I fell back into the bay.*

She hadn't seen Jake Denning in ten years, and although the man in the boat did resemble Jake—as she remembered him—there were certain things that didn't fit. For one, there hadn't been any indication from him that he recognized her, and she knew, without a doubt, Jake would never forget her. *A man doesn't forget a woman he asked to marry him—twice.*

Nurturing that small seed of doubt, she realized that she hadn't recognized his voice either. Sure, he'd been gasping for air when he'd spoken to her, but wouldn't she have recognized his voice with her perfect auditory memory? That gift gave her perfect pitch and a singing voice so many people praised. It also allowed her to pick up languages as quickly as Ryder did. She could even imitate voices, something Ryder could do too.

Would his voice have changed so much? No. Maybe his gasping for air affected his voice and that's why I didn't recognize it. She had to admit there was that possibility, along with the fact she hadn't been expecting to hear his voice.

Tossing the fern frond aside, she swam back and forth across the pool, forcing herself to listen to that gasping voice again. And there it was—that subtle, but unmistakable, Boston twang. With a whimper of defeat, she sank under the water and swam back to the falls. Again, she sat under them, letting them pour over her in a numbing deluge.

Jake Denning had been the first man to ever make her go weak at the knees or feel flustered when he smiled at her. She'd met him in New York during the year she'd rocketed to the top of the world of high fashion modeling. He was the first man she'd ever thought she was in love with. She spewed water from her mouth. "*Thought*, being the operative word," she gurgled out bitterly through the shower of water.

The need to breathe and think pulled her out of the falls. The shadows were deepening and she needed to get home before dark. Yet she was hesitant to leave until she'd decided on how to deal with Jake Denning. *He is the one man—no—he is one of the two men, I never wanted to see again.*

The inescapable truth that the man in her canoe was Jake Denning tore open more than one old wound. She hadn't seen Jake since the day before her contract to the Elite Modeling Agency had expired. Without a backward glance she'd fled New York for her home on a cattle ranch outside Glenwood Springs Colorado, grateful to shed her modeling persona and be free of a life she'd come to realize didn't suit her.

Jake's sudden appearance felt like a threat to her hard won peace and contentment. *I won't let him rob me of that, I won't. I've worked too long, too hard, to let him steal my happiness and peace by digging up the past. He won't be here very long, so maybe I can just avoid him.*

The image of the dead dragonfly lying at the bottom of the bay brought the inescapable thought that he might be stuck on Toolowa for a month—or longer. Another supply plane might not come for at least a month. It would be even longer before a supply ship came, if one came at all, which was doubtful these days. The war had disrupted the island's normal cargo and merchandise deliveries.

She grudgingly accepted the fact that there wouldn't be any way to avoid him, not for an entire month or longer, on such a small island. *There is simply no way around it. Sooner or later our paths will cross.*

With the sky dimming into twilight, she pulled herself out of the pond and started the three-mile trek back to her house. She had that long to decide how she was going to deal with Jake Denning.

3

JESSIE'S FRONT DOOR OPENED before she reached it. Her housekeeper, Triny, threw it wide and pounced on her. She was in her mid-forties, and a very attractive combination of her mixed ancestry. Her straight black hair, which sported one charming streak of white, along with her petite frame came from her Sumatra heritage. Her deep brown skin came from her Toolowan ancestors, and her vivid blue eyes from her English great grandfather. The details of her heritage were tattooed over her left eyebrow in the artful symbols of the Toolowan language, just as they were on every native Toolowan brow.

A beautiful design of swirls, loops, and geometric patterns arched over her brow, down the outside edge of her eye, wrapped around under her eye, ending precisely a half inch past its outside corner. Each loop, swirl, and geometric pattern was a family name. Chained together they formed a five-generation chart of her ancestors.

Triny danced from foot to foot, brimming with news. Jessie took a breath and steeled herself to endure the onslaught that, once started, might take hours to stop.

"Where's ya been?" Triny's small fists rested on her hips. "I's been waitin hours ta talk at ya. Tilly come un told me bout dose American flyers—once duh doc closed dem up in hospital—she say ya was dere, and even rescued one of um. Is dat true?"

Listening to Triny's English was always a trial. As hard as Jessie had tried, she hadn't been able to break Triny of some of her improper words and speech patterns. After three years of correcting her, Jessie had finally given up. Triny insisted she was just too set in her ways, and since Jessie could understand her, there wasn't any need for her to change.

To spare her ears, Jessie spoke to her in Toolowan knowing Triny would respond in whatever language she was addressed, and Triny's Toolowan wasn't subject to the same painful flaws her English suffered from. "Yes I was there, and yes I pulled one of the flyers to the surface—"

"And you were down going after the other one when the men showed up."

"That's right, and that's all I did."

"Takoa told Tilly, you were swimming after the second one, straight at three tiger sharks!"

Jessie groaned. Already the story was taking on a life of its own. That wasn't uncommon, but she hated to be part of *any* story that was of *any* interest on the island.

Triny was nearly drooling in anticipation of her answer. Even if she told Triny every last detail, by the time Triny ran off to tell everyone what she knew, there would be little truth left to the story. And of course, she would make Jessie out to be the heroine who had saved the day, single-handedly.

Still, Jessie decided the sooner she told Triny everything she was dying to know, the sooner she would go off to tell her news. Then Jessie could have some peace and more time to think—something she still needed. The trek back hadn't been sufficient to solve the problem of Jake Denning.

"There was only one shark." Jessie held up her hand to forestall any argument or questions, closed her fist, raised one finger, and repeated, "*One.*"

Triny's face fell; then brightened. "But if you hadn't been there to pull the first one over to your canoe, before the men arrived in the outriggers, the shark would have gotten at least one of those flyers, because I heard the whole bay was red with their blood."

"Yes, there was a little blood in the water, and, yes, that's probably what drew the shark. And since you seem to know so much about everything that happened, why don't you tell me about the two flyers and their injuries?"

The breath Triny drew made Jessie sorry she'd asked. She'd just yielded the floor to Triny, and it was going to be a filibuster. Before Triny could let loose, Jessie got out the last words she was sure she would get to utter for the next couple of hours. "Since I'm sure you have a great deal to tell me, let's go inside and get comfortable. I really don't want to stand out here on the veranda in my swimsuit and have a long discussion."

Triny gave her a squint-eyed stare as Jessie slid by her into the house, wagged her finger, and switched back to English—the language most commonly used on Toolowa since they had reached out to the world. "Dats another thing, folks been lookin fer ya duh whole afternoon. Why ya run off like dat?" Triny demanded, following Jessie into her bedroom.

Jessie pulled on a Chinese silk robe and slid her feet into a pair of comfortable mules, which her sister, Hannah, had sent to her for her last birthday, and ignored Triny's the question. "I'm starving. Can we continue this discussion while I eat?" she asked going back down the hall and into the living room.

"No we can't, cause ya can't eat nothin. Ya suppose ta be over ta da ambassador's for dinner." Triny looked at the clock. "In just over a hour. Shula come over ta remind ya da best part a two hours ago."

"Oh no." Jessie dropped into a padded rattan chair. She definitely didn't feel up to putting herself together to go anywhere tonight.

"Oh yeah."

Formal dinner parties at the Hamiltons were a monthly affair, and she'd forgotten it was tonight. *But after the events of the day, not to mention the past couple of weeks, Sam and Nora will understand if I simply bow out tonight.*

"Would you mind very much just running over there for me and telling them I'm just too tired to come tonight"— she clasped her hands together—"please?"

Triny stood over her, her hands again bracketing her hips. "I can't do dat. Shula say, ambassador say, da doc done patched up dose flyers and dey be coming ta dinner too, and you's expected. Ambassador thinks dey should meet da gal who saved um."

This information sent a shudder down Jessie's back. She rallied and asked, "So for all the blood that supposedly turned the bay red, neither of them suffered any great injury?"

Triny's eyes danced with what Jessie recognized as the joy of being able to impart some news about the flyers she didn't know.

"Well dah one ya pulled out got a shoulder full of coral dat poked through da canopy of da plane when it hit da reef, and it took da doc and nurse Tena most a two hours ta clean it out. His arm be bandaged up and in a sling."

"I'm glad he wasn't seriously injured, and the other one?" Jessie asked, keeping her expression neutral.

"He got lots a little cuts from da glass crashin in from da canopy when dey hit the water. And"—she gulped a breath, fixed Jessie with a suspenseful eye, and lowered her voice—"he helped get da other man out, den stayed down ta look fer duh pouch of secret papers he come ta give duh ambassador. Dats why he took sa long ta get out of da plane."

Jessie absorbed this information with more than a grain of salt. It was unlikely the flyer would have told anyone if he was carrying secret papers to the ambassador, but she was relieved he hadn't suffered any debilitating injury either.

"Well, thank heaven neither of them is badly hurt. Whichever one of them was flying that plane did a great job of getting it through the channel before the engine flared out and it nosedived and flipped over. His skill certainly kept them both from getting killed."

Triny gasped. "Duh engine was a fire? I didn't heared dat. Ya must a been real close if ya sawed dat."

"It flew right over my head," Jessie said with a wicked twist to her lips. "And"—she leaned forward—"it almost took my head off."

Triny clutched her chest with a horrified expression and sank down on the sofa.

Jessie couldn't help laughing over Triny's dramatics, even knowing she would make the most of that little tidbit. It felt good to laugh and release some of her tension, but going to dinner at the Hamiltons was out of the question. Especially when one of their guests of honor would be Jake Denning, and she would have to meet him again, after ten years, in front of all the island's elite, who would be sure to attend tonight.

"I believe I'll pass on dinner with the Hamiltons. So please just go and tell them for me."

"You can't," Triny said, sticking out her chin. "Sides, no woman in her right mind would pass up dinner with duh two most gorgeous men any gal on dis island has ever laid eyes on."

"Oh, and who would they be."

"Those two flyers a course. Tilly say every gal on duh island is mad about dem. Dey both sa big, dey make da palm trees look short, with shoulders wider dan I be tall. Some of da gals be in love with one, and some be swooning over da other, but most just can't make up dere minds."

Jessie received this exaggeration with a skeptical expression; then straightened in her chair, struck by a sudden thought. Casually, she asked, "Do these two paragons have names?"

Triny sniffed. "A course dey has names."

"And they are—"

"Major and captain."

"Those aren't names, Triny, they're military ranks."

"Well, no one say nothin bout names. Dey just hustle dem flyers into da hospital, and nurse Tena don't let no one in."

"Unless the major was just a passenger, I suspect he is the pilot, and the captain is his co-pilot."

Triny folded her arms across her chest, triumphantly. "Den I knows, which one be da pilot."

"And that would be?"

"People be sayin duh one dat got all dem little cuts be da pilot."

"That made more sense to Jessie. Jake hadn't been a pilot during the time she knew him. Of course, the war had transformed many men into things they never thought they would be. Yet somehow, thinking of Jake even co-piloting a plane was hard for her to picture. *Maybe Jake was just a passenger, but for what reason?*

The small mantle clock chimed the quarter hour.

"Gracious, if ya don't quit sittin round gabbin, and get ready, ya gona be late fer dinner."

"Me, sitting around gabbing—*me*?" Jessie protested getting up, resigned to her fate.

The thought of meeting Jake again in front of the island's high society made her nauseous. She swallowed hard and pressed her hand against her queasy stomach. *But maybe it's best to just get it over with so I can stop feeling sick about it. Besides, in front of all those people, Jake's pride will keep him from doing or saying anything that will intentionally embarrass either one of us,* she tried to reassure herself. Still, the jitters growing in her stomach persisted, and she had to admit, she was more than just a little nervous about how Jake would react when they were *introduced.*

4

JESSIE WALKED BACK INTO HER BEDROOM with mounting anxiety and opened her closet. She'd grown up as a cowpoke, more at home in ranch boots and jeans than dresses and silk stockings. She could throw a lasso with dead eyed accuracy, brand cattle, and tame mustangs. It wasn't until a New York modeling agent approached her, during a trip with her mother to Denver, that she'd given any thought to her appearance. He'd assured her of her potential, and the offer he'd made to help her step into the world of high-fashion modeling came at a moment in her life when she was desperate for a new direction.

Her transformation from cowpoke to high fashion model was jarring to say the least. At first, she enjoyed being fussed over by makeup artists, hairstylists, and designers. By the time she was six months into her modeling career, she hated all the fuss that went into transforming her into every woman's ideal and every man's dream. All the overdone makeup and hairdos became a bother that took too much time, and disguised who she really was.

After she left that world behind, she kept herself simply groomed, and it again became a rare thing for her to think about her appearance. Frankly, she just didn't need to. The combination of her Irish and Nahtow Indian heritage had given her a remarkable natural beauty that needed no enhancements. Her willowy—six-foot, three inches—figure could make anything she wore look good, even glamorous. However, tonight she decided to take the time to make herself look her very best.

She'd always had the ability to take Jake's breath way. She knew that because he'd told her so an endless number of times and that was exactly what she intended to do tonight. *If he isn't able to breath, I will have the upper hand right from the start, and be able to direct, and—hopefully—keep the conversation in safe channels.*

"Let's see now." She tapped her pursed lips, as she scanned her wardrobe.

In the last thirty-five years, after deciding to reach out to the world, Toolowa had established trade with many of the countries bordering on the Indian Ocean. Jessie loved the styles and fabric from all over Indonesia and India that flowed into the island and her closet bulged with them. Her wardrobe also held outfits she would be comfortable wearing for any occasion in the United State too.

I think tonight calls for something exotic. The Indonesian gown her dressmaker had finished just a week ago caught her eye. She'd intended to save the gown and wear it to the big New Year's Eve party the Zenderly's always threw, but decided she needed the extra confidence wearing it would bring her tonight.

Her expression was positively wicked as she stepped into the floor length, fitted dress, with a straight-line bodice and a front slit that reached her knees. She topped the emerald sheath with a gold-lace kebaya—a traditional over blouse worn by most women in Indonesia.

The kebaya had long sheer sleeves, with sculpted lace covering her forearms and wrists, shoulders, back, and a deep V neckline. Its molded tuxedo style was cut away in the front with long swooping tails in the back. It brought out the gold thread that ran in a swirling pattern through the emerald sheath.

The mirror told Jessie this outfit was everything she'd hoped it would be. Sitting at her dressing table, she put on the emeralds the grateful people of Toolowa had given her for coming to "enlighten", as they put it, their children. She'd been reluctant to accept such an extravagant gift, but the Toolowans' outpouring of love and generosity had finally convinced her to accept them. She took them not knowing where or when she might ever wear them. Surprisingly, she'd found occasion to wear them often.

Her position as a teacher was a highly respected one on Toolowa. Upon her arrival, she learned she was expected to move in the highest social circles, which included being invited to dine with diplomats, trade executives, and any visiting dignitaries that came to the island. The company she kept included: the ambassadors from the countries Toolowa had established trade with, the island's doctors, dentists, and their families, the other teachers on the island, the council of judges, and of course, the Zenderlys—the islands ruling family.

The opportunity to mingle in such a diverse world of people revived the social skills Jessie had acquired as a model. She felt comfortable in the presence of both the small and the great. Of course wearing a knockout dress never hurt, and tonight she needed to score a big knockout.

"I guess if I'm going Indonesian," she said to her reflection, "I should wear my hair up." She reached for her brush and stroked it through her auburn hair. The tropical sun had added very becoming gold highlights that danced in the glow of the lamp light.

When she'd first arrived on Toolowa, she'd almost cut her hair off, due to the heat and humidity. However, the native women assured her she would acclimate and convinced her it would be a crime to cut off such beautiful hair. They taught her how to do it up in simple ways that kept her cooler and didn't take any fuss. She was glad she'd listen to them and had just let it keep growing. Her hair was so naturally curly, that cut short, it probably would have ended up looking like a pile of frizzy foam on her head. Letting it grow gave it weight, transforming her curls into long loose waves.

Searching through the dressing table drawer, she found a pair of carved jade rods. Twisting most of her hair into a rope, she coiled it onto her head and anchored it with the rods, leaving a few shorter strands to hang in gentle curls around her face and neck. Satisfied, she applied a light dusting of rouge to her high Nahtow cheekbones, darkened her lip just slightly, slid into a pair of gold sandals, took a fortifying breath, and decided she was ready to meet Jake Denning.

A WANING THREE QUARTER MOON was already rising in the evening sky when she left her house. It lit the wide lane she followed, but she wondered if it was beaming friendly encouragement down on her or glowering sardonically over the ordeal that lay ahead of her.

She arrived at the Ambassador's home a bare ten minutes before dinner was due to be served. Shin, the Hamilton's Burmese butler, opened the door before she reached it. Dressed in a formal white jacket and bowtie, he gave her a rare smile as she stepped through the door. "You are especially lovely this evening, Miss Jayling."

"Thank you, Shin. Am I the last guest to arrive?"

"No, Doctor and Mrs. Snyder, who are bringing the Americans, have yet to make their appearance, but everyone else is present," Shin said, leading her across the polished hardwood floor of the foyer to the living room where hors d'oeuvres and drinks were being served.

The jitters in her stomach, calmed. *Good, he isn't here yet.*

When Jake arrived, and the rounds of introductions were made, she would be introduced to him according to her place in the room. If she could manage to be somewhere in the middle of the room, surrounded by a group of friends when they were introduced, the introduction would be short. It wouldn't be polite to keep the other guests waiting while Jake lingered over one introduction.

But what she needed the most was to have Ambassador Hamilton, Sam, or his wife, Nora, say her name before Jake could use the one name she never wanted to hear again—the only name Jake, and everyone else, had used during her time as a model. She hoped that when he was told her real name, it might confuse him enough to keep him from saying that one terrible word. He might even think she wasn't the same woman he'd proposed to in New York—but that was too optimistic a hope.

Shin escorted her as far as the living room. She stepped into the room, which was softly lit with oil lamps. It was decorated with a subtle blend of fine furnishings that came from all over Indonesia and as far away as India and Africa. The decor was adorned with large arrangements of tropical flowers. Their sweet fragrance wafted through the room like incense.

Friends smiled their welcome. She exchanged a few words with her host and hostess, was waylaid by several gallants who took her hand and murmured compliments until she managed to escape them and move into the general hubbub of the room. A glass of fresh, pineapple-mango juice was handed to her and a tray of hors d'oeuvres offered, before she spotted the situation she was seeking.

Two of her fellow teachers, Marcus and Lenoir Jorgenson, were standing in a more shadowed area of the softly lit room. Both were long lanky Swedes—the perfect cover for her. They were talking with Teneacia Chang, who went by Tena. She was the Eurasian chief nurse of Toolowa's hospital, and Jessie's best friend.

Tena wasn't native born, but like Jessie, had been invited to work and live on Toolowa. At twenty-nine, she was a year older than Jessie was, and considered tall for a Eurasian woman. Her five-foot nine-inch stance and vivid violet eyes were characteristics she'd inherited from her English father. From her Chinese mother, she inherited a flawless complexion and straight raven-black hair. Her exotic beauty had made more than one man sigh. It belied her fireball energy, industry, and efficiency, things many men found intimidating. They were characteristics she and Jessie shared.

She waved an inviting hand at Jessie.

With a little maneuvering, Jessie managed to situate herself precisely where she wanted to be in her friends' circle of conversation, so Marcus—who was as tall as she was—stood between her and the entrance to the room. Lenoir and Tena stood on either side of her. Marcus would block Jake's view of her when he entered the room, keeping her from being the first person he saw. Her position would also allow her to peek out around Marcus and get a good look at Jake before they were introduced.

Lenoir touched her arm. "There hasn't been this much excitement since—"

"Your arrival on the island, Jessie," Tena said, her lips twitching.

Jessie smirked. "The arrival of another teacher on Toolowa can hardly compare with a plane crashing into the bay."

"Maybe, but you did cause quite a stir among the men when you arrived," Lenoir said.

Marcus chuckled. "She still is."

Jessie changed the subject. "I'm surprised those American flyers are coming to this dinner party. Don't they need to rest and recuperate after their ordeal today?"

"Both of them are young and strong and neither was badly hurt. If Paul," Tena said, referring to Dr. Snyder, "had tried to keep them confined, he would have had his hands full. Besides they seemed pretty anxious to meet with the ambassador, talk with Edmund, and schedule a meeting with the judges' council."

"That sounds a little ominous. Especially when you consider their arrival was unexpected," Jessie said, and took another sip from her glass.

Lenoir leaned in and confided, "That's why those who frequently bow out of the Hamilton's dinner parties are all here tonight. Everyone is hoping to get the low down, not to mention, they're all dying to see those flyers."

"Including us," Marcus said dryly.

Lenoir put her elbow in his ribs.

Jessie and Tena laughed.

It was true that the monthly dinner parties Samuel and Nora Hamilton always held had been sparsely attended of late, but tonight the entire island's leadership and elite were crowded into the Hamilton's living room.

The sound of voices in the foyer drew everyone's attention. Adjusting her position, and crouching slightly, Jessie hid behind Marcus.

Shin escorted the final guests into the room.

Jessie peeked around Marcus. Her jaw dropped. She snapped her head back, and the tremor that ran through her sloshed her punch over the side of the glass. Trying to steady the glass, she wrapped her other hand around it and only managed to slosh more punch over its rim. Then to make matters worse, the jitters in her stomach turned into angry hornets, causing her heart to drum so hard, she was certain everyone in the room could hear it.

It was her worst nightmare—times two. Standing in the high arched doorway, towering over Jake Denning, was Sky Brannigan.

The room went silent, and suddenly felt hot and airless to Jessie. She couldn't seem to draw a breath. The rhythm of her heart pounded out a single panicked message—escape! *I've got to get out of here.* The French doors leading to the veranda were only five feet behind her. Cautiously, she took a small, shuffling step back. *When the introductions start, I can slip out the doors. With everyone's attention on Jake and Sky, no one will see me leave.*

In the hours after seeing Jake, she'd resigned herself to meeting him again—no matter how difficult or unpleasant. However, at that moment, no amount of earthly fortitude could strengthen her enough to face the man that had walked away from her without a backward glance, and shattered her life. The mere thought of facing Sky Brannigan, especially in front of all these people, made her quake and went way beyond a nightmare. *It would be like coming face to face with the devil himself.*

She took another step back.

Tena took hold of her arm and whispered, "Where do you think you're going?"

"I—ah—need some air, I'm feeling a little woozy," Jessie mumbled and pressed her sticky glass into Tena's hand.

The ambassador began the introductions with the chief judge. As a matter of protocol, he was always introduced first because he was in fact, His Royal Highness, King Edmund Chan Tommu Zenderly. It was a title he no longer used, but one that was clearly emblazoned over his left eye, which artfully listed his royal ancestors back to the beginning of Toolowan recorded history.

Edmund, as he insisted his friends call him, was a big man, with a muscular body. His features were bold and often lit with humor. His silver hair was cut short in the same fashion as American men, but he wore a traditional lava-lava topped with a tailored shirt and light jacket. No tie ever had, or ever would, encumber his neck.

Queen Menaloni Ruth Zenderly was introduced next. She was elegantly slender, and stood nearly eye-to-eye with her husband. She wore an expensive sarong topped by an elegant lace kebaya. She welcomed the American flyers warmly as they were introduced. After the extended introduction of the rest of the royal family, which included the Zenderly's married daughter, Beth, and Lowa, the younger of the Zenderly's two sons, the next introductions moved along quickly.

Jessie watched Jake and Sky move around the room, getting ever closer, with a growing sense of panic. She had to make a break for it now, before they saw her and she was trapped.

"Please just tell Nora I needed to leave," she whispered into Tena's ear and walked as quickly as her shaky legs would take her to the French doors.

Her hand reached for the doorknob.

"Amazon?"

The word, tinged with a Bostonian twang, skewered her in the back.

5

AGAIN, THE ROOM WENT SILENT. Jessie could feel the eyes of the entire company riveted on her back. Her fingers ached to take hold of the doorknob, wrench open the door, and bolt into the night. Instead, she turned—though she couldn't imagine why she was doing it.

"I thought it was you." Jake made a beeline for her. "But I was pretty shaken up when I saw you, and I've been wondering all afternoon."

The disarming smile she'd mastered during her year as a model automatically sprang like a defense to her lips. She forced her eyes to stay on Jake's astonished ones as he came across the room, not allowing hers to glance over his shoulder at Sky.

Jake took her hand and raised it to his lips. "You still take my breath away," he murmured, his voice as warm as a caress. "And I swear you're more beautiful now than you were ten years ago. That dress is spectacular. I can't begin to tell you what a wonderful surprise it is to see you."

"I'm"—Jessie swallowed the lump in her throat, conscience everyone in the room was hanging on their words, watching their every move, and forced the words out—"surprised to see you too, Jake." She pulled her hand from his and gestured to his bound up arm. "I'm glad you weren't badly injured in the crash."

"I have to tell you that when I looked up through the water and saw you with the sunlight shining all around you, I almost swallowed half the bay. I thought you were a mermaid. He gave her his lady killer smile. "Thanks for hauling me out of the drink."

"So did I," a deep voice growled over Jake's head, "But *Amazon* is a much better description, isn't that right—Jessie?"

The hornets in her stomach went into a frenzy. Her head jerked up and her eyes flared into Sky Brannigan's brilliant blue ones. She experienced a moment of déjà vu, but if she'd seen an instant of stunned pain in his eyes, it disappeared, and cold condemnation seemed to replace it.

His eyes traveled slowly over her.

Locked jawed, she tried not to blush, but heat flared up her neck and into her cheeks. That terrible word coming out of his mouth felt like an intentional slap. It made her so angry she wanted to shriek or throw something at him, and she might have, if her punch glass had still been in her hand.

The numerous small cuts on Sky's face, barely registered in the back of her mind. All she could see was red. *How dare he insult me like that in front of all these people, and why should he anyway? He was the one who walked away.* Now with a single word he'd told her what he still thought of her.

"You know this gorgeous Amazon too?" Jake asked Sky.

"Small world, huh?" Sky kept his eyes locked on her. "And the name she goes by these days—unless of course it's changed—is Jessie Garrison."

"How do you two know each other?" Jake's head swiveled between Sky and Jessie.

Before Sky could answer she quickly said, "Sky's sister—that is his cousin—is married to my brother."

"That's right. We're kind of related—in-laws in fact."

"Well this day just keeps dishing up more and more surprises," Nora Hamilton said. Always meticulously groomed, Nora was a consummate hostess of ample proportions, with expressive hazel eyes, and a soothing manner. "I will have Shin rearrange the place cards so you three can sit together at dinner and catch up with each other. But right now, we better finish the introductions before dinner gets cold."

With obvious reluctance, Jake and Sky let Nora draw them away from Jessie, and the introductions continued.

Nora's thoughtful suggestion that the three of them be seated together for dinner made Jessie feel like a condemned women, sentence to be tortured before she was executed.

"Why didn't you tell me you knew those guys, and what's with all this *Amazon* stuff?" Tena asked under her breath.

"I haven't seen either of them in years, so I don't *know* them—anymore, and Amazon was a name I went by a long time ago."

"Don't know them? Ha! You're related to one by marriage, and both are obviously smitten with you, and I want the whole Amazon story, my friend."

"Tena I really need some air, could you make my apologies to—"

"Gentleman." Sam Hamilton brought everyone's attention to him. "If you will please choose a lady and escort her, we will go into dinner."

Jessie bolted for the French doors, but only managed to take a couple of long strides before a big hand wrapped around her upper arm.

"May I escort . . . *the Amazon,* into dinner?" Sky asked softly.

His hand ran down her arm, and clasped hers—holding it prisoner. His touch was achingly familiar. The caressing feel of his fingers as they wrapped around hers, lifted her chin. They pushed her back toward memories she had sealed up, and would never allow herself to look at or feel again.

He stared pointedly down at her left hand, devoid of rings.

She wanted to snatch her hand back and slap him for adding so pointedly to her humiliation in front of all these people. They only knew her, and saw her, as a trusted teacher. Now she would have to answer questions about the one year of her life that had destroyed all her dreams. She tried unsuccessfully to stifle the trembling in her fingers as Sky placed her hand in the crook of his arm, furious with herself for so obvious a betrayal of her feelings. Right now, she needed to be as unfeeling as a mannequin.

"I think I have as much claim on escorting Am—that is—Jessie into dinner as you do, Major, maybe more." Jake took her other hand, and placed it in the crook of his bandaged arm.

"Oh, and just what gives you precedence over my claim on her as *my* sister-in-law, *Captain*?" The velvet edge to Sky's voice was a warning Jessie recognized.

Jake smugly said, "The fact that she saved my life this afternoon."

The way Sky's long fingers were caressing her hand, holding it in place, told Jessie he wasn't going to relinquish his claim. Every stroke of his fingers was torture. The hornets in her stomach began to fly up her throat. Their sting threatened to make her burst into tears. She had to do something before she completely humiliated herself. She quickly scanned the room and found her deliverance standing just a few feet from her.

Oliver Stone was a man no one ever noticed. The only distinctive thing about him was his prominent Adams apple, made more prominent by the bowties he always wore. Somewhere in his thirties, and single, Oliver was one of the dentists on the island. If Jessie had been asked what color his eyes were, she couldn't have said. Even now in the soft light of the oil lamps, she wasn't sure, but she was sure of one thing—he would rescue her. It would be a short reprieve, but one she desperately needed in order to salvage her composure.

"You will both have to forgive me, Major, Captain," she said, barely able to control her voice. "But Mr. Stone asked to escort me into dinner when I arrived, I'm afraid you will both have to defer to him." Jessie gave Oliver a slightly trembling, though thoroughly enchanting, smile. She pulled her hands from beneath Jake's and Sky's clinging fingers and walked over to Oliver.

He showed a moment of surprise, but he rose nobly to the occasion. Drawing himself up with triumphant pride, he took Jessie's hand, tucked it into his arm, and without a backwards glance, they walked out of the living room.

Jessie took slow, deep breaths as they joined the parade down the long candle lit hallway to the formal dining room. Her heart, that was beating as though she'd just run several miles straight up hill, began to slow. Her spiraling panic wound down—slightly, and now that Jake and Sky's hands no longer held hers, rational thought returned.

She began thinking, furiously. *How am I going to get through dinner with Sky and Jake breathing down my neck and everyone else watching us?*

They entered the formal dining room where Shin had just rearranged the place cards so Jessie could be seated between her two *old friends*. Oliver located her chair and gallantly seated her. She murmured her heartfelt thanks. He smiled regretfully at her and moved down the table to his own place.

By the time everyone was seated, Jessie was still fighting for control of her emotions, but had decided on a plan of action. *I've got to keep myself from being the object of any conversation between Jake and Sky. I won't allow my whole life history—or at least what each one of them knows of it—to become antidotes told over the dinner table to entertain everyone at my expense.* Undoubtedly, Sky and Jake would compare notes on her, but she wasn't going to sit there and let them do it here and now.

Additionally, she was determined not to allow either one of them to pull her into a personal discussion. Trapped between them as she was, she could think of only one way to reach her goals. Jake had called her Amazon because he didn't know her as anything else. Sky had used the term derisively, but that was what she was going to give him tonight—a taste of the Amazon. *That should keep Jake in line, and throw Sky off balance—I hope.*

After Reverend Arnold, the minister of one of the island's protestant congregations, offered a blessing on the food, she set herself to the task.

"So." She gave Sky the Amazon's smile that never failed to bring men to their knees, and was rewarded with an intake of breath, followed by the wrinkling of his brow. "What brings you two to Toolowa in such a dramatic and unexpected way?"

The question instantly drew everyone's attention—just as she knew it would.

Sky's eyes cut to the ambassador at the head of the table.

Every eye followed his.

Samuel Hamilton was an astute man that used his kindly—almost cherubic—face and gentle manners, to outwit, out maneuver, and wheedle out of people things they would never readily confess to a less innocent countenance. His head moved almost imperceptibly.

"Just a little business," Sky said.

Jessie gave Sky a teasing pout. "Surely it's more than just a *little* business for you to have come all this way."

His eyes narrowed, as though he knew what she was doing, but he was saved any further explanation by the ambassador. "I think it would be best if we deferred that discussion for tomorrow."

Jessie shrugged and touched Jake's injured arm, giving him the Amazon's smile. "Perhaps you could tell us what happened to your poor plane?"

Jake responded with a dashing grin. "I'm afraid there isn't much of a story there."

"No, there isn't," Sky said in an "I'm pulling rank" kind of tone and took over telling the story.

Jessie turned back to him, agog with curiosity, playing the dimwitted paper doll men always expected the Amazon to be.

Puzzled inquiry wrinkled Sky's brow. He cleared his throat and addressed the room, still attentive and waiting. "We flew out of Australia with a tail wind behind us. We were making very good time until we ran into a thunderstorm."

"We had a very intense thunderstorm this morning that blew in from the south," Nora said.

"The storm we hit came from the south too and was probably the same storm that visited you. Before we could climb above it we got hit by lighting."

Nora dropped the knife she was using to butter a dinner roll. "You must have been terrified."

"It wasn't exactly a picnic." Jake chuckled. "But Sky—that is Major Brannigan is a great pilot."

Sky waved away the compliment. "Fortunately, the storm clouds didn't exceed our plane's ceiling, and we were able to get above it."

"On one engine?" Queen Menaloni asked.

"We were lucky enough to still have both at that time, but before we got past the thunderstorm the left engine flared out. The lightning must have damaged it."

"Oh my, how did you keep from going down?" Nora asked.

"We didn't." Jake grinned.

"If we were going to stay in the air, we had to get the fire put out," Sky explained.

"So the Major cut that engine and just dropped us back into the storm. The rain put out the fire."

"You must have one very cool head," Edmund said, complimenting Sky.

Jessie coughed and picked up her water glass.

Sky glanced at her, a slight flush heightening his color and said, "We managed to make it out of the storm without getting hit again by lightning. By then we were more than half way here, and since that plane is capable of flying on one engine, we just kept coming, slow but steady."

"But why did it flame out just as you got into the bay?" Jessie asked with genuine interest, forgetting her pretense.

Sky's eyes came back to her and lingered with an expression she couldn't read. It was disconcerting, she had always been able to read him—*but that was a lifetime ago,* she reminded herself.

"I don't know for sure," he said. "It might have gotten damaged by the lightning too or just given out after doing the job of keeping us aloft for so long on its own."

"Lucky for us it lasted until we got here. If it hadn't—"

"We would have been fish bait." Sky finished Jake's thought.

"The whole thing gives me the shivers," Doctor Snyder's wife, Emma, a prim English woman, said.

Jessie pursed her lips in a thoughtful pout while the salad was served. "It leaves you stranded here for a while, doesn't it?"

"It does," Sky said.

"Well, since you're going to be here for a while, you might like to know something about Toolowa," Jessie said.

The suggestion worked like a charm.

6

EDMUND ZENDERLY CLAIMED THE FLYERS' attention and immediately took up his favorite subject. "It isn't known how long ago our ancestors came to Toolowa."

Thank you! Jessie took a long sip from her water glass, hiding her relief and the triumph that tugged at her lips.

Edmund leaned over his salad plate. "We only have a few rock pictographs that tell us they must have arrived here well before a written language evolved. What we do know from the pictographs is that they were a seafaring people, blown here by contrary winds."

"What do you mean by *contrary* winds?" Sky asked.

Tena, sitting across from Sky, set down her water glass and answered, "Virtually all the people whose ancestors found Toolowa were brought here by rare gales that came from the northwest."

"On Toolowa the wind almost always blows from the southeast. Occasionally we get winds, like today, that blow just from the south. However, at least once a year, during the cyclone season in the Indian Ocean, we get very fierce winds that blow from the north and west," Edmund said.

Jessie picked up her salad fork. "Over the centuries, those cyclones literally blew people to Toolowa."

"You see, the natural flow of the prevailing winds, and the ocean currents, pushed the early explorers in the Indian Ocean away from Toolowa," Marcus Jorgenson said. "Only those caught by a cyclone were driven to it, and in a way, that was a blessing. Toolowa was hidden from the world for many hundreds of years. Those who did find it, found a virtually untouched paradise."

Troy Lind, an Anglo-Saxon looking man and a judge on the ruling council, who could trace his ancestors back to the dawn of recorded history on Toolowa, took up the story. "The early written records tell us that those who rode the cyclone winds to Toolowa were welcomed and given citizenship. It was believed the Great Spirit brought them into Toolowa's safe harbor."

"In fact," Queen Menaloni said, "that is what Toolowa means—Safe Harbor."

A waiter removed Edmund's salad plate. He leaned back as the next course was served. "We are a blend of many races, cultures, and ethnic backgrounds. The culture that evolved here, through the random selection of people the wind brought, is as unique as many of the plants and animals that inhabit Toolowa."

Throughout the four-course meal of fish, lamb, poultry, and shellfish—each accompanied by a different kind of fresh fruit or vegetable, seasoned with Toolowa's unique spices—Sky and Jake were regaled with the history of Toolowa. Their attention was so completely claimed by Edmund and those who were enthusiastically recounting Toolowa's history that Jessie had little fear the conversation would have the chance to become personal.

Savoring her small triumph, she sat back and tried to relax, but her stomach was still entertaining hornets. She ate little and remembered nothing of the meal when it was over. Luck was with her, and the historians remained robust in their endeavors to expound Toolowa's history all the way through dessert.

"Toolowa is certainly an anomaly, and I don't understand how it escaped conquest during the age of exploration." Sky set his napkin next to his dessert plate and leaned forward. "Why weren't you conquered by one of the powerful European countries that made port here during that time? No other small island nation was able to withstand their superior arms when they were bent on conquest."

"Nevertheless, we did withstand them." Edmund's subdued voice immediately dropped a cloak of silence over the room.

"How?" Sky asked.

"Let's just say . . . that on Toolowa we have always known how to discourage unwanted visitors," Edmund said quietly, his expression veiled.

"We are very selective about who we allow to live here—even now," Troy Lind said.

"Considering we literally crashed this party, I hope you don't think of us as unwanted visitors," Jake said.

Smiles from around the table quickly assured the flyers of their welcome.

"The people of the United States were some of the first we invited here," Edmund said. "We even have a small number of Americans, who we invited to live among us, that are now Toolowan citizens."

"Like Jayling." Troy nodded at Jessie. "We gave her citizenship before the end of her first year on Toolowa."

Jake frowned thoughtfully at Edmund. "But didn't you say that only those who rode the cyclone winds to get here were allowed to become citizens."

"Ah, but Jayling—although invited to come—still rode a fierce wind to get here," Edmund said mysteriously.

The bewilderment deepened on Jake's brow. "Are you saying a storm brought Am—Jessie here?"

"The cyclone winds people ride to Toolowa now are mostly metaphorical. However, those they bring to us are still seeking safe harbor," Menaloni said.

Jessie felt Sky's and Jake's eyes on her, waiting for her explanation. The hornets in her stomach started buzzing around again. No one knew her reasons for needing Toolowa's sanctuary, and she wasn't about to discuss it, especially considering the cyclones that had driven her to Toolowa were sitting on either side of her.

The heavy pause that hung over the room told her there were many who would like to know her reasons. Even shy Oliver leaned forward, expectantly.

She lifted her chin. "My life was unexpectedly blown off course. Fortunately, a cyclone wind found me, and I rode that wind to Toolowa where I started a new life."

"Where did you hear about Toolowa, and how did you *ride the wind* here?" Sky asked, stiffly.

"She came with us." Sam gestured to his wife. "You see, a couple of weeks after Jessie graduated with her teaching degree, she headed home."

"I needed a little counsel from my parents when the plans I'd made for my life after college fell through," Jessie said and congratulated herself on the complete lack of emotion in her voice.

"When she arrived home, she found her parents entertaining us," Sam said.

"Sam is a friend of my dad's from his Rough Riders days."

"That's right, and after the Rough Riders, I went into the diplomatic corp."

"Which took us to Europe," Nora said.

"That hasn't allowed me to see Jack Garrison for nearly fifteen years, although we have kept in touch. So when I was appointed as ambassador to Toolowa—"

"A place he'd never heard of before." Edmund grinned.

Sam chuckled. "True. In fact Toolowa isn't even on the world map."

Nora touched Sky's arm. "We just had to take President Roosevelt's word on it that Toolowa existed."

"Nora and I decided since we had to cross the country to catch a ship for Hawaii, we would stop off and see the Garrisons on the way."

"That stop was a very profitable one for the people of Toolowa," Menaloni said, allowing a waiter to remove her dessert plate.

"That's right." Sam leaned back in his chair and folded his hands across his protruding belly. "You see, during our stay with the Garrisons, I received a phone call from the state department with a request from Toolowa that I recruit and bring an elementary school teacher with me because Toolowa was losing one of theirs to retirement. That request had me at my wits end. I didn't have a clue where I was going to come up with a teacher before we were due to sail."

"My arrival on the scene, along with my need for a new direction in my life, was an answer to both our prayers," Jessie said.

"How did your folks feel about you moving half way around the world to a place—I'll bet—they'd never heard of?" Sky asked.

Jessie shrugged. "My parents helped me weigh the pros and cons. In the end they both felt good about my decision to go with Sam and Nora. It immediately allowed me to start a new life. And I have to say, that coming to Toolowa was the best decision I've ever made." Jessie's radiant smile captured the company.

Menaloni smiled back across the table at her. "We will always be grateful for the wind that brought you to us, Jayling."

"Why do you call her Jayling?" Jake asked.

Before Menaloni could answer, Oliver Stone jumped in. "In Toolowan the name means, captive heart," he said, smiling at Jessie.

"You see she captured our hearts the day she landed. Everyone knew immediately that she belonged here," Menaloni said.

A swell of agreement ran around the room.

Sky glowered at her. "So you are no longer an American citizen?"

"I hold dual citizenship," Jessie said proudly. "Toolowa is as much my country as the United States is now."

"Do you intend to spend the rest of your life here?" Sky asked.

Jessie gave him an elusive smile and blotted her lips with her napkin.

With dinner at an end, the company prepared to continue the evening by enjoying the entertainments Nora had set up in the drawing room.

Men began helping ladies from their chairs.

Sky jumped up and pulled out Jessie's chair. As she rose from the table, she thanked him with the Amazon's most beguiling smile and felt gratified by his baffled expression.

Jake was on his feet by then too. Both offered her their arms.

"You're both so gallant, but where I'm going you can't escort me."

"And just where would that be?" Sky asked.

"Into the lady's room," Jessie said and escaped.

She pushed through the door of the lady's room and collapsed onto a maroon velvet lounge. *I made it through dinner,* she congratulated herself. But knew she now faced the most dangerous part of the evening. *Both of them will try to corner me into a private conversation, and I know they will insist on walking me home. I can't let that happen.* Her brow wrinkled in thought. *I guess I could play the Oliver Stone card one more time, but that's so unfair to Oliver. I don't want to get his hopes up again.*

The situation she found herself in made her head throb. She rubbed her temples searching for a way out of the dilemma that wouldn't give any of her numerous admirers the wrong impression. Her life had just become impossibly complicated, and she didn't need to add any more unexpected twists to it.

"What should I do?" she asked her reflection in the full-length mirror hanging on the wall across from her, and then jumped when Tena came through the door.

"So this is where you're hiding." Tena chuckled. "Those two gorgeous men"—she sighed dramatically—"who are making all the maidens' hearts on this island beat faster tonight, with the exception of my own, are lurking just inside the door of the salon. They're eyeing each other with, what I can only describe as, territorial male expressions. That tells me they're determined to out maneuver each, and the winner will pounce on you."

"I can't go back out there, Tena, I just can't."

"Well you certainly can't hold up in here for the rest of the evening."

"I would like to hold up here until those two are off this island," Jessie said, rubbing her temples more vigorously.

"Just how much *history* do you have with those guys?"

"More than I care to explain—especially tonight."

"So what are you going to do? I think they're prepared to wait you out, my friend."

"I don't know. It took all my wits to get through dinner. Now my brain has shut down, and I can't think anymore."

Tena's lips twitched. "Letting Edmund hold their attention through dinner was a brilliant move."

"It was a desperate move, and I don't have any left."

Tena dropped onto the lounge next to her in a delicate cloud of violet chiffon, put her elbows on her knees and rested her chin in her palms. "We've got to get you out of here before they send someone in after you."

"Yes! If I leave now, I won't have to fend off a tête-à-tête with either of them or ward off having one or both of them walk me home." She put supplicating hands together. "Help me—*please!*"

"Okay. But with those two hanging around the door like a pair of vultures just waiting to swoop in and devour you, we'll need a diversion to get you out of here unseen."

"Maybe Shin will help."

"Yes," Tena said with a calculating gleam in her violet eyes. "I believe I might be able to enlist his aid, but you are going to owe me a lengthy explanation for all the trouble I intend to go through for you. Agreed?"

"Yes. I'll tell you anything you want to know, just help me get out of here."

"Have you got a piece of paper and a pencil?"

Jessie opened her small gold evening bag and brought out the required items.

"Write a note to Nora, making your apology. Tell her you have a headache and I recommended you go home and rest."

"Well at least that won't be a lie. I do have a headache, a *double barrel* one," Jessie said as she wrote the note to Nora.

"Now, I'll go back out there and give this note to Nora. Keep this door opened a crack. I'm going to have an unfortunate accident with Shin and a tray. When you hear the crash, make your break. Hopefully, the diversion will be enough to hold your . . . *old friends'* attention for the few moments you will need to get out through the side door."

"Thank you, thank you." Jessie hugged Tena.

"You can expect me on your doorstep in the morning for my payoff."

"Come early, before Triny gets there. I'll have breakfast ready."

7

JESSIE RUSHED HOME as fast as her delicate sandals would allow. She glared at the sardonic light the moon cast upon her, listening for any sounds of pursuit behind her. Hot tears pooled behind her eyes, but she refused to let them fall. *Why . . . why after all I have been through to build a life for myself—when I am finally at peace, content with my life and who I am—is this happening now?*

She came through the door of her bungalow and found Triny asleep on the sofa. Tempted though she was to let her go on sleeping and not have to answer her questions about the evening, Jessie gently shook her shoulder. "Triny, it's time you went home."

"Ya back sa soon?" Triny peered at the mantle clock.

"Yes. I have a bad headache and I'm going to bed." Jessie held up a hand to ward off whatever was about to come out of Triny's open mouth. "Please, I promise to answer your questions tomorrow, but not too early. I want to sleep off this headache. You can come about noon."

Triny yawned. "Ya shur ya don't needs my help fer den?"

"I'm sure."

"Well if you's shur ya don't needs me, den I be here at noon."

Ten minutes after Triny left, Jessie was in bed staring up at her high beamed ceiling. Being hit with Sky Brannigan's open scorn had been humiliating. It was even more painful than she'd imagined, and she had tried to imagine what it would be like to meet him again, but that was a long time ago.

Looking into his judgmental, condemning eyes brought back her old enemy—the feeling of being tarnished, but that hadn't been the worst part of it.

Over the years she'd let the memories of him go, and one by one she'd replaced them with new memories, happy ones. His touch made all those old memories rush back at her like a shockwave. The effort it took to keep the memories of Sky and how much she'd loved him at bay had exhausted her. *That's probably the reason I have a headache. Still, I would rather endure the headache than give into the memories or touch those long forgotten feelings."*

She moaned into her pillow, rubbed her temples in a futile effort to ease her pain, and continued to fight against the memories that assaulted her. But she couldn't keep the day Sky walked out on her from bursting through her defenses. The back of her throat burned with the effort it took to keep the sobs that choked her from escaping, but nothing she did kept the tears from flowing. *No . . . no . . . NO! I won't cry over you any more, Sky Brannigan.* She'd believed all the tears she could ever cry over him had been spilt. Now she knew that wasn't true, and she despised herself for it.

She threw aside the thin sheet that covered her, *I won't let you take any more of my life from me, destroy any more of my heart—or rob me of my hard won peace.* Jumping up, she padded noiselessly out the open door of her bedroom, through the open door adjacent to hers and into another bedroom.

Here the moon was allowed to shine like a nightlight through the open shutters of the window. Bending over a small bed, she gazed into the angelic face of her three-year-old son, Kanoa. With gentle fingers, she tousled his curly gold hair. *He will probably hate his curls when he grows up,* she realized sadly. *But I will always love them, and adore him.*

Her love for her son filled her, and her peace returned. She'd found all the love and acceptance she needed in this one little man. She knew that no matter what mistakes her past held—and she couldn't deny she'd made some bad ones—Kanoa would always love her.

She drank in the scent of Kanoa's baby soft skin, now flushed with sleep, and laid her hand against his forehead. He felt warm, but not feverish. The fever had finally broken three days ago. That allowed her to bring Kanoa home from the hospital.

He'd been bitten by a matoo. The amphibious reptile was one of the unique creatures that inhabited Toolowa. They lived in and around fresh water, or had. Over the centuries, too many people had died from their bites. The Toolowans had hunted and slaughtered them without mercy, determined to exterminate them. In the past three years, no one had been bitten by one. That led the Toolowans to believe they had finally eliminated the pest from the island. Now all the fresh water ponds and streams were again being searched.

Jessie sat in the rocking chair next to Kanoa's bed and took his hand. The past two weeks had been the longest, hardest ones of her life. A matoo always bit deep and hung on. The one that bit Kanoa clamped onto the bottom and top of his left foot. It, along with his leg—all the way up to his knee—had swollen to three times its size in a matter of minutes.

If Tena and Takoa hadn't been with them and acted without hesitation, the bite would have been fatal. Takoa killed the beast with his knife and pried its jaws from Kanoa's foot. Tena tore a strip of cloth from her sarong and applied it as a tourniquet around Kanoa's swelling calf. After giving Kanoa a priesthood blessing, Takoa ran the five miles to the hospital with Kanoa in his arm.

Dr. Snyder had already injected Kanoa with the anti-venom before Jessie and Tena finally reached the hospital. He told them another few minutes without the anti-venom, he'd spent years developing to fight the matoo's poison, would have been fatal for Kanoa. Still, during the first twenty-four hours, Dr. Snyder was afraid Kanoa wouldn't live. If he did live, Dr. Snyder warned Jessie his foot and leg might still have to be amputated.

Hearing that, Takoa sent for his father. Edmund came, and together they administered another blessing.

The news of Kanoa's encounter with a matoo spread over the island in a matter of hours. Other teachers willingly took over Jessie's classes. For the first forty-eight hours she hadn't left the hospital, not until Dr. Snyder pronounced Kanoa out of danger.

How many decades did I age in those first forty-eight hours, my sweet little man? And how many more over the next few days until I knew you would be able to keep your leg and foot?

During his time in the hospital Kanoa had been heavily sedated to keep him from thrashing around with the intense pain the bite caused. With nothing to do but wait to see if his foot and leg would respond to treatment, Jessie spent the days in her classroom giving her students their final exams and all night in the hospital with her nearly comatose son.

Gratitude filled Jessie. She knew it was the priesthood blessings that had saved Kanoa's life and spared his foot and leg from amputation. Her love beamed down brighter than the moon upon her baby so peacefully submerged in his carefree sleep, even though that sleep remained partly medication induced.

Keeping Kanoa off his feet would have been impossible except for the sedatives. His foot was still bandaged where the matoo had bitten him. Matoo bites were slow to heal. Kanoa wasn't supposed to walk on it until the wound was completely closed and all the swelling in his leg and foot were gone.

She examined his leg and foot and took a relieved breath. The swelling was virtually gone. In the morning, she would unwrap his foot and check on the bite. *Hopefully, it will only be a couple more days before he can start to walk again.*

She rested her elbows on her thighs and put her chin in her hands, feeling the accumulated days of worry and fatigue. By the time she was allowed to bring Kanoa home, almost two weeks had passed since she'd slept in her own bed.

This morning, Triny spotted the exhaustion she couldn't hide. Triny decided Jessie needed a few hours just to rest, relax, and recuperate, before she ended up in the hospital too. Jessie protested, but when Tena came to check on Kanoa at noon, she and Triny ganged up on Jessie and forced her out the door for the rest and relaxation they were determined she should have. Reassured Kanoa was out of danger and his sedated state would keep him from needing her, she gave in and went canoeing, snorkeling, and finally napping on the bay.

Kanoa's thumb was still wedge into his slack mouth. In his other arm, he clutched a stuffed dog, dressed in a nightshirt. Jessie tugged his thumb from his mouth. His lips reflexively made a tight O. His brow twitched, and his eyes fluttered open.

"Mama," he whispered, holding out his little arms.

She scooped him up and held him close.

He hugged her neck.

That simple gesture was a powerful cure. She tucked his head under her chin, and with his ear resting against her heart, she leaned back in the rocking chair. Wrapped in her little man's arms, everything else that had happened today seemed monumentally unimportant. She rocked Kanoa, again centered in the life she loved until her head quit pounding, allowing her to drift into a restful sleep.

8

AFTER STARING INTO THE DARKNESS FOR HOURS, Sky was still reeling with elation. *I've found her. I've finally found her, and in a place I didn't even know existed until three weeks ago.* Countering his elation, his gut twisted with apprehension, and he couldn't keep from replaying the scene that had ended their relationship.

After four years, he still felt like howling out his frustration over his self-righteous pride and couldn't keep from berating himself. "Jerk, moron, idiot! Take your pick, Brannigan, or apply them all. That's what you were, and that's undoubtedly how she sees you now."

He jumped out of bed and paced the floor. *I can't change the past, but maybe the Lord has finally accepted my penance and given me a second chance to win Jessie's heart. But is that even possible?* He dropped back onto the bed. *How do I begin to make up for all the pain I caused her?* The scorn of self-loathing twisted his lips. "Maybe I should begin by offering to let her use me as a punching bag for as long as she wants," he said to the wall of his room in the embassy.

Once Dr. Snyder determined Sky and Jake wouldn't need to be hospitalized, Ambassador Hamilton had Shin prepare rooms for them. After one of the most traumatic days of his life, Sky was more than ready to retire when the party finally broke up.

He'd never crashed a plane before, and even though it was a more or less controlled crash, he wondered if he would wake up in the morning with gray hair at his temples. Already there were bruises along his right side. His shoulders and back also ached from the whiplash of the plane hitting the water and flipping over. He never, ever wanted to go through that kind of experience again.

Still, hearing Jake utter the one word he truly hated, to the one woman he'd never gotten over, made the trauma of the crash pale by comparison.

The barrage of emotions that had stormed him when he saw Jessie had been so intense they'd nearly knocked him down. Well, until the pure, blinding fury of understanding propelled him forward. That word "Amazon" coming out of Jake's mouth, answered the one question that had haunted him.

Jake, who'd become his friend and teammate when the Jersey Reds merged with the New York Jewels, shortly after Sky started playing pro basketball, was the man Jessie had betrayed him with—he was dead certain of it. It had been there in both of their faces.

The feelings of betrayal he thought he'd let go of came crashing back, magnified by new understanding, and—he had to admit it—jealousy. He'd been green with it when Jake walked right up to Jessie, as though their relationship was still intimate, and without missing a beat, began exuding charm.

The urge to throttle Jake had put a glint in his eyes and a growl in his voice when he'd spoken to Jessie. He'd instantly regretted the harsh comment that leaped off his tongue. It wasn't what he'd planned to say—if he was ever allowed to see her again.

"I'm such a stupid jerk." He groaned. "This is my one heaven sent shot, and I've already started off wrong."

Yet, that cruel comment sparked the clash between his eyes and her magnificent ones. They told him she still felt something for him. "Loathing, no doubt," he muttered. *But at least she didn't react with cold indifference.* Her trembling hand confirmed she still had feelings for him. *Even if what she felt was loathing, it means I can still make her feel, and that's a good thing—I hope.*

THE TROPICAL BIRDS, chattering their welcome to the sunrise, jarred Sky out of a restless sleep. He listened to them, his mind a little fuzzy, trying to drift back into the much-needed sleep that had eluded him most of the night.

But the events of the past twenty-four hours pushed through the haze into the forefront of his mind.

"Jessie," he whispered. "I was such a self-righteous fool."

He'd always been able to win over the women he wanted—not so with Jessie. She'd forced him to be patient. *And she was right to do it,* he acknowledged. Because of her, he finally let go of his cocky self-centeredness. Jessie had challenged everything about him. She never agreed with him if her opinion differed from his. She never just went along to please him. She fought for her opinions, worked for mutual solutions to their disagreements, and through it all, helped him grow. He loved her for doing that, and for sticking with him through that hard process.

The first rays of sunlight peeked through the window. He laced his fingers behind his head and took up where he'd left off last night—planning his campaign to again win Jessie's love. Her bare ring finger, and the fact no one contradicted him when he said her last name at the party, made hope flow like a shot of adrenalin through his veins. *Could it be that she hasn't married because she hasn't gotten over me—still loves me?* He knew it was a desperate hope, but her naked ring finger fueled that hope.

His hope was short lived.

Jake's expression when he took her hand made Sky's lips disappear into a hard line. Then he smirked with grim satisfaction. After Jessie disappeared from the party, Jake took up flirting with Teneacia Chang. He'd spent nearly the whole evening at her elbow. They seemed to get along famously. Sky hoped that meant Jake didn't harbor any lasting feelings for Jessie. Jake had always been a ladies man, and Sky rarely saw him with the same girl twice.

"Why settle for one dish when you can sample the smorgasbord," Jake liked to say.

This was one time Sky was glad Jake felt that way. There had been several other attractive women, besides Jessie and Tena, at the party. Certainly, there was enough of a smorgasbord on the island to entertain Jake and keep him away from Jessie. *And I'll make sure he stays away. Even if I have to drop a warning, or something harder, in his ear,* Sky decided, peeling back his light blanket.

He spotted a towel, a brown geometric patterned lava-lava, and a clean tailored shirt, neatly arranged over a chair. His uniform, that had been hastily laundered yesterday, was gone. *No doubt to be laundered again,* he surmised. He gathered up the items so carefully laid out for him and went into the adjoining bathroom his room shared with Jake's room.

Under the guise of concern for his sister-in-law's headache, Sky had asked and received directions to Jessie's house from Nora Hamilton. Washed, shaved, and wearing Toolowa's native dress, he stepped out the side door of the embassy and into a glorious sub-tropical morning.

A pleasant moment of déjà vu touched him. He hadn't worn a lava-lava since his missionary days in the South Sea Islands. It brought back memories of the people he'd taught the gospel to, members he loved, and how much he'd enjoyed life in the islands.

The cool morning breeze brushed over him with the fragrances of the jungle as he walked along a palm-shaded path. It was too early to visit, but he wanted to find Jessie's house before his meeting with the council of judges, which was scheduled for ten o'clock. As soon as it was over, he intended to head straight for Jessie's house, before Jake could.

Jessie's disappearance last night hadn't surprised him. *It was obviously a reaction to seeing Jake and me again after so many years. Either one of us would have been bad enough, but both of us at the same time, that must have been terrible for her.*

His initial reaction hadn't made the situation any easier for her either. *Why did I say what I did to her last night? Was it the shock of seeing her? Did that trigger my old feelings? Or was it that knockout dress and the way all the men were ogling her—especially Jake—that made me react the way I did.* He wanted to apologize for what he'd said— and so much more.

That dress had reminded him of the first time he'd seen her as the Amazon on the cover of a magazine at his brother's house. She was the most alluring woman in the world, and obviously thousands of men felt the same way.

Jessie hadn't wanted him to see the pictures of her as the Amazon. He'd respected that request and had never looked for her on the covers of old fashion magazines, not even the ones he knew his sisters-in-law had, until a few months after he started playing pro basketball.

While waiting for a haircut in a barber's shop, he'd come across an old fashion magazine with Jessie on the cover. At first, he'd glared at it in disgust. The Amazon was a name that fit her to a T. He'd decided right then to find as many of her magazine covers as he could, and burn them in effigy, hoping to burn her out of his heart forever. She hadn't been worthy of a place in it. Seeing her as she really was on the covers of all those magazines, and then burning them had been an exorcism—only it hadn't worked. *How could it? I knew from the moment I met her there would never be anyone else for me, but her.*

The lane from the embassy intersected with another larger one. He turned left and followed the palm and banyan tree lined lane that ran parallel along the perimeter of the beach to the north. Through tiny gaps in the tropical vegetation, he caught glimpses of the white sand and the aquamarine sea.

He still felt frustrated that he'd learned virtually nothing about Jessie's life on Toolowa at the party last night. Not that there had been much opportunity with people plying him with questions about himself and what he was doing here. Still, throughout the evening whenever the chance presented itself he'd asked discreet questions about her.

In the end, the only things he'd learned were, she loved being a teacher, and the school where she taught had just let out for a two-month planting and Christmas vacation. He found it odd that Jessie's friends, even after learning they were in-laws, seemed hesitant to tell him anything specific about her personal life. The one other thing he'd been told repeatedly was that everyone on the island loved her. *Well so do I! But has teaching been her whole life for the past four years?* It seemed very unlikely.

As he continued along the path, he thought about how Jessie would react to a visit from him. *I'm sure she would prefer a visit from a rattlesnake.* Dour resolve set his jaw.

Want it or not, I am going to see you today, Jessie, and you are going to listen to me, even if I have to abduct you to accomplish that goal.

He counted the smaller paths that broke off from the one he was on until he came to the fifth one. Turning due west, he followed a narrow track into the jungle for about fifty yards until he came to a small clearing.

A white stucco bungalow with a red tile roof and a deep covered patio sat inside a neatly trimmed hedge of bright red flowers. A wooden gate, set in the hedge, opened onto a stone path that led up to the front door. Flowering trees overshadowed the house from behind. Coconut palms, banana trees, and a fruit-bearing bush he didn't recognize, stood next to a vegetable garden.

Staying just inside the cover of the jungle, he gazed at the house. It was so picturesque that he had to fight the urge to move closer. Even the woodwind chimes on the porch beckoned him with an improvised song of welcome.

Lost in speculation and a genuine appreciation for Jessie's home, he was caught off guard by the sound of a man clearing his throat. He spun around and recognized Oliver Stone—the man that had escorted Jessie into dinner.

Oliver looked him over with disapproval, clutching a delicate bouquet of yellow flowers with a card carefully inserted in between the blossoms. "I do hope you aren't planning to disturb Jayling this early in the morning. Only gifts or notes are brought at this time of day and you don't have either, unless you've already put something on her porch."

"I . . . didn't bring a gift. I just came to see where . . . *my sister-in-law* lives so I can visit her later today."

"Perhaps you would like a lesson in the proper protocol for visiting a single woman on Toolowa."

Sky had taken an immediate dislike to Oliver at the party, mostly because Jessie had chosen to go in to dinner on his arm. That victory, along with his referrals to Jessie as Jayling during dinner, had burned under Sky's collar.

Now his obvious distain for Sky's ignorance of native customs tightened Sky's jaw. But Sky knew the value of following native customs. He decided they might be especially important if he was going to score points with Jessie. "Sure"—he shrugged—"but as a relative, am I bound by the protocols other men have to follow?"

Oliver seemed to consider the question before he replied. "Not if you were a blood relative, but you aren't, are you?"

"No. I'm not."

"Then it would only be polite to follow our customs."

"What are the Toolowan customs?"

"Come with me, and I'll show you." Oliver slid around Sky and walked down the path.

Sky followed him through the white wooden gate in the hedge and up the stone path to the porch, eagerly digesting every detail of Jessie's home. Oliver put a finger to his lips and mounted the three steep steps onto the veranda. Sky stayed at the bottom of the steps, observing this Toolowan ritual with interest.

Scattered over a table and a set of padded wicker chairs sat a number of small gifts, all with notes attached. Oliver set his offering in the middle of the table, came back down the steps and motioned for Sky to follow him back down the path.

When they re-entered the jungle, Oliver said, "At this time of the morning, gifts are left as a sort of calling card. The card attached to a gift either expresses some sentiment the giver simply wishes to convey or is a request to visit later in the day."

"And what are the appropriate visiting hours?"

"From two to four in the afternoon. However, if Jayling has other plans and doesn't wish to have visitors, she will hang a red scarf on her gate. In that case, no one with good manners will disturb her."

"Let me get this straight. If I don't declare my intention to visit by leaving a gift, I'm not allowed to simply drop by and visit during the proper visiting hours?"

Oliver gave him a disdainful stare. "A single man, interested in pursuing a closer relationship with Jayling wouldn't. It would be very impolite."

"I see. So how long do I have to deliver a calling card gift?" Sky asked as they walked back to the main lane that led into the business district of the village.

"If you hurry you can acquire something suitable and have it on her doorstep before she arises."

"And what time would that be?" Sky asked, finding it hard not to resent this man's obvious knowledge of Jessie's habits.

"She is usually in her garden before the sun rises above the channel plateau. You wouldn't want to deliver anything after that time."

"Thank you." Sky stopped on the intersecting lane that led back to the embassy.

Oliver gave him a curt nod and kept walking.

Sky watched the dentist for a few moments, and then sprinted up the path.

He'd seen a cluster of hanging orchids from his window. They would be a perfect calling gift. Declaring his intent to visit might not be wise, but if he showed Jessie he respected the Toolowan customs it might sway her decision to see him. He went through the front door of the embassy and quickly sought out Shin.

Fifteen minutes later he was again on Jessie's porch. He felt a moment of guilt as he cleared the other gifts she'd received from the table and placed them carefully on the crowded wicker chairs. Then placing a large fern frond in the center of the table, he draped the vine of large orchids over the top of the frond, stood back to evaluate the effect, rearranged a few of the trailing flowers, making them drape over the edge of the table, and slid his card between the feathery fingers of the fern.

9

KANOA'S ATTEMPT TO ESCAPE HER LAP woke Jessie. She tightened her arms, reflexively.

"Get down, please?" he asked, imploring her with his bright green eyes.

Yawning, Jessie blinked at the strong sunlight that poured through Kanoa's window. She'd slept longer than she usually did, but couldn't regret it. She felt calm, refreshed, and secure in her world.

"And just where do you think *you're* going, my little man?" She tugged Kanoa into a hug. "The doctor said no walking until your foot is all better." She fixed him with a stern eye, "You don't want to go back to the hospital, do you?"

"No!"

"Then you will just have to be a very good and patient little man for a few more days and let me carry you around."

"No." His brows drew together thoughtfully. "Crawl."

"Your knees will get tired of doing that pretty fast. It would be easier if you just let me carry you."

"Not a baby!"

"No, but if I let you crawl, you must hold your foot up."

"Okay."

Jessie set him on the floor and watched him scurry across it like a lame crab. When he reached the door, he sat down and grinned.

She bit back a laugh and tried to look grave. "All right, you can crawl, but do you really want to do it all the way into the kitchen? Or would you rather go piggyback?"

Kanoa's face lit with the smile that never failed to lift Jessie's heart and fill it with love.

"Piggyback," he said, and held out his arms.

Hoisting Kanoa onto her back, Jessie galloped into the kitchen. She set him down in his booster seat, shook a coconut, drilled a hole in it, inserted a straw, and handed it to him. "Sit tight while I go see what the fairies brought us for breakfast."

Kanoa grinned and began to suck on the straw.

The fairies were Jessie's explanation to Kanoa of why their porch was covered with small tokens of gratitude or admiration each morning. The bounty left on her front porch had made her uncomfortable at first. There was always so much more than she could use, and she felt guilty receiving so much when there were families on the island whose needs were so much greater than hers were.

Tena told her the gifts would probably taper off in time, explaining it was pretty common for new people on the island to be inundated with morning gifts of welcome and admiration—especially a single woman.

Jessie wanted to pass along what she couldn't use to the needy, but was afraid it might offend the givers. Tena assured her what she did with the gifts was strictly up to her. No one would feel offended if she chose to share her gifts. That helped Jessie accept the custom more readily, especially since the morning gifts didn't taper off, at least not much. Using her position as a teacher, she passed along what she couldn't use in her weekly visits to her student's homes.

A light breeze ruffled her loose hair as she stepped out her front door. Instantly, she was drawn to the exceptionally beautiful offering on top of the porch table. All the other gifts were arranged on the four chairs surrounding the table. Never had there only been a single gift on top of the table. It was set out as though it was of more importance than those crowded onto the seats of the chairs. This unusual configuration made her approach the table almost warily.

Orchids were a highly prized gift. They didn't grow in the wild on Toolowa. The first orchids had been imported from India and Australia. The hybrids developed from those orchids had been carefully cultivated. They brought those who knew how to grow them a substantial income. A single orchid would have caught her attention and marked the gift as special. The cascading bouquet of seven delicate blooms, so artfully displayed, was more than extravagant.

She plucked the envelope from its carefully situated place in the fern frond, afraid Oliver had mistaken her need for rescue as a gesture of encouragement. Reluctantly, she looked at the envelope, recognized the handwriting, and felt the need to sit down. She stared at the way he'd written her name. He'd done it just as he always had in his letters, with a tiny heart replacing the dot over the "i" in her name.

He's mocking me! After what he'd said last night, it was all she could think of. She crushed the envelope and dropped it on top of the fern frond. She wanted to reach out and sweep the orchids from the table, but couldn't. They were so lovely she couldn't destroy them, even if they were being used to mock her. *I'll have Triny take them to Clara Nayar. At least Sky's cruel joke will bring a little cheer to a grieving widow.*

Jessie stepped away from the orchids and picked up a decorative woven basket filled with rolls. She stacked the rolls up on one side, added a cluster of dates, a papaya, two kiwis, a pineapple, and a bunch of bananas to the basket, reading each card as she added the items. All of the fruit came from her students. Additionally there were several gifts of art, also from her students. She admired her student's creativity and glanced at the additional flower offerings, distressed to find Oliver's bouquet.

Discouraging him from pursuing her had been one of her more painful experiences on Toolowa. Thankfully, six months ago, he'd quit bringing her morning gifts. Now with one desperate act, she'd reignited his interest. *It serves me right—using poor Oliver like that.*

She left the rest of the morning gifts where they were and went in to feed Kanoa breakfast.

After their breakfast of fresh fruit and rolls was finished and cleaned up, Jessie dug out Kanoa's favorite toys from his toy box and set them next to him on the Oriental rug in the living room. They played with the die-cast cars Grandpa and Grandma Garrison sent Kanoa last Christmas until Tena came through the door, holding Sky's crumpled card.

Tena waved the card. "I take it that glorious bouquet of orchids is from someone you don't care for. Could it be from one of your American admirers?"

"It is. And I don't want to hear *anything* he has to say."

Tena's brows arched. "That bad, huh? Well I'm here to get the whole scoop, like you promised, so start dishing it out."

Jessie jerked her head toward the kitchen, got up and snatched the note from Tena's hand. "Auntie Tena and I will be in the kitchen if you need me," she said to Kanoa. "Remember you are not to walk, and hold your foot up when you crawl, okay?"

"I be good," he said and went back to building a garage of wooden blocks for his cars.

"I may have to fire Triny." Jessie dropped into a wooden chair at the kitchen table. "Kanoa's English is sounding more and more like hers every day." She blew out a breath. "Being a single, working mother definitely has its challenges."

"You could solve that problem by marrying Oliver."

"Very funny." Jessie slouched in her chair. "I take it you saw his bouquet?"

"I did, but if you're set against the idea of marrying Oliver, you could always marry Fenton, Chin-ho, or Tallen. Their flowers were very pretty too," Tena said teasingly.

Jessie gave her friend a sour expression. "If you're quite finished rubbing salt in my wounds, can I get you something to eat before you tell me what happened after I left the party last night?"

Tena waved a dismissive hand. "I don't need anything." She sat down across the table from Jessie and immediately took a roll from the morning gift basket, which still sat on the table. Leaning forward, her violet eyes danced. "After you left, your *friend*, Jake, attached himself to me like a barnacle on the hull of a ship."

"Did he? Well, I'm not at all surprised. When I met him in New York, he had a big reputation as a ladies man. Jessie clicked her tongue, disgusted. I guess nothing has changed with him."

"Apparently not. He even made a pass at me when he walked me home."

"That's Jake to a tee. But what did you expect when you let him attach himself to you and then walk you home."

"I only did that so I could pump him for information about your relationship with him."

"So what did he tell you?"

"All about how bowled over he was by the *Amazon,* your whirlwind romance, and how devastated he was when you left. Do you know he even tried to find you?"

"You're kidding!"

"I'm not. He told me he didn't know your real name. He said no one did, except your agent—who by the way—was killed in a car accident the day after you left. That kept Jake from being able to go after you."

Jessie swallowed and blinked. "I'm . . . truly sorry about Burt. I liked him, he was a good agent."

"Why was Burt the only one who knew your real name?"

"I insisted on that as part of the contract I signed. My folks weren't happy with my decision to become a model. So, I decided not to tarnish the family name with my unacceptable career choice. Burt was the one that gave me the name, Amazon."

"How original," Tena said dryly, "but if you and Jake were in love, I would think you would have at least told him your real name."

"He was never in *love* with me, and I only *thought* I was in love with him for a very short time."

"Tell me." Tena absently broke off a piece of the roll and popped it into her mouth. "And don't leave out a single detail," she mumbled with her mouth full.

With a resigned look, Jessie told Tena about being introduced to Jake by Burt at a party. "I was unduly flattered by his attention and full-court-press charm."

"If last night is any indication of the way he works, I think most girls would be bowled over by Jake, especially considering how handsome he is."

Jessie crossed her ankles and leaned back in her chair. "To be fair, I think Jake was drawn to me because I was a country girl, and that made me stand out from all the sophisticated women he knew."

"What drew you to him, other than his physical charms?" Tena asked propping her elbows up on the table, still nibbling on her roll.

"He grew up on a dairy farm in rural Massachusetts, and could speak my language."

"Your language?"

"Livestock."

"Ah." Tena popped the last bite of the roll into her mouth.

"I can't tell you how refreshing it was after nearly nine months in New York to finally meet someone I had something in common with. That was a rare thing for me. Most of the people I was introduced to felt like aliens from another planet."

"But," Tena said, when Jessie hesitated.

"But, I also have to admit, I was drawn to Jake because he was a couple of inches taller than I was, and that made me feel very feminine, something my height often robs me of. He also dazzled me with his debonair sophistication. I fell for him like the green country girl I was."

"Well after seeing him in action last night, I can't blame you. He's definitely got more than his share of charm and knows how to use it."

"That he does, but the rose-colored glasses I saw him through shattered after about six weeks. Once he felt sure of my affection for him, he stopped doing things with me that I liked to do. He kept telling me I needed to let go of the childish things I enjoyed and let him guide me into more sophisticated tastes."

"Oh and how did he propose to do that?"

"By integrating me into his world, which meant we mostly just went to high profile events where all the beautiful people go to see, and be seen."

"So, you didn't enjoy hobnobbing with the rich and famous."

Jessie picked up Kanoa's coconut and began to pluck at its hairy shell. "Believe me; being in a room with so many over blown egos isn't enjoyable. Not only that, but attending all those hifalutin parties with Jake made me realize he would never love anyone more than he loved himself. To him, I was just a paper doll he enjoyed using to attract the photographers. My role in his life was to pet his ego, build up his star athlete status, keep my mouth shut, and smile *adoringly* at him when we had our picture taken."

"Sounds like the country girl grew up pretty fast."

"Unfortunately, I didn't grow up fast enough."

"How so?" Tena asked, taking a banana from the breakfast basket and peeling it.

"I got tired of feeding Jake's ravenous ego and being used as a publicity draw for him. I decided to break up with him. By then I knew I wasn't cut out for the high life, and I wasn't going to renew my contract with the Elite Modeling Agency. It was almost up, and I wanted to spend my last few weeks in New York doing the things I wanted to do."

"Like what?"

"I wanted to do some of the dumb tourist things Jake wouldn't do with me." Jessie looked sheepishly down at the coconut. "I hadn't been to the Statue of Liberty or to the top of the Empire State Building. There were also a couple of the Broadway plays I'd been dying to see. I wanted to enjoy doing those things without having them turned into publicity events for Jake."

Tena snatched the coconut, making Jessie meet her eyes. "How did you do the dastardly deed?"

Jessie explained about going to Jake's party with the intention of breaking up with him.

"Good move—not doing it on your turf—I mean. It's always easier to walk out the door rather than try to evict someone from your house when you want them to leave, if they don't want to go."

"Well, it wasn't a good move."

"Why."

"Imagine my surprise when I woke up the next morning in Jake's bed with a monstrous headache and a diamond the size of Mount Rushmore on my finger."

Tena's mouth dropped open.

"Exactly." Jessie gestured at Tena's slack jaw. "Jake sweetly told me that we'd gotten carried away after announcing and celebrating our engagement at the party, but I didn't have to worry about anything because he loved me and intended to make an honest woman of me in short order."

Tena slumped back in her chair. "Oh, Jessie, I'm so sorry. Are you're sure you and he—"

Jessie's anguished expression answered her question. "I can't even begin to tell you how I felt."

"Try!"

"I was terrified"—Jessie massaged her temples—"because I couldn't remember what had happened, and I was dumbfounded by what I'd done. Jake put on the charm and told me he had a couple of away games so he'd be gone for the next week, but as soon as he got back we'd get married, and I should start planning the wedding."

"And you just went along with that? No questions asked? Didn't you want to know how it all happened?"

"I didn't have to ask about that. I knew *how* it had happened," Jessie said, and explained about drinking the liquor—she thought was wine—for courage.

Tena leaned forward. "Do you think Jake intentionally got you drunk or put something into that drink to make you cooperative? There are such drugs you know."

"I have no idea. He was always telling me I ought to let my hair down more, you know, relax my standards. He may have put something in my drink or just encouraged my drinking once I started. But the bottom line is; I chose to take that first drink. So what happened was my own fault."

"Okay, so it was your own fault. But I'm surprised you believed everything he told you. That's not the Jessie I know."

"No, but the *Amazon* that woke up in Jake's bed was paralyzed with fear. I was terrified I might be pregnant, and wouldn't have a choice about marrying Jake. So, I played the happy fiancée and fled his apartment as soon as I could. A few days later, I found out I wasn't pregnant."

"I bet that was a monumental relief."

"Yeah, monumental." Jessie blew out a breath. "Then the night before Jake told me he would be home from his road trip, I stopped into a little French restaurant to get some takeout. I spotted him with a well-known blond in a booth at the back of the restaurant. They were all over each other." Jessie leaned her head back against the wall behind her chair and shook with laughter. "I have never felt such relief."

"So I see."

"It made it easy for me to break up with Jake. I sent him his ring with a note detailing what I saw and told him not to darken my door again. I thought that was the end of it."

"Wasn't it?"

"No. The day before my contract with Elite expired he showed up at my last photo shoot and made a weeping, pleading scene, begging me to marry him. It was so embarrassing and not at all like Jake. I told him to take a hike, and that was the last time I saw Jake Denning. The next morning I was on a train out of the Big Apple, grateful to be free of the Amazon—and her life!"

"So you haven't seen him since then, and don't feel anything for him now?"

"No—on both counts. Still, seeing him last night was a painful reminder of everything that year in New York cost me."

"And just what else did it cost you—besides the obvious?"

Jessie's jaw locked. She took in a breath through her nose and blew it slowly out through her mouth.

Tena leaned toward her.

"It cost me happily ever after with—Sky Brannigan."

10

JESSIE WAS GRATEFUL TENA DIDN'T PRESS HER to continue. Instead, they sat silently listening to Kanoa make boisterous car noises in the living room.

There were no real cars on Toolowa. Kanoa learned about cars from the movies the supply planes brought. The people in the bay area always enjoyed the third Saturday of the month, when they would gather in a large outside amphitheater for an evening at the movies. From the moment a car raced onto the screen, Kanoa had been obsessed with them. His die-cast cars were his most prized possessions, along with the tan-colored stuffed dog he dragged with him everywhere. He couldn't go to sleep without puppy in his arms. Jessie didn't mind the dog in his bed, but routinely had to search it and remove several cars; afraid he would roll over on one and hurt himself.

The silence in the kitchen dragged on as Jessie fought to keep the emotions churning inside her from showing. She knew she hadn't succeeded when Tena reached over and squeezed her hand.

"You're still in love with Sky, aren't you?"

"No!" Jessie said vehemently, pulling her hand away. "I am *not* in love with Sky Brannigan—anymore. But . . . part of me still loves . . . the memory of him."

Tena frowned. "I don't understand what you mean."

Jessie sniffed and straightened in her chair. "I mean, I have never *before* or *since* felt for a man what I felt for Sky. It was—magical, just like a fairytale." Her face twisted. "Until it came crashing down on me like a nightmare."

"Tell me." Tena gently prompted.

"The moment I met Sky, I felt inexplicably drawn to him, but I resisted it."

"Why did you resist him when you felt drawn to him?"

"Because of my tarnished past and how squeaky-clean he was. But he was so persistent, and I was so attracted to him." She told Tena about the first simple touch of their lips on New Year's Eve and feeling his longing to deepen that kiss. "His restraint led me to believe he truly meant what he said about wanting to get to know me. I was even more encouraged by his willingness to hold off any demonstration of physical affection to allow us to forge a relationship without muddying the waters by adding the distortion of physical attraction."

"I can see how important that would be to you. It's important to me too," Tena said, and they exchanged knowing looks.

"Yes, and I began to hope that if we held off on the physical affection, he would come to see *me,* not the Amazon. Just as his cousin, Hadlee, eventually saw and fell in love with my brother, Ryder, for who he was. It took time for her to see past his responsibility for her mother's death and find the good man he'd become. One she eventually knew she wanted to be with for all time."

"Their story is so remarkable," Tena said when Jessie finished telling her about Ryder and Hadlee. "I admire them so much for pressing forward against such ugly opposition."

"So do I, and it was their courage that gave me the courage to try with Sky. Only I didn't tell him right up front about my moral lapse. I kept telling myself it would be better to wait until his feelings for me were strong enough to weather what I'd done."

"Mama," Kanoa called from the living room. "Come see my garage."

Jessie and Tena scooted back their chairs and hurried into the living room.

"I believe you have a budding architect on your hands," Tena said, admiring the garage.

Jessie crawled around the cleverly built two-story structure, inspecting it closely. "I think you're right. It's a terrific garage, little man. Your uncle Ryder would be very proud of you."

Tena ruffled Kanoa's curls. "It's a work of art. One that deserves a cookie—or something."

Kanoa beamed.

"All right, you can have a couple of cookies, but you have to eat them over a plate. I don't want to clean cookie crumbs off the rug." Jessie pointed a finger at Tena. "Since this was your idea, you can just go get him the cookies."

Tena returned with three cookies on the biggest plate Jessie had in her kitchen.

Jessie lifted a brow and took the plate.

Tena shrugged. "I thought it might help keep the carpet clean."

"We can only hope." Jessie set the plate down next to Kanoa and asked, "Do you need anything else?"

"No," Kanoa said and bit into an oatmeal-raisin cookie.

Tena took hold of Jessie's arm. "Just holler if you do, we'll be in the kitchen." She pulled Jessie back down the hall. "Now where were we?" she asked, settling back into her chair. "Oh, I know, you and Sky had decided to put physical affection on hold."

"We did, and it made our first real kiss so much more meaningful." A tremor ran through Jessie with the memory of that kiss, so full of his desire to assure her of his genuine feelings for her. "Do you know that kiss made me cry?"

"Made you cry?" Tena asked, puzzled.

"Yes, and just like you, he didn't understand my tears over that kiss, but I have never been so affected by a kiss. He apologized, concerned I thought it was too soon, and was distressed by the kiss."

"Were you?"

"No, I'd been longing for it and was a very willing participant. When I told him how he'd made me feel, he gave me that intoxicating smile of his, kissed me again and confessed he was in love with me. That made me start crying all over again. It felt so much like a fairytale—that whole summer did."

Tena plucked a few dates from the basket and popped one into her mouth as Jessie described that magical summer when she and Sky had signed on as members of Ryder's construction crew.

"The days we worked were long and exhausting, but the evenings always belonged to us."

"What did you find to do in the wilds of Colorado to entertain yourselves?"

"We had wonderful conversations, hidden away in our special place by the river. We laughed and talked and dreamed to its musical accompaniment all summer. And oh, Tena, the rambling walks we took through the meadow under the magnificence of the stars."

"You make it sound like you were the only two people in that camp."

"There were times when it felt like that. However, Ryder insisted on a curfew for our after dark outings and required us to join the nightly campfire before retiring. Even under his watchful eyes, Sky and I would snuggle up together around the campfire and enjoy the songs and outrageous stories the crew told." She made a face. "We also endured a lot of good-natured teasing."

"So that summer was paradise." Tena got up and poured herself a glass of water.

"Yes, except for one argument, and it was a doozey."

Tena sat back down, took a sip from her glass, and leaned forward. "Do tell."

"It began when he asked me to marry him before school started again in the fall, and I refused him."

"Why in the world would you do that when you were so much in love with him?"

Jessie blew out a breath, rocked back in her chair and explained about her desire to complete her education, and the reasons she wanted to do it at a different college than the one Sky was attending.

"I can understand that. Being at the same college probably would have weakened your resolve not to marry him before you graduated."

"That too. However, I also didn't want to tell Sky about what happened between Jake and me, not until he truly saw me and loved me for who I really was. At that point in our relationship, I felt as though he was still being blinded—at least some of the time—by the Amazon."

"I know the problem." Tena threw Jessie an understanding look. Then popped another date into her mouth and wiped her hands on a napkin. "And that was the basis of your refusal to marry him?"

"Yes, and when I wouldn't give into his pleading and sweet talk, he got frustrated, and we argued."

"But he gave in?"

"He did. He even apologized for trying to pressure me into getting married before I was ready and gave me the most beautiful bouquet of wildflowers."

When Jessie didn't continue, Tena guessed, "So he went back to BYU, while you stayed in Colorado."

"Uh-huh. I dried that bouquet of wildflowers and kept them on my desk as a sort of incentive and reminder of what Sky was willing to sacrifice for me."

"That *was* quite an extraordinary sacrifice."

"It was, and it meant so much to me." Her throat suddenly felt tight, she cleared it and said, "The next three years were filled with almost daily letters and weekly phone calls. They motivated me and continually reaffirmed my goal to graduate at the same time Sky did, so we could begin our life together. They were the lifeblood of our courtship, the constant affirmation of Sky's love, the reward of each day when I came home overloaded with homework. Most importantly, our letters allowed us to do what I desperately wanted. We came to understand each other's minds, learned how to talk out our differences, compromise, and unify our dreams." Jessie's voice quivered and died away. With a wave at the note, she explained about the heart over the "i" in her name.

An unexpected tear trickled down her cheek.

Tena handed her a napkin.

She blew her nose and straightened in her chair. "Through it all, we grew into one heart, our souls wielded by an unbreakable bond—at least that's what I thought had happened. Except, when I finally told him about my moral lapse, his love wasn't strong enough, deep enough, or enduring enough."

"When did you finally tell him?"

"When he was trying to formally propose to me." A bark of bitter laughter exploded from Jessie. "Nice way to ruin a proposal, huh? But I couldn't accept Sky's proposal until I confessed my secret. I wanted to go into our marriage being completely open and honest with him."

"Telling him was the right thing to do."

"Yes, and when he stormed out my door, I told myself our love was strong enough to weather the mistake in my past and he would come back." She shivered, hugged herself, and gazed out the window.

"What happened?"

Jessie inhaled a slow breath and blew it out even slower. "I sat up that whole night, waiting for him to come back. He didn't. Not that night—not ever."

"Oh, Jessie, I'm—"

She waved away Tena's sympathy and said, "Then a few days after he walked out on me, Hadlee came to see me. She told me Sky had called his parents from Kansas City to tell them he wasn't going into the family business. He'd decided to go east to look for work and said he would let them know where he ended up and what he was doing, as soon as he'd made up his mind. When his mom asked him about me, the only thing he said was"—she paused and swallowed—"he was glad he hadn't made the mistake of marrying me."

Tena reached across the table and squeezed her hand.

"Hadlee was so furious with him that she could barely get the words out. I think she cried as much as I did." Jessie leaned her head back against the wall and drew in a ragged breath. She hadn't let herself think about or remember her relationship with Sky for a very long time. Doing it now felt like a self-inflicted wound.

"I knew the first time I met you that there was grief hidden inside you," Tena said, her eyes overflowing with Jessie's pain. She wiped her tears away with the napkin Jessie handed to her and said, "I've never asked because it's often better to let the scars of old wounds fade rather than to continually tear them open."

"I agree, and I haven't wanted to touch the scars Sky left. There are things about them that are so far reaching and painful that I can't bear to feel them again and again."

Tena touched Sky's card. "I think I understand now why you don't want to read what's in this card."

"I don't have to read it to know how he feels about me. Last night, he said it all in one word. There will never be any understanding or forgiveness in his heart for the *Amazon*."

"Jessie, I don't know why he reacted the way he did. But I watched him during dinner, and I can tell you that the way he kept sneaking peaks at you, when he thought no one else was looking, and what those looks told me, spoke volumes about the way he feels."

"Just what do you think you saw?" Jessie asked. She respected Tena's ability to read people's emotions and moods. That ability had kept Tena alive after her mother died and her brother abandoned her.

"Mostly, I saw sorrow and regret."

Jessie scoffed. "I've no doubt that's what you saw, but you're misinterpreting the meaning. I can tell you unequivocally that he's *sorry* he ever met me, bitterly *regrets* ever getting involved with me, and now, to top it off, he's had the terrible misfortune to run into me again."

"No!"

"Yes!"

Tena pointed to Sky's note, "There's one way to know for sure."

"Who said I want to know?"

"All right then—I want to know."

Jessie scowled at her.

Tena held her breath.

With a flick of her finger, Jessie sent the note spinning across the table and into Tena's lap. "Be my guest."

Tena snatched up the envelope, opened it, and pulled out Sky's note. She read it silently and then pushed it across the table. "You need to read this."

Jessie pushed it back. "I don't want—"

"Yes you do!" Tena shoved it back again. "And if you won't read it, I'll tell you what it says."

Jessie glared at her. "Then tell me—if you must!"

"Dear Jessie, there is so much I want to apologize for, and say to you. Please, may I come and see you this afternoon? Sincerely, Sky."

11

AFTER DELIVERING THE ORCHIDS, Sky went for a walk along the beach, trying to get the lay of the land, but he was back in the embassy by breakfast. He again thanked Shin for letting him have the precious orchids, which Shin had so lovingly cultivated.

The Hamilton's proper butler simply said, "For Jayling, they are gladly given."

It was perfectly understandable to Sky that Shin, along with everyone he talked with about Jessie, seemed captivated by her. People were always drawn to her. He thought about the class of second grade students she'd student taught. He'd surprised her with a visit, and sat in on her class. Using a myriad of teaching techniques, including stories and games, along with her magnetic personality and glorious voice, she'd engaged her students in learning, easily holding them all—including him—spellbound.

Shin led him into the cozy breakfast room, just off the kitchen. Sam Hamilton was the only person in the room.

"Good morning, Major," Sam said, setting aside the book he was reading.

"Good morning, sir."

"Take a seat." The ambassador's hand swept the table. "You will find breakfast is a very casual affair here, and you can drop the sir. Just call me Sam, like everyone else on Toolowa does."

Sky hesitated before taking a seat. "Will Mrs. Hamilton be joining us?"

"I doubt it. She prefers having a tray in her room—unless the guests in the house include women."

"What about Captain Denning? Have you seen him this morning?" Sky asked evenly. He wanted to have a heart to heart chat, *or maybe knuckles to chin,* he admitted, with his co-pilot as soon as possible. Something he hadn't been able to do last night because Jake had insisted on walking Teneacia Chang home.

"I believe Captain Denning went to the hospital to have his shoulder checked. I'm afraid he had an uncomfortable night."

Good, Sky thought uncharitably, thinking of his own largely sleepless night, *because I'm sure Jessie had an even worse one than either one of us.* "How long ago did he leave?" Sky asked, filling a plate with eggs, pancakes, and fresh fruit from the covered dishes on the table.

"About an hour ago. I imagine he'll be back shortly."

Sky was working on his second stack of pancakes when Shin escorted a haggard looking Jake into the room.

"How's the shoulder?" Sky asked, swallowing a mouthful of pancakes.

"It hurts like—"

Sky's warning glare clipped off Jake's colorful expletive. "Did the Doc give you some painkillers?"

"Yeah, and he said there might be more coral in my shoulder than he thought. The wound is red and swollen. I'm supposed to take it easy and go back to the hospital in a couple of hours. After his rounds, the doc wants to examine it again."

"Poke around in it, you mean," Sky said.

Jake winced and took a seat.

Sky helped his handicapped co-pilot load up a plate and watched him dig in with enthusiasm.

"I'm glad to see your injury hasn't affected your appetite," Sam said. He leaned back in his chair, considering the two pilots. "I'm surprised you two skyscrapers can fit into a cockpit. What did you two do before the war?"

"We played pro-ball for the New York Jewels. Center." Sky bobbed his head and finished off his pancakes.

"Forward," Jake mumbled with a mouth full of eggs.

Sky wiped his lips and set aside his napkin. "I also flew cargo on the side. My family owns an airfreight business. I grew up in the air, and fortunately, cockpits in cargo planes are bigger than the ones in fighter planes."

"I didn't start flying until I met Sky. He taught me to fly cargo planes to help me supplement my income in the off-season. Thus the difference in our ranks," Jake said.

"You two are cargo plane pilots?" Sam lifted a skeptical brow.

"Sometimes—when we're not flying bombers," Sky said.

"Or troop transports," Jake said.

Sky grimaced. "That's what's sitting at the bottom of the bay."

"Why would the U.S. military send a transport plane to Toolowa?" Sam asked, his gaze shifting between the major and the captain. "For that matter, why would they send *any* plane here? Toolowa isn't being threatened by the war—as far as I know."

"With respect, sir, maybe that explanation better wait until our meeting with the council of judges. What we were sent here to do will take time to explain," Sky said.

Sam glanced at his watch. "All right, I can keep my curiosity in check for another thirty minutes."

Jake set his fork aside and pushed back from the table, looking better than he had when he entered the room. "Sir, may I ask why Edmund Zenderly goes by the title of chief judge instead of his royal majesty? Most kings wouldn't want to settle for the title of judge when they could be reverenced as *your royal majesty.*"

Again, Sam consulted his watch. "I think there's just enough time to tell you that story. And, Jake, just call me Sam." He leaned back in his chair and told them about the arrival of the short wave radio that had opened up the world to Toolowa. "They began receiving broadcasts from around the world. One of their favorites came out of Salt Lake City."

"Let me guess," Sky said. "It was the Mormon Tabernacle Choir's *Music and the Spoken Word,* wasn't it?"

"That's right. They were so impressed with the program that they got in contact with the Mormon Church, and the church immediately sent missionaries. They gave Edmund a Book of Mormon. He was particularly taken with one part in the book where a king, named Mosiah, frees the people from the rule of a monarchy by setting up a free government ruled by elected judges."

"So the people elected Edmund to be their first chief judge," Sky said, jumping to the correct conclusion. "The people here must hold him in very high esteem."

"They revere and love him so much, that at their insistence, Edmund's election is for the duration of his life."

"So he holds both titles," Jake said, resting his bandaged arm on the table.

"Yes, but when he dies, the monarchy will die with him."

"What about his sons? How do they feel about that?" Jake asked, referring to Takoa and Lowa who'd rowed him to shore after the crash.

"Oddly enough, his sons are fine with that. Neither of them act like royalty or expect to be treated like they are."

"Amazing." Jake shook his head with disbelief. "If I were a prince I would want to be treated like one."

"Will the next chief judge also be elected for life?" Sky asked pushing back from the table.

"No, he will only hold the office for five years. If he wishes to continue as the chief judge he must run for reelection."

"Are there term limits, like in the states?" Sky asked.

"No, it's possible for a man to be elected chief judge and retain that title for the rest of his life by being reelected every five years."

"If the Mormon's sent missionaries, I'm assuming there were converts," Sky said.

"Yes there were, and there are several congregations, or what they call wards, here on the island."

"Nice to know, since tomorrow is Sunday," Sky said.

"I take it you're a Mormon."

"I am."

"Well you will be in good company then. The Mormons on Toolowa include the entire Zenderly clan. We will go by the church on our way to the council building. After our meeting with the judges, Edmund can tell you when his ward meets."

Shin walked into the room and bowed. "I do hope breakfast was satisfactory."

Sky and Jake were quick with their thanks and praise.

Sam chuckled. "Shin isn't seeking compliments. His pride would never allow anything he considered second rate on this table. It's just his subtle way of telling me it's time we were on our way, if we don't want to be late for our meeting."

12

SKY TRAILED JAKE AS THEY FOLLOWED SAM along the broad lane that traced the shoreline of the bay. The natural growth of the tropical jungle along the lane was neatly manicured, thwarting the lush bushes and vines natural inclination to choke the lane. Sky admired the beauty of giant ferns, flowering creepers, red periwinkle bushes, towering palms, candlenut trees, banyans, and many other kinds of flora unknown to him. Like the other end of the lane that ran toward Jessie's house, he could see the brilliant sun reflected off the bay and the white sand of the beach intermittently through the dense foliage.

Toolowa reminded him more of the islands he'd spent his mission on than Hawaii did—where he'd initially been based at the beginning of the war. Hawaii had been taken over by the military, at least Oahu had. There was too much noise and too much civilization to suit Sky. Here on Toolowa, the island seemed to have adopted only those modern conveniences that made life more comfortable without detracting from the island's natural tranquility.

The breeze touched him with ghostly fingers. The music of tropical birds encouraged hope, and the unspoiled beauty of the sea, with its steadfast rhythmic sound, soothed his growing tension over the coming meeting. Even the simplicity of the buildings had a calming effect on him. All of it felt like an antidote to the complex, screaming war machines that had filled his life for three endless years.

A poignant longing ached inside him. *If only I could leave the war behind me and just stay in this peaceful place . . . with Jessie.* He wrenched his mind from that daydream. He couldn't afford to tease himself about that. *Even if Jessie wanted me to, I couldn't stay,* he admitted.

But—if she'll let me back into her life—I'll come back after the war is over, and we can make a new start.

He was pulled abruptly out of that absurd hope by the question Jake put to Sam. "Besides deciding who can live on Toolowa, what are the day-to-day responsibilities of the council of Judges?"

As they continued south along the lane that ran around the perimeter of the bay and into a more heavily populated area that the Toolowans referred to as the village square, Sam explained. "As you learned last night, Toolowa is partly a communal society. One of the judges' foremost duties is the allocation of property. You see, no one actually owns the land, not even King Edmund Zenderly."

Sky's brows lifted. "Interesting, but if no one owns the land, how do the judges decide who gets to live where?"

"When a person is granted citizenship, or a new family is formed, the council of judges meets to consider the needs of the person or family. They take into consideration profession, preference in location, and the family or person's needs in terms of size and space to accommodate them. Then they allot them a stewardship with the responsibility to improve and maintain their stewardship."

"What happens if someone wants a change in location? Or their family's needs change?" Jake asked.

"Then they simply petition the council and their request is given fair consideration. A vital part of the judges' job is to help the citizens of Toolowa be happy and content with their circumstances—and that isn't too hard to do, either."

"Why?" Jake asked.

"Because people here are content with a simple life. Family is their most prized possession."

"They've got that right," Sky said forcefully.

"Agreed," Sam said and pointed at the conglomeration of buildings just ahead. "That is the village square."

Sky smiled. There was nothing square about the rambling configuration of public buildings life in Toolowa revolved around. He scanned the sprawling hodgepodge of structures that were terraced along either side of the lane.

As they walked along, Sam pointed out the hospital and dentistry, two schools, half a dozen trading posts and stores, and just as many churches. All the buildings shared the unity of thatched roofs, but each was built on unique lines with a wide variety of materials ranging from wood, to rock, to plaster, which gave them a charming individuality.

Sky noted the location of the LDS meetinghouse, amazed at the diversity of religions represented by the churches, and admired the carefully controlled landscaping. Here again, the jungle was held in strict compliance by the workers he watched busily manicuring the grounds.

The broad lane rose gradually through the terraced square and prompted Sky to ask, "Where does the lane end?"

"It goes all the way up to the airstrip on the island's southeastern plateau," Sam said and told them about the tree dotted savannah, featuring a freshwater lake that covered the center of the island. "Most of the savannah, this side of the lake, is cultivated land. Those who managed and worked in Toolowa's spice and herb fields lived up on the plateau along the shore of the lake. However, most of the Toolowans live scattered along the perimeter of the bay in the cool of the tropical forest. Only a few preferred to live in the mountainous southern and western regions of the island as sheep and goat herders."

When they reached the center of the square, where the outdoor amphitheater for public meetings, parties, and movies was carved out of the hillside, they stopped to look at it.

"How many people can the amphitheater hold?" Sky asked.

"All the people in the bay area," Sam said and added, "There's another one like it near the lake, but it isn't quite as large."

"I'm impressed," Sky said, turning away.

They took the left fork in the main lane that ran along the ocean side of the square. It led them toward the council building's red tile roof, which stuck out in stark contrast to the rest of the square's thatched ones. Through an arched portico of stucco, accented by timber beams, they entered the building and followed the covered walkway around a lush open-air garden.

Sky lagged behind to admire and inhale the scent of a profusion of unusual blossoms, and then hurried to catch up with his companions as they passed a number of closed doors until they came to a set of open double doors. He ducked his head under the doorframe of what appeared to be a formal conference room. Fortunately, the ceiling was tall enough to accommodate his six foot, ten inch stance. He surveyed the room and made a mental note to watch out for the three large ceiling fans that whirled above a low table surrounded by cushions that sat in the center of the room.

A group of people stood with the chief judge. Sky recognized Troy Lind, Lily Apo, Pendow Hun, Tamrin O'Malley, Lin Pow, and Birdie Tyloa from the previous evening's dinner party.

The group's cheerful chatter ceased. Edmund shook their hands in formal welcome and showed them their seats at the table.

When everyone was seated, crossed legged, on the comfortable cushions around the low table, Edmund called the meeting to order and reintroduced the island's ruling council of judges.

Last night at the dinner party, Sky had been surprised that of the seven ruling judges, three were women.

As if reading his mind, Edmund explained, "On Toolowa, men and women have equal opportunity to run for elected offices."

All of the judges with the exception of Edmund, who was solidly middle aged, were what Sky thought of as "getting up there" in age. They were gray headed, wrinkled, and somewhat withered in appearance. However, the previous evening had taught Sky not to be deceived by appearances. Each of them was quick witted, sharp minded, and very perceptive.

"Major Brannigan, Captain Denning." Edmund nodded to each of them. "According to our laws and customs, all those who arrive on Toolowa uninvited—though not unwelcome," he said and smiled reassuringly at the flyers, "must meet with this council and justify their reasons for coming to Toolowa. That may sound harsh, but very few people are allowed to come to Toolowa and even fewer are allowed to remain. The island's resources will only support a certain number of inhabitants and we like to keep that number well below what the island can support."

"I can appreciate that," Sky said. "Toolowa is a paradise. It would be a shame if it were overrun with too many people, as other island kingdoms have been. Captain Denning and I want to thank the people of Toolowa for their timely rescue, excellent care, and cordial hospitality—considering our uninvited, and unexpected, arrival."

He would have continued, but he was interrupted by the council members. The smiling council patted the table lightly with the tips of their fingers.

Edmund quickly explained this gesture of appreciation for the flyers praise and gratitude.

When their fingers stilled, Sky said, "Our business on Toolowa wasn't meant to keep us here for more than a week. But with the loss of our plane, our stay will be prolonged, unless this council can arrange to get us off the island."

"I'm afraid we can't," Tory Lind said. "The war that has engulfed much of the world has curtailed our contact with those who have become our friends and allies. Where we used to enjoy weekly visits from trade merchants throughout the Indian Ocean, Australia, and even the United States, we now have contact only on a somewhat erratic basis."

"The last cargo ship that made port here came two months ago," Birdie Tyloa said in a reedy voice.

Lin Pow craned his short neck around Sam so Sky could see him. "The last cargo plane that brought mail and a very limited supply of goods and fuel came three weeks ago."

"It came out of Perth, and we were told it was unlikely another ship or plane would come for several weeks," Lily Apo said.

Sky frowned. "Are you in danger of running out of basic supplies to sustain the people of Toolowa?"

"Oh no," Edmund said. "Our ancestors lived here very well for thousands of years without any outside contact."

"As do we," Tamrin O'Malley, said in a soft Irish brogue.

"The disruptions to our regular communication and trade patterns are due to the needs of the war and the danger to ships and planes in the Indian Ocean that follow set schedules. But this does not concern us as much as we worry things may not be going well for our allies, and this is the reason their visits are now so sparse," Troy said.

A fly buzzing around the room landed on Edmund's arm, he swatted at it and said, "You see, with only one shortwave radio on the island we don't have a secure line of communication with the outside world. Scheduling cargo ships and planes over the radio would endanger those who bring them. Therefore, we never know for sure when the next ship or plane will come."

"Even the war news we receive can be weeks old," Pendow Hun said.

"What it means, Major, is that you and Captain Denning may be here for quite a while," Sam said.

Jake lifted his injured arm and rested it on the table. "I can think of a lot worse places to be stranded. I wouldn't mind biding my time on Toolowa."

"But that's not what we came here to do," Sky said. He turned to the ambassador sitting on his right. "We came here with orders to evacuate you, and as many of the Americans living here who wanted to go with us."

The room went still. The constant chatter of the birds and sound of the surf came in clearly through the large open widows. Overhead the fans whirred.

Sam's clear astonishment gave way to guarded concern. "Why?" he asked Sky.

The judges leaned in.

"Ambassador, we believe there is a credible threat to Toolowa. And the War Department feels it is in your best interest—and that of the forty seven U.S. citizens living here—to leave as soon as possible."

Before Sam could respond, Edmund jumped in. "What kind of threat is Toolowa facing?"

"Invasion," Sky said bluntly.

A chorus of inhaled shock erupted around the table. Edmund raised his hand, stilling them. "What makes your government believe we are going to be invaded?"

"And how soon?" Troy asked.

"Your Honor." Sky addressed Edmund as he had been instructed to do when they sat in council. "What I know of this matter is convoluted at best, but the War Department is taking it seriously, so seriously they authorized me to offer to take you and your family off the island too."

Another wave of astonishment ran through the room.

"I think you better tell us what you know, Major," Edmund said.

Sky took a breath and chose his words carefully. "The Navy has been working to clean the enemy out of the Solomon Islands since the battle of Guadalcanal. About three weeks ago, they came upon a boat floating seventy-five miles off one of the more remote islands. The boat held a woman and her dead child." He paused, took out his handkerchief and wiped his brow.

"How could a woman found floating in a boat in the Solomon Island be connected with a possible invasion of Toolowa?" Troy asked.

"The woman had a very distinctive tattoo around her left eye," Sky said running his eyes over the tattooed left brow of each council member.

"What was her name?" Edmund asked.

"Timora Jensen."

There was a collective intake of breath. The council exchanged wary looks.

"Timora Jensen is Toolowan, is she not?" Sky asked.

"She is," Edmund said. "She, and her American husband, Roger, were banished from Toolowa nearly three years ago."

"Banished?" Sky asked.

"Those who commit very serious crimes are banished—irrevocably—from the island," Edmund said, and quickly added, "but that is extremely rare."

"What do you do to those who commit minor crimes," Jake asked.

"We have no prisons here. We don't believe they have any beneficial effect on those that break the law. Instead, for minor crimes, we impose fines of time or money, or ostracize people for different lengths of time, depending on the crime. They're sent into the southern mountains for the length of their sentence, living as they can."

"And you find that effective? Wouldn't their family and friends simply help them out on the sly?" Jake asked.

"No, because if they are caught they too are ostracized, and the time is doubled," Birdie said, cooling herself with the additional efforts of a silk fan.

Sky pulled the discussion back on track. "What did the Jensens do that caused you to banish them?"

"They smuggled some spice and herb seeds off the island and were caught arranging to smuggle more," Edmund said grimly.

Leaning in, Sam said, "You see, Toolowa has many plants that don't exist anywhere else in the world."

"Over the centuries the Toolowans learned to cultivate and mix the unique herbs and spices that grow on the island. Our herbal teas are so distinctive and original that when we decided to start contacting other nations, we used them to begin our trading ventures. Now our teas and the spice blends we make for vegetables, meat, poultry, and fish, generate our main source of income," Edmund said.

"Which would be depleted if the plants could be grown elsewhere," Sky said and acknowledged, "That's what happened to the unique spices like nutmeg and mace that were smuggled out of the Spice Islands by France and England."

"Exactly," Troy said. "So you can see why it is vital to our growing economic endeavors to protect our unique plants."

Jake shifted his injured shoulder, repositioning it. "How many Toolowans work in the spice fields?"

"Over half," Edmund said. "However, the increasing demand for our herbal teas and spice mixes has required us to clear and cultivate more of the plateau every year. That requires virtually everyone on Toolowa to work for a few weeks of the year in the fields."

"Is that how the Jensens were able to get a hold of the seeds they smuggled out?" Sky asked.

The aged heads of the judges solemnly nodded.

"At least they didn't get more than a small shipment off the island, and so far, we haven't heard of any herbal teas or spice mixes to rival ours," Troy said.

"Didn't they also manage to smuggle out something else?" Sky directed the question to Edmund.

Edmund silently consulted his council.

Sky watched the judges' various expressions of hesitation turn into a united consensus and returned his attention to Edmund.

"After the Jensens were banished, we wondered if they might have stolen one other unique kind of seed and its products. But if they did, I'm sure we would have heard about it."

Sky scanned the faces of the judges, and said grimly, "You're about to."

13

MURMURED APPREHENSION ran through the room. Everyone's eyes fastened on Sky.

"Timora Jensen was delirious when she was picked up by a U.S. destroyer. The doctors who attended her found her ravings . . . intriguing. They began writing down what she said. It was a chilling puzzle with too many missing pieces. When she occasionally became lucid, she filled in some of the missing pieces."

Sky reached for the glass of water sitting next to his hand and drank. His mind kept wandering to Jessie, something he couldn't afford to let it do right now. This meeting was too important. Resolutely, he mentally reviewed his orders, arranged the details of what he would tell the council in his mind and formulated the questions he needed answers to.

He set the glass aside. "I need to know more about Roger Jensen and what else he took from here so the military can assess if there's a credible threat to Toolowa."

"What exactly would you like to know," Edmund asked.

"How long did Roger Jensen live here, and what did he do for a living?"

Tamrin O'Malley leaned forward. "Didn't Timora answer those questions for you?"

"We had more pressing questions and didn't get that far—before she died."

Shock ricocheted around the table.

Edmund's brow wrinkled with pain and sorrow. "Her parents will need to be told."

"I will take care of it," Troy said quietly.

Edmund nodded and said to Sky, "Roger Jensen was invited to come to Toolowa as a Methodist minister. He came highly recommended by his church. The people here took to him right away, and he established a respectable congregation."

"When did he arrive?" Sky asked.

"In nineteen thirty-nine, just after the harvest," Pendow Hun said authoritatively. Besides being a judge, he was also one of the islands historians.

"And when were the Jensen banished?"

Lin Pow frowned over the question for a moment, and then said, "Almost exactly two years later."

"How long had the Jensen been married?"

"About a year," Lily said.

"They were expecting their first child," Birdie said.

"That made banishing them very difficult for Timora's family, although they agreed with the council's decision," Edmund said.

There was no regret in the expressions of the judges for that decision. Sky wondered if there would be by the time he finished telling them what the Jensens had done. "Where in the States did Roger Jensen come from?"

"He said he hailed from Alabama, and he did have a lazy southern drawl," Sam said.

Sky lightly tapped the table, fitting together what he'd learned with what he already knew. *Things are beginning to add up.* He became aware that the judges were anxiously waiting for him to tell them about the invasion he had alluded to earlier.

He rested his forearms on the table, wishing for a chair with a back he could lean against, and plunged in. "It may interest you to know that the man who called himself Rodger Jensen was in fact Bertram Ballford. He fled Alabama and the U.S. in January of nineteen thirty-nine, before he could be apprehended and prosecuted for embezzling church funds, blackmailing several of his parishioners, and performing underage marriages."

"Oh my." Birdie's fingers pressed against her lips as though to apologized for her outburst. Then with a puzzled look she said, "He came with such glowing letters of recommendation from his church."

"Those letters were genuine." Sky assured her. "They were about the real Roger Jensen, who unfortunately died in an accident in Hawaii while enroute to Toolowa. The military dug up evidence that makes them believe Bertram Ballford followed Roger Jensen to Hawaii. Ballford knew about Jensen's invitation to come and live on Toolowa, so his very timely, *accidental* death played right into Ballford's hand."

"You believe Ballford murdered the real Roger Jensen, don't you?" Sam asked.

"Yes."

"He really did hoodwink us, didn't he?" The wrinkles in Lily's gentle face deepened with dismay.

"You and many others," Sky said sympathetically. "Alabama was the second place he embezzled church funds. The first place was in Mississippi, where he was really from."

"Roger Jensen or Bertram Ballford was an all-around bad guy," Jake said.

"Indeed he was," Tamrin said. "So just where did he go after he bamboozled us?"

Sky rubbed a hand along the back of his neck, and stretched it. "Timora mentioned three places—in her ranting—where she and Roger had lived. We investigated the locations and found verification of the peculiar incidences she muttered about during her delirium."

"What kind of incidences?" Pendow asked.

"The mysterious, sudden, and simultaneous deaths of several people in each location the Jensens took up residence."

"Timora told you about these deaths while she was delirious?" Lin Pow asked Sky, astonished.

"Apparently, in her mind, she was laboring under a heavy burden of remorse and guilt. She blamed herself for what had happened to those who died in the first two places she and Roger lived, after they left here."

"Where did they live?" Troy asked.

"Well now that's a very curious thing. They went to New Caledonia from here, and from what we've learned, Roger Jensen again worked as a Methodist minister." Sky paused to roll his shoulders, feeling the bruises and pains the impact of the crash had inflicted, still wishing for a chair back to lean against, and pushed Jessie out of him mind for the umpteenth time.

"He slid back into his old habits of embezzling church funds, but was caught, literally, with his hand in the till. Five parishioners held him while the police were called. When the police arrived, Jensen was gone, and all five parishioners were dead. All of them had traces of a gray dust on their bodies and appeared to have died of suffocation. Autopsies verified that."

Birdy emitted a strangled sound that drew Sky's attention. She quickly dropped her eyes. Sky let his move around the table. There were varying expressions of horror and outrage, but Edmund's was by far the most distressed.

"You said Timora spoke of three places they had lived. How many more people died in the other places?" Edmund asked.

"I can't answer that, because we aren't sure how many died in the third, fourth, and fifth incidences," Sky said.

Lily moaned. Tamrin, sitting next to her, laid a comforting hand on her arm as Sky continued.

"After the Jensens fled New Caledonia, they turned up in Nuku'alofa Tonga. The significance of that didn't dawn on us until we put it together with Timora's nationality. Then we recognized that their line of flight was significant as both New Caledonia and Tonga are on roughly the same latitude as Toolowa, and have similar climates. In both places, the Jensens tried to grow some unusual plants, but they had to run before the plants matured. In each place they destroyed the plants before they left."

"What made the Jensens leave Tonga?" Sam asked. "Were they recognized? I'm sure by then they must have been on an international wanted list."

"They were, except by the time they got to Tonga they had changed their names, altered their appearances, and started in with a brand new ploy. Now they were William and Ellen Jackson, botanists, looking for investors to back the development of several new varieties of herbal teas. After the Tongans tasted the *Jackson's* unique teas, many were so impressed that they invested their life savings in the Jackson's tea plantation venture."

Troy groaned, shaking his head. "How many people invested their money?"

Sky puffed out a breath. "Dozens. In fact they made quite a killing there, and as soon as they had a substantial nest egg, they tried to run."

"Why didn't they just stay there and grow our herbs and spices?" Pendow asked.

"From what we have been able to piece together, the Jensens weren't very good at growing the Toolowan herbs and spices, nor would they initially let anyone help them. Not only that, but Roger Jensen didn't seem to be as interested in developing his plantation as he was in wielding power over the lives of other people. That's why he got into the ministry. Not passing himself off as a minister on Tonga limited his influence in Tongan society."

"Good," Pendow Hun said loudly.

"Yes, but after about eight months, when the tea plantation didn't take shape, the investors demanded an accounting. Timora's fragmented account of the investors meeting with them made it sound like things got pretty ugly when her husband refused to return the money."

"What happened?" Troy Lind asked.

Sky's jaw hardened thinking of Timora's hysterical account of that meeting. For all the horror she'd felt over what happened, she'd still helped her husband do it. "Again the Jensens fled a volatile situation leaving seven people dead, with the same suffocated expressions and gray dust on their bodies as those on New Caledonia."

Lily moaned. "I don't know if I can bear anymore."

The lines around Edmund's mouth deepened. "We must hear all of it. The responsibility for all those who have died at the hands of the Jensens is ours."

"You aren't responsible for what the Jensens did," Sky said.

"But we are," Edmund said tightly. "The incidents you have described tell us the Jensens took the seeds and products of a very deadly plant called yunga." He paused, his face working through painful emotions. "I told you last night our ancestors had their ways to discourage invaders. During the age of exploration and conquest by the European nations, our ancestors ruthlessly repelled them with yunga."

"So that was it," Sky murmured.

"Yes," Edmund said quietly. "The secret of the yunga plant has never left this island before. Our isolation for so many millenniums kept the secret safe. When we opened Toolowa and began to allow others to come here, we were very careful who we let live among us. Only those we deemed worthy of citizenship know the secret of the yunga plant. We depend on their loyalty to protect our secret."

"Isn't that dangerous? Haven't you had incidences where the citizens have used it on each other?" Sky asked.

"Not in many generations," Troy said. "We are a peaceful people, content with a simple life. There is little strife on Toolowa. However our history tells us hundreds of Toolowans died, over many generations, learning to use the yunga plant. Their fear and respect for the yunga plant caused them to enact laws to protect the people and the secret of the yunga."

"Now, only a trusted group of Toolowans are allowed to process and store the yunga. Permission to use it in any of its forms must be justified by this council and then administered by those who are stewards over the yunga," Edmund said.

"So, the yunga must be processed to be used?" Jake asked.

"No," Edmund said. "The fruit is deadly if eaten, but it is not the only part of the bush that is. The leaves, bark, wood, and roots are equally deadly."

"How fast does the yunga grow, and how soon can it produce fruit?" Sky asked.

"A bush is fully mature and fruit bearing by the end of two years," Lily said.

Jake held up his hand. "But that's not how the Jensens used the yunga to kill their victims. They didn't live in either New Caledonia or Tonga long enough for a yunga bush to mature."

"That's true, but there are ways to use yunga against an enemy that don't require the bush to be fully mature." Pendow said.

"What ways?" Sky asked.

Lines of despair creased Edmund's forehead. He ran a hand through his thick graying hair and straightened his back, as though he'd made up his mind. "When our ancestors learned how poisonous the bush was, they decided to rid the island of the yunga. They cleared them from a section of the jungle and brought them all together to be burned"—a spasm of pain seized Edmund's face—"everyone who inhaled the smoke from that fire died."

Sky leaned forward. "You're kidding?"

Grim lines bracketed Edmunds mouth. "No, and inhaling the ash is just as deadly. The smoke and ash act more quickly than even eating the fruit."

"If it's that deadly, can touching it kill you?" Jake asked, alarmed.

Tamrin patted Jake's hand. "Casual contact will not hurt you. Still, over the centuries the people noticed that the yunga bush wasn't used by birds to nest in or plagued by insects. That encouraged the people to experiment. They soon found uses for the plant and cultivated it for its repellent properties."

"For example?" Sky asked.

"There is another unique bush on Toolowa called kabant. Its stem produces a thick creamy substance. When mixed with small quantities of the yunga's crushed fruit it produces a very effective insect repellent," Troy said.

"That's right," Tamrin said. "The mixture is used around doors and windows to keep insects and rodents out of our houses. If applied monthly, a home can be virtually rodent and insect free."

"But if you were going to use it to kill a large group of people quickly, as our ancestors did, then the wood smoke or ash is the most effective way. The wood ash is sifted into a fine powder. Blown into the air, everyone that inhales it will die within a few moments," Edmund said.

Sky stared thoughtfully at Edmund, drumming his fingers on the table, trying to process everything he'd learned. It didn't add up in his mind. If the Jensens had used the ash to kill, which Sky reasoned was the most likely scenario, why hadn't they themselves died, as the Toolowans who burned the first bushes had? He pressed his palms against the table. "If your ancestors initially died from the smoke how could they use it or the ash on invaders and live?"

"Because the antidote to the poison is in the plant itself." Edmund reached for a small bottle on a shelf behind him and emptied the contents into his hand. He opened his palm and showed Sky and Jake a number of shiny green seeds. "Before the fruit ripens to its red hue, the seeds are extracted, dried, and crushed. A dose of the seed powder—taken daily—will make a person immune to the poison of the yunga. It takes nearly a month to develop full immunity, but after that, all that is needed to maintain immunity is to take a small daily dose."

"Amazing," Sky muttered.

Birdie Tyloa leaned forward and revealed, "You and Captain Denning were each given your first dose of the seed powder when you were put in the hospital."

Jake drew in a sharp breath. "What?"

"We knew you would be staying with us for a while and thought it best to protect you," Troy Lind said.

Sam looked over at Jake and confessed, "You both took it again this morning at breakfast in your pineapple juice."

"Of course if you don't wish to continue taking it, we won't force you." Tamrin again patted Jake's hand.

"Considering we don't know how long we are going to be here—along with the fact Toolowa is facing the threat of invasion—Captain Denning and I will continue to take the seed powder. Thank you," Sky said.

Edmund put the seeds back in the bottle and returned it to the shelf. "Good. If we are facing invasion, then we will have to decide whether or not to use the yunga—as our ancestors did." His face clouded. "The secret of the yunga has been kept here for generations untold. Now through our carelessness, it has left our shores and been used to kill innocent people."

"And not so innocent people," Sky said.

"Who else did the Jensens use it on?" Lily asked Sky.

"The Japanese."

The room simmered with inquires.

Edmund held up his hand. "Tell us."

"The Jensens left Tonga on a stolen boat. It was well equipped and powerful. In Timora's delirium, she told us that the Jensens searched some of the remote Islands in the Solomon's until they found one that was largely uninhabited. The few people living on the island were simple and trusting. It didn't take long for Roger Jensen to win their support and loyalty. Here the Jensens did try to grow the rest of spice and herb seeds they had taken from Toolowa."

"And the yunga too?" Pendow asked.

"That too, but the island they chose was closer in latitude to the equator. The herbs and spices didn't do well with no dryer, cooler season. The yunga seeds they stole never even sprouted."

"Thank goodness," Birdy said fervently.

"Timora seemed glad about that too. Repeatedly, in her delirium, she was torn between her joy over their dwindling supply of what she kept calling "seed powder", and her fear that if they ran out, they would no longer be able to use what she termed the "deliverance plant"—if they needed too. In her lucid moments, she told us the natives were beginning to resent Roger. The herbs and spices that were supposed to bring them untold wealth were failing, and the natives were tired of providing for the Jensens with nothing to show for it."

"What did the people do?" Pendow Hun asked.

"Timora said they were asked to leave the island. However, when the first gunboat of Japanese landed searching for food and water, needing a place to hide until they could make contact with their battleship group, Roger went out to meet them alone and seemingly unarmed. When he returned all the Japanese soldiers were dead. That again won him the support and loyalty of the natives. They looked on him as their protector."

"How many did he kill?" Lin Pow asked.

"Unknown. But according to Timora, they repelled two more small landing parties before the fourth party came. That group was larger, much larger. Roger didn't have enough of the yunga powder left to subdue all of the Japanese. Some died but not all. They took the island and interrogated Roger until he told them about the deliverance plant. He used his knowledge to buy his life, with the promise to supply the Japanese with all the deliverance powder they could ever use. The Japanese left the island two days later, with Roger."

The implications of that hung in the air.

Sky shifted again on his cushion, trying to ignore his aches and concluded his tale. "The natives, who survived the Japanese's retribution for the deaths of their comrades, came after Timora as soon as the Japanese left. She and her daughter escaped their vengeance in the boat the Jensens had stolen in Tonga, but there was little fuel left, and they didn't have time to take food or water with them. Sadly the Jensen's daughter, Kelja, died after three days on the water. When we found Timora, she'd been drifting for five days."

The judges were silent after Sky finished. He listened to the whir of the overhead fans, the ocean's rhythm, and the sound of children laughing somewhere in the distance. The judges' distress was palpable. No one seemed able to break through the dark gloom that hung over the room. It was a heavy cloud the fans couldn't disperse. Lily's wet gleaming eyes poignantly expressed the tragedy they all felt.

The clock on the wall behind Edmund was creeping toward noon. Sky hoped the meeting would end soon. He was sure the judges would want to discuss what he'd told them privately.

The look Sam exchanged with him told him the ambassador had questions he wanted to discuss too. Sky wasn't sure how he was going to get through that meeting, but resolved to answer all the ambassador's questions before two o'clock. He was determined to be on Jessie's doorstep by then. The need building up inside him to see and talk with her was growing. Keeping his mind on this meeting, as important as it was to the Toolowans' survival and his own, now that he was trapped on the island, was taking an ever-increasing effort.

The thoughts Sky was lost in, were suddenly broken in on by Jake. He asked the last questions in Sky's mind. "How could the Jensens have stolen the yunga and the antidote without you knowing about it? Don't you inventory what's stored?"

"We do," Edmund said. "However, there is one time they could have stolen it without our notice. The yunga and the antidote are stored in sealed jars. When it has been stored for a year, it is considered diminished in its potency. The jars are emptied over the western edge of the island, into the sea. The Jensens were on a disposal team two months before they were banished. It is possible they emptied their jars into other containers and hid them to be retrieved later."

Shame faced, Troy admitted, "We didn't think about that possibility until a week after the Jensens left Toolowa."

"Even then we weren't too concerned," Tamrin said. "We thought the potency of what they could have stolen would be poor."

A shroud of guilt seemed to descend on Edmund as he said, "Obviously, we were wrong."

14

JESSIE WAS ONLY HALFWAY THROUGH WEEDING her vegetable garden, which hadn't been done in over two weeks, when Triny came through the gate.

"Hi, Triny," Kanoa yelled, before he went back to constructing a new dirt road for his cars. His knees were caked with Toolowa's rich black soil, but his foot was well wrapped, and he was still holding it up when he crawled.

Jessie was grateful he had recovered enough to be outside in the dirt. That was a cause for rejoicing, and she said a silent prayer of thanks.

Her rejoicing was short lived.

Triny marched over to her like an execution squad of one. "I knows all bout last night! So don't try ta deny ya knows doze flyers. An I means both a dem. My sister, Shula, say, ya bout fell over wif surprise—and not da good kind neither." She bracketed her hips with her hands. "Then ya up and runs off soon as dinner be done." She paused to exhale disgust. "Why ya don't tell me yesterdee, dat ya knowd dem big handsome flyers?"

"I don't know them—anymore, haven't seen either one in years," Jessie said, yanking out a weed with undue force and feeling better for it.

Triny sniffed and glared down at her. "Ya cuts me ta da bone! Me thinkin we be friends, and you's holdin out on me. How's I spose ta has anybody's respect when I has ta hear bout stuff you's spose ta tell me, from Shula?"

Jessie sat back on her haunches, and wiped her brow with her shirtsleeve. "Forgive me Triny"—she shaded her eyes against the glare of the sun—"but I need you to move so I can finish weeding this row."

"Well! If dats da way you's gonna be, I just take mysef off and do what I be paid for." Triny turned on her heels.

"Lunch be ready in thirty minutes." She threw over her shoulder, and stomped off.

"I have a thirty minute reprieve," Jessie said to Kanoa, who was rumbling a truck along his newest roadway. He paused and smiled at her, and that made everything right in her world. The only other smile that had ever had that effect on her had been . . . she jerked her mind away from those memories.

The front door banged shut behind Triny.

Jessie waggled her trowel at Kanoa, and confided to her little man, "What I really need is a reprieve from my past." She grimaced and went back to the therapy of weeding. *Unfortunately, Sky Brannigan taught me all too well that I will never get that reprieve. I'm stuck with my past, and the consequences of one drink that altered my whole life.* "No, all eternity," she muttered, viciously ripping out weeds.

She stopped her assault on the weeds after she finished the row, wiped her brow, and gazed up into heaven. "Why did I let Tena read that note?"

You know why. At least be honest with yourself, her conscience demanded. *You wanted to know what he said as badly as Tena did—no—more!*

Kanoa stuck out his tongue and blew a raspberry sound, now moving a racecar along his new road.

"Exactly," Jessie said, agreeing with the rude noise. "That's precisely how I feel." She started tugging on a stubborn weed in the next row, gave up, and sat down in the dirt. "Oh Kanoa, what do I do now?"

Kanoa stopped playing with his cars, looked at her solemnly, and said, "Have lunch?"

Jessie covered her mouth with her gloved hand, smearing dirt on her face, and laughed.

SKY WALKED JAKE TO THE HOSPITAL after their meeting with the council. They found Tena at the nurse's station and Jake immediately described the pain he was in and requested more painkillers.

Tena consulted his chart, gave him a shot, and assured him—and his growling stomach—he would be well fed while he waited for the medication to take effect. "I expect you will be here for a few hours. Dr. Snyder wants to take a meticulous look around in your wound."

Sky gave Jake's back a consoling thump, wished him luck and headed for the embassy. *At least I won't have to worry about Jake interfering with my plans.* He checked his watch. It was twelve thirty. *Good. With luck, I'll be able to answer all the ambassador's questions over lunch and be on Jessie's doorstep right at two o'clock—when visiting hours start.*

As he started up the lane to the embassy, he thought about the other bouquets of flowers on Jessie's porch. *Maybe I better get there a little before two and stake my claim,* he mused, shooing away a persistent bee. *If I can talk her into taking a walk with me, I can eliminate any interruptions from her other suitors,* he schemed, entering the embassy.

Nora Hamilton's presence at lunch foiled Sky's plan. Sam wouldn't let him bring up the subject of their meeting with the judges. Instead he directed the conversation toward Sky. Nora seemed especially interested in Sky's family and background.

Sky admired the interrogation skills Nora had learned from thirty years of marriage to a diplomat in the delicate questions she asked about his relationship with Jessie. He deftly deflected her questions with vague answers, while he watched the clock and ate as fast as polite manners allowed.

It was nearly one-thirty before Sky and the ambassador retired to his office to talk. Sam sat in a wing-backed chair near an open window and motioned for Sky to sit in the one opposite him, so they could enjoy the breeze.

Without preamble, Sam said, "You're no simple pilot with orders to collect a few American's. You're an intelligence officer."

"Yes sir," Sky said. "But my orders, which are now at the bottom of the bay, were to inform you and the council of judges of the situation and enlist your support in persuading all the Americans to leave Toolowa. The plane Captain Denning and I were flying could have taken all of them."

"And the other part of your orders?"

"I was to learn all I could about the deliverance plant, assess the threat, and relay that information without delay."

"And you were supposed to be back in New Caledonia in a week—right?"

"Yes, sir."

"So no one will miss you before then?"

"I'm afraid not. This mission is under radio silence. We don't want the enemy to know what we believe they may be up to."

"The ramifications of letting the yunga fall into the hands of the Japanese are unthinkable."

"They are, and we can't let that happen. The yunga is just the kind of thing the Japanese are looking for to revitalize their war effort. We have them pretty much on the run throughout the Pacific, but if they could get their hands on the stores of yunga the Toolowans have, it could change the war's dynamics."

"Yes." Sam drummed his fingers on the arm of his chair. "All they would need to deliver the ash powder would be impact bombs and the right wind direction. Or have those confounded kamikazes pilots deliver the ash— wherever they choose."

A chill crawled down Sky's spine. "That's it in a nutshell." He leaned forward, "I'm surprised the judges were so open with us about the yunga. Timora told us it was a highly guarded national secret."

"It is, but what you told the judges' council has changed everything. The secret has escaped Toolowa and has now become a grave threat to her people."

"How much processed yunga powder do the Toolowans possess, and where do they keep it? You know that's going to be the enemy's primary target."

"I don't know how much yunga powder they store. Not being a citizen, I'm not on a disposal team, but I do know where most of it is stored. Not the exact location, you understand, just generally."

"Most of it?"

"I haven't been there, mind you, but most of it is kept in a cave in the western mountains."

"That's not very efficient. Any ground invasion will come from the bay. If the yunga is clear across the island, how can it be of use in defending the people? The island would be captured before they ever reached the yunga."

"Enough is kept here in the bay to repel any invader, I assure you."

"Where is it kept?"

"That, I don't know." Sam sat forward. "Are the Toolowans really going to need to use the yunga to repel an invasion?"

"I'd say the possibility they will be invaded is high."

The mahogany clock on the mantle chimed one forty-five.

Sam leaned back in his chair and said somberly, "Why don't you lay out for me a few of the most probable scenarios and how much time you think we have before the enemy arrives on our doorstep."

With the clock ticking away his plans for the afternoon, Major Brannigan reminded himself of his duty, resigned himself, and plunged in.

15

IT FELT LIKE RUSH HOUR IN NEW YORK CITY to Sky as he urgently pressed through the throng of people meandering down the wide bay lane. More than once he was forced to stop, while a group of neighbors blocked the lane, visiting with each other. It was after three, and the afternoon shadows were lengthening.

Sky wanted to shout out his frustration with everyone's snail pace. It was wonderful that life on Toolowa was so relaxed that no one was in a hurry. In any other tropical paradise he would have felt the same way. Except, this obscure paradise was home to the one woman he had all but given up hope of ever finding again.

He consulted the watch that had mysteriously appeared on the nightstand in his bedroom. He had less than an hour to reach Jessie and say the things that had been growing inside him since he'd come to his senses—a year after walking away from an eternity with the only woman he wanted to spend it with.

When he'd humbled himself enough, he went to Colorado to find her. Her family refused to tell him where she was. Even his own parents and cousin, Hadlee, sided with the Garrisons. They told him it was too late and he should move on. That might have discouraged him, but it was more what they didn't say, than what they said, that kept him hoping, praying, and searching. If she had gotten married, they would have thrown it in his face—no one did.

He jostled, dodged, and even cut through the jungle until he finally made it to the path leading to Jessie's house. He barreled down it at a dead run. Her house came into view before he reached the edge of the small clearing it sat in. He skidded to a halt just inside the trees.

A bright red scarf flapped in the breeze on Jessie's gate. The sight hit him like a hard elbow to the solar plexus. He glowered at the gossamer no trespassing flag. Its fringe fluttered gently in the breeze, jeering at him.

Was it my gift that made her put out that red scarf? None of the morning gifts were still on the porch. He scanned the front yard. At least the orchids didn't appear to have been thrown aside or trampled in the yard. There was no sign of his card either, but were they the reason Jessie wasn't receiving visitors? *Was I wrong to respect the native customs, and ask for permission to see you, Jess?* Torn by a fierce internal debate, he continued to stare at the offensive scarf. *Should I just be patient and try again tomorrow? Or do what I really want to do and go through that gate and pound on the door.*

He took a step forward.

The door to Jessie's house opened. Jake stepped through it.

Sky scuttled back into the protection of the trees.

Jake turned back to the door. He blocked Sky's view of Jessie, but he knew she was there. Their voices mingled with the wind chimes, keeping him from understanding what they said.

Jake's head bent to Jessie's.

Jessie's hand ran along Jake's arm.

He's kissing her! And she—she's letting him! Rooted to the spot, he was too stunned to do anything but stare.

After a moment Jake's head came up, he backed away, and walked down the steps of the porch. When he reached the gate, he stopped and waved to Jessie, standing in the door. Smiling, she returned his wave and shut the door.

Sky quickly jogged down the path until he couldn't see the house, went around a bend, and stopped. He opened his fisted hands and wiggled his fingers, letting the blood flow back into them.

Jake's footsteps drew near.

Sky spun around and met Jake at the bend in the path. "You've been to see the Amazon."

"Yeah, Tena gave me directions to her house after the doc quit torturing me, but I guess I wasn't supposed to visit. She has this scarf on her gate. It's like a do not disturb sign. I didn't know about it, but she was nice enough to let me come in anyway."

"I guess I'd better not go and pay my respects then."

"Probably not."

"What did you two talk about?"

Jake shrugged. "Just old times."

"Do tell," Sky said through a tight jaw, lifting an interested brow as they walked along the path.

"I met her in New York when she was at the top of her game. I mean she was all the rage. Every guy who looked at her fell for her."

"You included?"

"Me included . . . and not just because she's the most gorgeous woman I've ever seen, either." Jake stopped and put a hand on Sky's arm. "Do you know she not only knows basketball, she plays it, and she's *good* too? That was the punch that did me in."

"You were in love with her?"

Jake gave him an incredulous expression, but his answer was evasive. "What guy in his right mind wouldn't be? She was every guy's fantasy—still is. And I'll tell you something else." He paused. "She's the one woman that broke my heart." He shook his head as though he still couldn't believe it.

Sky snorted.

"I know you think all I do is love them and leave them. But with Amazon—"

"Her name is *Jessie*."

Jake shrugged, "I guess I'll always think of her as Amazon, It just fits her better, and she was almost my Amazon." He shrugged. "You probably won't believe it, but we were even engaged."

Stunned, Sky pushed down a surge of anger. When Jessie had confessed her other sins to him, she hadn't told him she'd been engaged to the man she'd . . . . He unclenched his jaw and reminded himself, *it doesn't matter.* "That does surprise me," he said. "But, obviously, you didn't get married, so what happened?"

"I messed up, and she wouldn't give me another chance. The day after I pleaded with her to reconsider, she vanished, and I haven't seen her since." He paused as they came to the lane leading to the embassy and ran a hand over his bandaged shoulder. "Seeing her again made me remember why she's the only girl I ever came close to marrying—and you know," he said thoughtfully, "I think with a little gentle persuasion, she might even be willing to let me rekindle that flame."

16

IT WAS AFTER FIVE THIRTY when Jessie and Kanoa left the hospital. Jessie covered Kanoa mouth as he yawned and stretched. He'd awoken from a short nap just after Jake left. Jessie was glad Jake had come during Kanoa's nap. She almost laughed. *Jake came and went without finding out anything about my son.*

The sun was slanting to the west, but still shone on the bay as they made their way along the lane, heading for home. Jessie never tired of the sparkling sand, the turquoise water, the sound of the surf mingled with the calls of exotic birds, or the feel of the tropical breeze blowing around her. She breathed in the complex aroma of salt, seaweed, and fish on the breeze, grateful she'd gone to see her parents the weekend the Hamiltons had stopped in Glenwood Springs. It still amazed her that she'd found her place in the world so far from her home and family.

She hugged Kanoa as he rode on her hip. He wiggled his lightly bandaged foot, encased in a red rubber boot. His foot had improved so much, Paul said he could start to walk a little, but he was to take it slow and keep it dry. Jessie thought tomorrow would be soon enough to start.

They were nearing the path to the embassy when Jessie spotted Jemma Gunley's mother coming along the lane. Jemma was one of Jessie's students, one that worried her. She hadn't done well on her final tests, and Jessie wanted to spend some of the planting vacation helping Jemma catch up with the other children her age, before the next school year started.

She stopped Mrs. Gunley and briefly explained her concerns about Jemma. Mrs. Gunley listened gravely and asked questions. Jessie shifted Kanoa to her other hip as she outlined the help Jemma needed.

Kanoa began to fidget. He tugged on Jessie's sleeve. "Want to walk on the beach."

Jessie shook her head, continuing to talk with Mrs. Gunley.

"Please?" Kanoa begged, bouncing on her hip.

"Just a minute, and then we will." She apologized to Jemma's mother and began to suggest possible times Jemma could come for tutoring.

Kanoa's bouncing increased. Jessie set him on his feet, keeping hold of his hand. He tugged against her grip.

"Excuse me," Jessie said to Mrs. Gunley. She crouched and took hold of Kanoa's other hand. "You're being very rude," she said gently. "I need to talk with Mrs. Gunley a little longer. After I finish, we can walk on the beach."

"Go now."

"You know you can't go into the water."

"Won't," he said, shaking his head vigorously, making his golden curls bounce, "Just go to the boats."

Jessie saw that the outriggers were pulled well up onto the beach. It was pretty far and she didn't think he could make it. When he'd tried walking in the hospital he'd found his foot was still pretty sore.

"Well." She hesitated, and then gave in. "You can go through the trees to the sand. Sit down and wait for me there. When I'm done, we'll go to the boats, okay?"

Kanoa's curls bounced up and down.

"Promise," Jessie said insistently.

"Promise," Kanoa said brightly.

She let go of his hands. Her business with Jemma's mother would only take another minute or two and she could keep an eye on him through the trees.

Kanoa took an exuberant step and immediately whimpered. He thrust out a quivering bottom lip.

"Just take it slow and don't go any farther than you promised. I'll carry you down to the boats when I come."

Taking small, tentative steps, Kanoa shuffled away.

Jessie again apologized to an indulgent and smiling Mrs. Gunley. Then she explained more fully her concerns about Jemma and what she hoped to accomplish with the tutoring sessions she wanted to schedule for the next four weeks.

REACHING THE EDGE OF THE TREES, Kanoa ventured onto the sand, took a few steps, and stopped.

His mouth dropped open.

A giant emerged from the ocean with hair whiter than the sand. He picked up a towel and began to dry off his massive shoulders and huge arms. He looked in Kanoa's direction and smiled.

Hypnotized, Kanoa couldn't help himself. He hobbled toward the giant. Mama had read "Jack and the Beanstalk" to him and he knew he should be afraid of giants. They ate little children and never smiled. So why did this one? His smile made Kanoa feel good.

The giant walked up to him. His smile faded. Kanoa knew what the giant felt because mama always wore that same expression when she was worried about him.

"Where is your mother?" the giant asked.

Kanoa waved at the trees. "Talking."

"Ah," the giant said, dropped to his haunches, and touched Kanoa's red boot with the bandage sticking out of the top. "You look like you've had an accident."

Kanoa looked into the giant's friendly blue eyes. "Matoo bite me."

"What is a matoo?" the giant asked.

"Bad, bad lizard! Kanoa in hospital long time."

"I'm sorry the matoo bit you, and you had to be in the hospital, Kanoa." The giant held out his enormous hand, grinned, and said, "But I'm very pleased to meet you."

Kanoa looked at his big white teeth, certain now that this giant had never eaten a child. He returned the giant's grin and put his small hand into the giant's enormous one.

"My name is Sky," the giant said and pumped Kanoa's hand.

Kanoa thought Sky was a very good name for the giant. His eyes matched the color of the sky, and surely his head could reach the clouds. Kanoa examined the giant's hand, still holding his, marveling at how big his hand and fingers were.

A woman's voice called Kanoa's name from beyond the trees.

Kanoa started. "Uh-oh, Mama is coming," he said, scooting behind Sky. "I not supposed to walk this far."

SKY STOOD UP, LETTING KANOA HIDE behind his legs, and looked toward the trees. He hoped he could explain things to his mother, so Kanoa wouldn't get in trouble for walking too far onto the beach. He shaded his eyes against the sun and blinked. His breath caught in his lungs, refusing to be expelled. He blinked again.

Jessie strode toward him.

He stared at her, unbelieving.

"Mama," Kanoa said nervously, cowering behind his legs and grasping his calves with his small hands.

"What did you promise me, little man," Jessie said stepping around Sky, ignoring him.

Sky felt like he'd swallowed his tongue. He opened his mouth to explain, but nothing came out. His brain refused to accept what his eyes and ears told him. The child had green eyes, like Jessie. He had curly hair, just like Jessie. His skin was even that light copper tone that came from Jessie's mother and her Nahtow Indian blood. The conclusion was obvious, but Sky couldn't make himself accept it.

Kanoa tried to dodge Jessie's hand by scooting around to the front of Sky's legs. Jessie snagged him and lifted him onto her hip. He reached out and took hold of Sky's huge fingers. "Sky a nice giant," he said. "I want him to come home with us."

Jessie looked up at Sky. "I see you've met—*my son.*"

Sky nodded, her words reverberating in his ears so loud he could hardly hear the waves break on the beach. "He's a—great kid," he heard himself say. "I—I didn't think you were married."

"There you are," Takoa called from down the beach. "I've been searching all over for you two."

Jessie threw Takoa an engaging smile. Kanoa waved at the man who'd hauled Sky to the surface of the bay after the crash. Jessie set Kanoa down and he hobbled toward the Toolowan.

"Your . . . husband?" Sky choked on the word.

Takoa scooped Kanoa up, tossed him in the air and caught him, making Kanoa laugh.

"No, although we do share a very special bond," Jessie said, smiling fondly at the pair.

"What about Kanoa's father?"

Jessie glared at him. "Although it's none of your business, Kanoa's father and I were never married." She gave him the Amazon's provocative smile and sauntered down the beach.

He immediately sensed that the Amazon's smile was intended as a slap—and it felt that way. Rooted to the spot, Sky watched her. She joined Takoa, slipped her arm through his, and together they walked down the beach.

Kanoa, riding on Takoa's broad shoulders, turned and waved.

Sky lifted a hand that felt like it weighed a thousand pounds, and waved at the smiling boy. Then he sat down abruptly and tore his eyes away from Jessie and *her son*. For the second time, Jessie had shattered a fantasy he'd been telling himself for three hopeful years. Just like before, it had been an illusion he'd dreamed up in his own mind.

How could I have thought she wouldn't change? Or that her life wouldn't move on—just because mine hasn't? How could I have deluded myself into believing her love for me was deep enough to compel her to wait forever for me to come to my senses? But he had believed it. *Why should she? After all, I was the one that walked away, not her. Fairytales, Brannigan. Why are you always telling yourself fairytales—and believing them?*

WITH HER THOUGHTS CAREENING in too many directions, Jessie laughed with Kanoa over something Takoa said, although she had no idea what it was. She wanted to kiss Takoa for his timely arrival.

Spotting Sky coming out of the ocean so close to Kanoa had made her heart start battering her ribs, while paralyzing her feet. She tried not to think about how she'd felt at that moment, but the feeling continued to churn in her stomach.

Last night, the Hamilton's use of oil lamps and candles for a softer effect had blurred Sky's face in shadows, and she'd intentionally avoided looking at him whenever possible. However, behind the cover of the trees, with the sun accentuating his features, she'd stared her fill.

He'd lost his baby-face. She wondered if it was the additional years or if the war was responsible. Regardless, he was even more handsome with his matured features and the different way he now cut his sun-bleached hair, than she remembered. He'd obviously spent a lot of time in the sun and surf too. He had the sharply defined muscles of a swimmer, accentuated by his deeply tanned skin. His teeth had flashed brilliantly in the sunlight when he'd smiled at Kanoa. He was downright devastating. The intense attraction she'd felt for him the day they met, came roaring back at her. Admitting that, made her feel ill.

Even worse, the way she'd felt when he'd stooped to talk to Kanoa—she sucked in a breath, answered a question Takoa put to her, and pushed that treacherous feeling away. She couldn't bear touching that feeling again. Still, it had set off a panicked need to rescue her son, which finally freed her feet.

Racing down the beach, she hadn't dared to look at Sky. Until he'd given her the perfect opening to . . . *shock him,* she admitted. A pang of pure spite flushed over her. It surprised her. She hadn't known that feeling was in her and felt ashamed. Still, she couldn't deny that Sky's dumbfounded expression, when he learned Kanoa was her son, had filled her with a fierce satisfaction. *He deserved to be blindsided by that one for his self-righteous condemnation of me.*

She held in the harsh laugh tickling the back of her throat. Topping off Sky's shock with her lack of a husband, and the truth that she hadn't been married to Kanoa's father would surely keep Sky from ever wanting to speak to her—she hoped. No, she knew. *It will definitely keep him and his moral superiority from ever darkening my door again with morning gifts or requests to see me, and that's just fine with me.*

THE SUN DISAPPEARED beyond the western mountains of Toolowa. The turquoise color of the bay faded into shimmering silver. Sky sat in the sand, staring out at the cliffs surrounding the bay and the channel that led out into the open sea. He was glad for the growing shadows that hid his grief.

He'd found her only to learn he'd lost her so completely, so irrevocably, so eternally, he couldn't contain his feelings. The Jessie he'd known had been overcome by the Amazon. There was no other way to explain it. Why else would she have thrown Kanoa's lack of a father and her single state at him with no embarrassment? It even explained why she was in this backwater, isolated little kingdom.

The moral standards of Toolowa, notwithstanding all its churches, were probably like many of the islands in the South Pacific—extremely lax. *Is that why Jessie came here?* His conscience savaged him. *I'm to blame for what she's become. What I did must have solidified her long held belief that all men would ever see in her was the Amazon. Did she just give up trying to fight off that image and find a place the Amazon would be comfortable living? In a society that wouldn't condemn her, as I did?*

He tried to accept the truths his eyes, and her lips, had confirmed, but somehow couldn't believe it. The Jessie he loved had a deep and abiding testimony. She'd stood up to him and declared her worthiness by virtue of repentance. *She was right to feel that way too, because it was the truth and yet . . . .* He'd seen her willingly kiss Jake, the man that had cost her, her virtue.

He had to wonder about her relationship with Takoa too. She and Takoa seemed quite cozy. *Is Takoa, Kanoa's father? Their names even rhyme. Yes,* he decided with certainty, *she is very much at home with Takoa, and she did say they had a very special bond. What else could it be, besides Kanoa? But then why aren't they married? Their affection for each other is obvious.* That thought badgered him until a more appalling one trumped it. *Unless they can't marry because he's already married!*

Sky stretched out on the still warm sand, laced his fingers behind his head, and wondered about the divorce laws on Toolowa as the sky faded into gray. He couldn't reconcile it. The only thing his cousin Hadlee would tell him about Jessie was that she was happy with her new life, and her family was happy for her. *They couldn't possibly be happy about her being an unwed mother . . . unless of course, they don't know.*

Could she have changed so much? Could our breakup have caused her to reject everything she believed in to the extent she has become the immoral and deceitful Amazon she thought I believed her to be? Could the Jessie I knew really turn her back on all her values and beliefs? He didn't want to accept that idea. But how else could he explain Kanoa and what she'd told him.

No! He pushed aside his doubts and sat up with a growing conviction. He was a good intelligence officer, and something about what Jessie told him didn't add up. *I know her, and I know she would never give up her fundamental values.* Still, he couldn't kid himself. He knew now he would never have another chance to win her.

What she'd told him today was meant to disgust him. It was her way of telling him the bond between them had been severed—forever. *Even if that's true, I'm going to find out what's going on in your life Jess, and if nothing else, I still owe you an apology and an acknowledgment that what I did to you was wrong.*

He gazed up at the growing number of stars and vowed, "I'm going to make that apology and ask for your forgiveness, Jessie, whether or not you want me to, or care if I do. And if what I did to you caused you to turn your back on your values, then I'm not going to rest until I've helped you turn your life around—no matter how long that takes." It was the least he felt he owed her in restitution for what he'd done to her.

17

JESSIE WAS PREPARED TO SEE SKY when he walked into the chapel for sacrament meeting.

She'd been able to avoid crossing his path during Sunday school, thanks to her calling as a teacher in junior Sunday school, which met separately from the senior Sunday school. The gospel doctrine class, she knew Sky would attend, always ran over time. Still, she'd decided to insure her escape from him by letting her class out a few minutes early.

He took a seat in the back of the chapel on the aisle, looking surprised and confused when he spotted her. *I'll just bet you're confused. Here I am an unwed mother sitting on the stand in sacrament meeting.* She eyed the side door at the front of the chapel. *At least it won't be hard to get away after the meeting is over.*

As the chorister, she had no choice but to sit on the stand in front of the congregation. Every time she looked up, Sky's eyes were glued to her. The only way she could avoid his stare was to keep her focus on her songbook or her lap.

Her hackles rose. *I will not be cowed by Sky Brannigan's stares.* With deliberation, she let her eyes roam the congregation as she always did, keeping them mostly on Kanoa.

He was sitting on Takoa's lap in the front row, smiling and waving at her as she directed the music. She suppressed her amusement as she directed the sacrament song. Takoa had his hand's full keeping Kanoa still and quiet.

After Tena played the last notes of the sacrament hymn, they both left the stand, while the deacons lined up to pass the sacrament.

At least I won't have to keep avoiding Sky's eyes until I go back up on the stand for the closing song. I wonder if they'll bore a hole in the back of my head before then.

Tena sat down next to Takoa. Jessie sat on his other side. He passed Kanoa to her. She folded him into her arms and whispered a reminder of what he needed to do during the prayers and the passing of the sacrament.

SKY TRIED TO KEEP HIS MIND ON THE MEETING but found it an impossible task. Jessie was stunning in a trim yellow dress that fell just below her knees. Her flower-adorned hair cascaded down her back and triggered a yearning in his fingers. He wanted to run them through her fiery, gold-laced locks.

It had taken him by surprise when he walked in and saw her on the stand. Not having seen her at Sunday school, he'd assumed she didn't go to church anymore. After Sunday school, he'd thought about paying her a visit, but couldn't. Nora Hamilton was expecting him at lunch. He didn't dare refuse, not after skipping out on dinner last night.

At lunch, he'd learned it was customary not to intrude or visit on Sunday's unless prior arrangements had been made. It was a family day, and a day of rest that was respected on Toolowa. His desired tête-à-tête with Jessie would have to wait for one more day . . . *unless I can corner her after this meeting.* His mind went to work on how he could accomplish that goal.

When the sacrament was finished, Takoa's arms encircle both Tena and Jessie's shoulders. Sky's jaw tightened. He knew from the Hamilton's party that Tena was single, and he'd learned in Sunday school that Takoa was too. *So what's going on? Who is Kanoa's father, and why is Takoa acting as if he owns both Jessie and Tena.*

Throughout the meeting, Takoa's arms rested around the shoulders of one or both women—when he wasn't holding Kanoa.

Anyone would think he's romancing both women at the same time, and they don't appear to mind. Sky glowered, over this new distortion to the picture he was developing of Jessie's life. He struggled with it and finally admitted that the more he saw and heard the more confused he felt. Trying to untangle Jessie's life was the equivalent of being lost in a maze.

Yet, as perplexed and pained as he felt over all he'd learned about Jessie's life, he enjoyed watching her son. Kanoa was an active little boy. He bounced between the three adults that tried to keep him corralled until he finally escaped Tena and ran up the steps to the stand.

Bishop Troy Lind welcomed him onto his lap. Kanoa sat for a few minutes before wiggling out of Bishop Lind's arms and coming back down. He immediately jumped up on the bench, looked backward over it, spotted Sky, and waved enthusiastically.

Sky couldn't keep from smiling. He wiggled his fingers in return.

Kanoa leaned down and said something in Jessie's ear, pointing his finger at Sky. Jessie pulled the youngster around to the front and held him on her lap for the remainder of the meeting.

He's a terrific little kid, outgoing, happy, and obviously loved by everyone. Jessie, or rather, Jayling, is too. That wouldn't be true if she was the terrible person she tried to lead me to believe she was. In fact, if she were so wicked she wouldn't have a calling or take the sacrament—unless of course she's done more repenting. Sky tried again to puzzle out the mystery of Jessie's life, but the more he tried the more frustrated he became.

He didn't sing much of the closing song. Instead, he just sat with the hymnbook in his lap, gazing at the most beautiful woman in the world, listening to her magnificent voice. It flowed through him and filled him with memories so sweet that he wanted the song to go on forever.

After the closing prayer, he jumped up and plowed up the aisle. Midway up, his progress was blocked by an elderly couple. He couldn't just push past them. While he waited impatiently for them to take the slow, careful steps that would unblock his path, Jessie slipped out a side door, followed by Tena and Takoa. By the time he made it out the door, they were gone.

You can only avoid me for so long Jessie. Sky tromped out his frustration along the beach, heading for the bay's southeastern cliffs. *I'll catch up with you, and we will talk.*

He deliberately avoided going north. The temptation to invade Jessie's privacy might be too great if he went near her home. *I need to make my confession, tell you how sorry I am, and ask for your forgiveness. I want answers too. And I intend to get them—one way or another—even if your life is no longer any of my business.*

His progress was arrested where the beach met the cliff that rose to the plateau. He leaned against an outcropping of boulders and gazed out over the water. Across the bay, a light shone briefly on top the northern plateau. It flashed twice. A light from the pier, which protruded out into the bay at almost the center point between the northwest and southeast, answered with two flashes. A light flared from on top the jagged tip of the southern plateau. Sky watched the second flash receive the same response from the pier that the northern flashes had received. Intrigued, he jogged back down the beach to the pier.

He was almost to the end of the pier before he recognized Lowa, Takoa's younger brother, and the other man who had pulled him from the bay. Lowa looked remarkably like his brother. Both men were heavily muscled and topped six feet by a few inches. Each possessed the exotic charms that Sky knew always appealed to women.

"It's a beautiful night to be out on the beach," Lowa said, when Sky reached him.

"Mind if I share it with you for a while?"

"I'd welcome the company." Lowa motioned for Sky to sit. "Night patrol is always a tedious business."

Sky loosened his tie and unbuttoned the neck of his white shirt. Both items had magically appeared, along with a pair of dark blue pants, on the chair in his room this morning, just like the watch, the shirt, the lava-lava, and the swimming trunks.

When he'd asked Sam about them and thanked him, Sam had just waved off his thanks. "It's a matter of pride for Shin to anticipate and provide you with everything you require."

"But the clothes must be custom made—nothing else will fit me, and I want pay for everything you've had Shin get for me."

"The cost has been taken care of."

"But—"

"It's been taken care of, Major," Sam said with finality. "However if you simply want to thank Shin for doing what he considers his job, I'm sure he'll appreciate that. And, if you don't want to be coldly rebuffed by him, you had better refrain from asking what things cost or offering to pay for them."

He took the ambassador's advice and didn't inquire about the cost of everything Shin had given him when he thanked the butler and received his formal acknowledgement.

Now, careful of his new pants, Sky sat on the edge of the pier and hung his long legs over the end. "I can't adequately thank you and your brother for saving my life."

Lowa waved a hand, dismissing Sky's gratitude—something he'd done at the ambassador's party. "I think you would have made it to the surface without our help."

"No I wouldn't have. When I saw Jessie swimming toward me I was so surprised I inadvertently blew out most of the remaining air I had."

"Did you recognize her?"

"No. Like Captain Denning, I thought I was seeing a mermaid."

Lowa chuckled. "I ought to tell you it was probably that mermaid that saved your life, if any one did."

"Seems to me, she almost cost me my life. I wouldn't have blown out the air in my lungs if I hadn't been amazed by her swimming like a streak straight for me."

"She was doing that to ward off the tiger shark that was coming up behind you."

Sky's jaw dropped. "Honestly?"

"Yes. Your blood drew it," Lowa said, gesturing at the numerous small cuts that were scabbed over and healing on Sky's face, arms, and hands.

"How close was that shark?"

"About ten yards away."

"Then why would Jessie swim straight for me?"

"To make it back off or distract it."

Sky swallowed, *It's a good thing she didn't know it was me, or she would have let that shark have me.* Horror prickled across his skin. Jessie had endangered herself to rescue him. Kanoa's impish smile danced through his mind. Anger flared under his collar. "A mother has no right to put herself in danger like that."

"Tell that to Jayling—if you can get her to listen."

Sky's jaw became a hard line. He was certain Jessie was deliberately avoiding him, because she didn't want to listen to him—about anything. That thought pushed him back into the first days of their acquaintance and almost made him smile. Jessie was the most independent, strong-minded woman he'd ever met. It was one of the many reasons he hadn't been able rid his heart of her. After Jessie, every woman he met was just too fragile, too dependent—too helpless.

He tamped down his fear for Jessie, but his determination to get her to listen to everything he wanted to say to her intensified. "Would Jessie's tactic have worked, if you and the other men hadn't jumped in when you did?" he asked.

Lowa's attention swung from the southern cliffs to the northern ones. "Most likely, but with more people in the water the chances are better of warding off a shark, especially one drawn by the scent of blood."

"Then I have more to thank you, Takoa, and Jessie for than I knew." Sky extended his hand. "Thanks, again. I hope I can catch up with your brother and Jessie to thank them as well."

Lowa shook Sky's hand. "So you and Jayling really are in-laws?"

"We are." Sky considered Lowa's dubious expression. "Did you think we'd made it up when we said it at the party?"

"It did cross my mind, but only for a moment. Then I wondered if . . . well . . . maybe your families don't get along very well."

"Why would you think that?"

Lowa shrugged. "Because there seemed to be a good deal of tension between you two."

Flashes of light from the northern cliffs saved Sky from any further discussion about his relationship with Jessie. He used the distraction to change the subject. He tapped the top of the lamp after Lowa responded to the signal. "Tell me about your signaling system?"

"Toolowans have always patrolled the plateaus above the channel cliffs, because every invasion—as far back as our recorded history goes—have come through the channel and into the bay."

"Is that because there's no other way to land on Toolowa from the sea?"

"Yes. Toolowa rises out of the ocean for a thousand feet to the plateaus on the north and southeast. On the south and west, it rises nearly five thousand feet to the tops of the mountains. Besides, the water is too treacherous to try to land a boat, even if there was a place."

"What are the island dimensions?"

"The island is roughly thirty miles wide by forty-five miles long. It's shaped like the skull of a prehistoric bird. The narrow channel into the bay is formed by the birds slightly opened beak, with the help of a sharp fang that sits in its wide lower jaw. If you were to walk across the island it would take a day to go from north to south, and a day and a half to cross the island from the western mountains to the eastern tip of the birds hooked beak."

Sky thought about the islands dimensions and out line, and then asked, "Do you still only patrol the plateaus above the channel cliffs?"

"No. Not since the Japanese invaded the Dutch East Indies and Burma. Now we patrol all of the northern, eastern, and even some of southern side of the island."

The light blinked from the spur of land that formed the fang on the south side of the channel. Again, Lowa responded.

"How often do they signal?"

"Every ten minutes. The two that report to me are at the end of their chain of watchers. The signal moves in a relay from the farthest western points, both on the north and south."

"What happens if someone in the chain doesn't report in?"

"If a one minute lapse occurs, then the next watcher in line sends three flashes and keeps his lantern on. Everyone else in the chain then relays three flashes too. That emergency message would reach me in a matter of minutes and I would send out a security detail to the station just west of where the lantern remains lit."

"How many men make up your shore watch?"

"Two hundred men and women."

"Women are part of your shore watch? Are they part of your security force too?"

Lowa shifted his position and chuckled. "We are very democratic on Toolowa. Anyone who wishes to be part of the watchers security force is welcome. However, there is a core group of security officers, under Takoa's direction, who are paid to keep order and protect the island."

So Takoa is your chief security officer?"

"He is."

"Does he do night watch too?'

"Yes, that's why he wasn't at the Hamilton's party. It was his final night on duty for the next three months."

"You rotate that, I take it."

"We do. One quarter of our force is always on night duty."

"That works out to only doing night duty once every four months. That's not too bad."

"Except when it's your month." Lowa groaned and fixed Sky with a pained expression. "Especially when you have a beautiful wife at home, like I do."

Sky clapped Lowa's shoulder, remembering his introduction to Lowa's very lovely wife, Petra, at the party. "I see your point." He looked across the star lit bay, focusing on the channel. "How deep is the channel, compared to the bay?"

Lowa seemed to consider his question before countering with one of his own. "How likely are the Japanese to come?"

"I see you know what I told the council. Is that because you're part of the security force?"

"Everyone knows. On Toolowa, every bit of news and gossip is known almost before it happens. Our grapevine is that good. So are the Japanese likely to come?"

Sky watched the waves roll under the pier. "My official statement for Toolowa's gossip mill is . . . I don't know. I was sent here to find out the truth about the deliverance plant, Timora Jensen told us about, and try to ascertain the threat to Toolowa. The war has turned against the Japanese. They need something big to turn it around."

"Could the yunga turn it around?"

"It is a unique weapon and used judiciously it could—if nothing else—prolong the war. But that depends on how much you have stored and how soon more could be produced."

The light from the north flashed again. Lowa returned it, and then he and Sky waited for the signal from the southern plateau. It blinked to life. All was well, at least for the moment.

Lowa responded and closed the cover of the lamp. "Are you working on a strategy to defend Toolowa, Major? Is that why you want the dimensions of the channel and bay?"

"I'm scheduled to meet with the council of judges and the head of island security—who I now know is your brother—tomorrow, to brainstorm ideas on defending Toolowa. If the island is invaded, it will be unlike any other Toolowa has seen."

"What are you saying?"

"That the sea isn't the only way an invasion can come—anymore."

18

JESSIE SAT AT HER DRESSING TABLE, braiding her hair
for bed, congratulating herself on escaping Sky after
church. She'd just finished the braid when a rapid series
of knocks pounded on her front door. She glanced at the
clock. It was after ten. There was only one person she
could think of who would have the nerve to disturb her,
and possibly wake her son, at this late hour.

She tightened the belt on her robe and headed for the
front door. *If Sky Brannigan thinks he can bully his way in
here at this hour, he has another thing coming.*

By the time she reached the living room, the door was
swinging inward. For the first time since she'd come to
Toolowa, Jessie wished she had a lock on the door. "Oh no
you . . ." Her words trailed off as Tena stumbled into the
house.

Her violet eyes were red rimmed and streaming. Her
perfect complexion was covered in red blotchy patches,
and her chest heaved with hard, erratic gasps. "It's over!
It's truly over and done. I had to . . . do it. He gave me . . .
no choice." Tena collapsed into Jessie's arms.

Jessie hugged her tight and made calming sounds as
though she was trying to sooth one of her students who
had just skinned a knee. When Tena quieted a little, Jessie
pulled her over to the couch and pushed her down onto it.
She went back to the front door, shut it, and returned to
her friend who was again sobbing and wiping her tears
away with the palms of her hands.

"Takoa proposed tonight, didn't he?"

The question brought on a violent bout of sobbing from
Tena.

Jessie left the room and came back with two
handkerchiefs. She handed both to Tena and sat beside

her, an ugly suspicion growing inside her. "Tell me what happened."

"I should . . . never have . . . started dating . . . Takoa, but he was so darn . . . persistent," Tena said, crying into her handkerchief. "I would have been happy with just his friendship."

"No you wouldn't. Don't kid yourself about that." Jessie knew all too well about trying to make yourself believe you could settle for a friendship when your heart longed for more. "You've loved him almost since the day you got here."

Tena's head bobbed as she buried her face deeper in the big handkerchief.

"And I know why you've held him off for so long."

Tena's muffled voice came from the depths of the hankie. "Do you blame me?"

"How could I, when I did the same thing."

"You tried so many times to get me to tell Takoa about my past, before we became more than friends, but I didn't understand why until you told me about Sky."

The suspicion Jessie was nursing grew into a certainty. "What I told you about Sky's reaction to my past made you reject Takoa's proposal, didn't it?"

"Yes," Tena's sodden voice said, her face still buried in the handkerchief.

Jessie jerked the soaked square of cloth out of Tena's hands.

Tena's head came up and Jessie held her friend's eyes. "Joshua Takoa Zenderly isn't Sky Brannigan. If I have ever seen a man who loves a woman unconditionally, it's Takoa and his love for you. His feelings for you won't change just because of what happened to you. Like me, he will simply admire you even more for what you have made of yourself. I don't know if I could have healed as completely as you have if I'd gone through everything you endured."

A grateful smile wavered on Tena's lips for just a moment. "I never would have healed if Takoa hadn't taught me the gospel. It saved me and made me whole." She shook open the second handkerchief. "I don't doubt Takoa would overlook my past, but that's not the main issue."

"Then what is?"

"Something I haven't been able to get out of my mind since the night of the party." Tena looked down at the hankie, and silently twisted it through her fingers.

Jessie waited; her stomach in knots. She knew what Tena was going through. It was still hard to believe that one, seemingly small, wrong choice had put her life on a completely different course. In her case, it was her own fault. But Tena was completely innocent of any wrongdoing. Yet, she too was suffering with long reaching consequences.

"Before Takoa proposed, he told me he was going to run for chief judge someday." Tena's chin trembled. "He wanted me to know he isn't content to just be the chief security officer on Toolowa. He wants to do more to serve his country and help its people."

"I have no doubt he will be the chief judge one day." Jessie squeezed Tena's hand. "And do a great job too."

Tena wiped her eyes and blew her nose. "I know he will, and that's the problem. I can't be the chief judge's wife."

Painful understanding etched itself on Jessie's brow. "It's very unlikely that anyone from your past will show up on Toolowa. After all, you've been here for five years, and it hasn't happened yet."

"I might have agreed with you until Jake Denning and Sky Brannigan showed up. Just one of them coming would have been enough of a nightmare. But to have both of them come here, and at the same time too." Tear's again rolled down Tena's cheeks. "I jumped at the chance to come to Toolowa because I was sure this would be the last place on earth anyone who knew me would ever find me."

"So was I. I thought I would never run into my past again—especially not on this obscure little island."

"But you were wrong." Tena crumpled the handkerchief into a ball.

"I was," Jessie said, knowing Tena's fears were real and all too probable. "But I think you should tell Takoa, and let him decide."

"No!"

"So what reason did you give him for not wanting to marry him?"

"I told him I didn't love him."

Jessie rolled her eyes. "As though he would believe that!"

"He didn't. So, I told him I didn't want to be the chief judge's wife, and I wasn't about to stand in the way of his dreams. I had him then," she said grimly. "He couldn't take back what he'd already told me he wanted. He tried, but I asked him to leave. Being a gentleman, he didn't have a choice."

"I'm so sorry." Jessie smacked the back of the sofa, making her palm tingle. "So much of your pain—and Takoa's too—is my fault." She'd encouraged Tena to go out with Takoa and encouraged him to persist when Tena kept resisting his efforts to deepen their relationship. "If I couldn't have happily ever after, I at least wanted you two to find it. I should have minded my own business and left well enough alone."

"It would have happened anyway." Tena hiccupped on a sob. "Like you said, as soon as I saw him I knew I wanted to be more than friends. One's heart is a hard thing to deny; particularly when it is being hard pressed by the person it desperately wants."

"Tell me about it." Jessie sniffed and took hold of Tena's hand. "It's going to be awfully hard for you to see him all the time now."

Tena straightened her back. "That's why I'm leaving on the first boat, plane, floating log, or even with the Japanese, if they show up first."

"No." The word trembled out of Jessie's mouth. She tightened her grip on Tena's hand. "You can't mean that. What would I do without you?"

"Maybe you should come with me—now that Jake and Sky both know where you are."

The idea did have a certain appeal. Already the rumors were flying. Jake seemed to have told anyone who would listen how she'd broken his heart, and that he longed to have her back. She knew the people of Toolowa believed what he was saying, and it was good fonder for the rumor mill.

It was especially juicy after the cream of Toolowan society had seen Sky's strong reaction to her and the tussle the two had started over taking her in to dinner. Mrs. Gunley had even been bold enough to ask her which one she was in love with, after she'd set up tutoring times for Jemma.

They won't be here forever. The military will come for them. Still, now that they know I'm here, will they leave me alone, once the war is over? She frowned over the idea of leaving, while Tena blew her nose.

She hated what Jake was telling everyone and refuting it didn't seem to do any good. *I don't believe Jake has been carrying a torch for me all these years. I'm just a convenient diversion. Once he leaves Toolowa, I'm sure he won't give me another thought. But Sky is a different story.* Her gut told her Sky had a definite agenda, if his note hadn't. His touch told her that too. He could turn out to be a reoccurring plague that would come back to infect her. *Maybe it would be better to leave Toolowa and lose myself, one more time, in another remote corner of the world.*

Her eyes became shards of green glass. "No! I'm done running. I've run as far as I ever intend to. Jake and Sky have cost me too much. I love my life here. I won't let them cost me that. I won't!"

19

SKY DUCKED UNDER THE DOORFRAME of the judges' council room and sat down on a cushion at the big oval table. Jake sat down beside him. Takoa took the seat on his other side.

Outside the council room windows, the darkness was just beginning to fade. Sky rubbed his eyes and scanned the faces of the judges, unable to detect any weariness. Instead their aged features held an intense urgency. *Maybe elderly people are more productive the earlier it is.* He covered a yawn. *Personally, I'm more productive if I spend the wee hours of the morning in bed.*

Edmund brought the meeting to order and said, "Major Brannigan, we would like to thank you and Captain Denning for attending this meeting. We value your expertise and experience in military affairs and would like to have your input."

"You're welcome," Sky said. "We're anxious to help you in every way we can."

The fingers of the council members tapped the table in appreciation until Edmund said, "This council has deemed is wise, in the event we are invaded by the Japanese, to make plans to deal with the enemy. We have devised two differing plans of action, which we will present to the people. The plan the people choose will be the one we follow—it is our way." He gestured to Tamrin O'Malley. "Judge O'Malley will outline our first plan."

Tamrin O'Malley leaned forward and said in her soft Irish brogue, "We find it unthinkable to simply turn the yunga over to the Japanese. At the same time, there are many who also find it unthinkable to take the life of another person. Therefore, the first plan we will present to the people is to immediately destroy all our stores of yunga, along with the yunga groves and as many of the bushes in the wild as we can. We will then peacefully surrender the island to the Japanese—should they come."

Sky inhaled sharply. "With respect, I strongly advise this council against simply surrendering Toolowa to the Japanese."

"Why?" Tamrin asked.

"Because the Japanese retribution against this council and the people of Toolowa for destroying the yunga will be—severe."

"That's true," Jake said grimly.

"The Japanese are fond of beheading those who thwart with their plans. If you destroy the yunga and surrender the island, no one in this room will survive. All of you will be executed as examples to the people of what their disobedience will cost," Sky said brutally.

The faces of the judges remained placid.

Edmund said quietly, "There are those among us who would rather die than take the life of another person, no matter how good the reason. We respect their feelings and want our people to have this option, even knowing what it will cost."

Sky looked at Takoa for help in convincing the council not to offer this option to the people. Takoa said nothing, his face impassive, but his eyes were hard.

"What is your other plan?" Sky asked.

Edmund nodded at Troy Lind. Judge Lind said, "There are also many who feel it is our right and duty to defend our homes and families against any who would take away our sovereignty and enslave us. As did our forefathers, we would use the yunga, and any other means we can devise, to keep the Japanese from taking Toolowa." Judge Lind took a resolute breath and said, "Should the battle go against us, we will ensure that all the yunga is destroyed. No matter what the cost, we will not allow the Japanese to take possession of the yunga."

Beside him, Sky heard the relieved sigh Takoa expelled before the Toolowan said, "Then with the councils' permission, may I take Major Brannigan and Captain Denning on a tour of the island? Their knowledge of the enemy and the kind of warfare we may face will be invaluable in helping us devise a strategy to defend Toolowa—should the people vote to do so."

The judges' fingers again tapped the table. When they stilled, Edmund asked, "Are you and Captain Denning willing to go with Takoa, Major?"

"Yes," Sky said emphatically.

"Then we will leave today," Takoa said.

"When you have completed your tour, and are on your way back, send us word. We will schedule the village meeting for that evening, outline the plans for our people, and learn their will," Edmund said, concluding the meeting.

The sun was just rising when Sky and Jake left the council chamber with Takoa.

"How soon do we leave?" Jake asked Takoa.

"Immediately," Takoa said.

"Then I'll need to stop by the hospital and get more pain killers.

Sky had been keeping an eye on Jake all through the meeting. He was torn between ordering him back to his bed until his shoulder improved, and letting him come on tour of the island. In the early morning light, Jake had a decidedly gray tinge beneath his tan, and his expression was pinched. He'd spent the previous day in bed, per the doctor's orders, but it hadn't help, at least not that Sky could see.

"I'm not sure I should let you come, Jake," Sky said.

"The only thing wrong with me is a sore shoulder. It's nothing I can't handle with the help of a few pain pills."

Sky's better judgment told him not to let Jake come, but was overpowered by a nagging fear of leaving Jake alone in close proximity to Jessie for a few days. "All right, you can come as long as you keep up, but if you slow us down, I'll order you to turn back," he said, justifying the decision by reminding himself that Jake had great instincts for strategy and tactics. *Besides*, he rationalized; *it's going to take every bit of brainpower the three of us possessed to come up with a viable plan to defend Toolowa.*

"Understood." Jake grinned.

"So what do we need to bring?" Sky asked Takoa as they entered the hospital.

"Nothing," Takoa said. "I'll take care of everything."

They stopped at the nurses' station and found Tena going over patient charts. She glanced up and immediately let her eyes fall back to the chart she was holding. "What can I do for you?" she asked.

Sky's brows lifted. Tena's voice was politely cool, her posture stiff, he face carefully blank.

"I need a supply of pain pills," Jake said. "We're going on a tour of the island and I'd like to be comfortable doing it."

Tena's eyes came up. She looked at Sky, glanced at Takoa, and dropped her eyes. "How long will you be gone?"

"A couple of days, maybe three," Takoa said.

She found Jake's chart, and hurried into the dispensary behind the nurses' station. A few minutes later, she came back out with a bottle, gave Jake instruction on how to use the medication, turned on her heels, and quickly went back into the dispensary.

Jake popped a few painkillers, declared himself fit to tour the island and ready to brainstorm a plan to defend it. Sky nodded a little doubtfully, and the three of them plunged into the jungle equipped with only the clothes on their backs and Takoa's water bag.

Traveling light allowed them to move faster, and Takoa assured them that there was plenty of fresh water and fruit along the way to quench their thirst and satisfy their hunger. When they stopped for the night, they would be fed and housed by his uncle who oversaw all the spice and herb production on the plateau, making it unnecessary to bring camping equipment.

They took their first break at the small waterfall Jessie and Kanoa like to frequent. Kicking off their boots, Sky and Jake plunged into the pool after Takoa. They cooled off and drank deeply before again pushing upward toward the rolling savannah above the bay.

Sky kept throwing glances back at Jake as the trail got steeper. His co-pilot's jaw was fixed into a hard line, but he was keeping up.

The conversation between the men was minimal as they climbed out of the steep jungle bowl the bay sat in and onto the savannah. They stopped under the tropical canopy to catch their breath and cool down after the long uphill climb, before venturing out into the blazing sun.

Sky wiped his brow and neck with a handkerchief, feeling distracted. He just couldn't keep Jessie out of his mind for more than a few moments. Not even the gravity of a possible Japanese invasion, and the need to come up with a plan to thwart it, kept his mind from wandering back to her.

Aggravated with himself, he frowned at Jake, who was bent over and bracing his hands on his thighs, and asked, "You all right?"

Jake ran a forearm across his brow, sweating profusely. "I'm okay—just hot." He rolled his sleeves up a couple of notches and poured some of the water from Takoa's canvas water bag over his head.

All of them donned the goofy palm frond hats Takoa quickly constructed before they again took up their march. A ninety-minute hike across the tree dotted savannah brought them to the northern rim of the island, near the point where the hooked upper beak of the bird began.

Sky stared out across the vast, empty sea. Then noticing Jake's attention fixed on the sea, he again evaluated his co-pilot.

Jake's ridged expression, relaxed. He closed his eyes and inhaled the stiff breeze that blew across the savannah. His breathing slowed.

Good signs, Sky decided. He hoped Jake would be okay now. Hiking across the rolling savannah would be easier, but hotter.

Satisfied with Jake's condition, Sky's focus shifted to their guide. Takoa's mood seemed subdued, almost depressed, more so than Sky could attribute to the threat confronting Toolowa. *He looks like a man who has just lost his best friend, or his girl. The question is, who is his girl— Jessie or Tena.* He was sure one of them was, *but which one*—and then it hit him.

Those few minutes they'd spent in the hospital so Jake could get more pain medication from Tena had been electrically charged. It reminded him of the atmosphere between him and Jessie when their eyes locked at the ambassador's dinner party, and left him with no doubt.

Takoa was definitely in love with Tena. *Something must have recently gone wrong between them.* That certainty just added to Sky's confusion. It brought up even more questions about Takoa's close relationship—*no, his too close relationship*, Sky amended, *with Jessie.* He glanced at Jake and choked down the urge to ask Takoa directly about his relationship with Jessie, along with a few pointed questions about Kanoa.

The Toolowan seemed to sense his thoughts and as though to return Sky's focus to their job, said, "From this vantage point you can see anything that tries to approach Toolowa from the north or northeast."

"A good location for surveillance," Jake said.

"Yes. Regardless of which plan your people choose, from now on, you're going to need to station a twenty-four hour watch along this northern edge—not just a night watch," Sky said.

Takoa nodded. "I'll arrange that as soon as we get back."

"Good," Sky said absently, still trying to put Jessie out of his mind, but he couldn't let go of the questions that nagged at him. *Jessie, I have to talk to you. It's driving me crazy not knowing what's going on in your life. More than that, I have so much I need to say to you.* However, here again, his duty thwarted him. For the next few days, he had to focus his mind on helping Takoa come up with a solid plan to defend Toolowa, one he hoped the people of Toolowa would vote to support.

Again, mopping his neck, Sky forced his mind back to the task at hand. Far below him, he watched white caped waves crash against the base of the cliffs. "If access to the rest of the island is as impossible as this, it's no wonder every invasion has come by way of the bay."

Their lookout point stood on a small rise. It not only allowed a good view of the sea but of the savannah too. Sky turned to the west. In the distance he could see the jagged outlines of the western mountains. He turned south and saw the cultivated fields of herbs and spices, the silver-blue shimmer of water reflecting off Lake Akalowa, and the southern mountains that stood up like sentinels until they reached the bird's lower beak and flattened out.

Unlike the lightly forested upper beak of the bird, the lower beak was grassy and nearly treeless.

Considering what he'd seen so far, Sky concluded that if the Japanese dropped paratroopers onto the island they would do it on the wide expanse of the savannah. *They'll probably drop the paratroopers on the western side of the lake, beyond the most heavily populated area on the savannah. If they do that, and then land a large body of troops by sea as well, the people on the island will be surrounded by their troops.*

"If Toolowa decides to fight, the most important thing we need to do is keep from having to fight on two fronts. We don't want to find ourselves surrounded," he said to Takoa and unfolded the strategy he was sure the Japanese would use if they invaded Toolowa.

Frowning, Takoa listened intently and said, "Then before we head for the lake, I need to take you to the end of the bird's beak, where the channel begins. Perhaps we can think of a way to keep a ship from entering the channel."

IT WAS AFTER DARK by the time the trio reached the large rambling lakeside home of Takoa's Uncle Henry. They were welcomed warmly by his aunt Myah, and fed a superb meal of fresh fish and exotic vegetables, seasoned with spices the two flyers had never tasted. After thanking the Zenderly's for the delicious meal, they bedded down for the night in one of the two huge dorm rooms attached to the back of the house by a covered walkway.

The dorm rooms—each of which could sleep fifty people—were used as overflow accommodations. They housed the seasonal workers who came from the bay twice a year for two weeks to help with the planting or harvesting. Fortunately, the dorms had just been prepared to receive the onslaught of people due to arrive from the bay next week to begin planting.

It was still dark, and Sky felt as though he'd only been asleep for a few minutes when he was awakened by Takoa the following morning.

"I'll go get our breakfast, you get Jake up," Takoa said as he crossed the room to the outside door.

Sky groaned, rubbed a hand across his beard-roughened jaw, and sat up in his hammock. It had been a surprisingly comfortable bed. He felt the urge to just lie back down and go to sleep again, but they had a lot of ground to cover today, before they headed back to the bay.

"Jake"—he poked his copilot, sleeping in the hammock next to his—"wake up. It's time to get going."

Jake responded with a low moan.

Sky swung his legs over the edge of the hammock. "Hit the deck, buddy," he said and went into the bathroom.

He yawned and stretched to shake off the last vestige of sleep. He lathered his face, hoping Jake had slept as well as he had, but worry badgered him.

Yesterday, during the final hour of their trek, Jake had fallen behind, his strength flagging and obviously in pain. At dinner he'd wolfed down his food faster than polite manners allowed, pleaded fatigue, and headed for their quarters.

Sky had politely excused himself and gone with him, not only to give Takoa some time with his uncle and aunt, but also to make sure Jake was okay. Jake had given him gruff reassurances, but the door to the dorm room had barely shut behind them before Jake stripped down to his boxers, swallowed more pain pills, and climbed into his hammock.

Sky stroked a razor across his jaw with a sure hand, his concern for his co-pilot deepening. Jake's waking moan had been pain ridden. *Maybe I should send Jake back instead of letting him go any farther. That bottle of pain pills was nearly empty last night. He doesn't have enough of them left to make it through today, let alone tomorrow, which must mean he's in a lot more pain that he's letting me see.*

He struggled with the decision as he turned on the shower and stepped in. By the time he shut the shower off he'd decided Jake shouldn't go any farther. *I don't want to send him back to the bay. I don't want him anywhere near Jessie while I'm gone. Besides, Jake might not have the strength to make it back to the bay on his own. I'll order him* to stay here and rest until Takoa and I get back from the mountain fortress. Maybe by then he'll be feeling better.

He stepped out of the shower and reached for a towel just in time to hear a dull, but distinctive thud, come from the dorm room. He wrapped the towel around his waist and opened the bathroom door.

Jake was lying in a heap on the floor. Sky rushed to his side. He rolled Jake off his wounded shoulder, found a rapid pulse, and felt his forehead. *He's burning up.*

Sky ran into the bathroom, soaked a towel in cold water, and dashed back into the room. He wrapped Jake's head in the towel, and then reached for his wrist. He was frowning over Jake's rapid pulse when Takoa walked in with a basket of fruit and hot bread.

"We've got to get Jake back to the hospital—now. He's got a raging fever, and just look at his shoulder and arm."

Takoa gaped at Jake's enflamed wound and angry red arm and bolted for the door. "You get him dressed, I'll get a stretcher and some help," he called as he ran.

Sky pulled on his BDUs, and laced up his boots.

Jake's BDUs were hung on a peg attached to the thick beam that supported his hammock. Sky grabbed the pants and worked Jake's legs into them, tugged them up over his boxer shorts, around his waist, and fastened them. Then decided that was enough clothes to wrestle Jake into for the moment. Taking the light blanket from the hammock, he covered Jake with it.

Before Takoa came back with a stretcher and six sturdy bears, Henry and Myah Zenderly were bending over Jake.

Henry so closely resembled his older brother Edmund that when they were introduced, the previous evening, Sky wondered if they might be twins. Henry chuckled and told him people often thought that when he was introduced. The grave expression he now wore deepened the resemblance and reminded Sky of the one Edmund wore when he'd learned what the Jensens had done with the yunga.

Worry grew in Myah's lovely hazel eyes as she quickly and efficiently inspected Jake and issued orders. "Put him on the stretcher, and take him into the bathroom. We must get him into the shower and cool him down, now!"

20

JESSIE WAS TRYING TO COAX KANOA into finishing his dinner, when Tena walked into her kitchen. Jessie lifted an inquiring brow. Tena didn't usually come to visit her at dinnertime.

"I need to talk to you," Tena whispered glancing at Triny putting dishes into the sink, "without the islands gossip chain in attendance."

"Okay." Jessie gave up on the squash Kanoa refused to open his mouth for, washed his face and hands, and lifted him out of his booster seat.

"I'm going to put Kanoa to bed," she said to Triny's back as she and Tena left the kitchen. "You look just like Triny does when she's about to burst with news," Jessie whispered as they passed through the living room.

Tena shut the door to Kanoa's bedroom as soon as they were inside. "*News* is just what I've got, but I don't want it all over the island in the next five minutes."

"Okay, so what gives?" Jessie set Kanoa down on the bed and took his pajamas from a chest of drawers.

"Six men came off the savannah this afternoon. They carried a covered stretcher into the hospital—with Jake on it."

"What?" Jessie stopped removing Kanoa's shirt to stare at her friend.

Tena flopped down in the rocking chair and rocked back. "Jake was unconscious, and his symptoms led Paul to the conclusion that he has coral poisoning."

"I've never heard of coral poisoning," Jessie said tugging off Kanoa's shirt, and then trying to get him to hold still so she could remove his shorts.

"That's because not everyone is susceptible to coral poisoning. In fact, this is the first case of it I've ever seen.

According to Paul, certain people can be very allergic to the toxins in some kinds of coral. Unfortunately, Jake seemed to be one of them."

Jessie pulled Kanoa's legs out of his shorts and asked, "Why didn't Paul spot that right off, when he first removed the coral from Jake's shoulder?"

"Jake didn't have any symptoms at that point. It took a while for the infection to get going. Apparently, it progressed so slowly at first that Paul didn't see it. Now, after all the exertion of touring the island with Takoa and Sky, the infection is full blown."

"So how bad is he?"

"Bad, real bad."

"Are you serious?"

"Yes. Jake only has a fifty percent chance of surviving."

Jessie stopped wrestling Kanoa into his pajamas, stunned to realize Jake might not recover from something as simple as cuts from the coral reef. "What's being done for him?"

"Paul is treating him with a sulfonamide drug, but it's a game of catch up, and at the moment Jake is losing. The next forty-eight hours will tell the tale—if you know what I mean."

"Does Sky know?" Jessie asked, buttoning the last button on Kanoa's pajamas.

"Paul had Lowa send out a coded call to find Sky and Takoa and tell them to come back as soon as they can."

"Good," Jessie said, tucking Kanoa into bed. He snuggled up with his dog, and Jessie began the nightly ritual of massaging his back. When Kanoa stopped wiggling and stuck his thumb into his mouth, she whispered to Tena, "You know, I never thought I'd say it, but I'm sorry for Jake. Is there anything I can do?"

"As a matter of fact, there is." Tena rocked forward. "When Jake finally came around, he asked to see you."

Jessie put a finger to her lips as Kanoa's eyes fluttered shut. A few minutes later, he stopped sucking his thumb and let out a soft sigh. Tena quietly opened the door, and they crept out of the room. Neither said a word until they reached the backyard and began unpinning the clean clothes from the clothesline.

"Did Jake say what he wanted?"

"No. He just begged me to ask you to come."

"*Begged you?*"

"Yes."

"I can't image why. He's already been to see me, and we did all the reminiscing I ever care to do."

"That bad, huh?"

"Yeah." Jessie dropped a bunch of clean dishtowels into a woven basket. "Jake seems to remember our time in New York fondly, which is odd considering the way things ended between us. He made it very clear that he would like to take up where we left off."

"Do you believe he still has feelings for you?"

Jessie put a handful of clothespins into a bucket. "I know what he's been telling everyone. But I think he's just being his usual lady-killer self, hoping for some diversion while he's stuck here. And, since he knows me, he's just starting with his most obvious option."

Tena helped Jessie fold a sheet, set it into the basket, and then leaned against the clothesline pole. "I see your point, but his request to see you sounded pretty urgent. You are, after all, the only person he really knows on this island, besides Sky. Jake's scared, and I don't blame him. His condition is very serious."

Jessie hung the bucket of clothespins on the end of the clothesline and picked up the basket. The smell of sun-dried clothes made her inhale deeply. She really didn't want to go see Jake. He'd pushed rekindling their romance hard, and the last thing she wanted to do was encourage him—or give the gossip chain more fuel for the fire.

Her conscience pricked her. *If he's as bad as Tena says,* and she knew Tena wouldn't have come unless Jake's condition was very serious, *then maybe I should go and see him. It's normal for Jake to want comfort in a time of need. Besides, since he knows me, I'm the logical choice.* Still, she didn't want to get any closer to Jake than necessity dictated. Stalling, she asked, "What about Sky?"

"Assuming the callers reach him quickly, he and Takoa will probably get back from their *tour* sometime tomorrow."

The way Tena said "tour" lifted Jessie's brows. "I take it the *tour* has something to do with the meeting they had with the judges' council yesterday morning. Triny was all a buzz with it, but I didn't really listen."

Tena stretched out on a lounge chair on the back veranda. Jessie set the basket down and sat next to her. She pointed at the open window.

Tena flashed the okay sign and whispered, "I'm sure it does, but I didn't ask when Jake told me about the trip. Takoa and Sky were with him when he stopped by the hospital yesterday morning to get more painkillers. Being near Takoa is more than I can bear. I made the mistake of looking at him." Tears glistened in her violet eyes. "It was all I could do not to burst into tears. He looked at me with such hurt confusion." Tena wiped her eyes with the clean dishtowel Jessie handed her. "I gave Jake the pain killers and . . . ran."

"You need to tell him. You owe Takoa the truth, even if you're determined not to marry him. Don't leave Toolowa and let him wonder for the rest of his life. That would be cruel and unfair."

A red parrot with green wings and a blue tail landed on the clothesline and began to caw at them.

Tena sniffed. "If I didn't know better, I would say he is agreeing with you and lecturing me."

"Does that mean you'll tell Takoa the truth?"

Tena scowled at the bird. "I . . . I will—sometime before I leave."

The bird increased his noisy recital.

"I think he's lecturing me too," Jessie said.

"Does that mean you'll come and see Jake?"

"Well . . . I won't be able to see him until tomorrow evening. Tonight and tomorrow morning are booked full of tutoring. I had to do some pretty fast-talking to get some of my students to agree to it. Spending their vacation doing more school work is a tough sell." She stood up and picked up the laundry basket. "Tell Jake I'll come and see him around five or six tomorrow evening." She paused. "Let me know if he gets any worse, and I'll come right away."

21

THE ISLAND'S CALLING CHAIN was as effective as any phone system—and almost as fast. It sent messages by way of birdcalls and whistles. The encoded message, which only someone from the security force could understand, caught up with Sky and Takoa just after dawn. By then they were almost half way back to Lake Akalowa, following their tour of Toolowa's mountain fortress.

"Jake's condition is getting worse," Takoa said and explained that Paul wanted Sky to return to the bay as quickly as possible.

They pushed themselves hard, but it was after three in the afternoon when they finally dropped off the southern plateau and into the bay area. Sky didn't go to the embassy to shower or eat. Instead, he went directly to the hospital and found Dr. Snyder.

"How is he, Doctor Snyder?" Sky asked, mopping his brow with the tail of his shirt.

"It's Paul," Dr. Snyder said, and then gravely reported he was pumping painkillers and sulfonamide drugs into Jake via an intravenous tube. "I had to sedate him too."

"Why?"

"Because when he's conscious he gets very agitated, and that only aggravates his condition."

"So there's nothing more you can do?"

"I'm sorry. I'm afraid all I can do right now is keep pumping in the medication, make him as comfortable as possible, and wait and see."

His tone was so heavily guarded that Sky felt the first real flutter of alarm. "Be straight with me, Paul, what are his chances?"

"At the moment . . . less than fifty, fifty."

Sky's stomach rolled over. "Are you serious?"

"I'm afraid so. Jake seems to be having a very bad reaction to his encounter with the coral. Coral poisoning isn't too unusual. However, most people don't have the kind of severe reaction to it that Jake's experiencing. I've pulled more coral out of the people of Toolowa since I started practicing here than I can remember, and no one has ever reacted like Jake. Fortunately, I saw a few bad cases of coral poisoning when I lived in Australia near the Great Barrier Reef. If I hadn't, I wouldn't have known what was happening to Jake."

"Is there anything I can do?"

"I'm afraid not. It's a waiting game now. So you might as well go get cleaned up and have dinner. Come back and see Jake after that. The sedative should be starting to wear off by then."

"Okay," Sky said and started to leave.

"Oh"—Paul put a hand on his arm—"there is one thing you can do. Tell that sister-in-law of yours, Jake keeps asking for her. Even in his sedated state, he mutters her name. I don't know what's between the two of them, but if you could convince her to visit Jake it might do him some good. If she could calm him down, I wouldn't have to sedate him again."

Sky's jaw tightened. "I'll do that," he said and strode down the hallway. *So Jessie hasn't been here.* That revelation both elated and somehow irritated him. It seemed to answer the question of how Jessie felt about Jake, but it bothered him that she apparently felt no compassion for Jake's suffering and the life threatening condition he was facing.

Walking back to the embassy, Sky reviewed the details of the plan he and Takoa had talked over, prayed over, and finally settled on to defend the people of Toolowa—knowing Sam would expect a report.

They had decided that destroying the yunga and protecting the people of Toolowa were their main objectives. Trying to fight against the Japanese's superior weapons, to keep them from taking the island, would cost the lives of too many people. In accordance with that, their plan included putting Henry Zenderly in charge of destroying the cultivated groves of yunga bushes up on the savannah and sowing the ashes into the ground. Every citizen would have the responsibility to destroy the yunga bushes around their homes, and a task force would be set up to destroy the rest of the wild yunga bushes, which mostly grew in the bay area. That project would begin immediately.

Takoa's security force would be in charge of setting up a twenty-four hour surveillance system and assigning people to man the various stations Sky had suggested to Takoa on their tour of the island. They would also execute a two-pronged defense of the channel. In the best-case scenario they would prevent a ship from entering the bay. *But that's a long shot,* Sky had to admit. Mostly, what he hoped to do was to slow down the enemy's ground assault from the bay, and give the rest of Takoa's security force time to set off the booby traps he and Takoa planned to plant along the trails out of the bay. The surveillance teams, which would report on the enemy's progress across the island, would also need time to get into place and secure their positions.

Then, to keep from fighting on two fronts—should the Japanese drop paratroopers onto the savannah—everyone on the island, not involved in surveillance or the limited resisted they planned to stage, was going to retreat into the Toolowan's mountain fortress during the next week.

The fortress was a valley surrounded by a ring of very rugged peaks. It was only accessible by a single route, and the keyhole entrance was steep and easily defensible. *Even with primitive weapons,* Sky reflected.

There was a fresh water lake there and the entrance to a vast catacomb of caves. The Toolowans had used those caves to store supplies for hundreds of years. The caves would provide shelter for the people, and the provision stored there would allow them to live comfortably for months or withstand a long siege. *But it won't come to that. As soon as the Japanese are sighted a distress call will be continually sent out over the shortwave radio.*

Sky felt good about the plan and knew Takoa did too. Takoa had left him at the hospital and gone directly to the judges' council building. They were waiting to hear and discuss the plan he and Takoa had devised, before Takoa presented it this evening at the meeting for the people living in the bay area.

The following evening, the judges were scheduled to meet with the people that lived in the mountains and along the shady, tree-covered shores of Lake Akalowa in the amphitheater near Henry Zenderly's home. After that meeting, the judges would tally the people's votes.

He and Takoa were expected to attend the meeting on the savannah too. The judges wanted him to again tell the story of Roger and Timora Jensen. They also wanted Takoa, as chief security officer, to outline the island's defense strategy.

When the embassy came into view, Sky's feet slowed. Tonight's meeting wasn't due to start until eight. *That means I don't need to go back to the hospital until seven. Now if I can just avoid the ambassador until dinner at six,* he mused, entering the embassy through a side door. *I'll have time to go see Jessie.* That desire had been thwarted for six long days. *Nothing is going to stop me this time.*

Clean clothes were waiting for him when he came out of the bathroom after a prolong shower. They were neatly laid out on the chair in his room, just as he knew they would be. The dirty ones he'd dropped there were gone. He donned his shirt, wrapped the lava-lava around his waist, tucked it in, and slid his feet into the pair of sandals that sat on the floor in front of the chair. *Shin truly is a marvel.* They fit perfectly. He felt profoundly thankful he wouldn't have to continue to wear his combat boots everywhere he went.

He cracked opened his bedroom door and peeked out. *Now if I can just escape without being waylaid by either of the Hamiltons, or Shin, I will be one happy man.* With no one in sight, he opened the door wider and cautiously poked his head out. *It's now or never.* He dashed out of the bedroom and through an outside door at the end of the hall.

It was just after four o'clock, past polite visiting hours, but Sky had already decided that wasn't going to stop him. Not even the red scarf would. Still, he almost shouted with relief when the Jessie's bungalow came into sight. There was no red scarf on the gate. Unlatching the gate, he boldly went through it, paused to latch it, and marched up to the front door.

He knocked loudly and waited impatiently. When no one answered, he knocked again with more force.

Still no one came.

He was about ready to try the door, to see if it was unlocked, when it started to turn. It moved in a jerky sort of way, but finally opened.

"Sky giant!" Kanoa beamed up at him.

Sky dropped to his haunches and extended his hand. "Hi, buddy, how's your foot?"

Kanoa put his hand into the one Sky offered. "I walking good now."

"That's great." Sky ruffled his curly hair and asked with a grin, "Do you know we're related?"

"What is related?" Kanoa cocked his head, his fingers still wrapped around one of Sky's fingers.

"It means we're family."

Kanoa's eyes widened. "Are you my papa?"

Sky's arm encircled Kanoa. "Can I tell you a secret?"

"Uh-huh."

"You have to promise not to tell."

"Okay."

Sky looked at him suspiciously. "We'd better make it an oath. Hold up your little finger."

Kanoa held up his hand, closed his fist, and raised his little finger. Sky wrapped his huge little finger around Kanoa's and pumped it once.

"Okay. Now that you've pledged to keep our secret, I'll tell you what it is." Sky cupped his hand around Kanoa's ear and whispered, "I'm going to do everything in my power to become your papa."

The moment the words were out of his mouth, Sky knew he shouldn't have said them. It wasn't fair to put that idea into Kanoa's head and raise his hopes when Sky's own were so dismal. He knew the likelihood of again winning Jessie heart was—*next to impossible?* But he had to admit, what he'd said was exactly what his heart wanted and what he intended to do.

Kanoa wrapped his arms around Sky's neck. "When—when will you be my papa?"

"It may take a while, but I'll tell you how you'll know."

"How?" Kanoa bounced up and down.

"When your mama kisses me," Sky said wistfully, "then I'll be your papa."

A door banged at the back of the house, followed by footsteps coming down the hall. "Where in da world has ya got ta child," a shrill voice demanded.

"Triny," Kanoa said, tucking himself in closer to Sky. "She's watching me, while Mama's gone."

Sky felt the sharp spurs of disappointment dig in. *How much longer am I going to have to wait?* He set his jaw. *I'll wait here all night if I have to, or at least until I know where to find you, Jess.*

"If ya don't answer me, I swears—" Triny's mouth dropped open as she came into the living room.

Sky rose with Kanoa in his arms. Triny's chin followed his rise, tilting backwards until Sky was afraid she would tip over. Her hand went to her chest.

He gave her the melting smile that never failed to work on women. "You must be Triny," he said, holding out his hand.

She swallowed convulsively and stepped forward, her delicate hand getting lost in his. "My stars but ya's bigger and handsomer dan anybody's been a sayin."

Struggling with the twitch that tugged at his lips, Sky said, "And *you* are prettier than I was led to believe too."

Her free hand fluttered dismissively. "I just be plain old Triny, but if I be twenty years younger, I be swoonin over ya like all da silly gals on dis island be doin."

"Well, since you refuse to be anything more than my friend, what do you say we work on that? May I come in?"

Triny threw up her hands, "Where be my manners. A course ya can come in."

Sky ducked and stepped into the living room. This was Jessie's home, and he wanted to explore every inch of it, but more than that, he wanted to feel welcome here. That desire intensified when he immediately spotted the piano. The longing to have Jessie sing to him pulsed through him. He looked away and went on to admire the room's high beamed ceiling, open design, and large heavy furnishings. He could picture Jessie here. The room suited her with its uncluttered comfort. It felt like home—like the home he wanted with Jessie.

He set Kanoa on the Oriental rug in the midst of a mound of die-cast cars and trucks.

Triny took hold of his arm and practically pushed him onto the sofa, before cozying up beside him.

"So you babysit for Jessie." Sky tossed out his first fishing line, tentatively.

Kanoa's head came up from his cars. "Not a baby! Mama say, I a little man."

"Forgive me," Sky said. "I can see you are indeed a little man, and I won't forget it again."

"Okay," Kanoa said and went back to running his cars across the rug.

"I does sit for Jayling, but I be more dan dat," Triny said with pride. "I be her housekeeper, an very good friend. Nobody knows Jayling better den me."

Sky gave Triny a dashing grin. He'd been an intelligence officer long enough to recognize a deep well when he met one, and he'd just found what he perceived as an almost bottomless one. If anyone could tell him what he wanted to know about Jessie, along with all the dirt there was to know on this island, Triny was the one. He settled in and prepared to pump her for all she was worth.

An hour and a half later, Sky walked back through the gate and latched it. No one watching him would have been able to tell he was angry—furious in fact. What he wasn't sure of was who he was angriest with, Jessie, or himself. As soon as the house was out of sight, he tromped down the path, muttering to himself.

22

JESSIE HURRIED ALONG THE BAY LANE, grateful the long day of tutoring was behind her. *At least I was able to spend the time I wanted with Eli. Now if he will just do the work.* She blew out a frustrated breath. It was unlikely with no support at home.

Eli's parents weren't particularly interested in his education, so when she suggested tutoring to improve his math skills, they left the choice up to him. *As though an eight year old would volunteer to spend his holiday being tutored,* Jessie smirked. *Well at least he agreed to do some practice problems, but I better check on his progress in a day or two.*

With that decision made, her thoughts shifted to Jake. No one had come for her during the night, which made her hope Jake was doing better. *Maybe he's out of danger.* Guilt pricked through her optimism as the hospital came into sight, and she decided to stop and check on him.

Paul was just coming out the door of the hospital after his own long day when Jessie reached it. Before she could ask, he said, "If you're here to see Jake you might as well go home. He's still sedated and it will be a good hour or more before it wears off. I'm going home myself to grab some dinner before I come back and check on him."

Jessie gasped with alarm. *If Jake has to be sedated—*"Is he that bad?"

"The sedation is just to keep him quiet and let him rest. I'm going to let it wear off and then see how he is."

"When should I come back?"

"You could drop by for a few minutes before the village meeting, I'm sure he'll be awake by then."

"Okay, I'll be back then," Jessie said feeling relieved. *If Paul is going home for a while then Jake can't be too bad,* she reasoned. *I can go home, have dinner, and get cleaned up without feeling guilty.*

She left the hospital, tired, hungry, and needing a hug from her little man, still worrying over the poor progress of a few of her students. *What more can I do to help them?*

With her mind completely absorbed by ideas on how to inspire her struggling students, she turned onto the path to her home and collided with Sky's chest before she even realized he was there. The impact threw her off balance.

His arms came around her, keeping her upright. He held her firmly, but not crushingly, and yet she felt bruised by his embrace. Not with the kind of bruises that leave ugly discolorations on the skin, but the internal kind, the kind that lingered forever on the heart.

She couldn't deny he'd left ugly bruises, and deep scars there. She thought she'd gotten past their pain. *No—that isn't true.* She knew she hadn't, but she had learned to ignore the throbbing.

The warm familiarity of his arms seemed to press unbearably around her until she wanted to cry out. She pushed against his chest, unable to hold back the blush she felt staining her cheeks. "Let go!"

He tightened his hold and scowled at her. "You lied to me."

"I did no such thing." She wrestled an arm free, brought up her hand and drew it back.

He caught her hand as she swung it. Released her, let her back up a step, crossed his muscled arms over his chest and stood like a roadblock in front of her. "That's hardly the proper way of thanking me for keeping you from landing on your backside in the dirt."

Jessie wanted to refute his conclusion but couldn't. If he hadn't caught her, colliding with his rock hard chest would have sent her sprawling backwards. "All right, thank you. Now if you will excuse me, I'm in a hurry."

He stood his ground like a bull moose, a determined glint in his eyes. "You aren't going anywhere until I get some answers."

"I don't owe you any answers." She lifted her chin. "My life is none of your business." She tried to step around him, but he countered her move, forcing her, if she didn't want to end up in his arms again, to take another step back.

"You wanted me to believe you were an unwed mother, and Takoa was Kanoa's father."

"I am an unwed mother, and Takoa is Kanoa's father in every way that really counts," she said, trying to edge around him.

"His Godfather." Sky blocked her attempt, putting himself toe to toe with her. "I should have guessed it was a fa'a'amu kind of arrangement. Families in Tahiti give their children to extended family to rear—for various reasons—all the time."

"It's not that kind of arrangement. I helped rescue Kanoa's mother from a sinking boat after a cyclone. She died a few minutes after giving birth to Kanoa in my canoe. No one even knew her name." She stepped sideways and gained a foot, then lost it when he again countered her move.

"Why did you adopt him?"

"Because his birth mother begged me to; he looks like me, and . . . I wanted him." She faked a step toward his open side then jumped the other direction. But again found herself toe-to-toe with him, doing a weird sort of dance as he countered every move she made to get around him. "You're going to make me late for dinner."

"No, you'll make yourself late by not answering my questions,' he said, again folding his arms across his chest. "Why did you want me to believe you are an unwed mother?"

Jessie hazarded a glance at him and realized that behind the angry glint in his eyes there was a humorous sparkle too. On some level he was actually enjoying the dumb little dance they were doing.

It suddenly reminded her of all the one-on-one basketball games they'd played and how he'd cheat to win. It always happened when she managed to get around him and line up a shot. Invariably, he would catch her in his arms, lift her off her feet, and kiss her to keep her from scoring.

His quirked up lips told her he was remembering those games too. That irritated her even more and made her hand twitch with the urge to smack the smug expression off his face.

"I didn't *make* you believe anything. I simply stated the facts. *You* are the one that decided I was an unwed mother. Besides, you wouldn't have believed anything else of *the Amazon*."

His face fell, and Jessie knew she'd scored a hit. She took advantage of the moment and tried to lunge around him.

He caught her in his arms again. "You're wrong about what you believe I think about you."

"Am I?" She pushed against his chest, broke free of his arms, and took a few steps back, feeling far more rattled than the circumstances dictated. "Then why did the first words out of your mouth proclaim to one and all that the best name for me was Amazon."

Sky's shoulders drooped. "I'm sorry for that unwarranted crack."

The sound of women talking made both their heads jerked in the direction of the oncoming voices. Loud, cheerful chatter came down the lane from the direction of the town square.

Sky lowered his voice to a soft growl, "Why didn't you just tell me Kanoa was your *adopted* son?"

"I won't stand here and have this conversation with you." She lunged forward, trying again to push past him.

He caught hold of her arms. "All right, but we are going to have a conversation, and it can either be here and now, or you will agree to meet me somewhere when we can have some time and privacy." He pulled her close, until they were again toe-to-toe.

His breath brushed her brow and his lips were far too close to hers. Her knees almost buckled with the traitorous, and nearly overpowering, yearning that hit her.

"If you refuse this very reasonable request, I will come and get you and carry you off into the jungle."

Her heart was beating out of control, and not just because the voices coming down the lane were closing in on them. She knew exactly what the set of his jaw meant. Audacity had always been Sky Brannigan's calling card. He would make good on his threat.

"All right," she said, hearing the note of desperation in her voice. "I'll meet you."

"Tonight."

She wanted to refuse, but the voices were close enough now for her to recognize them, even though the jungle foliage kept her from seeing the women.

Tilly and Shula were Triny's younger sisters. After their parent's died in a flu epidemic, which swept the island when Triny was fifteen, Triny made her sisters go to school while she supported them. She wanted them to learn to talk properly and make something of themselves. Both had done just that. Tilly worked as Judge Lily Apo's secretary, and Shula was the head of housekeeping at the American embassy. The three single women shared a home and were the last people Jessie wanted to know her business.

"Okay." She quickly agreed.

"Where, and when?" Sky asked, still holding her arms.

She swallowed and lowered her voice. "Follow the path that starts on the east side of the church. It leads to a clearing. I'll be there after the town meeting."

"You better be there no later than fifteen minutes after the meeting ends, or I'll be coming after you." He let go of her and extended his hand, took hers, and pumped it. "Thanks for the directions," he said loudly as the women came into sight at the juncture where the path to Jessie's house met the lane.

"You're welcome," she said brightly, with a glance at the two suddenly silent, gaping women.

Sky stepped aside, letting her go past him.

"Thanks again," he called after her as she walked sedately down the path.

She heard him say good evening in his most charming voice to the women, and listened to them giggle before she rounded a curve in the path and was hidden from their view.

Feeling more than a little shaken and thoroughly disgusted with herself, she ran for home.

23

TORCHES RINGED THE AMPHITHEATER and ran down between the crowded rows of wooden benches. Sky sat on the platform at the bottom of the theater with Takoa and the council of judges, watching it fill to overflowing. The people of Toolowa were indeed diverse. The variety of hair colors, skin tones, and their vastly different ethnic features made Sky feel like he was looking out over the crowd at one of his basketball games in New York City.

He searched the multitude for Jessie and finally spotted her. She dropped onto a bench next to Tena, near the top of the theater. Kanoa stood on the bench between the women and waved down at him.

Takoa returned the wave and Sky wondered if Kanoa meant the wave for Takoa or him, maybe it was meant for both of them. He lifted his hand and waved, started to make a comment to Takoa, and stopped. The Toolowan's eyes were riveted on Tena.

Thanks to Triny, he now knew the details of Takoa's romance with Tena and about their break up, even though a frustrated Triny didn't know the reason. It explained Takoa's moodiness over the past few days. His tight-lipped refusal to be drawn out on his personal relationships with either Jessie or Tena was due to a broken heart. Sky felt a deep pang of empathy for him. He knew all too well how it felt to be hopelessly in love with a woman who didn't want him anymore.

Although Sky hadn't been able to draw Takoa out on his personal life, Takoa had been very open about his love for Toolowa, its people, and his desire to serve and protect them. *Kanoa couldn't have a better example to pattern himself after,* Sky admitted, as Edmund stood, and the people of Toolowa instantly quieted down.

"I know the news of the American plane that went down inside the bay has reached everyone. Thankfully, the two pilots aboard the plane survived the crash. For those of you who don't know, Captain Denning is in the hospital suffering from coral poisoning. Right now his condition is grave, but Dr. Snyder and the hospital staff are doing all they can for him. If you wish to help him, I'm sure he would welcome your prayers in his behalf."

A chorus of assent and well wishes ran through the crowd, along with the stomping of feet.

Edmund held up a hand, and silence again descended. "Most of you know the reason the Americans came to Toolowa. For those of you who don't, it grieves me to tell you they came to warn us about the possible invasion of our island by the Japanese."

The Toolowans' outrage and fear rolled together and boomed down at those on the platform like a crack of thunder until Edmund again raised his hand. "The council of judges believes the threat our American allies came to warn us of is credible, but you must judge that for yourselves."

Sky stood at Edmund's invitation and related Timora Jensen's story. Those sitting near Timora's grief stricken parents and family reached out to comfort them in their grief and shame.

When Sky finished, Edmund asked if his people found the threat to be credible.

The thundering of feet answered him.

"Then we must decide what to do about this threat. Your judges have two differing plans to present, but they are open to suggestions. Each of you has the right to ask questions, or propose a different solution to this problem. After we outline our proposals, the floor will be open to entertain any other ideas. At the end of one hour, each person will vote his or her conscience. The plan that receives the most support is the one we will use. Is everyone in agreement with this?"

Again, there was a thundering of feet. Edmund held up a hand, and yielded the floor to Tamrin O'Malley.

A low hum ran through the crowd as she presented the plan for destroying the stores of yunga and peacefully surrendering the island. At her invitation, Sky stood and explained the possible consequences of this plan. Then Takoa took the floor and outlined the plan he and Sky had come up with to defend the people of Toolowa. He told them, frankly, that this plan would undoubtedly cost lives.

Questions were asked and answered to the best of the judges, Takoa, and Sky's abilities. When there were no more questions, Edmund opened the floor to any other comments or suggestions.

A bent and wizened man, thin and bowed down with age, but strong with conviction stood. He was Queen Menaloni's elderly father, Kaylawnu Potapoo, a highly respected and greatly beloved man. "I strongly support the defensive strategy that has been outlined for us. However, I would like to propose an element be added to that strategy, which I believe will keep the Japanese from taking the island."

The proposal Kaylawnu made was met by silence.

Sky felt the hair rise on the back of his neck. He watched the people with growing horror. A kind of peace settled over them, some even smiled. That quiet serenity was as unnerving as the elderly man's proposal. Sky stared up at Jessie. She and Tena had their heads together, whispering urgently.

Edmund raised his hand and, it seemed to Sky, even the insects and the lapping of the waves stilled.

"We will vote," Edmund said.

SKY STILL FELT STUNNED by the people's decision as he walked along the path behind the church. The defense plan he and Takoa had devised had been overwhelmingly accepted. He was thankful for that, but then, so was Kaylawnu's addition. Even Takoa stood in favor of it, as did Tena and Jessie. It was one more thing he now urgently needed to talk about with Jessie.

Kaylawnu's addition to their defense strategy was so drastic that Sky knew it would change life on Toolowa for years to come. Still, he had to admit that it also held a kind of preemptive brilliance, which might be the best way to save the lives of the people on Toolowa, but the sacrifice would be staggering.

When he reached the small clearing, he swept it with the flashlight Shin had given him. The light revealed a worn wooden bench sitting in the center. He walked over to it, sat down, snapped off the flashlight, and let his eyes adjust to the darkness.

The clearing punched a hole through the jungle canopy, opening it to the sky. Countless pinpoints of light shimmered above him, softening the blackness of the night. Their twinkling brilliance was boosted by a waning crescent moon. Sky's attention swiveled between the bright clusters of the stars and the path he'd entered the clearing by, waiting expectantly.

The sounds of the night suddenly stilled. He came to his feet, feeling Jessie's presence rather than seeing her.

"Here."

He spun toward the sound of her voice as she slipped into the clearing on a beam of starlight as graceful and lovely as a wood nymph. For a moment, he was surprised by the direction of her arrival. She'd entered the clearing from a place that—he felt sure—wasn't connected to any path. At least he couldn't detect anything except a dense wall of jungle at her back, but then he didn't know this island, not the way she did.

It reminded him of all the stories she'd told him about her Uncle Zedekiah, the last full-blooded Nahtow Indian, who'd spent many summers with her family. As a child and teenager, she'd roamed the mountains with him learning the ways of the Nahtow. With him as her teacher, she'd become especially good at moving soundlessly across any kind of terrain. Sky had always admired the way she could silently appear and just as mysteriously vanish.

Her stance at the edge of the clearing was that of a wary doe, ready to spring away at the least sign of danger. It told him one false move from him, and she would bolt. If she ran back into the jungle, not even the aid of a flashlight would help him track her.

This was his chance, maybe his only chance, to say all the things he yearned to tell her. But at the moment, all he could do was gaze at her.

A shaft of pale moonlight lit her face. In the four years they'd been apart, her remarkable beauty had come to full flower, but it wasn't the beauty of the Amazon. Now it was something much more refined, confident, regal, and that somehow made her seem, untouchable.

He drank her in like a tonic, one that could cure him of all his suffering, if he could just find the right words to draw her to him. However, he saw that the task wasn't going to be an easy one. Her eyes were wary, her stance poised for flight, her jaw a line of defiance.

"Thank you for coming." He stepped to the end of the bench.

"Stop!" She held up a hand like a barricade and drew back, letting the jungle brush her sides.

He stopped, hardly daring to breath.

"I'm only here because of your threat. And since you had the last words—four years ago—when you walked out on me, I think I deserve to have the first ones now."

"Agreed," he said, standing perfectly still.

She stepped back into the clearing, walked along its edge, and stopped, now even farther from him.

He smiled inwardly. *At least the bench is no longer between us.*

"I've buried our past with all the tears and grieving I ever intend to give it, and I won't let you dig it up again. I'm not interested in anything you have to say about it."

"Please Jess—"

"No"—she took a step toward him, her hands fisted— "it's my turn, and I'm going to have my say." She marched to him and came to a stop a few feet from him. Her face worked through some painful emotion before she said, "All I want to do is . . . apologize, ask for your forgiveness, and . . . *thank you.*"

Her declaration blindsided him. Over the years, he'd tried to imagine what she might say to him if they ever met again. Of all the things he'd imagined, what she'd just said had never entered his mind. Her unforeseen attitude sent his stomach into free fall. It felt like she was preparing to slam a door in his face and bolt it with finality.

He searched the green eyes that could bewitch the devil himself. Those expressive eyes used to tell him what she thought, how she felt. Now he could read nothing of what she felt, although they held his with unflinching fortitude.

"I should have told you about my . . . moral lapse, before we got in too deep. For that I'm truly sorry and ask for your forgiveness. You had every right to expect me to be . . . innocent. I deceived you, and then expected you to shrug off what I'd done. I knew right from the start I wasn't what you thought I was, but I deluded myself. I wasted your time and hurt us both. I'm sorry for that too, and I don't blame you for walking out on me. I just got what I deserved and—"

"No!" He couldn't bear to listen to even one more word. This wasn't at all how this conversation was supposed to go. He was the one who had been wrong—dead wrong. What he'd done to her had been despicable. He desperately wanted to make that confession, apologize, and plead for her forgiveness. "Jess—"

Her hands shot up.

It halted his words and the step he took toward her.

"And"—she repeated stubbornly—"I want to thank you for the very ugly, but valuable, lesson you taught me."

"What lesson?"

"That I'm irrevocably tainted and no good priesthood holder will ever want me."

A strangled sound caught in Sky's throat.

She held up a warning finger and used it to punctuate her words. "*Thank you,* for helping me to understand that," she said somberly. "Your rejection has, and will, continue to save me the pain of ever telling another man what I told you. Facing and accepting my tainted condition has allowed me to move on with my life, see a different future, accept a different path, and find contentment." She took a step back. "So there's no need for you to make whatever apology you referred to in your note. I don't need, want, or deserve it."

"Are you finished?" he asked through clenched jaws, when she didn't continue.

She nodded curtly.

His fingers ached to brush back the strand of wavy hair the breeze fluttered against her cheek. She was within reach of his arms. He forced them to stay at his sides.

"Do you think we might sit down for a minute?" He gestured to the bench.

She threw him a suspicious look and shrugged. He backed up and sat on the far end. She sat gingerly on the other end, her body poised for flight.

What she'd said flayed his soul. He'd never felt such penetrating guilt. The wounds he'd inflicted on her were so much deeper than he'd ever imagined. The tone of her voice and her averted face told him she truly believed that no good man could ever love her enough to see beyond her past mistakes. *My rejection made her feel so unlovable that she has cut herself off from the very idea of ever being worth to marry. That's my fault, and I have to convince her she's wrong.*

He understood now how impossible it had been for her to tell him what had happened with Jake, especially at the beginning of their relationship. *That was another unrealistic expectation I imposed on her, without her knowledge.* The years had taught him that her heart had needed time to believe in his love, before she'd felt confident enough to share the secret her soul harbored. That understanding made him see why she'd held him off for so long.

"Jessie," he said softly, and unconsciously reached for her hand. "I'm the one who needs—"

The sound of laughter coming toward the clearing made them both jump to their feet.

Sky glared over his shoulder. *No! Not now!*

He identified both a male and a female tone to the playful laughter and it occurred to him this clearing must be a popular place for sweethearts to meet. He quickly turned back to Jessie to suggest they make a hasty retreat.

She was gone.

Switching on his flashlight, he plunged into the jungle from the direction she'd come. *She can't have more than a moment's head start on me.* He swung the light in an arch, pushing through the dense foliage, searching for any movement of the ferns, or a glimpse of her long auburn hair.

Nothing moved.

24

SING LEE, ONE OF THE STUDENT NURSES at the hospital, pounded on Jessie's door at three in the morning.

She was a petite little thing with honey colored hair and warm hazel eyes. Unintentionally, she made Jessie feel big and awkward. It was a feeling that always disconcerted Jessie. She loved her height, but Sing Lee's fragile air of sweet innocence made every male that crossed her path feel the urgent need to protect her. That was something Jessie wouldn't have minded inspiring in a man—at least she wouldn't have some years ago. Somehow, Sing Lee always made her remember that desire.

"You need to come," Sing Lee said, stepping through the door. "Captain Denning is worse, and he's asking for you. Doctor Paul says, he's at the crisis and may be . . . dying."

"Can you stay with Kanoa?"

"Yes, I can stay until you come home."

"I'll show you what to do if Kanoa wakes up, and you have to feed him breakfast. Triny will be here by nine o'clock. She can take over for you then—if I'm not back."

Five minutes later, Jessie ran along the lane to the hospital with only a glimmer of moonlight to guide her. The night was alive with the constant hum of nocturnal insects, accompanied by the rippling of the waves against the shore. That peaceful duet did nothing to calm the turmoil in her mind.

She couldn't have refused to go see Jake, especially not since Paul thought he might be dying. The terrible part was—she didn't know if she could find the compassion to comfort him. What had happened between them had been her own fault, but she couldn't help feeling he'd taken advantage of her at a time when she definitely hadn't been herself, and he certainly must have known it.

Already, she'd forced herself to put aside her feelings and had gone to the hospital before the town meeting, but Jake had still been too groggy to talk to her. She'd meant to stop by after her rendezvous with Sky, but had been too upset to do it.

Tena met her as she rushed into the hospital. "Tell me," she said, gasping to catch her breath.

"He's almost at the crisis." Tena took her arm and propelled her along the corridor. "We'll know in the next hour."

Paul met them at the door to Jake's room. "Thank you for coming, Jayling. Jake keeps asking for you. There's something weighing on his mind that he seems to want to tell you. His agitation over the matter is making things worse and I don't want to sedate him again. He needs all his energy to fight the infection. Do your best to calm him down." He patted Jessie's hand. "Once he unburdens his mind, his anxiety may subside. At least I hope it will."

"I'll try," Jessie said, took a deep breath and followed Tena into the room.

Tena took a seat next to the door, close enough to watch Jake, but far enough away to give Jessie and Jake some privacy.

The room was dimly lit, but even in the inadequate light, Jessie could see how sickly pale Jake was. His usual meticulously combed hair looked like a tornado had hit it, and his face was covered by a two day old beard. There were dark shadows under his closed eyes too.

Jessie sat down in the chair next to the bed.

Jake's eyes opened bright with fever and etched with pain. "You've come," he said, feebly reaching out his hand.

Jessie grasped it, and his arm went limp as though the effort to reach out for her had taken all his strength. Sympathy and pity, she hadn't expected to feel, filled her.

She gently squeezed his hand. "Everything is going to be all right, you just need to be quiet and rest."

His grip on her hand tightened painfully, and she felt grateful he still had that much strength left in him, but she didn't want him to use it up with anxiety.

"Will you stay with me? Until—until it's over?"

"Yes, I won't leave you until you're better. I promise."

He closed his eyes, and his grip slackened.

Jessie covered their clasped hands with her other one, strategically placing her fingers on his wrist. His pulse was fast—too fast.

She searched for some words of comfort and encouragement, murmuring whatever came to mind.

After a minute, his pulse slowed and his pinched expression relaxed.

"Sing to me, Amazon," he whispered, calling her by the name he knew her by, the one that had connected them so long ago.

The request, and the name, pulled her back into a memory. They had once danced on the small terrace of her New York apartment to the music of a street band that had drifted up from the sidewalk. She'd sung the song the street musicians were playing. He'd been astonished by her voice and had requested she sing to him often after that. He'd also coaxed her into singing for a few parties they'd attended. Everyone told her when she quit modeling she should go into the music business. She'd even been approached by two Broadway producers, but found she had as little ambition to pursue a singing career as she had for a modeling one.

"Is there anything in particular you would like to hear?"

He moved his head slightly from side to side, as if speaking took too much effort.

The tune to a lullaby she often sang to Kanoa to comfort him when he woke in the night with a bad dream, or just couldn't sleep, drifted through her mind. She hummed the melody as an introduction and then began to sing it in a soothing tone.

Jake's eyes closed. His lips curved up on a sigh.

SKY ARRIVED AT THE HOSPITAL OUT OF BREATH after sprinting the distance from the embassy. He stopped Paul, coming out of another patient's room, got the latest update on Jake, and headed for his room. He cracked open the door, aware Jessie was already there, in time to listen to her finish the lullaby she was singing.

Her voice ignited memories so precious that he found himself blinking back tears. They flowed through his mind with every note she sang.

That Sunday when he'd first heard her sing a duet with her brother, Ryder. The love song she'd sung in his ear while they danced in the little nightclub called Smooth Sounds. The countless magical evenings they'd wandered the meadow, while they were employed to help Ryder build the bridge on the Tulliver's ranch. They'd danced together all that summer to the music of the river, the breeze, and Jessie's incomparable voice.

The last time he'd heard her sing had been at her college graduation. The song had been one of hope for a class now ready to take on the world. That had been the day he'd betrayed her, failed her . . . lost her.

He let Jake's door close, but kept it from latching, still yearning to listen to the sound of Jessie's voice as she finished singing. What he couldn't bear was watching her tenderness with Jake. It was a bitter reality, but Jake had far more claim on her than he did. Even now, he wondered why they hadn't married—after what had happened between them.

When Jake had said he'd messed up, Sky was sure he knew what that meant. Jake never could keep his eyes from roaming. *Is that why Jessie didn't give him another chance when he begged and, by his own admission, pleaded with her to forgive him and marry him? Is that what will happen to me when I beg for a second chance?*

He sat down in a chair outside Jake's door just as Jessie started to sing again. *You have no idea what I would give to have you hold my hand and sing to me again, Jess.* He dropped his head into his hands and gave himself up to the sweet agony of her voice.

JESSIE FINISHED THE SONG on a whispered note, and let the silence draw out, hoping Jake was asleep.

His hand twitched in hers.

She raised her eyes and found his open, watching her.

He gave her a flickering smile. "Thanks."

"Shhh. Close your eyes and I'll sing another song for you."

He did, and she sang another lullaby. His fretful expression relaxed, replaced by a peaceful one.

When she finished, his eyes opened and held hers. "I need to tell you something—privately."

"It can wait until you're better. Right now you just need to be quiet and rest."

"No! I need to tell you—now!"

"All right," she said, patting his hand, trying to calm him down. She twisted around and asked Tena, "Would it be all right if we had a few private minutes?"

"I . . . suppose." Tena stood. "But only a few, and if anything changes come and get me—immediately."

"I will." Jessie waited until the door shut behind Tena before she asked, "What do you need to tell me?"

"It's about Burt."

"Tena told me he was killed in a car accident just after I left New York."

"It's not about that."

"Then what?"

SKY WAS HOLDING HIS HEAD in his hands, lost in the wonderful memories of the past, when a pair of shoes stopped in front of him. He looked up at Tena. "How is he?"

Tena took the seat beside him, laying a gentle hand on his arm. "Jessie's presence is helping. He's calmer now."

"Good. Can I go in and see him?"

She withdrew her hand, and stood. "Jake asked for some privacy. You'll need to wait until Jessie comes out. I told her to keep it short." She took a couple of steps and stopped. "I'll be at the nurse's station if you need me."

"Thanks," he said, before dropping his head back into his hands, fighting the conflicting feelings of worry over Jake's condition and the fear of what might be happening between Jake and Jessie.

Five interminable minutes ticked by before Jessie flung the door to Jake's room open.

Sky leaped to his feet. Jessie's expression doused him in fear. He took hold of her shoulders and demanded, "What's wrong? Is Jake all right?"

"Paul! Where's Paul?" Without waiting for an answer, she jerked free of his hands, let go of Jake's door, and ran down the hall toward the nurses station.

Sky caught Jake's door before it closed. In the recessed lighting, he could just make out Jake's face. It was deathly white. His mouth was opened, slightly. One long arm hung over the side of the bed in an oddly flung out way. He stared at that limp hand with its motionless fingers unable to force his feet to step over the threshold and into the room. He willed Jake's hand to move. *Just wiggle your fingers, or twitch, if nothing else.* But Jake's hand continued to hang lifelessly over the side of the bed.

The pounding of running feet, jerked him around. Paul, Tena, and Jessie race toward him. He let go of the door. It shut, closing off the sight he didn't want to accept. He stepped aside as Paul and Tena reached it. They rushed through it. Jessie skidded to a halt beside him.

"It happened so fast," she said, hugging herself. "One moment he was talking to me, the next he—he just . . . stopped."

Sky blinked, trying to take in what she was saying and what it meant. The answer was there in her pale face. She was trembling too, but her eyes were dry. Instead of tears, there was something angry and haunted in the depths of her vivid green eyes that he'd never seen before and didn't understand.

An icy hand clutched his throat. He pulled his burning eyes away from hers, suddenly needing to be alone.

"Where are you going?" she called after him as he shot by her and lengthened out his stride.

He charged through the outside doors of the hospital, a step ahead of the feelings that threatened to overtake him. *Not again, not again, not again,* his feet pounded out the rhythm as he raced up the lane.

Turning sharply at the church, he sought the privacy of the clearing behind it. *Surely, it will be empty this time of the morning.* Aided only by intermittent starlight, he stumbled along the path until he found the clearing.

It was silent and empty. He fell onto the bench and gave vent to his feelings of both grief and guilt.

From the day he and Jake met there had been a bond between them, and something more when they were on the basketball court together. People called them the psychic twins. They played off each other with a harmony and rhythm that people said was like magic. Their ability to read each other on the court was a draw that sold tickets, lots, and lots, of tickets.

Sky found it odd that as in tune with each other as they were on the basketball court; they were completely out of tune off of it. He disapproved of Jake's life style, and Jake often told him that his religion robbed him of all the fun life had to offer. Despite all that, they had developed a strong friendship. Each learned to accept the other's right to be who he was and found things in the other to respect. When the war broke out, they signed up together, went through training together, and managed to stay in the same outfit. By then, Jake had become like another brother to him.

How many bombing runs did we do together? How many times did we make it home on a prayer? How many emergency transports did we do? How many times did we save each other's lives? Too many times to count, that's how many. Sky slammed the palm of his hand against the seat of the wooden bench. *And how many times in the past few days have I wanted to throttle Jake, because of Jessie and what happened between them?*

He was fighting the same old battle, only this time his feelings of betrayal were directed at Jake. He knew Jake had felt the estrangement between them since the night of the Hamilton's dinner party. Jake had even asked if he'd done something to make Sky angry, but Sky had been too angry to talk about it.

Jessie was the one subject he'd never discussed with Jake. And now that he finally knew what had happened between them, he hadn't been able to look at Jake without feeling a deep seeded resentment, or the unsettling desire to do him bodily harm.

Grief welled up in him for the loss of his friend, even while the anger he felt for Jake lingered. He knew he had to let go of that anger, just as he *had* let it go with Jessie—because she'd been right. What had happened between her and Jake had been none of his business. It was over and done before he met either one.

Now Jake was gone. He'd left the world without knowing or understanding why Sky had backed away from their friendship.

"I'm sorry, Jake," Sky whispered, his voice blurry with feeling.

25

PIERCED BY A SHARP SHAFT OF SYMPATHY for Sky's evident distress and grief, Jessie's immediate urge was to follow him. After all, Jake had been *his* friend.

"Almost like brothers," Jake had said, during his visit to her house. "Ones that disagree about a lot of things, but we've always taken care of each other's backs."

Jake's death is so stupid, so pointless, and that makes it even worse. She wavered for a moment then went after Sky. Her determination only lasted for a few paces before a swamp of ugly emotions caught her in a quagmire. She dropped onto the nearest chair and stared down the corridor at Jake's closed door, trying to wade through her murky feelings. *How can I comfort Sky over Jake's death when I'm not even sure how I feel about it?* That thought made her wince with shame, but didn't subdue the anger she felt toward him.

What Jake had told her just before he died thrummed in her brain, growing louder and louder. The ramifications flew at her like an emotional wrecking ball. Only the shield of her towering anger kept that wrecking ball from demolishing her on the spot.

If only Burt hadn't died . . . she felt the anger build toward hatred. "But if he were alive," she said through her teeth, "I would probably be in prison for his murder." And if she was truly honest, she felt the same way about Jake.

Her anger must have been visible because the student nurse who walked by practically hugged the other side of the corridor.

I must look like I'm ready to kill someone, and I probably would, except both the men I'd like to murder are already dead. That thought made her slump in her chair. She leaned her head back against the wall. The anger that had hit her with such ferocity ran down the drain of self-pity. She felt a sardonic laugh bubble up inside her, but it came out as a sob, and a sudden torrent of tears.

Jake's door opened.

Tena came out and hurried over to her. Jessie straightened in her chair, wiping her eyes.

"Well, that was a close one!" Tena collapsed onto the chair beside her. "I really thought he was gone—"

"What?" Jessie grabbed Tena's arm. "Are you saying Jake isn't—dead!"

"He came awfully close. His body almost gave out after giving everything it had to the fight. Thankfully, Paul was able to revive him, and his fever has finally broken."

"Does that mean he's going to be all right?"

"It most certainly does." Tena drew in and blew out a relieved breath.

"Good," Jessie growled the word through her teeth, "because as soon as he is—I intend to kill him!"

Tena stared at her. "What's the matter with you?"

Jessie jumped up. "Never mind, I've got to find Sky. He thinks Jake's dead."

"And just how are you going to do that?" Tena called after her as she ran down the corridor.

THE STARS WERE BEGINNING TO DIM with the growing light in the east, when Jessie started her search for Sky. Past experience told her he would go to ground and hold up somewhere until he worked through his emotions. That eliminated the embassy, or the beach. One held people that would ask too many questions, the other was too public. Pausing, she said a silent prayer, listened to the impression that came, and headed for the path to the clearing behind the church.

He was sitting on the bench, his forearms resting on his thighs, his head in his hands.

Soundlessly, she crossed the clearing to the bench. "Sky," she said, lightly touching his arm.

He leaped to his feet, and turned away, nearly knocking her down, though not intentionally.

"If you're here to comfort me over Jake's death, I don't need it. You can't possibly understand how I feel—felt about Jake."

"That's not why I came," she said to his back, his anger surprising her. "I came—"

"No, I don't suppose it is." He jerked around. "Especially since I don't see any tears in your eyes for him." He peered down at her through the gloomy shadows filling the clearing. "But why aren't there? Surely there should be, after all you and Jake meant to each other—did together."

"Stop right there!" She jabbed a finger into his chest. "You have no idea how I feel about Jake, and it's none of your business anyway."

"No, but surely you should shed a tear for a man you must have once loved."

"I didn't come here to talk about my past relationship with Jake. I came to tell you—"

"How sorry you are he died in such a pointless, absurd way—like so many others." Sky ran a forearm across his eyes, and something in the way he said "like so many others" caught at Jessie's heart.

"Like what others?" she asked, trying to read his face in the predawn light.

His fists clenched. "Like all the people who shouldn't have died in this stinking war."

She didn't fall for his blustering rhetoric. The hurt was too plain, too deep, too personal not to see, and then it came to her with gut retching certainty. "Have you lost your brothers?"

As though her question opened a floodgate, he dropped back onto the bench, emitting an anguished sound. It was something she had never heard or seen him do. He always put up an impenetrable front of self-control, unwilling to show what he perceived as weakness. Her heart ached for him, and she felt a desperate need to comfort him.

She sank onto the bench beside him and put her arms around his shaking shoulders; awakening something in her that she'd told herself was dead.

"Tell me," she whispered, hoping to comfort him, but dreading what he might tell her.

He leaned into her, his head resting against the side of hers. "Jed," he sobbed, "shot down . . . a month ago. He saved his carrier from a kamikaze attack. His body . . . couldn't be recovered."

The words were inadequate, but she said them anyway, "I'm so sorry." Her arms tightened around him. "Of all your brothers, Jed was my favorite."

"Mine too," Sky said, and expelled a shattered laugh full of memories. "He's the one I shared a room with growing up. The one I fought the most with and got in trouble with. But he always knew when I needed him. He never failed me, even if that meant giving me a piece of his mind."

Jessie didn't try to hold in the pain she felt for him and his family as Sky shared his feelings for Jed. She sniffed, pulled back a little, and brushed a tear from his cheek. "How are Lynda and Eric doing?"

His eyes again spilled over. "It's Lynda, Eric, and"—his voice broke—"Jenny." He took several deep breaths before he continued. "Jed was wounded a little over a year ago. He was sent stateside for a few months to recover. Jenny was born just two months ago. He never even got to see her."

She drew him back into her arms, cradled his head on her shoulder, and cried with him. "Being a single parent is hard enough with just one little one, but with two, what will Lynda do?"

"She and the kids have moved in with Mom and Dad. That has been the biggest comfort for all of them. For Lynda it's a blessing to have Mom tend the kids while she works. She won't let my folks take over supporting her, but she loves being there with them. It makes her feel like she is still part of our family and that's helping her cope."

"With no family left of her own to rely on, I'm glad Lynda has your folks. And I'll bet your mother is thrilled to have babies permanently in the house."

"Mom loves the arrangement. She says Eric looks and acts so much like Jed that it will be like watching him grow up all over again."

"That must be such a comfort to her, and Lynda too, being able to see Jed in his son—I mean."

"It is," Sky said as dawn suddenly burst above the eastern cliffs of Toolowa.

Rays of yellow light shot across the sky, turning it from silver to pale blue, and dispelling the night's cloak of darkness with astonishing suddenness.

Jessie became uncomfortably aware of Sky resting in her embrace. Not only that, but somewhere in their mourning over Jed, Sky's arms had encircled her.

Her mouth felt unaccountability dry. His face was much too close to hers. It was so close that the barest movement of either of their heads would bring their lips together.

It had been easy to comfort Sky under a cloak of darkness that hid her from his view and kept her deeper feelings veiled, but the growing light would undoubtedly reveal things she didn't want him to see.

She dropped her arms from around him as though he was a lightning rod, and she was afraid at any moment the lightning building between them would strike.

As the light overhead grew into a new day, she tried to scoot back a bit.

Sky's arms didn't budge. If anything, they tightened around her until she felt like breathing was impossible. That giddy sensation she'd always felt when Sky held her afflicted her, making her tremble.

"It was Jed that finally brought me to my senses."

"About what?" she asked, just before the answer dawned on her. She dropped her head and focused on her white knuckled hands, not daring to look up into those blue eyes that had always had the power to make her melt.

"About you." His lips brushed her temple.

Her elbows flew outward, breaking his embrace. She leaped to her feet and stepped back. "I told you, I've buried our past. It's dead, Sky. Please don't dig it up."

"I listened to what you wanted to say about it, and I think it's only fair for you to let me have my say too," he said, rising to his feet.

Her laugh had a broken quality to it that she couldn't control. He was still too close, and she took another step back. "After four years is there really anything left worth saying?"

"There is for me, and I won't walk away from you again, without saying it. *I can't,*" he said, closing the gap she'd opened between them.

She didn't want to do another silly dance with him. She stood her ground and looked up at him. Was that pity she saw? She could stand almost anything, but his pity. If what he wanted to do was apologize for running out on her without a word and breaking her heart, she didn't want to hear it. She knew it would force her to feel that pain again, that loss.

"I've already told you my life has moved on. I'm happy, and I don't need or want anything from you."

"But I *need* and *want* something from you." He reached for her hand.

Desperate now, she did the only thing she could think of to end the conversation. It was underhanded, and her conscience pricked her, but she did it anyway. "It will have to wait. Right now Jake needs us. He isn't dead. That's what I came to tell you."

"What?" Sky gripped her shoulders.

"We were talking when he suddenly went limp, lifeless. When he didn't respond to me, I dropped his hand and ran for Paul."

"His hand hanging off the bed like that was so unnatural, so still. That's what made me think he was dead."

"And I was sure he was when his grip went slack and he didn't seem to me to be breathing."

"When I looked through the door at him, I didn't think he was breathing either."

"According to Tena he was, but he was also as close as anyone can get to being dead. She said his body had just given all it could to fight the infection and he was completely exhausted. His fever broke about five minutes later." She felt Sky's muscles relax into relief. "Tena says he's going to be just fine." *At least until I kill him.* Her teeth sank into her lower lip holding back the ugly laugh she felt working its way up her throat.

Abruptly, Sky let go of her and sat down. "Jake's really alive and going to be all right," he said as though to reassure himself. He sagged back against the bench, took a long deep breath, blew it out, and slowly rose to his feet again. "I don't care what happened between you and Jake all those years ago in New York. It doesn't matter. It never did."

The raucous laugh that croaked out of her came of its own accord. It was tinged with a bitterness she couldn't conceal any more than she could stop the hot flush of anger that climbed her cheeks. She cocked her head and glared up at him. "So, just how long did it take you to come to that brilliant conclusion, Einstein?"

"It took one, long, brutal year of trying fruitlessly to exorcise you from my soul, and a hard kick in the pants from Jed."

"Gave you a piece of his mind, did he? Good for him. I always admired the way he could put you in your place."

"He did that all right."

"Just what magic words did he say that reached your heart, when nothing I said did?" Her tone was biting, but held a genuine curiosity that she couldn't hide.

Sky took her hand and pulled her toward the bench. "We better sit, this might take a while."

Jessie resisted him, digging in her heels, regretting she'd asked the question that put the scars on her heart in jeopardy of being torn open. More and more she was fearful of what the scars hid. She didn't want to hear what he had to say. At least that's what she'd been telling herself since she'd learned the contents of the note he left with his morning gift.

Still trying to wiggle out of the situation she said, "What about Jake? Shouldn't we go see him?" She despised herself for the note of panic she heard creep into her voice. "He must be wondering why we aren't there, and I did promise to stay with him until he was better."

"He is better, and I'm done waiting," Sky said with a finality she knew too well. He sat and dragged her down beside him. "It's my turn," he said, and claimed her other hand.

"Let go!"

"Only if you promise not to run away again!"

"All right," she said, needing the sensation his touch sent through her to stop.

His grip loosened, she snatched her hands from his and scooted backward to the other end of the bench.

"Does my touch disgust you that much?"

She didn't answer. She couldn't. Not and tell the truth, something she was fighting against with increasing futility.

He huffed out a breath. "Now where were we?"

"Jed's magic words," she said. "You were going to tell me what they were."

"What they were nearly blew me away," he said, shaking his head. "They made me feel small and petty—ashamed. They made me stop fighting what I felt for you. What I still want to have with you."

26

JESSIE'S HEART HAMMERED as though it knew these were the last beats it would take before Sky tore off the scars that had mended and protected it—after he'd demolished it. In an odd way, she was grateful for those scars, which had developed slowly over time. They'd sealed up the pain and hid the hurt away. Eventually, with the help of her little man, her heart had begun to feel alive again, hold joy again, and even feel love again.

She knew her heart would never heal again if the scars were ripped open. The desire to run away was nearly irresistible. At the same time, a desire to know what Jed had said to Sky, which had made him let go of his anger and decide her past didn't matter, grew.

Ultimately it was a single painful question that held her there. *If he changed his mind about my sullied past, still loved me, and wanted a future with me, three years ago—* and even now his expression told her that was true—*why didn't he come after me?*

She lifted her chin, he was going to tear her heart open that much was certain, but she wouldn't give him the satisfaction of knowing it. "So what did Jed tell you," she said with a bravado she hoped was convincing.

"No one else in my family knows what Jed told me." Sky hesitated for a long moment. "It was about Lynda's past. The things she did before she joined the church, made what happened between you and Jake seem insignificant by comparison."

"Did you tell Jed what I did?!"

"No. But he knew how I felt about you. He figured there was only one thing that would make me let go of you. He told me whatever had happened in your life, before we met, couldn't compare with what had happened in Lynda's life. But none of it mattered, because the atonement had made her clean, worthy, and whole."

She stared at him, her pain too acute to speak. Then the truth spit from her mouth. "So—unlike you—Jed's love for Lynda was deep enough, and enduring enough, to survive her past transgressions." A pitiful sardonic laugh followed the words. "Lynda is truly a blessed and fortunate woman. She may have to endure years of separation from Jed, but he will always be hers. And ultimately, they'll get to spend forever together."

"Yes, they will." Shame flushed above the collar of Sky's shirt and spread upward, but he set his jaw, leaned forward, and proclaimed, "My love for you is just as deep and enduring."

"Is that why I haven't heard from you in four years?" Jessie asked, her temper rising.

He slid across the bench in less than a heartbeat, gripping the back of the bench with one big hand. The other one shot out in front of her and landed on the side rail, effectively trapping her.

"I went to your family exactly one year after I left you," he said, his voice desperate with pleading, "Not one of them would tell me where you were, not even Lee. When I pressed her, Ryder and I almost came to blows. They said you were happy with your new life, and they weren't about to let me make you unhappy ever again. Even my parents told me it was too late."

Jessie could feel the blood drain from her face. A dizzy sensation swirled around her. *He came for me. Why didn't anyone tell me—or even ask me if I wanted to see him.*

"I was the one that was unworthy four years ago, because of my stupid pride." He lifted his hand from the side railing and brushed a long strand of hair from her cheek. "I'm so ashamed and sorry for what I did to you—to us. *Please*, forgive me."

"I told you, I don't blame you for how you felt."

"I know I don't deserve a second chance, but I'm . . . *begging* you for it." He placed his fingers under her chin and gently coaxed her to look at him. "I have never stopped loving you, not for a single moment. Even when I was trying to hate you and push you out of my heart, I couldn't do it. It was impossible when all I've ever been able to see—from the very first moment we met—is forever in your eyes."

The world stopped as he held her eyes captive. Breathing was as impossible for her as breaking away from his blue gaze.

"Believe me, Jess"—his fingers stroked her cheek—"there hasn't been anyone else. There never will be."

The scars on her heart gave way, exposing a yawning emptiness where Sky's love for her had lived. His love and understanding would have meant everything to her four years ago. *But what are they worth to me now?*

His eyes brimmed with love and pleading.

She was bombarded with emotions so powerful and conflicted that she found she couldn't say anything. It was all she could do to just keep breathing.

The caress of his hand against her cheek broke her paralysis. She leaped to her feet. Too much had happened in the past few hours, and minutes. "I need time to think about this," she said and bolted into the jungle.

SKY DIDN'T FOLLOW. Her parting words rang with a terrible kind of justice. They were exactly the same words he'd said to her the day he'd walked out on her. He dropped his head back into his hands, trying to hold the hopelessness at bay. He'd laid his heart bare at her feet, put his life and happiness in her hands—*just like she did.*

The agony she must have endured, waiting for him to come back, tore through him. *I know I deserve to, but how long will I have to wait for your forgiveness, Jess? And can you ever love me again?*

She hadn't given him any reason to believe that she still felt anything for him. *And yet, there was a look in her eyes, just a moment, when I told her I'd come for her.* The thought ignited an ember of hope inside him. He pleaded with heaven to help him fan that ember to life, but it was too small to last. *It will serve me right if it takes four years for her to tell me how she feels about me.* He stood up, *but that won't stop me from telling her how I feel about her, every chance I get.* He strode across the clearing and down the path to the church. *Right now, though, I need to see Jake and tell him how grateful I am that he's alive.*

JESSIE PLUNGED INTO THE JUNGLE following a faint track known only to the islanders. It took her into a grotto obscured by ferns and jungle vegetation. In the dark privacy of the sheltering cavern, she threw herself down on the jungle carpet and released all her pent-up feelings.

Stop it, stop it, stop it, she railed against her tears. *None of it matters anymore. I have a good life, I have a son, I'm happy, I am!* "I don't need Sky Brannigan to be happy!" Her voice echoed with trembling bluster into the depths of the grotto.

At least be honest with yourself, her heart demanded.

"All right, I admit it. I—I do still love him, but love wasn't enough to hold us together four years ago, and it isn't enough to bring us back together now!"

In the distance, she heard the clang of the town bell. It always rang as soon as the sun cleared the cliffs above the bay, announcing the beginning of a new day. *I have to get home. There's so much to do, before we'll be ready to leave for the mountains—if that's how the rest of the voting turns out.*

She pulled herself from the floor of the grotto, brushed the gecko that clung to her hair off, and came out into the veiled sunlight under the jungle's canopy. Inhaling and exhaling, she took several breaths in an effort to calm her overwrought feelings.

It wasn't like her to let her emotions get the best of her. She thought her feelings for Sky had died, the year after he left her. It was disconcerting to know that wasn't true. All she'd really done was bury them inside her scared heart. Sky's declaration had forced her to admit they were still there, and very much alive. She didn't want to feel anything for Sky Brannigan, and she hated the fact that she did.

She inhaled another calming breath, "I won't let Kanoa see me like this—I won't." She plunged into the jungle. *By the time I get home, one way or the other, I have to be in control of myself. Kanoa is already too wound up about going into the mountains. And I can't—I won't—let Triny see me like this. She sees too much as it is. I don't want her badgering me about Sky, or Jake.*

27

THE PEOPLE OF TOOLOWA VOTED resoundingly to defend themselves. With that decision, three busy days of sorting and packing went by for Jessie. She managed to avoid Sky, although every morning he left a gift in the center of her veranda table with an expression of his love. That prompted her to hang out her red scarf to keep him from visiting, which, thankfully, he respected.

On the fourth morning, Jessie was working in her garden when she heard the latch on her gate clink open. She twisted around, ready with a curt dismissal, but it wasn't Sky.

Sam Hamilton walked through the gate.

Relief immediately replaced apprehension. Smiling, she rose to her feet and dusted off her knees.

"I didn't expect to find you digging in your garden," Sam said by way of greeting.

Before she could answer, Kanoa squealed, "Grandpa Sam!" He ran to Sam and tugged on his pant leg.

Sam lifted the little boy into his arms and tickled him. Kanoa roared with laughter, and Jessie was hit by the one truth she'd been running from most of all. Kanoa wanted, needed, a father. Every man her son met, he seemed to cling too. She knew he loved Takoa, and Edmund and Sam were like grandfathers to him, but that wasn't the same as having a live-in father.

Her conscience seared her with guilt. *I knew Kanoa would grow up without a father when I adopted him.* Still, she had to confess that although Kanoa might be enough for her, she wasn't enough for him. *That will be especially true the older he gets*, she acknowledged, while admitting she had no desire to entertain marriage just to provide Kanoa with a father.

Sky's pleading eyes haunted her. If she truly loved him—and she did—and he wanted her, something she was now certain of . . . then maybe she should just give him another chance and see what happened. *Kanoa obviously likes Sky,* she acknowledged. *But love isn't enough for me,* she reminded herself fiercely, and then wondered, *but if Sky's love isn't enough, then what would be?*

"Why are you working in your garden, when you should be packing?" Sam asked putting Kanoa down and interrupting her brutally honest reflections.

"I'd like to take as many fresh fruits and vegetables with us as I can," she said, pulling off her work gloves, and pushing a loose strand of hair off her forehead.

He nodded and studied her with a concerned and slightly quizzical expression. "Nora and I haven't seen much of you since the night of our dinner party. I'm thinking it's because of our guests."

Jessie didn't want to lie, but she didn't want to tell the truth either. Instead, she leaned over and picked up her basket of vegetables. "I know I haven't been a frequent visitor of late. I'm sorry about that. How do you and Nora feel about everything that's going on?"

"That's exactly what we want to know from you. You know I promised your parents I'd take care of you, and I have a feeling I've done a pretty poor job of that lately."

Jessie knew Sam's subtle probing was well meaning, and she still thought of him as the Cavalry that had come to her rescue, taking her into a new world that had brought her joy and peace. But at the moment, she didn't want to confide in him.

He laid a hand on her arm. "Jessie, Nora and I are concerned about you. We aren't deaf, and from what the gossip chain is saying, you must be very uncomfortable right now with both Sky and Jake on the island."

Jessie swallowed and looked away.

Sam's arm came around her in a fatherly gesture of concern. "We don't want to pry into your business, but we are worried about you and Kanoa. We want to be sure you have all the help you need to be ready to leave."

"I do, and I will be ready," Jessie said, grateful for the change of subject. Her gaze swept her home and garden.

She watched her son race his cars along the extensive network of dirt highways he'd created. The sting of tears threatened her composure. "Still, it will be hard to leave."

"I was truly astounded by Kaylawnu's suggestion and the Toolowans' acceptance of it."

"I was too, but you have to admit, it's the surest way to keep *all* the yunga out of the hands of the Japanese, and it's a good defensive move too." She blew out a sigh of resignation. "You know we have to do it. The Japanese will come wearing protective gear, making the yunga useless against them."

"And surrendering it to them is unthinkable. I know that, but burning the island seems so extreme."

"It does. But in the long run, if there isn't even a single yunga bush left for the Japanese to get their hands on and use against our unsuspecting allies, think of the lives it will save."

"I agree, but will the people really be safe in the mountain fortress from the fire?"

"They will. I know you haven't been there, but the fortress's vast network of caves will be our fire shelter."

"But can we defend it against a Japanese assault?"

"Yes. Even if the Japanese try to bomb us or drop paratroops into the fortress, we'll be safe."

Sam's eyes widened. "I hadn't thought of that."

"Don't worry. The caves will protect us against bombs, and the paratroopers dropping from the sky will be easy targets as they descend."

"But some might make it."

"Even if a few do, without landing in the lake or on the cliffs of one of the peaks, they won't be able to reach the caves before they're cut down—but I doubt that will happen. As soon as the Japanese are sighted we'll set fire to the island. That will keep them from dropping their paratroopers. They won't drop them into a fire, and the fire will drive the ones that come by ship back into the sea."

"The fire will only protect us if the wind blows from the west, something it usually doesn't do."

Jessie took his hand. "I know it's hard for you to understand, or believe, but I know when Edmund calls for the wind to come from the west, it will."

Sam's eyes searched hers. "You're very much like your father. He also has faith in things I've never been able to understand, and yet I admire you both—and Edmund too." He shrugged. "I can't argue against faith."

"Believe me when I tell you, Sam, that there is enough faith on this island to bring the wind from whatever direction we need it to come. The Lord will hear the pleading of this people. Of that, I have no doubt."

"Then come to dinner tonight and bring Kanoa, help Nora feel what you have just made me feel. She is afraid— very afraid—and I don't know how to comfort her."

Just as Sam had been a grandfather to Kanoa, Nora had been a grandmother. Jessie wanted to comfort and reassure her, but she didn't want to run into Sky, not yet, not until she knew and understood everything that was in her heart.

Sam seemed to read her mind and said, "Sky will be at the hospital all evening. He's having dinner with Jake, who, as you may already know, is improving by leaps and bounds."

"I have heard, and I'm glad for him."

"So will you come to dinner and help me calm my wife's nerves?"

Jessie bit her lower lip, hesitated, and then nodded.

"Good. We'll expect you about seven."

28

NORA CLUNG TO JESSIE'S HAND. "I wish you would let Sam walk you home."

Jessie gave Nora a reassuring hug. "I've been walking myself home from your house this late at night for years, and nothing has ever happened to me."

"But that was before—"

Jessie gave Nora another squeeze and laughed. "The Japanese aren't out there." *However, someone else might be, and I definitely want to be gone before he gets back or I run into him on my way home.*

She stepped out the Hamilton's door and breathed in the damp night air, more disturbed than she'd expected to be by Nora's fears. In all the years the Hamilton's had served in various diplomatic positions, they had never found themselves in a dangerous situation.

Jessie had patiently explained to Nora that the situation might not ever be dangerous. The Japanese might not come. After all, a venture so far south in the Indian Ocean would be very risky. If they did come, the island would be set on fire before they could land.

Already the ignition points for the fire had been set up. The yunga groves, west of the lake, had been burned and people were now moving into the fortress. Once the people were all there, they would prepare to defend themselves against the Japanese, or—if the Japanese didn't come—they would simply wait out the war.

At the village meeting, Sky had made it sound like the war might be over in a matter of a few months. That meant if the Japanese didn't come they wouldn't even have to rough it for too long. Once the war was over, they could all go back to their homes with no more harrowing an experience than camping out for an extended period.

Jessie stepped off the veranda and walked briskly down the dark lane, heading for a narrow path that would take her home in a more direct line. She'd almost reached the cut off when a star generated apparition materialized out of the darkness in front of her.

An embarrassing squeak of fright escaped her when a pair of hands grasped her arms.

"What are you doing out so late, and alone?" Sky asked his voice rough with concern.

"Having dinner with the Hamilton's, and trying to calm Nora's overwrought nerves," she said on a relieved breath, stepping back.

The moonless sky deepened the night's darkness. The light from the stars was barely adequate to allow Jessie to navigate her way home. They made Sky's hair appear white, and his teeth positively gleamed when he smiled.

"Did you succeed?"

"I guess . . . maybe." She shrugged. "I don't really know. She's awfully upset about having to move into the mountains . . . among other things."

"How about you? Are you upset about moving and— *other things?*"

It was a loaded question, positively explosive, and the reason she'd been avoiding him for the past four days. "At the moment"—she covered a yawn—"my only concern is getting home to bed." *Without being pursued by you.*

"I'll walk you."

"No! That is, no thank you, I know the way, and it's late. There's no reason you should postpone getting to bed just to walk me home."

"I'll walk you," he said stubbornly.

She opened her mouth to argue, and then decided it would take longer to squabble over the matter than to just let him walk her home and be done with it. "If you must."

"Thank you." He tucked her hand into his arm, covered it with his, and started back down the lane.

"Wait." She tugged on his arm. "If you insist on walking me home, there's a faster route."

"Okay. I'll pilot—you navigate."

Pulling Sky back a few steps, she led him off the lane and onto a nearly invisible path. Her visual memory wasn't perfect like her mother's or her brother's. Still, compared to most people, it was far superior, and frequent use of this path allowed her to maneuver deftly even at night. With sure steps, she led him along the faint track.

Unlike the well-maintained public lanes on the island, the only thing that maintained this narrow trail was the feet of its users, trampling any vegetation that dared to grow. With each footstep, they churned up the odor of dead and decaying plants. It drifted on the breeze, wrinkling Jessie nose.

The constricted path kept them close together. Sky's fingers caressed hers while she carefully picked her way over the familiar ground, searching for the landmarks that kept her on course. His silent caressing touch ignited her senses and made her skin tingle. Its poignant familiarity sparked a battle between her mind and her heart. *It would be so easy to respond to him, and just give into my heart.* But her heart had been wrong about him before, and she didn't trust it anymore.

She ducked under a low hanging vine, brushing it aside with her free hand. "You'll need both hands to keep from being slapped by branches and getting tangled in vines."

As though to prove her point the slap of a branch sounded over her head. It was followed by a muffled grunt from Sky. He released her hand, and she quickly removed it from his arm.

He stopped, and rubbed his cheek. "I know you don't want to talk about us, and I won't press you . . . at least not tonight. But don't you even want to know how Jake is doing? You haven't been to see him since the night he almost died, and he's been asking for you."

Jessie started down the path again, ignoring his question. She knew all she cared to know about Jake Denning. *Besides, if I went to see him, I might kill him.*

"I assume you know that's where I've been all evening." He smirked ruefully. "I'll bet you knew I'd be gone or you wouldn't have been at the Hamilton's, would you?"

She paused and said, "Sam told me you would be gone, when he invited us."

"Us? Who came with you, and why isn't *he* walking you home?"

"Kanoa was my escort." Jessie pushed aside the large fronds of a fern that blocked the path and stepped around it. "Shula volunteered to take him home after dinner, put him to bed, and stay until I came home."

"That was nice of her," Sky said, clearly relieved. "It's amazing how loyal the staff of the embassy is to the Hamiltons. I've noticed how often they go out of their way to take care of the Hamiltons' needs, and those of their guests. Every morning Shin supplies me with just the kind of clothes I need."

Jessie looked back at him with pride in the giving spirit and endless hospitality the people of Toolowa seemed naturally endowed with, and tripped over a protruding tree root.

Sky caught her elbow, keeping her from falling, held on, and stopped. "Jess, why haven't you been to see Jake?" he asked again.

The darkness hid Jessie's scowl. Whether or not she spent time with Jake was a subject she didn't intend to discuss with Sky. Besides, she was still so furious about what Jake had done to her that she wasn't sure she could answer without bursting into tears.

"I know you have feelings for him, or you wouldn't have kissed him—the day he came to your house to visit. I heard you sing to him in the hospital too."

"Kissed him?" Her outraged woke the jungle inhabitants and set off a chain of chirping, cawing, and humming complaints. Pulling her elbow from Sky's hand, she tromped down the path.

He followed closely on her heels.

"Yes, *kissed him*," Sky said, overtaking her with his long strides and walking beside her. "I watched you two say goodbye. I saw him kiss you, and . . . you certainly didn't seem to object. That tells me there still must be something between you two."

Her arm shot out in front of him, bringing him to a stop. "There's a tree blocking the path just around this bend," she said, and cautiously moved forward.

The tree had fallen sometime in the past week. It had taken her and Kanoa by surprise when they used the path on their way to the Hamilton's for dinner. Fortunately there had still been enough light to navigate around the obstacle with little difficulty. Now, in the darkness, it would require greater care if they weren't going to be gouged and scratched by the branches of the massive tree.

They stopped several feet beyond the reach of the downed tree's grasping branches.

"The best place to climb across the trunk is a few yards to the left. There aren't any branches there."

Carefully picking her way through the undergrowth, she followed a parallel path to the huge tree trunk. When the tree's branches finally stopped, so did she.

Moving in cautiously, she reached the tree and patted the bare trunk. "Here."

Sky put his hands on the waist high trunk and swung over the top. Jessie prepared to follow. She placed her hands on the trunk and—sucked in her breath as her feet left the ground. Sky lifted her over the tree and set her down, his hands still on her waist. She wanted to back away, but couldn't with the tree trunk directly behind her. He grinned down at her and she knew he was congratulating himself on very neatly pinning her between him and the tree trunk.

His breath tickled the curls on her forehead. She averted her face. He was much, much too close, and her wayward heart was doing summersaults.

"After what happened between you and Jake, I guess there will always be some . . . feelings between you two," he whispered miserably.

His continual probing spiked her anger. "Nothing happened between me and Jake, not ten years ago, and not on my doorstep!" she said, before her resolve, never to tell him what Jake had done, could stifle her anger.

Sky gripped her shoulders. "What do you mean nothing happened between you and Jake ten years ago?"

Her laugh was as serrated as her feelings. Her mind shouted at her to shut up, but she was too angry. Once again he'd thought the worst of her. In that moment she knew there would be a certain bitter satisfaction in telling him the truth.

"You heard me. Nothing happened between me and Jake ten years ago, *nothing!*"

Sky gaped at her. "But you told me you woke up in his bed, and he was there with you. Now you're telling me nothing happened?"

She pushed against his chest. He released her and she started to side step him. His hands shot out, encircling her waist. She gasped out a protest as he lifted her off her feet, sat her on the tree trunk, and then sat down beside her.

Her anger drained away as quickly as it had come. "I guess I should be grateful Jake was cut by the coral. If he hadn't almost died, he wouldn't have felt the need to confess his sins, and I would never have known the truth."

"So what really happened," Sky asked gently.

"It was a setup. My agent, Burt Cummings, arranged it to make me stay in New York and sign a new contract."

"But why did Jake go along with the setup?"

"For the money, he needed the money."

Sky's arm slid around her, pulling her close. The gesture was so comforting that she didn't object.

"I think you better start at the beginning, honey. I'm afraid I'm not following you."

She brushed at her cheek and leaned into his shoulder. It was such a solid shoulder. She had to admit, it felt wonderful to lean against his strength. Something she'd done so many times in the past. His strength had always comforted and buoyed her up, but it had also failed her— when the final test came. That thought so saddened her that the emotions she'd been drowning in for days gushed out without warning.

Sky wrapped her in his arms, leaned his cheek against her head and rocked her, murmuring endearments.

On a final sniff she said, "I told Burt I wouldn't be signing a new contract a month before I left. He almost came unglued. He tried everything from guilt over the jobs he'd already signed me up to do, to telling me the Elite Modeling agency would triple my salary if I signed a three year contract."

"Wow, weren't you even tempted?"

"No, I just wanted out. Burt asked me if Jake knew I was leaving. I told him Jake was throwing a party to celebrate his return to basketball, after a wrist injury, and that I planned to break up with him after it was over."

"If Burt knew you were going to that party intending to break up with Jake . . . then what made him think—"

"I'm getting there," she said on a sniffle. "He called and told Jake I was going to break up with him after the party. It didn't exactly come as a shock to Jake. I'd been breaking our dates for the past couple of weeks, hoping he'd just get the message and quit calling."

"Not Jake, he'd never believe any woman didn't want him."

"That's Jake all right." She lifted her head and straightened her spine. "And apparently no woman had ever broken up with him before. He told me he was angry, 'really steamed,' as he put it, when Burt informed him of my intentions."

"I can just imagine."

"Jake confessed he was angry enough and in debt enough, to some *very bad people,* to be persuaded by the money Burt offered him into going along with Burt's plan to keep me in New York. Burt was sure if I was forced to stay, he could get me to sign a new contract."

"Why was Burt so rabid about you signing a new contract? Surely models come and go just like pro athletes do. Even if they're great, they only hold the spotlight for a while before some new kid shows up and takes it. It happens all the time."

"Yes, but before he discovered me, Burt was on the verge of bankruptcy and being fired. He'd contracted with a few other models he thought would do very well only to have them bomb, costing Elite thousands of dollars in lost contracts. When I rose to the top so quickly, Burt did too. He told Jake I was his gold mine, his ticket to staying on top as an agent. Apparently, the Elite Modeling Agency saw it like that as well. They told Burt if he didn't get me to sign a new deal, they would fire him. But if he could, they would double his commission."

"So what really happened the night you ended up in Jake's bed?"

"Jake drugged my drink, and then poured a couple more drinks down me, just for good measure. When I started getting tipsy, he slipped a diamond ring on my finger and told everyone at the party we were engaged."

"So that's how your engagement happened."

"He told you, did he?"

"Oh, yeah. He also informed me, after his visited with you, that he had every intention of rekindling the flame he felt sure was still there."

"Never say die, that's Jake's motto with women."

"You're right about that. So what happened after you two got *engaged*?"

"He poured a few more drinks down me. When I passed out, he put me in his bed. 'To sleep off the booze,' he told everyone."

"Why that no good—"

"Yeah, but at least as soon as he deposited me in the bedroom, he went back to the party. Burt's wife Agnes took over from there. She wasn't happy about the plot, but she liked living high and fast. She set the scene up to the last detail so I'd think Jake and I had—well you know." Jessie felt the blush and was grateful for the darkness. "Jake was never in the room until I began to stir, and Agnes was in the closet watching him the whole time he was. She told him if he did anything improper, she'd blow the deal. She said she wouldn't be a party to rape."

"But she had no problem being part of a con."

"Apparently not." Jessie paused as an owl hooted overhead. "Living the high life does terrible things to some people."

"I hope I never meet your agent. I don't think I could keep from killing him, if I did."

"You won't. He died in a car accident the day after I left New York."

"That only leaves Jake for me to vent my wrath on." The muscles in Sky's arm knotted.

Jessie could almost hear his teeth grind. "You'll have to stand in line for that right," she said grimly. "I have first dibs."

"No wonder you haven't been to see Jake."

She blew out a breath and gazed up at the heavy canopy of trees overhead, catching an occasional twinkle of a star through the swaying of the breeze driven branches. "I'm still so angry, I can't trust myself to be anywhere near him—not yet."

"And now that *I* know what happened, it may be a while before I visit Jake again too," Sky said through his teeth.

"Don't stay away from him on my account, because as furious as I am with Jake, and Burt, none of it would have happened if I hadn't willingly taken that first drink—and that's the whole, unvarnished, ugly truth. She laughed derisively. "That one drink was the key to the entire plot, and I took it because I was nervous . . . well, almost terrified about breaking up with Jake." She looked into Sky's eyes, something she'd been avoiding. "That one reckless, wrong decision changed the course of my entire life."

"It wouldn't have, if I hadn't been the most pious fool on the planet." He blew out a breath. "Oh, honey, can you ever forgive me for failing you?"

"I did that a long time ago." She laid a gentle hand on his cheek. "But going our separate ways was really for the best."

"Don't say that, Jess. I couldn't bear losing you again," he said turning his lips into her hand and kissing her palm.

She inhaled sharply and snatched her hand away. The satisfaction and exoneration she thought she'd feel by telling him what had really happened with Jake, tasted like defeat. Somehow, it brought home the fatal flaw in her relationship with Sky with absolute clarity.

What had been wrong with their relationship four years ago, and what was still wrong, and would probably always be wrong—a barrier to any future they could have together—became stunningly clear in her mind.

It was a painful truth to accept, but she couldn't ignore it now that she'd seen it and knew what it meant. "Burt and Jake just did us a favor—"

"No—"

"Yes. I thought we'd become so close, so in tune, our souls so unified that nothing could tear us apart—not even my past. That was the kind of love I thought we had."

"We did—"

"No we didn't. That kind of love is grounded in trust, and that's something we didn't have, something we both lacked. Trust is so fundamental to true and lasting love that what we felt couldn't have survived in the long run, and in fact—*didn't*."

"But it has, I still love you as deeply and intensely as I ever did. I love you more now than I did even then." His arms tightened around her, insisting she believe him.

She pulled herself out of his arms, feeling an immediate loss and a deep loneliness. "Face it, Sky, down deep, you don't trust me. Think about the conclusions you've jumped too just since we've met again. You thought I kissed Jake, but I didn't. Oh, he tried, but I wasn't about to let him. I turned away and all he managed to kiss was my cheek."

"Well, from where I stood it sure looked like you kissed him," Sky said defensively.

She rolled her eyes and tucked her hands under her legs to keep him from taking them. "Then you jumped to the conclusion I was still a loose woman when you met my son and I told you I hadn't been married to his father. It didn't even cross your mind that Kanoa was adopted until Triny blurted it out."

"Okay, I'll admit—"

"I'm not done yet," she said wearily. "I also saw every glare you threw at Jake, and even poor Oliver, at the Hamilton's dinner party."

"Ok. I'll admit it. I was jealous."

"Can't you see that's just another form of distrust?"

"No," he said stubbornly.

"Well it is," she said and changed tactics. "Suppose for a moment that we're married."

"Now you're talking." He tugged on her arm, pulled her hand out from under her leg, and held it.

"Can you really tell me you would trust me to work in an office full of men who you knew would flirt outrageously with me? Or even trust me to carry on a casual conversation with a neighbor you thought had his eye on me?"

"Of course I'd trust you. I just . . . wouldn't trust them. I know how men's minds work."

"Sky, can't you see that it isn't really them you mistrust, but me? If you trusted my feelings for you, other men's attraction to me wouldn't bother you, because you'd be secure in my love for you. You'd know my heart belonged to you and couldn't be interested in anyone else."

Sky grinned broadly. "I'm extremely glad to hear you say that."

Jessie groaned and slid off the log. "You know I was only pretending."

"But I'm not." Sky jumped off the log too.

"If you can't see what's wrong between us, then there isn't any hope for us, or a relationship."

"I admit it. I've been jealous and insecure. It's just . . . I always found it so hard to believe you could love a goofy guy like me."

"Well—I do."

His arms drew her close.

She flattened her hands against his chest, holding him off. "Sky, love wasn't enough to hold us together four years ago, and it isn't enough now. Consider it from my point of view. Do you really think I want to spend my life watching you growl and glare at every man that looks at me because you're afraid one of them will steal me from you?"

"I wouldn't do that, Jess."

"Oh yes you would. Think back."

"Okay, so I did in the past, but that's behind me now."

"Is it? I'm not so sure. And I refuse to live my life afraid to make the least little gesture of kindness or courtesy to another man because you might mistake my innocent gestures for something more. I couldn't live with the constant worry that I might do something to crush the fairytale image of what you believe I ought to be and send you running from me like I have the plague."

"I know you don't have any reason to trust me, but—"

"That's right—I don't. The truth is; I don't trust you any more than you trust me, and that's what's wrong with us."

"But that can change. We've both grown . . . we've learned—we're different now."

"Yes, but trust takes time. That's something we don't have. You can't stay on Toolowa. Sooner or later, the military will come for you. I don't want to start something we may never be able to finish."

"But I'll come back as soon as the war's over, and I really believe that will be soon."

"You can't guarantee me you'll survive until it is. I don't want to open my heart to you just to have it crushed again. More than that, I don't want Kanoa to love you and lose you. I can't let that happen to him."

"Aw, honey, there's no guarantee either of us will live even one more day, but we can't live our lives in fear."

"I agree, but I can't live my life without trust either."

"Then let's work on it, one day at a time—together." He tightened his arms around her. "What do you say, honey, is what we had worth one more try? I promise you, I'll never give you another reason to doubt me, my feelings, or my commitment to you—no matter what that takes. I'll even bite my tongue off to keep from growling at other guys when they ogle you."

She didn't doubt he meant it, and she wanted to believe him—and believe in him. *Could we learn to trust in each other?* She felt herself sink into his intoxicating blue gaze. There would never be anyone else for her. She knew that with absolute certainty.

"Isn't the hope of sharing forever with each other worth taking the risk?" he asked coaxingly, inching his face toward hers.

"I want to believe that," she murmured, pulling back. "But I don't know if I can, because it's not just my own heart I'm risking this time—its Kanoa's too."

"I know, but there's no risk involved for either of you. It's a slam-dunk, pure and simple."

Despite her fears, she lifted her face. Her hands moved up the front of his shirt, waiting for his kiss, wanting it more with each passing moment, even if it led to more pain in her life.

The town bell jarred the night.

They froze; their lips only an inch apart. Sky's head jerked up. Jessie's fingers curled like talons into the front of his shirt.

The bell rang twice in quick succession, followed by a pause and then three slower clangs.

"The Japanese!" they said in unison, and raced down the faint path to Jessie's house.

29

SKY AND JESSIE BURST THROUGH THE DOOR of Jessie's house. Shula shrieked, collapsing into a heap on the sofa. "I thought you were the Japanese. Thank goodness you've come. How long do we have?"

"The signal only indicated that the night watch has spotted something"—Sky paused to catch his breath—"not how far away it is or what it is."

"But we have to assume it's the Japanese." Jessie leaned over bracing her hands on her thighs, breathing heavily after their frantic run.

Sky pointed at the pile of luggage sitting next to the couch. "How close are you to being ready to leave for the savannah?"

"I'm ready right now. Tena and I were going to leave with the Zenderlys and a few other families tomorrow morning." She gestured to the bags. "A group of porters were going to accompany us and take all our baggage."

"You aren't going to be able to take all this with you now. Do you have just a knapsack of essentials? The rest can be brought up—if there's time—later. Right now I want you and Kanoa into the mountains as soon as possible."

Jessie's eyes narrowed. *He's acting like my husband.* She agreed with what he was saying, but she wasn't about to let him dictate to her or become dependent on him. Especially since she was still entertaining doubts about letting him back into her life—and heart. Heat flared in her cheeks as she thought about how close she'd come to kissing him. *I guess I should thank the Japanese,* she decided sardonically.

Her hands went to her hips, "You don't have to worry about Kanoa or me. We're perfectly capable of taking care of ourselves. Besides, you need to get back to the embassy.

Isn't it your responsibility to see to the ambassador's safety? And what about Jake?"

'The Japanese are welcome to Jake," Sky said and paused, running a hand through his short-cropped hair. "I didn't mean that, and you're right. I am responsible to help the ambassador, but not until I get you and Kanoa at least as far as the savannah."

"That will take the better part of a couple of hours, something you don't have." Jessie jerked her head at the open windows of the living room. The anxious sounds of people shouting grew. The commotion of a large crowd on the move filled the air. "Hear that, I'll have plenty of company and help on the way. You don't need to worry about me."

"You're just as likely to get trampled by that mob out there as helped. Whatever the night watch spotted won't get here for a while, and we won't even be able to tell who the ship belongs to until it gets light. There's enough time for you to come with me to the embassy. We'll collect the Hamiltons and take them up to the savannah too." He turned to Shula. "Now where do you need to go?"

"Home! I have to find Triny and Tilly."

"No uses don't,' Triny said from the doorway. "We be here, and we brung all da stuff we needs." She glared at her sister. "What's ya doin here anyways, Shula? Why ain't ya at da embassy?"

"Never mind that now," Jessie said. "The three of you, need to get going."

"I ain't goin no wheres wifout ya," Triny said.

The two squared off.

Sky intervened. "We don't have time to debate this." He pointed at the pile of baggage. "Which bag do you need Jess? Let's take it and get this caravan over to the Hamilton's. We'll sort out who's going with who when we get there."

Jessie pressed her lips together. Sky still sounded like a husband, but he was right. There was no point in continuing the argument. She tapped an overstuffed knapsack and talked down the hall. A minute later, she returned with a sleepy Kanoa. His golden curls were tousled, and his thumb was stuck securely in his mouth.

He cracked open an eye. His soggy thumb popped out of his mouth. "Sky!" he shouted and held out his arms.

Sky shrugged Jessie's large knapsack over his shoulder and took Kanoa from her. "Hey, buddy, how would you like to go on an adventure with me?"

Kanoa's eyes popped open. "Now?"

"Right now," Sky said, and walked out the door.

THE SOUNDS OF THE NIGHT closed in around Kanoa. Lying on a mat on Auntie Beth's screened in porch; he listened to the loud pulsating hum of the crickets, the constant croak of frogs, and the hooting of an owl somewhere close by. In the distance he heard people still moving along the lane, pressing on around the lake. Papa told him many of the people were determined to reach the mountains before morning.

Papa had wanted Mama to keep going too, but she had refused when Grandma Nora said she couldn't go any farther. There others that had decided to stop for the night too. He listened to them settling in on the grounds of Auntie Beth's home above the bay in the trees of the eastern savannah.

Beth was Grandpa Edmund's oldest daughter. Kanoa didn't know her as well as he knew his uncles, Takoa and Lowa, but he liked her very much, especially when she made his mat into a soft bed of sofa cushions and gave him a cookie.

Kanoa rolled over onto his side and peered up at the cot where his mama slept. On the other side of her, Auntie Tena also slept on a cot. They were sleeping inside the screened-in-porch, because Grandpa and Grandma Zenderly, along with Grandpa and Grandma Hamilton, had taken up all the beds in Auntie Beth's house. That was fine with Kanoa. He liked "camping out," as Mama referred to sleeping on the porch.

Camping was something Mama said he would have to get used to doing, because they were going to go all the way across the island to camp out in a secret mountain fortress. They would stay there until some people she called, *Japanese,* went home to their own country— wherever that was. When he asked Papa about the Japanese, Papa told him they were unfriendly people who he wouldn't want to meet.

Kanoa wiggled around in the soft cushions trying to find just the right spot to settle into, wondering where Papa and Uncle Takoa were right now. "Papa," he whispered and then clamped a hand over his mouth. That was a secret, and he shouldn't have said it out loud, at least not until Mama kissed Papa.

Pride swelled his chest and made him grin. Riding on Papa's shoulders all the way up to the savannah, towering over everyone, made him feel big and strong. No one on Toolowa was as tall as his papa. Even Papa's friend, Jake, wasn't as tall.

Tonight was the first time he'd met Jake, and he wasn't sure he liked him. He had slowed everyone down on their climb out of the bay, needing help up the steeper parts of the trail and stopping frequently to rest. Auntie Tena told him it was because Jake was still weak from coral poisoning, and that sounded silly.

I've been cut by coral lots of times, and it never made me sick. He thought about the problem for a few minutes, trying to figure out how coral could poison someone, but finally gave up trying to understand it. Rolling onto his back, he stared up at the open beamed ceiling above him and wondered why Jake seemed so surprised when they were introduced.

Jake asked Mama, his tone grumpy, why she hadn't mentioned Kanoa when he came to visit. Mama just shrugged and told him it had been naptime when he arrived, so she couldn't have introduced Kanoa anyway. Jake mumbled something about understanding now why Mama knew so many lullabies and dropped back to walk with Grandpa Sam.

Looking down from his perch on Papa's shoulders, Kanoa asked Mama who Jake was. She told him Jake had been a friend of hers—a long time ago.

Kanoa's teeth tugged on his lower lip. Then why hadn't Mama been friendly toward Jake tonight? When they had stopped for a drink of water, Jake pulled Mama aside.

Papa immediately started toward them. He and Papa both heard Mama tell Jake that now wasn't the time to talk about what he had told her. Then she quickly moved on and stayed away from Jake during the rest of the hike up to the savannah.

Kanoa again rolled over onto his side and looked up at her. She was so still and quiet he knew she was asleep. He wiggled around some more, trying to feel sleepy, but couldn't quite let go of his curiosity about Jake.

He was supposed to be Papa's friend too. At least that's what Papa had said, but Papa hadn't seemed to be too happy with Jake either. That reminded him that he wasn't happy with Papa, or Uncle Takoa, for not letting him go with them to see the Japanese ship.

Mama sighed, muttered Papa's name, and rolled onto her other side, facing Auntie Tena. He rolled over too, again facing out into the darkness through the screen. The night whispered with mysterious voices, and movements that didn't have anything to do with birds, insects, or people. It felt restless, just like him. A breeze made his curls dance, adding to the fidgety feeling crawling over him.

He knew why he couldn't sleep. In the rush to leave, puppy had been left behind in his bed. Snuggled up with puppy was how he always slept. Papa said he'd go back to get him, if he could. Mama said he shouldn't count on it. Beth gave him one of her daughter's teddy bears, but that wasn't the same. It had short round ears, and he missed pulling on puppy's long soft ears and having puppy's head tucked up under his chin.

He tossed the bear away and quietly got to his feet. With the stealth he used to leave his room at home and sneak into the kitchen to raid the cupboard where Mama kept the sweets, he tiptoed around the end of his mother's cot. So far, he hadn't been caught on one of his nighttime kitchen raids. With the confidence of that achievement, he made it to the screen door, leading outside. Reaching up tall, he unlatched the door, and stepped through, shutting it quietly behind him.

30

SKY SQUINTED THROUGH THE BINOCULARS into the sun as it broke the horizon and sent reflected rays of light shooting across the water, peering northeast. "Got her," he said to Takoa lying on his belly beside him on the edge of the cliff. He was silent for a long minute before he handed the binoculars to his anxious companion.

Takoa adjusted the focus, scanned the ocean in the direction Sky had, and came to an abrupt stop. "Tell me what I'm seeing."

"A number one class landing ship. That thing can hold up to three hundred troops. I'm afraid the Japanese mean business—but at least it runs too deep to enter the bay."

"And, thankfully, it isn't an aircraft carrier either."

"No, but that doesn't mean aircraft aren't on their way. They have planes we call Nells. They carry paratroopers, and have a twenty-nine hundred mile range. It wouldn't surprise me to hear them overhead by the time that landing ship is in the channel." Sky got to his feet, "This looks to be shaping up like an all-out invasion."

"Just like you feared." Takoa stood too. "And we aren't prepared for them yet."

"How long will it take for the men to get into position?"

"Another hour."

"I'm sure we've got that much time." Sky got to his feet. "Right now we need to get back and get the people still at your sister's home moving toward the mountains as fast as possible. I'm afraid we haven't got more than a couple of hours, at best, before the Japanese land their first troops on the beach. And although we haven't seen or heard any planes, I'm sure their paratroopers aren't far behind."

They hurried back along the path that ran beside the edge of the cliff, under the cover of the trees. Thirty minutes later, Beth's house came into view. As they neared, both men instantly became aware of a commotion and the frantic call that issued from everyone's lips.

"Kanoa," Edmund shouted, as they charged into the yard.

"What's happened?" Takoa asked his father.

"Jayling woke up an hour ago to find Kanoa's bed empty. We searched the house and the grounds. Now there are men out searching the path to the lake."

"Where's Jessie?" Sky asked as the first tentacles of fear took hold of him.

"She and Tena, along with Lowa headed back to the bay. Jessie thinks he might be trying to go home to get his stuffed dog. He was very upset last night that it had been left behind," Edmund said.

Fear churned in Sky's gut. "How long ago did they leave?"

"About fifteen minutes ago."

"Sir, you need to get these people moving toward the mountains, right now. I'll go after Jessie, and find Kanoa," Sky said.

"Wait." Takoa clutched Sky's arm, and briefly told his father what he and Sky had seen, and what it meant. "I'm going with Sky. If you don't hear from us, do what we planned."

"All right," Edmund said and started issuing orders.

Takoa let out a piercing whistle from between his teeth. It instantly brought a dozen young men to him. He told his security force that the Japanese would be landing in the bay in less than two hours. "I'm not going to order any of you to come with us. I know each of you has your own concerns, but with more of us hunting for Kanoa and Jayling, the better our chances will be of finding them before the Japanese land. We need to be out of the bay area before they set foot on Toolowa."

Not a single man hesitated. They bid their families a hasty farewell and urged them to hurry into the mountains. Then with Takoa and Sky in the lead, the little troop set off at a fast trot down the trail.

JESSIE RAN AS HARD AND FAST as her long legs would allow, outpacing Tena, and even Lowa. Unconcerned with their progress, she didn't even look back to see where they were. She was as close to hysterics as it was possible to get without falling over that precipice. Every moment that went by without knowing where Kanoa was, felt like an hour, every minute, a day. *Now I know what an eternity in outer darkness feels like.*

Skidding over loose rocks, she slipped, caught herself on the branches of a kabant bush, and rushed on. *Please, please, help me find him, Father,* she silently prayed, *please don't let anything bad happen to him.*

The trail was treacherously steep coming down to the waterfall. Jessie's reckless pace finally caught up with her. She stumbled over a patch of loose rocks, fell, and skidded down the trail, skinning both knees and the palms of her hands.

Before Lowa and Tena could reach her, she was on her feet and running again. She ignored Lowa's call to slow down and Tena's concern for her safety. Not caring about the pain throbbing through her bleeding knees and palms, she pressed on.

It seemed to her as though the trail had tripled in length, and it took far too long before she came out onto the village's main lane above the beach.

The rumbling sound of a boat engine drew her attention to the sea. Through the tangled bushes that conceal the lane from the beach, she glimpsed an amphibious landing craft half way down the channel. Her exhausted legs picked up speed, sprinting down the path to her home. *Please let him be there,* she prayed.

She had no doubt Kanoa had headed home to get his dog. Whether or not he'd made it was an agonizing question. Repeatedly, as she'd run along the trail that descended into the bay, she'd shouted his name—they all had. Now with the enemy about to land, she pressed her lips together, only opening her mouth to take in another gasping lungful of air. Her eyes swept back and forth along the lane, hoping to spot Kanoa coming down the path with his dog in his arms. But had he made it home? That question was the torment that sped her on.

He's barely three years old. Could he even stay on the trail all the way down to the bay without getting lost? It seemed unlikely, and yet, in the last few hours the feet of hundreds of people had crushed the lush undergrowth making the trail easily visible, while destroying anything that might indicate Kanoa had come this way.

Panic threatened her as her fear grew. This wasn't the same as the frantic race to the hospital after Kanoa had been bitten by a matoo, when the comfort of a priesthood blessing had mitigated her fears. Drawing in another labored breath, Jessie brushed away tears. Without the comfort of a priesthood blessing to sustain her hope, all she could do was pray, and she did that with all the fervor in her soul.

Bursting through her front door, she took a frantic look around the living room and bolted down the hall.

Kanoa's bedroom door was open. She flew through it.

"Kanoa!" She skidded to a stop. Her eyes riveted on her son's bed.

The dog was gone.

31

SKY'S BREAKNECK PACE BROUGHT TAKOA and his men into the bay area in record time. "Jessie can't be that far ahead of us," he said, as they hit the main lane that ran just above the beach.

"I hope she has found Kanoa," Takoa said, catching his breath as they slowed down.

The party stopped as the sound of a boat engine reached them.

Sky glanced at his watch. "The enemy has arrived exactly when we thought they would. That means we need to find Jessie and Kanoa and get out of here—fast."

Takoa gave the signal to move out. The dozen men that accompanied Takoa and Sky skulked along the main lane, peering out across the bay through minuet breaches in the jungle camouflage.

A speedboat raced across the harbor, armed with a forward machine gun, and manned by at least two dozen men—by Sky's estimate.

"That boat will land in under five minutes," Takoa said.

"You and your men need to head for Jessie's house. Keep her from coming back this way."

"But if she saw or heard that boat, I'm sure she'll leave the bay by another route. Most likely, she'll use the route behind my parent's home. It's steeper, but more direct." Takoa's brows contracted in thought, "What if she's there, but Kanoa isn't?"

"Get her out of the bay anyway."

"She won't go until she finds Kanoa."

"I don't care if you have to hogtie her, and have your men carry her out. I want her out of here right now."

"So do I. Tena is with her, and I don't want her here anymore than I want Jayling and Kanoa here."

The boat slowed as it approached the beach. Every man crouched along its sides with his gun at the ready. Ten yards from the beach, they cut the engine and dropped an anchor into the shallow water.

The moment the boat stopped, the soldiers cautiously began to disembark. They were a grotesque site with their faces concealed behind ghoulish gasmasks.

"It appears they've come prepared to be attacked with the yunga," Sky said.

"What if everyone on board the ship is wearing a gasmask?" Takoa asked.

"They won't be. The direction of the wind is at their back right now."

"Yes, but that will soon change," Takoa said.

"I know, so you better get going," Sky said as the enemy began to wade through the shallow water to the beach.

"Aren't you coming with us?"

"No, I need to see what these ghouls are up too." Sky frowned, puzzled by the situation. "There's only a couple of dozen of them. It's not the kind of assault I was expecting."

"Do you think they've come to try and buy the yunga instead of take it?"

"Not a chance. But the empty bay and beach may have spooked them. This might be just a forward reconnaissance team, trying to figure out if we mean to fight or surrender. They might even be waiting for their air support to arrive."

"We need to be gone before that happens."

"You will be. And when you find Kanoa, give me that bird call you were trying to teach me, so I'll know you're headed back out with everyone safely in tow."

"What are you going to do?"

"My duty. I'm going to disrupt the enemy and hopefully give you more time to find Jessie and Kanoa and get the people into the mountains."

"How?"

"I can hold them in the bay area for a little while by setting off the booby traps we planted on the trails leading up to the savannah."

"It's a good idea, but you can't stay in the bay area. You haven't taken the antidote for the yunga long enough to make it fully effective, a few breaths of the yunga ash could kill you."

"Not if I confiscate one of their gasmasks."

"That will be a very dangerous undertaking."

"Don't worry. I can take care of myself. You just get the people we love back to the savannah, and make sure your men are in place for the yunga drop."

"I don't like leaving you here."

"I'm not your responsibility. You have the people of this island to think about, so get going."

With a solemn nod, Takoa signaled to his men. They faded into the jungle, each following a different path toward Jessie's house.

Sky hunkered down into the heavy undergrowth next to the lane and watched the enemy.

THE SOUND OF A MOTOR HAD DRAWN HIM. Kanoa saw the goblins step out of the boat with wide-eyed terror. Each one carried a gun with a long knife attached to the end. All their faces were monstrous, and they talked in garbled words Kanoa didn't understand. Slowly, they fanned out over the beach.

Kanoa burrowed deeper into the sand beneath a pair of large palm fronds that had fallen to the ground. Well hidden under the fronds, next to the stout trunk of a coconut palm on the edge of the sand, he wrapped puppy tightly in his arms and watched the goblins move warily up the beach. As they came closer, a shiver skidded down Kanoa's back. *Are these goblins the Japanese?* "Unfriendly," was what Papa had said. And they sure looked unfriendly.

They stopped in a spear headed formation at the edge of the sand not ten feet from where Kanoa hid. He held his breath, not daring to move a muscle. The goblin in the lead said something, and the troop cautiously disappeared one by one into the thick vegetation above the beach.

When the last goblin disappeared, Kanoa counted to ten, just as Mama taught him to do when they played hide and seek, before he wiggled from his hiding place. His heart pounded as it never had before. Glancing back at the place the goblins had gone into the jungle, he ran along the edge of the sand toward a path that would lead him back up the lane to the waterfall and the savannah.

He'd gone about fifteen yards when one of the goblins jumped out of the jungle and grabbed him. Kanoa shrieked like the banshee his mama told him wailed in the night when something bad was going to happen. He kicked out at the goblin and bit the hand that held his arm. He even pounded with his fist against his assailant—never letting go of his puppy.

The goblin's fingers dug into the back of his neck. His feet left the ground. The monster shook him like a rag doll, shouted to his companions, pushed through the undergrowth, and stepped onto the lane.

A goblin with a sword strapped to his waist barked at the one who held him. Instantly Kanoa fell to the ground, landing hard. He scrambled to his feet, spinning in a circle, seeking an avenue of escape. All around him the goblins glowered down at him. Burying his face against puppy, he tried not to cry.

A goblin stepped forward, and Kanoa's fright abruptly turned into rage. The goblin tore puppy from him. With a shriek of outrage, his hands stretched up to take puppy back. The goblin laughed in a garbled way, dangled puppy out of his reach, letting him just brush puppy's paw with his fingertips before tossing him to another goblin. Kanoa ran to that goblin. He also laughed and dangled puppy by one paw. Kanoa jumped up trying to grab his dog, but the goblin tossed him back to the first one again. Crying with frustration, Kanoa raced back to try to rescue puppy, desperately jumping as high as he could for his dog.

SKY'S JAW WAS SO TIGHT it felt like it would crack. He fought the fury that threatened to rob him of any ability to think clearly, but it was unbearable to watch the soldiers torment Kanoa.

It was only a stuffed dog, but to Kanoa it was a friend, a playmate, a comfort. Sky knew it wasn't likely the soldiers would do him any harm, at least not yet, but his howls of fear and frustration were sure to bring Jessie.

He glanced toward the path to her house. *How much time do I have?* Jessie might already have heard Kanoa's wails and be on her way. Without a doubt, he knew what she would do as soon as she arrived. He couldn't let that happen. Out of time, options, and the ability to endure any more of Kanoa's tears, he laced his fingers on top his head and stood up.

"Why don't you ghouls pick on someone your own size, or better yet, why don't you pick on someone my size."

Puppy fell to the ground.

Kanoa dove for him and scooped him up as every head and weapon jerked in Sky's direction.

32

SKY STEPPED OUT OF HIS HIDING PLACE, walked forward a few paces, and dropped to his knees in a deliberate act of surrender.

"Sky," Kanoa cried, managing to dodge the hands that reached to catch him as he ran to Sky.

He clutched at the front of Sky's shirt. Sky bent down, letting Kanoa's arms slide around his neck. He laid his head against Kanoa's, his mouth next to Kanoa's ear. "Listen to me, buddy," he whispered. "When I tell you to go, I want you to run home as fast as you can. Your mama is waiting for you there. Don't stop and don't look back. Okay?"

Sobbing, Kanoa just jerked his head, his arms almost choking Sky.

Sky kept his hands firmly locked on his head, running his eyes over the enemy's insignias and ranks. "Do you speak English," he asked the silent man who wore the rank of lieutenant.

The lieutenant's hand went to his saber. "Enough to get the answers to the questions I will put to you," he said, his gasmask giving his words a wheezing sound.

Sky nodded and whispered into Kanoa's ear, "Go."

Kanoa leaped away.

Sky made it appear as though he'd knocked Kanoa away from him while getting to his feet and stepping toward the lieutenant. It effectively blocked the boy from the soldiers view as he scampered into the jungle.

Half a dozen soldiers leaped into the underbrush, where Kanoa had disappeared. A sharp command brought them back. They pointed their bayonets at Sky and pressed them against his chest.

"Back on your knees, GI," the lieutenant said.

Slowly, Sky complied.

"Your heroics won't save that child—or you," the lieutenant said and barked out something to his men.

Rough hands grabbed hold of Sky's arms, wrenched them behind his back, and tied his hands securely. Half a dozen soldiers stepped behind Sky, pressing their bayonets against his back.

The lieutenant stepped forward.

Even with Sky on his knees, the lieutenant didn't stand eye to eye with him. The breeze spoke to Sky's nose relaying the unmistakable odor of the sea, sweat, and—Sky's brows rose a fraction—fear. The lieutenant covered it with a careful inspection of Sky's uniform. "What is an American GI doing on Toolowa?"

"Taking a vacation."

The lieutenant backhanded his face.

Sky's head jerked to the side. He clenched his teeth, and slowly turned his head back to the lieutenant, staring directly into his alien eyes.

THE CAWING OF A BIRD stopped Jessie, Lowa, and Tena in their tracks. "Takoa and his men are coming," Lowa whispered and answered Takoa's call.

To the unknowing ear, the birdcalls sounded just like the real thing, but to any Toolowan the difference between the real thing and someone using a birdcall to communicate was unmistakable.

Takoa and his men intercepted Jessie, Tena, and Lowa creeping down the path from Jessie's house just as Kanoa's blood curdling screech split the air. It took both Takoa and Lowa to keep Jessie from barreling down the lane to rescue her son.

Jessie froze for a moment when she heard Sky's voice, her terror instantly intensifying. His challenge to the Japanese reignited her efforts to pull free of the arms that restrained her. Her fear for her son, and now Sky, turned her into a lioness. Silently, she writhed and thrashed. Her battle with the Zenderly brothers ended when Kanoa came charging down the path.

The arms that restrained her fell away. She darted out of the jungle foliage and onto the path. Grabbing Kanoa from behind, she scooped him into her arms and covered his mouth, before he could cry out. She was shaking so hard she was afraid she would collapse right on the spot.

Lowa and Takoa reached out through the vines and ferns, took hold of her arms, and dragged her back into the cover of the jungle.

"Shhh, little man. I have you now and everything is going to be all right," she hissed into Kanoa's ear.

He twisted in her embrace and wrapped his arms around her neck, nearly strangling her. Shaking with terror, he whispered back, "Sky giant, save me."

Jessie's heart expanded as though it would burst out of her chest and she prayed, *don't let them kill Sky, not after what he did for my son. Please help us find a way to rescue him too.* Then before Kanoa could say anything more she again put a trembling hand over his mouth and rocked him, murmuring reassurances into his ear.

Only twenty yards separated them from the soldiers that surrounded Sky. Everyone looked at Takoa, awaiting his orders. He motioned to them and with the stealth of many generations of jungle dwellers, the group moved toward the Japanese soldiers until they were close enough to watch the blood from Sky's split lip drip onto his shirt.

Takoa gave the birdcall telling Sky he had Jessie and Kanoa. The corners of Sky's mouth lifted.

"We have to help him." Jessie mouthed the words to Takoa, griping his arm.

He responded with a curt nod, his attention fixed on the soldier who seemed to be in charge.

The soldier spoke in slow, careful English, "Where are all the people? We were led to believe they would come out onto the beach and greet us with their unusual weapon."

Sky stared straight ahead. "Sky Brannigan, Major, United State Army Air Corp, serial number: 3, 2—"

"Do not try my patience, Major!"

"Name, Sky—"

Again, the lieutenant's hand flew like a whip across Sky's face. "How long have you been here, and how many American GIs are on Toolowa?"

Sky answered with a cold, blue stare of silence.

Jessie kept Kanoa's face turn away, keeping him from seeing what was happening to Sky. But her body jerked with the sound of the stinging slap Sky took, her distress escaping in a muffled whimper.

"Go with Lowa," Takoa mouthed. "He'll take you, Kanoa, and Tena out of here."

"No. I can't leave Sky, not like this, not after he rescued Kanoa," Jessie mouthed back.

She murmured into Kanoa's ear. He tightened his grip on her neck and shook his head, making his soft baby curls bounce. She tried again, this time prying his arms away and holding his hands. "I need you to be a brave little man, and go with Auntie Tena," she whispered.

Kanoa opened his mouth to protest, she gently laid her scraped palm over it. "Do you want to help Sky?" she asked with her lips pressed to his ear.

His curls bounced vigorously.

"Then you must go with Auntie Tena."

Crocodile tears rolled down Kanoa's cheeks, but he went into Tena's arms.

"Get him out of her," Jessie whispered urgently.

Tena cradled Kanoa, but insisted, "If we're not all going, I'm staying too."

"No you're not," Takoa hissed. "The three of you are leaving—now."

Jessie glared at him and shook her head, then whispered to Tena, "At least take Kanoa home and wait for us there. I don't want him to see what they're doing to Sky. Please."

They looked back at the lane just as the lieutenant's knuckles connected with Sky's right eye in another backhanded slap.

Tena flinched and took Kanoa.

Jessie hugged her and Kanoa, kissing both their cheeks.

Tena's hand reached out to Takoa. He took it and pressed his lips into her palm. Her fingers caressed his cheek. "Be careful, and signal me when it's safe to come back," she mouthed, pulled her hand from his and disappeared into a wall of undergrowth.

The sound of another slap made Jessie wince.

Sky's nose began to bleed.

"We better do something fast—before they decide to kill him," Lowa whispered.

Jessie's eyes narrowed. "I have an idea."

33

SKY TASTED THE BLOOD FROM HIS SPLIT LIP, thankful the lieutenant was only using his hand. *If he changes to his fist, I won't have any teeth left. As it is, I'm going to have a shiner to go along with my split lip and bloody nose.*

"Where are the Toolowans?" the lieutenant growled.

Sky shrugged.

The lieutenant's fist slammed into Sky's stomach. He doubled over, his breath coming out in a whoosh. The soldiers behind him grabbed his arms and wrenched him back up.

"I weary of this game, Major. Tell me what I wish to know"—the lieutenant drew his saber from its sheath—"or you will die right now."

"Wait—" Sky gasped out the word, trying to recover from the blow that had knocked the wind out of him. "Can't . . . breathe . . . yet."

The lieutenant raised his sword. "Where are the Toolowans? And how many GIs are on this island?" he asked again.

Sky sputtered, sucked in a solid breath, exhaled, and took in another one. "Toolowans . . . left. That kid . . . must have been overlooked . . . when they took off."

"Where did they go?" The lieutenant's blade slid beneath Sky's chin. The tip came to rest against his windpipe.

The sudden chatter of birds drew everyone's eyes to the breezy treetops. A flock of birds flew from the trees as though they'd been flushed out. The Japanese searched the impenetrable canopy above them. Nothing but interwoven branches met their gaze.

The lieutenant refocused on Sky. "Where did they go?" he asked again.

"Don't know," Sky said, untruthfully. "They were gone when I got here." *And that's the truth if you look at it from when I came off the savannah,* he almost grinned.

A heavy sigh wheezed out of the lieutenant's mask.

Sweat broke out on Sky's forehead. That long-suffering sigh told him his time was up.

A barked order backed the soldiers behind Sky out of the way.

The lieutenant swung the sword with both hands in an intricate dance in front of Sky, pivoted, and twirled the blade over Sky's head, sending horror shrieking down his spine.

The rush of the blade flew at the back of his neck.

Sky drew his last breath.

The sword came to an abrupt halt at the base of his neck. The touch of cold steel shivered through him.

The lieutenant spoke softly, "I will ask you one last time, Major."

Sky drew himself up and barked out, "Sky Brannigan, Major, serial number—"

The sword left Sky's neck, but the sensation was comfortless. The lieutenant pivoted on his heels, the air sang with the sound of the blade's motion, and the whir of something else.

Sky closed his eyes in a final prayer.

The whirring sound surrounded him. An instant later, a vine lasso, like the embrace of a grizzly bear, cinched around his chest. A sharp tug jerked him onto his face. At the same time, the jungle exploded with what seemed like the wail of a thousand savage voices.

Sky twisted his head to the side as he was dragged across the lane by the vine lasso and into the jungle. Before the jungle swallowed him, he managed to see a hail of coconuts fall from the trees. The enemy fell to the ground under the deadly barrage of coconuts, before they could raise their weapons. The barrage was accompanied by the swinging descent of Takoa and his men from the trees on the heavy vines that blanketed the jungle.

The vine lasso that dragged him, suddenly stopped.

Jessie yelled at him, "Don't take another breath."

Lowa rolled him over.

He caught a glimpse of the other man that helped Lowa drag him into the jungle just before Jessie fell to her knees and clamped her mouth over his.

The pain in his split lip was immediately forgotten. Too stunned to do anything, he stared up at her as she pinched his bleeding nose closed and breathed hard into his mouth.

From the lane, he heard the commotion of yelling men, both Toolowan and Japanese. There was the brief sound of gunfire, followed by a terrible gagging sound, and then silence.

Jessie released his nose, let him exhale, pinched it again, and immediately blew another hard breath into his lungs. He drew it in almost delirious with the feel of her lips covering his. The sounds of the men shouting faded from his conciseness. All there was in the world was Jessie, and her lips on his. He'd dreamed of it, longed for it, even prayed for it, and now he couldn't help himself. His lips moved against hers.

She jerked back, clamping a hand over his mouth. "I am not kissing you, you big idiot! I'm trying to keep you alive. Just take the breaths I give you, and no more nonsense, unless you'd rather die of yunga poisoning." She released his nose, let him exhale, and covered his mouth again with hers, giving him another breath.

He closed his eyes and took each breath she gave him, keeping his lips still under hers, aching to kiss her. He might have too, if his hands hadn't still been tied behind his back.

Takoa's voice penetrated Sky's longing. "We need to get Sky away from here. Upwind."

Jessie pulled back and put her badly scraped hand over his mouth. He resisted the urge to kiss it. At the same time feeling bereaved, her lips were no longer against his.

"Where? We can't take him onto the beach."

"Just around the bend in the lane to the south," Takoa said.

He and Lowa slid their hands under Sky's arms. Jessie let him exhale and then gave him one more deep breath. In unison, Takoa and Lowa hauled Sky to his feet, dragged him out of the jungle, and onto the lane.

Sky caught only a glimpse of the Japanese soldiers sprawled over the lane. Their gasmasks had been ripped off, and a grayish cloud hung in the air. Propelled by the Zenderly brothers, Sky held his breath and ran until he thought his lungs would burst.

"Stop," Jessie called from behind, yanked on his arm, pulled him around, drew his head down to hers, closed her mouth over his, and gave him another deep breath. He took in that life giving breath. Then, just for a moment, before she pulled her lips from his, he thought hers moved against his with something other than the necessity of giving him a breath.

"Thank you for rescuing my son," she said softly.

He felt dizzy with elation, *or is it just the lack of oxygen?* She had kissed him. Even if it was only for an instant, and in gratitude for rescuing Kanoa, still she *had* kissed him. Hope roared in his ear and he almost missed what Takoa was saying.

"You can breathe now." Takoa loosened the heavy vine from around his chest. Letting it drop, he reached behind Sky and untied the ropes that bound his wrists.

Sky blew out the last of the breath Jessie had given him and drew in a tentative one. Everyone watched him with wary expressions. He drew in another breath, and then another.

Takoa and Lowa smiled and thumped his back. Jessie let out the breath she seemed to be holding and sat down on a tree stump.

"You were supposed to get her out of here," Sky said to Takoa as soon as he was breathing normally again and could speak.

"Believe me, I tried, but not one of my men would help me tie her up and drag her back to the savannah."

"Traitors," Sky growled.

Jessie jumped up from the stump. "No, the people here are just much more democratic than in the States. Anyone can protect this country and its people, be they men or women."

"I know that, but you're a mother. You have no business putting yourself in danger to rescue me or anyone else, and don't tell me this wasn't dangerous. I didn't see much of what happened, but from what I heard you could have been shot." Shifting his attention to Takoa, he asked, "Was anyone shot?"

"A couple of the men were grazed, but their wounds aren't serious."

"Oh and just what's that running down your arm?"

Takoa glanced at his left arm and blinked as though he hadn't noticed before that he was bleeding. He shrugged. "Like I said—nothing serious."

"And just whose hair brained scheme was it that got you shot?" Sky asked, gingerly touching his right eye that was already beginning to swell shut.

"Wasn't mine." Takoa held up his hands.

"Whose?"

Jessie lifted her chin. "Mine."

"I should have known." Sky pulled her into his arms, hugging her tight. "I see you haven't lost your touch with a lasso. Thanks for saving my life and keeping me alive." He held her for as long as she permitted. When she broke away, he said to Takoa, "All of you need to get out of here."

"I take it you intend to stay here and get yourself into more trouble," Jessie said.

"I intend to do my duty."

"Your duty isn't any greater than mine," Takoa said.

"If you have a mind to help me with what I want to do, I'll take it."

"And just what do you intend to do"—Jessie tugged on his arm—"besides get yourself killed?"

"I intend to put a hole in that Japanese ship," Sky said to Takoa. "Are you game?"

Takoa grinned.

"Are you out of your mind?" Jessie asked.

"I haven't got the time to discuss the state of my mind, Jess. Please, just go find Kanoa and Tena, and get out of the bay."

"Lowa will take you," Takoa said and motioned to his brother. "I want you to get Jayling, Kanoa, and Tena back to the savannah and into the mountains."

Lowa hesitated, and then reached for Jessie's arm.
She pulled away from him and poked a finger into Sky's chest. "I don't know what you think you can do against a

ship full of Japanese, but it isn't worth your life. The plan you and Takoa came up with originally, and the amendment Kaylawnu proposed, will take care of the Japanese. Come back up to the savannah with us. There's no sense in getting yourself killed."

Sky's expression softened with the anxious tone of her voice. She was afraid for him. He wrapped his big hand around hers, capturing the one that poked his chest. Instead of jerking it away, she returned his clasp, her hand trembling, imploring him with arguments his heart couldn't fight.

"You have a duty to your son. I have one to my country, and I'm running out of time."

"How much time to you think we have?" Takoa asked.

Sky let go of Jessie's hand. "I'd say we have no more than fifteen minutes before the Japanese will start wondering why their scouting party hasn't checked in. So I need to tell—"

"Wait"—Takoa raised his hand—"do you feel that?"

"What?"

"The wind has shifted. It's coming from the northwest."

Sky consulted his watch. "Your father has called for the wind right on schedule."

"Yes, and that means the security force is in place for the yunga drop."

Sky's brows drew together. "Can you signal the men on the cliff from here and let them know when to start the drop? I need that to coincide with what I want to do."

A piercing cry came from deep in Takoa's throat. The sound was an odd orchestration of whistles and caws that rose and fell in pitch and tone. It rang through the bay raising the hair on the back of Sky's neck.

"What are you doing? I haven't told you what I'm planning yet."

"That call told the security force not to drop the yunga until I signal them, and to let my father know not to call the wind from the west unless we need it," Takoa said.

"It will also bring Takoa's men, and Tena," Lowa said.

A moment later, Takoa's men came down the lane carrying the enemy's gear. It included the gasmasks and a radio. They handed the radio to Takoa.

Sky eyed the radio and asked, "Do any of you speak Japanese?"

"I do," Tena said, coming up behind the men.

"Mama," Kanoa called, wiggling out of Tena's arms and running to his mother as soon as his feet were on the ground.

Jessie gathered Kanoa into her arms and hugged him tight.

Longing dug deep. Sky pushed it away and said to Tena, "If only you were a man."

"I can tell you what to say," Tena said.

"Yes, but I don't have the fluency needed to pull it off— make it sound right."

"But I do," a deep voice answered from beside him.

Jessie's vocal range was amazing. He'd forgotten she could imitate voices, even men's voices, and do it to perfection with her auditory memory. She'd fooled him many times with her voice, even made him jealous once when she answered her home phone in a male voice. It had taken a few minutes for her to convince him there really wasn't a man in her apartment. She told him she'd been answering her phone like that for a week, explaining the need to discourage an undesirable guy who was relentlessly pursuing her roommate, Alice.

Jessie shrugged. "There's still a lot you don't know about me," she said to the Toolowan's that gawked at her in amazement.

"No," Sky said. "You and Tena are getting out of here."

"That's right," Takoa said. "Lowa, Tusi, Jonah, get them out of here—now."

Jessie's and Tena's vehement protests were interrupted by a static laced voice coming over the Japanese radio.

34

EVERYONE LOOKED AT TENA when the voice stopped.

"They're asking for a progress report. Apparently, they heard the gunfire, and the patrol is a few minutes late checking in. So what do you want to tell them?"

"Tell them . . . the bay appears to be deserted, except for a GI you've captured. Ask them if they want the GI sent to the ship for questioning," Sky said.

"No!" Jessie shifted Kanoa to her hip and tugged on his sleeve. "I don't know what you're planning, but going aboard that Japanese ship is the same as committing suicide."

Sky took the hand that tugged on his sleeve. "Tell her what to say, Tena, and make it quick. We don't want them to get suspicious and send another boat."

"I won't say it." Jessie pressed her lips together.

"Toolowa needs your help, Jess, and I haven't got time to argue about it with you," he said, nodding at Tena.

Tena bit her lip as she thought for a moment. Then she spoke to Jessie in slow, precise phrases. Before she finished the radio crackled to life again, repeating the request for information. The interruption forced her to repeat the last part of what Jessie needed to say. "Now you better hurry, they're getting anxious."

Jessie handed Kanoa to Sky and took the radio from Takoa. She drew a resigned breath, gave Sky an agonized look, and pressed the button. The words Tena told her to speak came out in the lieutenant's voice.

Sky felt the chill all the way down to his toes. *The Garrison's*, he reflected, *are a family with some very unusual characteristics, and gifts.*

Jessie finished the message and released the call button.

No one breathed.

The silence seemed interminable.

The crackle of static hummed on the air. Again, the voice came over the radio.

Tena listened intently. Her eyes flew to Sky as the message concluded. "They've ordered the lieutenant to send you to the ship with a few of the men."

"Tell them we'll be on our way in twenty minutes. Oh, and tell them we want to make a reconnaissance sweep along the shoreline of the bay before we come," Sky said.

"Why do you want to do that? Jessie asked.

"Because I need time to do a little work on the boat before we get to the ship," Sky said, gently rubbing Kanoa's back.

The toddler had snuggled into his arms, obviously exhausted from a night without sleep. His deep, regular breathing told Sky he'd finally given in to exhaustion. He slept with one arm around his puppy, its head tucked under his chin, and his thumb hanging slackly from his mouth. His other arm rested along the side of Sky's neck, his curly head tucked under Sky's chin.

A kind of love Sky had never experienced filled his heart. In that moment, he knew he wanted to make Kanoa his son as much as he wanted to make Jessie his wife. His feelings were so intense that it took the full effort of his will to shut the door to those desires. *You have a duty to do, and you'll do it—just as Jed did—regardless of the consequences.*

Jessie gripped his arm. "Sky, don't do this—please."

"Tell her what to say, Tena," Sky said quietly, feeling Jessie's fear in the grip of her fingers.

Tena slowly said the words only she understood to Jessie.

Jessie pressed her lips together, refusing to say them.

Sky kissed Kanoa's curly head, handed him to Lowa and took hold of Jessie's hand. "I don't know if what I'm planning will work, but it's our best shot to protect your home and the people you love, without destroying everything on this island."

"Don't make me send you to your death."

"You aren't, because I don't intend to die."

"I'll never forgive you if you do," Jessie choked out the words and pressed the button on the radio. She finished the message and released the button.

Half a minute went by before the ship replied.

Tena relayed the ship's message to Sky. "You've got the go ahead for the reconnaissance sweep, and we're supposed to check in again in thirty minutes."

"That's all the time we'll need to get ready."

"And just what are you planning to do?" Takoa asked.

Sky grinned "I'm going to deliver that package I've been working on."

Takoa's eyebrows shot up. "How?"

"With the help of the Japs own boat. So I'll need a man who can drive that boat, an acetylene torch, and someone who can use it. I also need someone who knows the inside of the American embassy well, and all of them have got to be good swimmers."

As Sky explained his plan, he kept glancing at Jessie. Her lips were tightly compressed, and from time to time, she vaguely shook her head. When he finished his explanation, she stalked off.

"This is strictly a volunteer mission," Takoa said to his men.

Without hesitation every man raised his hand.

Sky quickly questioned the men and found several who had the skills and resources he needed. He chose the ones that would best fit into the Japanese uniforms, sent them off to get into one, and collect the items he required.

"I need all of you back here in fifteen minutes," he shouted after them.

They called back their acknowledgement, and Sky watched them until they disappeared around a bend in the lane. Then he excused himself and went to find Jessie.

He found her peering through a bush at the ship sitting between the cliffs, just outside the mouth of the bay.

"Jessie," he whispered, coming up behind her and slipping his arms around her.

She whirled in his arms, her expression a mixture of anger and fear. Her hands splayed out against his chest and for a moment he was afraid she would push him away. Instead, her finger clutched the front of his shirt.

"You are, without a doubt, the most stubborn, irrational man I've ever met! Or do you just want to outdo Jed, and win another posthumous medal to make your mother proud?"

Her words hurt, but he understood the fear that made her say them. He was afraid too. It was something the war had taught him to live with, but it never got easier, and this time the temptation to give into his fear was almost overpowering. If he was honest, what he really wanted to do was just take Jessie and Kanoa and make a run for the mountains. But he couldn't, not and live with himself for the rest of his life.

Giving in to the temptation that had been tormenting him, he ran his hand through her long wavy hair. "I adore you too." He smiled down into her stormy eyes.

She blinked rapidly and dropped her head onto his chest. "Don't do it"—her shoulder began to tremble—"please don't put me through this. Don't throw away the opportunity heaven has given us to find out if there's still a future for us." She gazed up at him, "You know I love you," she said as though the words were spoken against her will, and dropped her head back onto his chest.

He tightened his arms around her, resting his cheek against her hair. "And I love you." He kissed the top of her head. "It's never been a matter of love between us. I think we fell in love the night we met, in the middle of a pile of dirty dishes."

Her head bobbed beneath his. "But I had no intention of letting you know that, not when you were acting like such a peacock—so sure of your charm."

He smiled, cracking open the dried blood on his split lip and winced. "I know now that cockiness was a big part of my problem, I thought I was perfect."

"So of course you expected me to be perfect too. Nothing less would do for you."

"That's why I completely flunked out on the trust test, and I've been beating myself up about that for three—no four—miserable years." He lifted his head and put his fingers under her chin, coaxing her to look at him. "I'm not the self-righteous peacock that walked out on you anymore—just like you aren't the Amazon."

Her lips quivered. "I know. You proved that to me when you were willing to give up your life to rescue my son. I knew then that I could trust you—absolutely."

He pressed her to his heart. "I'm glad to know I have your trust, and I'm going to come back to you. The devil himself couldn't keep me from coming back now that I've found you again and know you still love me."

"That's easy to say, but you can't promise me you'll come back."

He held her eyes, adoring her with his. "Trust me. This time I won't let you down."

She pushed away from him, bristling. "Trusting you isn't the issue here. I know you mean to come back to me, and I can see that what you want to do isn't just mindless heroics. You believe you can help save this island and you're determined to do everything you can to accomplish that goal. But you don't have control over the outcome. So, it doesn't matter if I trust you or not. You've already made up your mind and how I feel just doesn't count."

He snorted, "Wrong card, Jess, because I could say the same thing to you about my feelings. I want you and Kanoa out of here, across the savannah, and into the Toolowan's mountains fortress before the Japanese start dropping paratroopers onto the savannah—cutting off any retreat you could have."

"And what happens if the ship calls back before you reach it, and I'm not here to take the call. The Japanese might blow you out of the water before you could execute your plan."

"That's a risk I'm willing to take." He cradled her face in his hands, "But I couldn't live with myself—or you—if I ran away right now when there's something I can do to keep the enemy from taking this island."

"There's already a plan in place to do that."

"Yeah, and part of that plan will cost the people of Toolowa everything they have worked for and built for the past—I don't know how many generations. Do you want that?"

"No, of course not, but—"

"No more." He grabbed her hand and headed for the privacy of a small grove of banyan trees.

It surprised him when she followed him without resistance, and willingly came into his arms, wrapping hers around his neck. She received his kiss, matching his intensity, and for a few precious moments the world was forgotten as the love they had never let go of for each other found expression, and new life.

I'm finally home again, after years of miserable, self-imposed exile. Sky deepened the kiss, banning Jessie tightly in his arms, never wanting to let her out of them again, and lingered for a moment longer in the dream that had sustained him for so many lonely years. With a groaning effort, he broke the kiss and stepped back from all he yearned to have.

Jessie pulled a handkerchief from her pocket and reached up. He caught her hand before she could wipe the blood from his face. "It's a very convincing touch." He grinned, causing his lip to bleed even more. "And when we walk down the beach, it will keep every eye on that Japanese ship focused on me."

He took the handkerchief from her and gently wiped his blood from her face.

"Don't leave me, Sky, not now, not when we've just found each other again. Don't risk this chance we've been given."

"Jess, I—"

"You said my plan to rescue you was hair-brained, but your plan is positively suicidal. Don't make me a widow before I get to be a wife—please."

He drew her back into his arms. "You can't even begin to imagine how I yearn to just stay here with you and never let you out of my arms again." His brushed back her long hair. "I promise you, when I get back, we're going to finish making the plans we started four years ago. But right now, I don't have any more time to argue with you. Just go get Kanoa, and"—He lowered his face to hers until they were nose-to-nose—"*get out of here.*"

Her eyes narrowed. "If you think one kiss, and one I love you, gives you the right to dictate to me, then you have another thing coming." She pushed against his arms, but he held on to her. "You have your duty to do, and I have mine as a citizen of not only Toolowa, but of the

United States as well. And that means I'm staying right here in case the ship calls again."

"*Fine*, but you won't get my vote for mother of year by putting yourself and your son in harm's way," he said, pulled her to him, kissed her, and stalked off.

35

SKY LED A SHORT PARADE DOWN THE BEACH to the boat, his hands tied behind his back with the same rope the Japanese had used to bind him. Following him marched four Japanese soldiers, their faces hidden behind gasmasks, their bayonets pointed at his back, each shouldering a heavy backpack.

The four Toolowan's posing as Japanese soldiers, Lotto, Gunner, Lu Chen, and Don, marched directly behind Sky, using his broad back and towering height to conceal themselves and their poorly fitting uniforms.

Sky prayed the enemies' hats and gasmasks would disguise Takoa's men enough to fool even the penetrating eyes of a pair of binoculars, which were undoubtedly watching them.

JESSIE BLINKED BACK TEARS, trying to control her fear, but it grew with each step Sky took toward the boat. She searched her mind for some kind of comfort and, for a moment, found one. *At least Kanoa isn't here to see this. By now, he must be sleeping soundly in his own bed, safe in Lowa's watchful care.*

She knew it had been a bitter order for Lowa to accept from his brother, especially since everyone knew why Takoa made it. He was protecting his brother. Lowa was the only man in the group who was married and had children. Beyond that, Takoa trusted Lowa with the life of his godson.

The small troop, heading for the boat, was almost there. *I can't bear to watch Sky walk out of my life again—I just can't!* But she couldn't make herself look away. She could still taste the blood from Sky's split lip, along with the tears that continued to trickle down her face and into her mouth.

Her breath had kept him alive, protecting him against the yunga. In turn, he'd brought her heart back to life, healing it fully with that one compelling kiss. *Oh, how I've missed your kisses, Sky, and the feel of your arms around me.* She also had to admit she'd missed his audacity; something he now paraded down the beach, walking fearlessly toward what she was sure was certain death.

His harsh words, just before he stalked off, still stung. The idea that she was a bad mother was a mean thing to have said, but she knew why he'd done it. If he died trying to protect Toolowa, he didn't want her to see it. More than that, she knew he wanted to protect her and Kanoa, and she loved him for it.

Next to her, Tena sat in the sand holding the radio, and weeping. Before Takoa and his men had moved out, he too, had tried to bully her into leaving. She'd stood her ground as determined as Jessie, reminding him that he had no right to dictate to her, and she had every right to play her part in protecting their country. Takoa had stomped off without letting her treat the ugly bullet-inflicted gash along his arm.

Jessie tore her teary eyes from Sky and peered at the rocky north shore of the bay. Takoa and the rest of his men were going to station themselves in the rocks. Takoa would give the signal to start the yunga drop, which they hoped would go a long way to helping Sky's plan succeed. He would then launch the rescue mission to pick up Sky and his men.

"What are you crying about?" Tena asked sniffing back tears. "I thought you didn't love him."

Jessie laughed derisively. "That's what I've told myself for four years. Adopting Kanoa helped me believe it too. But the moment Sky walked into the Hamilton's living room, I knew it wasn't true, and still I refused to admit it to myself. What's even worse"—she watched Sky march into the water—"he knows how I feel. He knows I love him. And yet, there he goes again, walking out on me, knowing the odds are even longer this time that he'll come back."

Sky's troop waded through the shallow waves to the boat. Two of the men steadied Sky, helping him board. The others quickly followed. Sky disappeared, sinking out of sight into the bottom of the boat. A couple of tense minutes dragged by before the boat's engine roared to life. Slowly it backed away from the beach and turned to the south.

"Good-bye, Sky. I wish . . . I wish you hadn't come back into my life."

"You don't mean that."

"Yes I do," Jessie said harshly, as the boat moved away. "If Sky hadn't come and forced me to see what my life is missing, I would still be happy with just my little man to keep me company and my place in the world."

36

DON DROPPED HIS BACKPACK NEXT TO SKY in the bottom of the boat and brought up a pair of binoculars, starting the ruse of scanning the island. His backpack held the Japanese gasmask Sky needed to protect himself from the yunga. Lu Chen dropped his too, and Lotto and Gunner retrieved them. Crouching down in the boat, they shrugged off the backpacks they also carried. Lu Chen's pack held a few tools and the hoses and nozzle for an acetylene torch. Lotto's held the tanks for the torch. Gunner's held the homemade bomb Sky had been working on for the past few days.

A button popped off the tight uniform Lotto was wearing as he untied the rope, binding Sky's hands. Gunner grinned, his own muscles stretching the seams of his uniform. He handed Sky the backpack with the bomb, and then took hold of the ones Don and Lu Chen had been hauling. The three men dragged the packs along as they belly crawled into the bow.

Originally, Sky and Takoa had planned to drop the bomb over the side of the channel directly onto any ship that dared to come down it. The arrival of their enemy, sooner than expected, had forced Sky to leave it behind in his rush to get Jessie, Kanoa, and the Hamiltons onto the savannah. He'd planned to come back for it, when everyone was safely on the way to the mountains.

Lotto unloaded the backpacks containing the parts of the torch, along with a heavy hammer and a dozen long wooded wedges. "Where do you want the hole?" he asked Sky, attaching the hoses to the acetylene and oxygen tanks and adjusted the gages.

"Here." Sky touched a spot in the bow as Lotto pulled on a pair of gloves, put his goggles on, and lit the torch.

The bomb would explode on impact, but the impact had to be hard enough to compress the blasting caps. Sky decided the protruding nose of the bow would provide the strongest point of impact.

"Give us as much time as you can," Sky called to Don and Lu Chen.

"Right," Don said, through the gasmask he wore. With his long hair tucked up inside a Japanese cap and pulled down low on his forehead he could—at a distance—pass for a Japanese soldier.

He suddenly raised his hand, waved it at Lu Chen, and pointed at the island. Lu Chen immediately slowed the boat to a crawl. They inched along as Lotto went to work with the acetylene torch, cutting through the hull of the boat.

Sky checked the bomb over. It was crude, but he knew it would do the job. All it needed was to be positioned it in the hole so that the blasting caps hit the ship first. When they rammed the ship with the boat, the blasting caps would ignite a primary explosion that would set off the main explosive.

How much damage the bomb would cause was something Sky couldn't predict. If the bomb breached the ship's hull, it would be right at the waterline. The ship would immediately start taking on water, and if enough of the crew was taken out by the yunga before they reached it, the ship might eventually go down without the needed crew to run damage control. That was the best-case scenario, but Sky wasn't betting on it. Mostly, he just wanted to cause enough havoc to slow the Japanese down and buy the people of Toolowa more time to get to the safety of their mountain fortress.

"We're running out of coastline," Lu Chen yelled through his gasmask.

"We need more time," Sky yelled back.

"Okay. We'll come about, sweep back the way we came, and then follow the coastline to the north," Lu Chen shouted.

He brought the boat around in the curve of the sharp lower fang, which hid them from the Japanese ship in the channel, and started back along the shoreline.

"How much time will that give us?" Sky threw the question over his shoulder at Lu Chen.

"You've got about ten minutes before we reach the north side of the bay."

"Okay tell me when we get there," Sky said watching Lotto's progress. "How much longer?" he asked Lotto

"I should be done by the time we hit the north side of the bay." Lotto said, just as he made the first breach in the hull.

The next ten minutes felt like a lifetime. A cold sweat broke out on Sky's brow.

"We're starting the sweep on the north side," Don called.

"This sweep will take less time," Lu Chin yelled. "So get your gasmask on, Sky. You need to be prepared before Takoa give the signal to drop the yunga."

Sky pulled on the gasmask and adjusted it.

"Done!" Lotto shouted.

"Should we head for the ship?" Lu Chen yelled.

"How much time before we hit the mouth of the bay." Sky yelled back.

"About three minutes."

"Okay, let's head for the ship."

Don handed Lu Chen a rope to tie off the wheel so the boat would stay on course once they went overboard and ducked into the bottom of the boat before anyone on the ship could get a good look at him. Of the four, he had the most Anglo-Saxon coloring and features.

Lu Chen was now the only one whose head was above the sides of the boat. Only he had some oriental ancestry. His uniform fit him better than his companions, and with the gasmask and cap to hide his features, he could easily be taken for one of the Japanese soldiers. He was good at handling the boat too, having served a few years in the Australian navy before coming to Toolowa. He slowly turned the boat to the east and lined it up with the ship's bow.

"Three minutes should be plenty of time to finish this job. And I want everyone off this boat just before we hit the mouth of the channel," Sky shouted over the roar of the boat's motor.

They gave him thumbs up, and Sky slid the bomb into the breach Lotto had cut through the hull. He held it in place as Lotto secured it, pounding wedges in around it to keep it from shifting or falling out.

"Give us a thirty second count down, Gunner," Sky shouted through his mask.

"There's the signal for the yunga drop," Lu Chen yelled.

From the bottom of the boat, Sky couldn't hear it. He glanced up and saw a gray cloud drop over the edge of the northern cliffs to the northwest of the ship and watched for a moment as it blew on the wind Edmund had called. It dropped down onto the ship, and Sky marveled for a moment at the faith of the islanders, saying a quick prayer of thanks. *Now if only the men aboard that ship aren't all wearing gasmasks. If they are, this island doesn't stand a chance of deflecting an invasion.*

He pulled his attention back to the bomb.

Lu Chen opened the throttle, finished tying off the wheel, and waved at Gunner.

"Thirty seconds," Gunner called.

Let's see if it holds," Lotto said.

Sky dropped his hands away.

The boat bounced over the in-coming tide, plowing through wave after wave. The bomb vibrated and shifted. Sky rammed it back into place, holding it steady so Lotto could pound more wedges in around the edges of the hole.

Lotto struggled to pound in the wedges as the boat bucked against the waves. He managed to pound in three additional wedges and quickly picked up another.

"Time," Gunner shouted.

"Everyone over the side—now!" Sky yelled.

"I'm not sure the bomb is secured," Lotto yelled back.

"It will just have to do." Sky grabbed him by the arm, yanked him to his feet, and sent him flying over the side of the speeding boat. The other three men quickly followed.

Even above the ship's powerful engine, Sky could hear the fearful shouts from aboard it and watched men drop to the deck, engulfed by the gray cloud the stiff breeze blew down on them.

The big forward gun on the ship boomed. The water on the starboard side of the boat exploded like a geyser.

The bomb jiggled.

Sky grabbed the hammer and pounded in two more wedges.

The bow of the ship rose up in front of him.

He dropped the hammer and leaped to his feet.

Gunfire peppered the deck.

The boat slammed into a wave rolling through the channel, knocking him down. He rolled away from the bow. Another wave hit the boat, sending him sliding backwards across deck and into the stern amidst more gunfire.

The ship's bow filled his field of vision.

He scrambled to his feet, slid along the deck, and grabbed for the railing on the port side. His feet went out from under him as his fingers caught hold of the railing. A bullet pinged off of it next to his hand. He heaved his body up again and launched himself into the air.

The boat rammed the ship dead on, and shattered like spun glass.

An instant later, an explosion rocked the bay.

37

TAKOA AND HIS MEN LEAPED TO THEIR FEET and ran for the outriggers tied near the rocks. Smoke billowed into the sky, filling the channel, obscuring their view of the ship. Another explosion, that seemed even larger, shot smoke and flames into the sky from the back of the ship.

"I didn't see Sky jump, did you?" Tusi, Takoa's strapping cousin, bellowed over the reverberating noise of a third explosion.

"No," Takoa yelled, releasing the line of the outrigger, "but I did see the others go over."

They pushed the outrigger into deeper water and jumped aboard. Two others followed. The outriggers flew over the water under the expert handling of the Toolowans.

"Over there!" Tusi pointed at the head that broke the surface of the water and the hand waving frantically at them.

Takoa steered the outrigger toward the man, rapidly closing in on him.

Shouts from the other outriggers confirmed to Takoa that the other three Toolowans had been sighted. The boats spread out to retrieve the swimmers.

"Did Sky make it off the boat?" Takoa asked Lu Chen as he pulled him aboard the outrigger.

Lu Chen unbuttoned the enemy's wet shirt and pulled it off. "I don't know. When I went overboard, he was still on board the boat. I surfaced after the bomb exploded."

Takoa let out a shrill whistle and the three outriggers converged. "Did anyone see Sky go overboard?" Takoa asked frantically.

"I didn't," Don said.

"Neither did I," Lotto said.

Gunner shook his head. "Me neither."

"The bomb wasn't completely secured by the time we had to jump, but Sky wouldn't let me stay any longer. He literally threw me overboard," Lotto said.

"And he was still working on securing the bomb when I went over," Gunner said.

Lu Chen finally said what they all feared. "I don't think he made it off before the collision and explosion."

JESSIE REGAINED CONSCIOUSNESS, gazing up at Tena. She blinked against the bright sunlight, unsure of where she was. Slowly her surroundings came into focus. Her brows knit, *why am I laying in the bushes looking up at Tena.*

She focused on the coconut tree above her head, but the swaying branches just made her feel dizzy. The strong smell of oil burning wrinkled her nose. The sounds that assaulted her ears were incomprehensible. She'd never heard such sounds on Toolowa. Then it all came rushing back at her like a torpedo.

She let out a horrific Nahtow mourning wail. It swelled out of her like the most natural sound she'd ever made, even though she'd only heard it once when it came from her Uncle Zedekiah—many, many years ago.

He had come to stay with her family for a couple of months. During that time he taught her the art of tracking. The chance to test her new skills came one morning when she sat down to breakfast and her mother told her Uncle Zed had gone on foot into the mountains just before dawn. Jessie decided to surprise him by tracking him down.

She found him in a secluded canyon, wailing like a lost soul. When she finally found the courage to approach him, he told her the death wail was something the Nahtow had been doing for hundreds of years to mourn the loss of those they loved. She reminded him that he and his wife, Yarley had been sealed together in the temple, and that meant they would have eternity together. He assured her, he knew that was true. Still, he felt his wife's loss, deeply, and he always allowed himself to mourn in the Nahtow way, on the anniversary of her death. It was his way of releasing the sorrow he would always feel over their separation.

Tena's hands covered her ears as Jessie's wail grew in volume. Jessie reached up and pulled Tena's hands away from her ears, letting the wail die away.

"He's dead! He didn't get off the boat. I counted them. Only four went overboard before the crash. All of them wore Japanese uniforms. None of them was big enough. He's dead," she cried, her chest heaving.

Tena leaned down and wrapped her arms around Jessie, hugging her tight. "It's a long way out. We can't be sure he didn't get off, just because *we* didn't see him. Takoa had a better perspective. You know he will search for Sky and find him."

Jessie's head thrashed back and forth. "Takoa won't find him . . . because . . . there's nothing left of him to find!"

"You don't know that for sure." Tena coaxed Jessie into a sitting position.

Jessie clutched her head, swaying in a drunken fashion, willing the world to stop reeling.

When Jessie quit swaying, Tena pulled her to her feet. "Let's go home, the explosions may have woken Kanoa, he might be scared. We can go there and wait for Takoa to bring Sky."

"No." Jessie pulled away from Tena, pushed through the ferns and bushes, and stumbled out onto the beach.

Tena followed. Together they watched the outriggers glide through the water and back to the rocks on the north shore.

One by one, Jessie counted the men the outriggers had hauled from the bay as they jumped out and waded onto the beach. "Four, they only rescued four." She dropped to her knees and doubled over. "Sky's lost to me—forever!" she cried, and let out another one of those terrifying wails.

Tena dropped down next to her. "We don't know yet. Don't give up hope. Takoa will keep searching for him until he finds him—you know he will. Let's go home, Kanoa needs you, and you need him." She tugged on Jessie's arm.

"Mama!"

Kanoa's voice brought Jessie out of the swirling darkness that threatened to take her away again. She sprang to her feet and reeled on wobbly legs, scouring the beach for her son. He was running toward her with Lowa sprinting after him. It was obvious Kanoa was trying to reach her before Lowa caught up with him.

"That little rascal escaped me," Lowa shouted, gaining on Kanoa.

Still drawing shuddering breaths, Jessie ran toward Kanoa. Barely able to see through her tears, she caught him up into her arms at a dead run and just kept running.

The gate to her bungalow was standing open. Jessie raced through it, burst through her partially open front door, charged through the living room and into her bedroom, collapsing with Kanoa onto her bed. She curled herself into a ball around her child and sobbed.

Kanoa put his little hands on her cheeks. "Why are you crying, Mama?"

Jessie couldn't bring herself to tell him. He'd never been confronted with the death of someone he knew before. It was an experience she didn't want him to have, not this young.

She knew Kanoa liked Sky. He'd talked about him every day since they'd met at the beach. How could she tell him he would never see Sky again, that he'd died to keep Toolowa safe. Dealing with that responsibility right now was more than she could bear. She hugged Kanoa tightly, unable to control the tearing sobs.

LOWA RUSHED INTO THE ROOM, breathing hard from running all the way back to the house.

It had required the full force of his will to tear himself from the spectacle of the Japanese ship going down in the channel, but he was still under orders to take care of Kanoa, Jessie, and Tena.

One look at Jessie's near hysterical state, made him try to take Kanoa from her arms.

"No," Jessie cried, swatting at his hands.

Kanoa kicked out against Lowa's gentle tugging. "No." He tightened his grip on Jessie's neck. "Mama needs me—she's sad."

"Lowa." Tena panted from the doorway. "Leave them be. Come with me. I need your help."

"It looks to me like Jayling's the one that needs help."

"Please." She beckoned to him.

He released Kanoa's arm and followed her from the room. As he door the shut he asked, "What happened?"

"Sky didn't make it off the boat before it hit the ship and exploded. We watched and counted the men that jump overboard, Sky wasn't one of them. We saw Takoa pull the others out of the bay."

Lowa's shoulders slumped. "I'm terribly sorry to hear that," he said sadly. "I know they are related by marriage, but I didn't think they were that close."

"They've been in love with each other for seven years."

"Why aren't they married then?"

"It's a long, complicated story, but they just found each other again. This was their chance to start over—now it's gone."

"What can I do to help," Lowa asked.

The sound of Jessie's grief now mingled with Kanoa's wails reached them. "We can't let Kanoa watch this for long. It's not good for a child to see such grief."

"So what do we do? You saw what happened when I tried to take him away."

"Go to my house." Tena pulled him to the front door. "There's a medical bag under my bed. Bring it to me. I'll give Jessie a sedative. What she needs right now is to escape her pain, if only for a little while. As soon as she goes to sleep, I want you to take Kanoa up to the savannah."

"He'll fight me the whole way."

"No he won't. I'll give him a mild sedative too. By the time he wakes up, your parents will have him. Grandpa and Grandma Zenderly will know what to do."

"What about Jayling? She's always so cool headed. It's *scary* to see her like this."

"I know. That's why we need to give her some time to grieve Sky's loss without the eyes of other people. I'll stay with her until she regains control of herself. Hopefully, when she's calmer, I can help her work through her grief."

"All right," Lowa said and went out the door.

He returned a few minutes later with Tena's medical bag in hand. She took it from him and quickly found a couple of syringes and the sedative she needed. Carefully drawing up the right doses, she flicked the syringes and dropped them to her side. "Jessie may not take kindly to having this injection. You may have to hold her down."

Lowa balked. "You better make it quick then. Keeping Jayling still will be like trying to tame one of those wild mustangs she told us she liked to break. Not only that, Kanoa might interfere too, and that little rascal won't hold anything back if he thinks we're doing something to his mama she doesn't want us to do."

"I know." Tena's lips quivered. "And watching you take them both on is going to be quite a spectacle."

"Just make that injection lightning fast," Lowa said. "I'm not in the habit of assaulting women and children— no matter how good the reason."

They crept down the hall to Jessie's door. It sounded like a pair of mad cats howled behind it. Lowa turned the handle carefully until it unlatched, swung it open, and charged in.

The element of surprise was on their side. Lowa came away from the brief fray with just a bruised jaw from the kick Kanoa landed while trying to defend his mama. Jessie proved to be too exhausted physically and emotionally to put up much of a fight, which allowed Tena to inject the sedative before Jessie knew what she was doing. But keeping Kanoa's squirming, little body still so Tena could give him his injection was a challenge Lowa would long remember. After the deed was done, it was only a matter of a few minutes before both Jessie and Kanoa were lying sedated on the bed.

The roar of a plane and a barrage of gunfire sent Lowa and Tena racing out of the house. They scanned the small patch of sky above Jessie's house and caught a glimpse of a plane bearing a star on its wing, fly overhead. Its guns blazed. The sound of a plane going down whined overhead, followed by the blast of a crash.

Lowa cheered. "That was an American plane doing the shooting."

"Then the plane we heard going down must be Japanese."

"It was probably carrying paratroopers, like Sky predicted. He said the Japanese had planes that could carry men from the Dutch West India to Toolowa."

"But how did the Americans know to come. Sky's mission was under radio silence."

"I don't know. But if the American's are here, Toolowa isn't going to be invaded." Lowa let out a victory whoop.

More planes roared overhead, followed by gunfire.

Lowa crushed Tena in a victory hug. "I need to go back to the beach, find Takoa, see what's happening, and find out if I can help."

"All right, but be very careful. The fighting might not all be in the sky, and who knows where the ones going down will fall."

Lowa started to move away.

Tena caught his arm. "Take care of Takoa. I couldn't bear it if anything happened to him."

"I thought you no longer cared for him."

"I will always love him."

"Then why won't you marry him?"

"There are good reasons why I won't allow him to marry me." She held up her hand. "Please don't ask me about them now. Just stay safe. Keep Takoa safe. And help him find Sky . . . if that's possible."

With a nod, Lowa started for the gate.

"Come and tell me what's happening," Tena called as he went through the gate and broke into a trot.

"I will," he yelled back, and ran.

The aerial battle was over by the time Lowa reached the beach. He watched more than a dozen American planes fly overhead in a tight formation, heading in the direction of the landing strip on top of the savannah, and let out an ancient Toolowan victory cry.

In the channel, the Japanese ship was gone. In its place sat a U.S. submarine. Takoa's outrigger was floating beside the sub. Uniformed men walked its wet deck, their faces covered with gasmasks.

Lowa watched Takoa climb aboard, and from the cliffs he heard the cheers of his people. Dropping to his knees, he clasped his hands together and rejoiced with a prayer of thanksgiving, and then rushed back to Jessie's to give Tena the good news.

"I'm so glad Toolowa is safe and relieved Takoa is too," she said, sinking onto the sofa.

"The callers have already reached Dad and Sam," Lowa said excitedly, sitting next to her. "I heard the message, just as I got here, that they are already on their way back. Messages are also being sent to the mountains right now. Everyone will be on their way home very soon."

"Then there isn't any point in sending Kanoa up to the savannah." Tena shrugged. "I guess we will just have to wait and see how things go when the sedation wears off."

"When will that happen?"

"I didn't give Kanoa a very heavy dose of the sedative. He may wake up before Jessie does. So I think it will be better if we put him in his own bed. Jessie will be able to sleep longer if we do."

Lowa took Kanoa into his room. Tena helped him settle Kanoa into his bed, with his puppy tucked under his chin.

"Now, why don't you go and find out more about what's happening. Then, please, come back and tell me when you can," Tena said, walking Lowa to the door. "And if you see Paul, ask him to come."

"Paul was already on his way to the mountains before we started for the bay to find Kanoa. He left with a caravan of stretches, carrying Jake and some of the other hospital patience, just after dawn. He wanted to get them into the mountains as soon as he could."

"That means the earliest he'll be back will be tomorrow night."

"But you're going to need some help with Jessie and Kanoa before then."

"I'll be fine for a while, but I'll need some help tonight."

"I'll find someone to come and help you as soon as I know what's going on and things settle down."

38

CAPTAIN LEWIS TREMANE, a balding, middle-aged man, shook hands with Takoa. "Zenderly," he said when Takoa introduced himself. "That's the name of the ruling family on this island, if I'm not mistaken."

Takoa smiled. "It was, but my family does not rule this island any more. We are a democracy, ruled by a council of judges. My father is now the chief judge. I am the chief of island security."

"You're doing a bang up job," Captain Tremane said. "From our position we could only see part of what happened, but we did see a small boat ram the Jap ship. That explosion not only provided us with the diversion we needed to launch our torpedoes undetected, but went a long way to sinking that ship."

Takoa's smile faded. "That explosion cost the life of one of your men."

"Who?"

"Major Sky Brannigan. It was his plan that helped you sink the Japanese ship."

Captain Tremane was silent for a long moment, and then said sadly, "It grieve me to hear that. Major Brannigan was a well-respected man in intelligence and reconnaissance. He will be sorely missed."

"All of Toolowa will miss him too. Especially me," Takoa said. He put aside his grief, and went on to detail Sky's plan. "Sky hoped that between the bomb and the yunga, we could at least hold the Japanese off until our people reached the mountains and we could burn the island."

"Burn the island?"

"Yes. We couldn't let the Yunga fall into the hands of the Japanese." Takoa paused. "Your gasmasks tell me you know about the yunga."

"Not really. We only knew what Major Brannigan suspected—until we saw your men drop it, and what happened to the Japanese out on the deck."

"You don't need the gasmasks anymore. The wind has carried the yunga away now."

Captain Tremane pulled off his gasmask, took a breath, and motioned for his men to do the same. "When we saw the gray cloud blow off the top of the cliff, we knew what you were doing. We hoped sinking the Jap ship would keep you from using it on us when we surfaced."

"Thank you for finishing the job Sky started." Takoa extended his hand.

Captain Tremane took it. "You're welcome," he said, and asked, "What about Captain Denning, who came with Major Brannigan to Toolowa? Where is he?"

Takoa explained about the plane crash, Jake's injury from the coral, and the resulting infection. "He has been very ill and was in no condition to take part in what we did, although he is now much better."

"Where is he?"

"Safe in our mountain fortress."

"What about your father and Ambassador Hamilton?"

"They were on the savannah near the lake, helping putting out the fire from one of the enemy's downed plane, when the callers reached them."

"How long will it take the news to reach the people in the fortress?"

"I'm sure the callers will reach them in the next hour. Before nightfall, everyone will be on their way back to their homes."

"Who are the callers?" Captain Tremane asked.

Takoa waved at the crowd standing on the edge of the northern cliff and explained their communications system.

"Amazing." Captain Tremane grinned. "I can see that Toolowa is as unique a place as I was told. I'm looking forward to meeting your father and the council of judges."

"Then you're planning to stay for a while?"

"Yes. Just to be sure the Japs don't call on you again."

"We're grateful for all your help, Captain, and we can provide comfortable accommodations for your crew on shore."

"Thanks, but that won't be necessary." Captain Tremane paused. "However, would you make a special call for your father, the judges, Ambassador Hamilton, and Captain Denning to come back as soon as possible?"

Takoa sent the messages in a series of chirps and caws. A few minutes later, he informed Captain Tremane that his father and Ambassador Hamilton were already on their way back to the bay, with the rest of the judges.

"They should arrive in a couple of hours," Takoa said and then suggested, "While we wait for them and news about Captain Denning's return, would you like a tour of the bay area?"

"I would," Captain Tremane said. He call for his lieutenant, and turned the submarine over to him.

They had just finished the tour of the town square when Takoa's attention was diverted by a call from Dr. Snyder. He paused to listen as the caller, from somewhere near the bay's rim, relayed the message from the doctor. When the caller finished, Takoa said, "That call was from Toolowa's head doctor. He and Jake, along with many of the sick and elderly, made it to the fortress a couple of hours ago. He feels it would be better for Jake to rest overnight. The frantic rush up to the savannah last night took its toll on Jake's strength. Jake is still weak from the coral poisoning, and Dr. Snyder doesn't want him to have a relapse. He has arranged for Jake to be brought back to the bay on a stretcher tomorrow."

THE TRICKLE OF PEOPLE returning to the bay from the savannah grew into a steady stream by the afternoon. Those who lived in the bay were accompanied by many who lived on the savannah and wanted to see the Americans and their submarine.

As soon as Edmund and Sam returned, Takoa and Captain Tremane met them at the council building. After the formal introductions were made, the council of judges and the American ambassador quickly organized a victory feast and celebration for the Toolowan and American heroes who had soundly defeated the enemy.

Takoa found he had little interest in either the feast or the festivities that were meant to celebrate his men's brave actions in saving Toolowa. Instead of helping with the preparations for that celebration, he spent the afternoon searching the channel for some sign of Sky, but with no success. As the hours dragged by, Sky's death began to weigh heavily upon him. He'd only known Sky for a very short time, but he had liked him. More than that, during their exploration of the island and their formation of a plan to protect it, he'd formed a deep respect for the Major. Sky had sacrificed himself to save Toolowa, and a people he barely knew, along with countless others that might have died if the yunga had fallen into the enemy's hands.

Not wanting to diminish the people's joy with his grief, Takoa stayed in the background while the final preparations for the feast were made. He was just about to take his place at the table when Lowa took him aside. His brother quickly told him about Jessie's reaction to Sky's death and Tena's concern for him. He fidgeted through the meal, pushing the food around on his plate, eating little. When the entertainment began, he took the opportunity to slip away.

Tena opened the door to his first soft knock. He fell helplessly into her large violet eyes and saw what Lowa had told him was true. She did love him. She could say she didn't, but her eyes couldn't. *That's why she's been avoiding me.*

They gazed into each other's eyes, his telling hers, what hers were unable to withhold from him.

"Why?" he finally asked.

"Why, what?" She dropped her eyes.

"Lowa told me, you won't allow me to marry you for some mysterious reason." He took her hand. "Don't you think I have the right to hear your reason?"

"Yes," she said, taking her hand from his and backing into the room. "And I had every intention of telling you before I left Toolowa."

"You're leaving Toolowa?" Takoa stepped through the door and shut it, staggered by this unexpected news.

"It's the best thing I can do for both of us, because I don't want to hurt you any more than I already have." Her chin quivered and she took a ragged breath. "Besides, it's too hard for me to see you all the time."

He again took hold of her hand. "Tell me why you won't marry me. I don't believe a reason exists that's so terrible it would make me back away from the eternity I want to have with you."

"I believe that too, and that's why I have to be the one to back away—for your sake."

"Tell me why." He pulled her toward him until she had to tilt her head back to see his face.

Her eyes filled with a grief that constricted his heart. He drew her closer. She pulled away from him, glancing over her shoulder in the direction of the hall. Takoa followed her gaze but didn't see or hear anything from the bedrooms.

She turned back to him. "Let's sit down."

As they settled on the couch, Takoa noticed she seemed to take particular care to keep the space between them as wide as possible. He leaned toward her expectantly, his hands clutching his knees to keep them from taking hold of hers.

"Do you know about Jessie and Sky?" she asked.

"Only that she is very upset about his death. I suppose that's to be expected since they were related by marriage. But what does Sky's death have to do with us?"

"More than you know." She slumped back against the cushions and told him about Jessie and Sky.

He listened carefully, a terrible suspicion growing inside him. "Is there something in your past you think I can't handle? Something you believe will drive me away from you?"

"No," she said, clasping her hands in her lap, "but it would bring you shame. It would rob you of the respect and position you deserve to hold in this community and the work you want to do." She glanced up at him and continued before he could speak. "I understood that the night Jessie saw Sky and Jake again after so many years. She came here to escape her past. She was sure this was the last place on earth her past would ever catch up with her. But it found her, and she's suffering all over again with her feelings for Sky and what is now lost to her."

Certainty pulsed through Takoa. "That's why you came to Toolowa—to escape your past."

"Yes and my past would hurt you—shame you." Her face was resolute. "I won't let that happen."

"Don't you think I have the right to make up my own mind about what will shame me?" he asked, sliding closer to her.

"No, because you would sacrifice everything you want to do with your life for me. I won't let you do that."

He took her hand, his long fingers closing over hers. "I can't force you to marry me, but *please* tell me why you're willing to throw away eternity with me."

"I haven't always been a virtuous woman," she said, averting her eyes. "In fact, for many years I was a—a prostitute."

Without concealing the pain and deep sorrow that pierced him, he asked, "Why did you become a prostitute?"

"I know everyone here believes I was born in Australia, but I wasn't. It took a few years for me to perfect the Aussie accent and speech patterns, before I sounded like a native."

"Where were you born?"

"In China; into a very well to do family. My English father was a high-ranking diplomat, but a dishonest one. He was caught embezzling government funds and sent to prison—where he died. My Chinese mother, my brother, Sung, and I were disgraced. We were left destitute and homeless. Sung and I begged in the streets for a year, before our mother died of hunger. Soon after she died, Yun, a man who owned a very exclusive brothel, approached Sung. He offered Sung a large sum of money to buy me. The money was enough to allow my brother to leave China and start a new life."

"Your own brother sold you into prostitution?"

"He was only my half-brother, and we were never close. But I didn't blame him for taking the opportunity to escape our shame and poverty."

"How old were you?"

"Nine."

Pain gasped out of Takoa. It twisted his handsome face. "How long?"

"Seven years—that felt like an eternity." Her voice hardened, "I was very popular with all the diplomats, trade barons, and politicians from different countries that patronized that exclusive brothel. I was a good actress too. I could turn myself into anything a man desired. My years there taught me how to deceive men and wheedle out of them treasures that I hid from Yun. But mostly, I learned how to get them tell me everything I wanted to know about them."

Takoa winced. "Why did you want to know anything about them?"

Her laugh sent a chill down Takoa's back.

"Because knowledge is power. The more knowledge I had about each of my customers, the more power I had over them. From the knowledge I gain about a particular customer, I devised a plan to escape the brothel. I did it too, with my own con game."

Tena's expression took on a deviousness that Takoa had never seen. The grief and pain he felt grew into a burning anger against her brother. "What did you do?"

"I simply made a very misunderstood diplomat from Australia fall in love with me. I convinced him that I was the only woman who would ever truly loved, appreciate, or understand him. He believed me, helped me escape, and drew up the paperwork giving me a new identity as an Australian citizen."

"Did you love him?" Takoa couldn't help asking.

"No, but I was grateful he got me out of China. When we arrived in Sydney, he set me up in a house near his office, a place he could visit without his wife's knowledge. As soon as I felt I could blend into Australian society, I changed my appearance, and disappeared."

"Where did you go?"

"I moved to Melbourne, changed my name again, and with the treasures I'd gotten from my customers as a prostitute, I attended nursing school. After I graduated, I was offered a job in Perth. I worked hard, and received several promotions. I was even offered the job as head nurse, due to my predecessor's pending retirement."

Takoa rubbed the dull ache in his temples, knowing there was nothing he could really do to sooth the pain of what Tena was telling him. "With such a bright future and all of Australia between you and the diplomat, why did you feel the need to run any farther?"

"That poor, misunderstood diplomat became a powerful politician in Australia. He toured Perth when he was running for a national office. I even saw him—although he didn't see me—when he inspected the hospital where I worked. Fortunately, the head nurse hadn't retired yet, so she was part of the entourage that toured the hospital with the politician, instead of me. But his visit terrified me. The invitation from Toolowa to come and be the head nurse here came a few days later. I took the job, certain my past would never find me here."

It was now all clear in Takoa's mind, and he loved her even more for trying to protect him from her disreputable past. He reached across the space that separated them and took hold of her hand. "So what you're really afraid of is having some former customer show up on Toolowa and recognize you."

"Yes." She tried to pull her hand from his, but he didn't let go. "I know you will be the chief judge someday, and Toolowa couldn't have a finer one. But I can't be the chief judge's wife. Toolowa is becoming more and more known in the world. Other countries want to send diplomats and trade executives." She paused. "Tell me how you'd feel if one of the men who came here to do business, or sign a treaty, was one of my former customers?"

"The possibility is very remote."

"That's what Jessie thought too, and her past comes from farther away than mine does, yet it found her."

He gently squeezed her hand, wanting to pull her close. "All right, so your past might find you here. So what? Do you really believe it will matter to anyone who knows and loves you? Or that I'd let any man say anything derogatory about you without severe consequences? The people of Toolowa love you. They wouldn't tolerate any slander against you."

"But that's just it"—she yanked her hand away and slid to the other end of the sofa—"it isn't slander, it's the ugly truth. You can't marry me and be the next chief judge. It would put you and the people of Toolowa in a position of shame. The people of Toolowa expect your wife to be someone they, and everyone else who comes to Toolowa, can respect. More than that, the people of Toolowa deserve to have you rule this country. They need you."

"And I need you! Do you really believe I want to be the chief judge more than I want to be your husband, or that I can't make a significant contribution to my country if I choose not to live my life in the spotlight? Lowa is as good a man as everyone believes I am. He will make a fine chief judge."

She jumped up from the sofa and took a frustrated turn around the room. "But the people want you. Even Lowa wants that—you know he does. You have a duty to this country, and I won't stand in the way of that. I can't."

He jumped up too, strode across the rug, and pulled her into his arms. "And I can't let you go. As much as I love Toolowa and her people, I love you more. I'm not willing to give up forever with you even for my country. I'd rather move to some remote place, in the farthest corner of the world, and have you for my wife than stay here and be the chief judge."

Her violet eyes probed his. "Would you?"

"Yes," he said, and kissed her.

She resisted him for just a moment before her arms slid around his neck, and she kissed him back. The intensity of her kiss gave him hope. It strengthened his determination to marry her and live anywhere she felt safe.

A wail of despair broke their embrace.

"Jessie." Tena dropped her arms from around his neck.

Takoa resisted letting her go, and held on. Nothing had really been settled between them. He was anxious to remedy that situation. His arms tightened around her.

Another moaning wail made him release her.

She hurried down the hall.

He went after her, determined not to let her out of his sight until he'd gotten her promise to marry him.

39

THE SEDATION WAS WEARING OFF and the sounds coming out of Jessie were medicated howls. Unlike the piercing wails of immediate loss that issued from her on the beach, these moaning wails were more desolate.

"Shhh, sweetie," Tena said, trying to make Jessie lie back down in the bed. "You're safe. Kanoa is too. He's asleep in his bed, so just lay back down now and rest."

Jessie looked wild-eyed over Tena's head at Takoa. "Did you find him?" She reached out her hand to him. "Tell me you at least found his body so his family can lay him to rest. They never found his brother's body, and his mother—oh his poor mother."

Takoa took Jessie's hand, coaxing her to lie back on the bed. He could feel her grief in the painful grip of her fingers.

Tena laid a hand on her forehead as she began to thrash about. "Her agitation has made her feverish. I wish Paul were here, I'm not sure I should give her another injection. Maybe she'll calm down if you just talk to her, help her understand what happened."

Sitting on the edge of the bed, Takoa drew Jessie into his arms. He held her gently and spoke to her in a soothing voice, his own heart torn with sorrow over the death of Sky Brannigan. "What Sky did helped save this island. He will always be remembered as a hero among us. His selfless act was one of the bravest things I've ever witnessed."

"Is the island safe then? Did his bomb sink the ship?" Jessie demanded.

He understood the note of desperation in her voice. She needed to know Sky's death had meaning. It would give her something to hold on to, be proud of, something she could share with his family to comfort them. He went over the scene again in his mind, but he'd been too far away to see what had happened clearly, and that was still troubling him. All he had to go on was what the others aboard the boat had told him, and that was far too little to be of help to Jessie.

Her wide, dilated eyes pleaded for the answers she needed to begin her search for peace.

What Captain Tremane said came back to him. "Jayling, what Sky did distracted the Japanese long enough so a U.S. sub could sink their ship, and in doing that we didn't have to burn the island."

Jessie's fingers curled into his shirt. "What are you talking about? I didn't see an American submarine."

"That's because we left before it surfaced," Tena said. "But don't you remember hearing more than one explosion?"

Jessie gasped. "Yes. I remember."

Takoa tightened his arms around her, feeling her tremble, "Sky's a hero, Jayling. His diversion held the enemy's attention long enough for the sub to get in to position and fire before the ship was aware of its presence. What he did saved this island."

Jessie went stiff and still in his arms. The color drained from her face. "No," she said with an unnatural calm. "That sub would have sunk the Japanese ship anyway, without Sky's diversion. He died for nothing—absolutely *nothing*."

She slumped against Takoa's broad chest and let out another one of those haunting wails.

Takoa and Tena exchanged alarmed looks.

Tena sat on the bed and added her arms to Takoa's. Holding Jessie between them, they rocked her, letting her wail out her grief until her voice finally gave out.

When she quieted, they laid her back, covered her up, and held a whispered conference near the door.

"I think I'd better stay with you two tonight," Takoa said, "in case Jayling gets agitated again. I don't want you to have to handle her by yourself."

"I'd welcome your help with Jessie—and Kanoa too." She glanced out the door. "I better check on him."

"Go. I'll stay with Jayling." He walked back to the bed, sat on the edge, and held Jessie's listless hand in both of his.

She stared at the ceiling as though he wasn't there.

When Tena returned, they assured Jessie they would stay with her for as long as she needed them.

Jessie nodded, closed her eyes, and turned her face away.

Takoa and Tena returned to the living room and sat on the sofa.

"Will you let me treat your wound?" Tena touched the makeshift bandage on Takoa's arm.

He agreed, but winced as she began to unwind the strip of shirt he'd used to wrap it.

"Hurts, does it?"

"I haven't had time to think about it, but yes."

Tena inspected the three-inch groove the bullet left in Takoa's left arm. "Thankfully, it has stopped bleeding and doesn't appear to be too deep, but it will need to be thoroughly washed to keep out infection."

She retrieved her medical bag from the chair across the room, and they went into the kitchen.

"Sit at the table," she said and filled a bowl with warm water.

"We didn't get to finish our conversation," Takoa said, watching Tena's long fingers as she cleaned and bandaged his wound. "I know you love me, and that's all that matters to me. Marry me, and we will live anywhere you want. Anywhere you feel safe from your past."

Tena finished wrapping the wound. "I've given you my answer," she said quietly, packing up her supplies.

Discouraged, but not defeated, Takoa let the subject drop—for the moment—and followed Tena into the living room.

They settled in for the night, taking turns sitting in the big overstuffed chair in Jessie's room while the other one tried to sleep on the sofa in the living room.

During the night, Kanoa woke on Takoa's watch. He left Jessie's room and hurried into Kanoa's. "It's okay, little man," he whispered trying to hush Kanoa.

"Mama," Kanoa cried, "I want Mama."

Takoa picked him up and took him into Jessie's room. "See your mama is sleeping, just like you should be."

"I want Mama." Kanoa pushed against Takoa's chest.

Takoa decided it was better to let Kanoa snuggle up with his mother, rather than wake her with a tantrum. He put him in Jessie's bed and tucked the blanket in around him.

Jessie moaned softly and, as though guided by instinct even in her sleep, curled around her son with a sigh.

Takoa's shuffling between the rooms woke Tena. "What's the matter," she whispered coming into Jessie's room.

Takoa pointed to the bed, "I think they'll both do better if they're together. They need each other for comfort right now."

"Yes." Tena yawned.

"Go back to sleep." Takoa pulled her out into the hall and hugged her.

"No it's my turn to watch them."

"There's no need, I'm wide awake now."

Actually, he hadn't been able to sleep all night. He kept playing the moment the boat crashed into the ship over and over in his mind, unable to rid himself of the nagging feeling that persisted in his gut. It felt as though he'd overlooked something, something important, but he couldn't make whatever it was come to the surface of his mind.

Restlessly he paced back and forth across Jessie's living room after Tena insisted she take over the watch. It was dawn before he finally realized what was nagging at him.

THE SUN, SHINING THROUGH HER WINDOW, woke Jessie. She squinted into its blinding glare, confused. *I never sleep this late.* A soft breath tickled her cheek, and she became aware of Kanoa in the bed with her. *Now why—*

A wail rose up from the deepest recesses of her soul and came out as a hoarse groan. It was all that was left of her voice. The hours of wailing had taken their toll. She wanted to stop but the grief she felt wouldn't let her.

Now she understood why her uncle wailed for the loss of his wife. Something in the act expressed better than any words the terrible grief and unbearable loss she felt. Somewhere in her mind, she knew she would eventually learn to live with the grief, but it would never go away. How could it, when she had finally accepted what her heart wanted and had admitted Sky was the only man she would ever love, ever want, ever need. Now the dream Sky's kiss had ignited was dead. She would never share her life with him, never belong to him, and neither would Kanoa.

She glanced at her son, with his thumb stuck slackly into his mouth, and knew he would never have a father. That truth made her feel like wailing even more. Her raw throat croaked out a wail that woke Kanoa. She rocked him and forced herself to tell him that Sky was dead. When he understood he would never see Sky giant again, his wails became as haunted as hers.

I have to stop, for Kanoa's sake, I have to stop, she berated herself, but she had never felt such soul rending grief, and the croaking wails just kept coming. They finally stopped when Tena ushered Edmund, Takoa, and Lowa solemnly into her room.

Takoa reached for his godson. Kanoa came willingly into his arms, tucking his head under his godfather's, he clung to his neck.

Edmund sat down on the edge of the bed and took Jessie's hand. "Jayling, I have been told about your feelings for Major Brannigan, and my heart is broken with yours. All Toolowa is in mourning for his loss. His name will always be revered here, and his sacrifice remembered among this people for as long as there is one Toolowan on the face of the earth."

Jessie had no voice left to express her feelings. Only the tears that poured from her eyes told Edmund what she felt. He held her in his arms, stroked her hair, and wept with her. Tena, Takoa, Lowa, and Kanoa did too.

When Jessie's emotions began to subside, Edmund asked; "May we give you and Kanoa each a blessing of comfort, Jayling? It is what the Lord can do, through us, to help you right now."

"Please," Jessie croaked out, and the Zenderly men laid their hands on her head.

THE ZENDERLYS LEFT THE QUIET HOUSE under Tena's watchful eye, with the promise to return in a few hours. Jessie was again sleeping with Kanoa tucked into her side.

Edmund closed Jessie's gate after they passed through, and paused. "I'll send Sam over as soon as he can get away. I know he is very anxious to see Jayling. At the moment, he's in a meeting with the American military leaders. I'm supposed to be in that meeting too," he said and hurried down the path.

Lowa laid a hand on his brother's arm as they watched their father disappear around the bend. "You seem as distracted as you are grieved."

"It's been bothering me all night," Takoa said.

"What?" Lowa asked as they walked down the path.

"Yesterday when Sky took off in the boat it was high tide."

"So?"

"The night we spotted the Japanese was a new moon. That means yesterday's high tide was a spring tide."

"So?" Lowa repeated.

"Do you remember what we used to do in our teens whenever we had a spring tide?"

Lowa's brows came together. "Yes, we would take out an outrigger and—" He stopped dead in his tracks and grabbed his brother's arm. "Are you thinking what I think you're thinking?"

"Yes, and I have to find out, for Jayling's sake I have to know."

"How much time is there before the next high tide?"

"Less than fifteen minutes, I think."

"I'll come with you," Lowa said, picking up the pace. "You know the tide won't be quite as high this time."

"Yes, but I have to try."

40

WHEN THE ZENDERLY BROTHERS reached the beach, the tide was nearly at its peak. Toolowa had two high tides per day that normally reach six feet. However, during a spring tide, which always came with the new moon or the full moon, high tide rose ten feet past its normal height.

"We better hurry. We need to be out there before the tide peaks," Takoa said, untying an outrigger and leaping into the sea.

Under the Zenderly brothers' powerful arms, the outrigger sped across the waves, passing the U.S submarine now anchored in the middle of the bay. The incoming tide fought them, but they pressed on with an urgency even the sea couldn't thwart. They came to a stop fifty yards inside the channel, where the bow of the Japanese ship had been. It was directly beneath a set of deep crags in the cliff's sheer face.

With the tide trying to take them back into the bay, holding the boat in position beneath the crags required a constant effort. Grimly they fought the tide and waited. Slowly they rose with the sea to within twelve feet of the crags.

It was only possible to reach the three vertical crags that ran into the cliff face at a spring tide, and then only by those with the strongest muscles and stoutest hearts. The practice of trying to jump up, take hold of the sharp rocks, hold on, and climb into the crags, had long been a rite of passage the young men of Toolowa used to prove their manhood. It was a test of both their strength and bravery.

Many had the strength to make the jump, but keeping hold of the serrated rocks while gravity pulled their bodies down took more than strength. It took an iron will to hang on while the rocks cut into fingers and palms. Many found it too painful, and inevitably let go, falling back into the sea.

Both Takoa and Lowa had tested their metal in their early teens at the crags without success. It had taken a few years of trying before they were big enough, strong enough, and determined enough to jump up, grab hold of the sharp edges of the crags, hold on, and climb in.

"Can you make it," Lowa asked considering the water line on the cliff face. "The water is a foot lower than yesterday, and I won't be able to help you and hold the outrigger in place too. We probably should have brought another man."

"It's too late to worry about that now. We'd never be able to go back and get out here again before the tide started to fall. Just hold the boat as steady as you can, and let's hope I'm still as good at this as I used to be."

Lowa grinned at his brother. "I have no doubt."

Takoa returned the grin. "I appreciate your confidence in me. Let's hope it puts more spring in my legs and resolve in my hands."

They waited impatiently as the tide rose another few inches before they paddled farther into the channel and brought the outrigger around.

"You better get into position." Lowa fought the strong incoming tide. Takoa slid to the center of the boat, got his feet under him, and crouched, ready to spring.

When Takoa was in position—waiting for the exact moment to spring upward, with his hands pressed against the wall of the cliff for balance—Lowa let the outrigger drift back toward the crags, holding it tightly against the cliff face.

The bow of the outrigger reached the mouth of the first crag. Takoa held his position.

Lowa back paddled, slowing the outrigger down, knowing the mouth of this crag would offer his brother the best chance. It was wider and held more places to grab hold. His muscles strained to keep the boat at a snail's pace and hold it against the cliff as the bow passed under the mouth of the crag. He let the outrigger slide another two feet, until Takoa was directly under the crag's mouth.

With all his strength Lowa brought the outrigger momentarily to a complete stop.

Takoa sprang into the air, his hands reaching for a hold on the edge of the crag.

Lowa thrust the outrigger away from the cliff face.

It was the standard procedure used to protect the jumper. If a jumper fell and hit the outrigger, he was sure to be injured, or damage the outrigger. Either scenario would keep him from being able to try again.

IT HAD BEEN MANY YEARS since Takoa had last done this daring deed, but it came back to him. As he sprang upward, his arms shot above his head. His fingers found a jagged knob and hung on, while his other hand locked into a deep serrated depression. The weight of his body fell with gravity, he grunted with the effort to hold on against the downward pull of his body while the razor-sharp rocks tore into his palms.

His will won, and for a moment after he secured his painful grip and quit swinging, he simple hung against the cliff face. He drew in a breath and let out a shout of triumph.

His brother echoed it from below.

Flexing his arms, he drew himself up until he could sit just inside the first crag with his feet dangling over the edge.

"Throw up the flashlight," he called to Lowa, wiping the blood from his palms onto his lava-lava.

"Hang on," Lowa called, brought the outrigger about and steered it back along the side of the cliff.

He paddled against the tide for fifteen feet before he again brought the outrigger around, let go of the paddle, and reached for the flashlight.

A few moments later, the outrigger was again under the crag where Takoa sat.

Lowa threw the flashlight up to him and yelled, "Good hunting."

Takoa caught the flashlight, waved, and carefully turned toward the mouth of the dark crag.

It was a long shot, and Takoa didn't kid himself about that. Still, it was just possible if Sky had been going overboard when the boat collided with the ship and exploded, that he might have been thrown upward by the blast into one of the crags. They were certainly wide enough and at spring tide, it was possible.

He entertained no hope that Sky had survived the blast. If he had, he would have been found yesterday when Takoa and his men searched extensively for him, but nothing had been heard or seen of him.

Twenty-four hours had passed now, and Sky was undoubtedly dead. Still, if his body could be recovered, they could send him back to his family. Takoa hoped that would bring Jayling a small measure of comfort.

Balancing carefully on a narrow ridge that ran in front of the crag, he stepped into it.

The crags were home to a colony of bats. Every evening they could be seen flying out of the crags in search of insects.

Takoa wrinkled his nose, the stench of bat droppings was overpowering. He turned back to the entrance, took a breath, and switched on the flashlight.

This particular crag was twelve feet wide and ran for fifty feet into the cliff face. Takoa knew he didn't have to go in more than a few feet. If Sky had been thrown into the crag, he would be close to its mouth.

Keeping his flashlight pointed down, he moved slowly, not wanting to stir up the bats. His flashlight revealed what he hadn't thought of. The floor of the crag was covered in dead bats. The yunga had penetrated the crag, and done its work. The death of the bats hit him with unexpected sorrow.

He swept the beam of his flashlight deeper into the crag, illuminating the names etched into the wall of the men who had conquered the crags. His name was etched next to his father's and brother's, along with his kin for many generations, but there was no trace of Sky.

Disappointed, he clicked off the flashlight and returned to the mouth of the crag. "Nothing but dead bats," he called down to Lowa still paddling the outrigger up and down the channel. "I'll try the other ones."

Looping the cord of the flashlight around his neck, he hugged the cliff face and slid along the narrow ridge of rock that ran between the crags.

The middle crag was the smallest one at a mere four feet wide, five feet high, and ten feet deep. It didn't have a floor. The sides of the crag slanted together but didn't quite join. Instead, they ended in a narrow fissure that could easily trap a careless foot.

Takoa took a deep breath of the clean sea air and held it. He ducked into the crag, bracing his knees on either side of the fissure. Nothing but dead bats and their droppings covered the steeply slanted walls above the fissure.

He backed out as hope drained away. "Nothing," he called down again to Lowa, and picked his way carefully along the ridge to the final crag. This crag was closest to the bay, and the tallest of the three, but its mouth was narrower than the first crag's.

In his mind's eye, Takoa thought it was too far from where the bow of the Japanese ship had been. He paused at the mouth of the crag, taking in several breaths of clean air, trying to get the stench of the bats out of his nose and throat, held his breath, switched on his flashlight, and stepped into the crag.

His breath rushed out of his lungs in a whoosh.

Sky Brannigan was sprawled on the narrow floor of the crag, still and dead, like the bats surrounding him.

Takoa let out a whoop that echoed through the crag.
No longer concerned with the foul air, he plunged in, his light fixed on Sky. He was lying on his stomach, his head facing to the side, his gasmask somehow still in place. Dried blood caked his right pant leg from calf to mid-thigh. His right arm lay down along his leg. The tip of his pinky finger was gone. Takoa leaned over examining the blood caked in his short hair, and the huge bruise on his right temple.

Grief surged through Takoa for this brave man. He pulled the gasmask from Sky's face, placed his hand on Sky's head, and gasped. It was warm to the touch. Anxiously, he ran a hand across Sky's brow. It too was warm. He grabbed Sky's wrist, and through the pounding in his own chest and ears, he felt a faint, erratic pulse. He dropped to his knees, humbled by this miracle that—in his experience—was without precedent.

"He's alive," Takoa bellowed, laid his hands on Sky's head, and by the virtue of the priesthood he bore, commanded Sky to stay alive.

41

THROUGH A VAPOR OF DARKNESS, Sky heard a voice. It was a voice he knew and loved. He couldn't quite make out what was being said, but he held onto the voice, pulling himself up through the darkness into a swirling gray fog.

The voice became clearer.

He felt his brows contract, and then her gentle fingers stroked his forehead. She was scolding him, but he found he didn't mind. Not as long as the hand that stroked his brow and the other one, he now felt holding on to his, were communicating her love.

The furrows deepened on his brow, as he became aware she was crying, and he was the cause. Her tears hurt more than the pain throbbing in his head.

The desire to comfort her brought him out of the fog. He forced the eye that wasn't swollen shut, from the Japanese lieutenant's blow, open and gazed into the emerald eyes that owned his heart. The words he wanted to say came out as an indistinguishable croak.

She reached for a glass and put a straw to his lips. It took an absurd amount of effort just to suck on the straw, but the water he managed to draw through it felt wonderful going down his throat. He took another long sip and swirled the water around his mouth before swallowing, his eye never leaving her face.

Her soft mouth trembled with words she seemed to want to say, but couldn't form.

For a long time, they simply looked at each other. He, out of the one eye he could open; she, through tears that continued to spill like a summer shower.

Both let their eyes do all the talking.

"I told you, you could trust me to come back," he finally said, hoarsely.

It was the wrong thing to say.

A tirade of fear and pain poured out of her that hurt him more than his leg, which was heavily bandaged and on fire, along with part of his right hand. He let her cry and rant out all her pain and grief, knowing her Irish temper needed the outlet, along with her nerves. He rejoiced to know how much she cared, even while he felt guilty for causing her so much grief.

From what he could glean through her somewhat disjointed discourse, the American military had shown up, sunk the enemy ship, shot down their paratrooper planes, and saved the island.

"I wonder what made them show up in the nick of time," Sky croaked. "Not all the top brass were convinced the Japanese would come after the yunga."

"Captain Tremane, the sub's commander, said your commanding officer is rather fond of you. So when you didn't get back on schedule, he got worried."

"Nice of my commander to send the Cavalry—so to speak—after me."

Jessie tisked her opinion of that statement and said, "Don't get too puffed up. They didn't plan to come after you—at least not right away—not until the navy got wind of a troop transport heading our way. They decided they'd rather the Japanese didn't land on Toolowa and sent a sub, along with a squadron of fighter planes."

"I'm glad they got here when they did."

"Yes." Jessie's voice took on a dangerous edge. "Their timely arrival means your heroics were completely unnecessary."

Guilt and chagrin struggled for control of Sky's bruised face. "I'm sorry, honey. If I'd known help was here, I probably wouldn't have done it, but I didn't, and I couldn't just let the Japanese land."

She sighed heavily and relented in a gentle voice, "I know." Then soothing his guilty brow, she told him what Captain Tremane had said about his diversion.

"I'm glad it wasn't all for nothing."

"Maybe not, but I'm sure the sub would have sunk the ship anyway. And during the twenty-four hours you were presumed to be dead, I was in—well you know perfectly well where I was. Thankfully, Takoa and Lowa found you in the bat crags and blessed you—to keep you alive."

"Did they?"

"Yes."

"Remind me to thank those two. It seems rescuing me is becoming a full time job for them." He paused, and tilted his head. "Just what and where are the bat crags?"

She explained Takoa's inspiration and the Zenderly brother's search of the bat crags for him. He concentrated, trying to remember, but nothing past the moment he threw himself from the boat came back to him.

"I wish I could have seen the sub sink that Japanese ship," he said, wistfully.

"I'll just bet if you'd known it was out there ready to fire on the ship, you would have still done exactly what you did and missed seeing it go down anyway."

Sky shrugged a stiff shoulder. "Maybe."

Jessie bristled. "Don't try to deny it, Brannigan. You enjoy standing nose-to-nose and spitting in the face of danger, without any regard for how I feel. You are, without a doubt, the most reckless man I've ever met. Why I should care what happens to you is beyond me. No doubt, you'll always be a source of pain to me, if I—"

"Jayling," he interrupted entwining his fingers with hers. Her gasp told him that endearment, coming from him, had caught her off guard. "Have mercy."

Her jaw tightened. "If only I didn't love you and could walk out that door."

"But you do. So stop all this caterwauling and kiss me before I die of longing."

Her laugh had a definite soggy sound to it. She sniffed, tossed her fiery hair over her shoulder leaned down and gently kissed him.

When she would have broken the kiss, he caught hold of the back of her head and deepened it. The pain of his numerous wounds was forgotten as she kissed him, expressing her love. In return, he tried to tell her that she meant everything to him and he wasn't ever going to let her go again.

"Papa!" a childish voice yelled as Kanoa bounded into the room, interrupting their kiss.

Sky smiled so wide he cracked his split lip open again.

"Papa?" Jessie asked, her head swiveling from her little man to her big one. "Just what have you two been cooking up behind my back?"

Kanoa gushed out the secret. "Sky giant told me when you kissed him he would be my papa—and you were kissing him. I saw you," he said bouncing up and down and taking hold of Sky's hand.

"That she was." Sky grinned.

"So that makes you my papa."

Jessie arched a brow. "Not quite. Sky and I would need to get married, and he would have to adopt you, before he'd be your papa. And we haven't settled that yet." She fixed cool eyes on Sky. "I'm not sure I want to marry you. Not when you have no qualms about running off into danger—leaving me to suffer over it."

"I guess I should have told you about the blessing President Grant gave my mother after Jed died."

"Are you talking about President Heber J. Grant, our prophet?"

"Yes, he's been a family friend for years. He even married my folks, and all my brothers."

"What did he tell your mother in the blessing?"

"That if she faithfully served the Lord, and her sons kept their covenants, she wouldn't lose another son in the war."

"And you didn't think to tell me that, before you ran off to play hero? Ooo, I could just . . . scream."

"I'm sorry, honey, but I didn't even think about it," he said, letting his sorrowful eye plead his case. "Please forgive me."

"Yes, Mama, forgive him and marry him. I want him to be my papa," Kanoa said, taking hold of her hand and putting it in Sky's.

"Jess"—Sky moaned—"this isn't the way I envisioned making my marriage proposal to you. I wanted it to be the most romantic moment of your life. Not only because I adore you and you deserve it after all I've put you through, but because I first need to grovel at your feet and beg for your forgiveness for my self-righteous pride that has cost us too many years together."

"Stop." She put a finger to his bleeding lip. "I've already accepted your apology and forgiven you a long time ago. Besides, what I really want from you is to be treated like a queen for the rest of eternity. That should be enough to make up for your pride—and your heroics."

"But I don't even have a ring to put on your finger, and I want one there. I want every man alive to know you belong to me."

"I do too," she said reaching for her purse. After a short search, she pulled out a red velvet box.

Sky eye bulged. "I don't believe it! You kept it?!"

"Ah-huh, and . . . I've never opened it."

"Why not?"

"Because I couldn't bear to see what I'd lost, and could never have with you, because of one wrong choice."

Shame rode Sky hard. All she'd suffered, and the years they'd lost were his fault. "I'm surprised you didn't just throw it away. Why would you keep such a painful reminder of a man who let you down so badly?"

"Because it's the place I've kept my heart—all these years."

A tear slid over the rim of Sky's eye.

Jessie leaned over and kissed it away.

"That's where my heart has lived too—inside that box, waiting, hoping, longing, praying," he said, taking the box from her.

She dropped to her bandaged knees, winced, and then dazzled him with the Amazon's smile. He basked in that glorious smile with the absolute certainty that he would never have to worry about her giving it to another man.

She tugged on Kanoa's hand, and he knelt too. With both of them holding his hand she asked, "So, will you marry us?"

"Yes," Kanoa said. "Will you?"

Sky couldn't keep from grinning. Blood from his split lip ran down his chin, but he didn't care. "I'm the one that's supposed to be on my knees doing the asking—no begging."

"I don't think you'll be up to kneeling anytime soon. Besides, you aren't just getting me. You're getting a very special packaged deal. So will you?"

"It's a terrific deal."

"Does that mean yes, or no?" Kanoa demanded.

"That, my son, is a very definite yes!" Sky said, opening the velvet box.

Jessie gasped. "Oh, Sky, it's gorgeous."

He took her hand and slid the ring onto her finger.

She raised her hand, admiring the large marquis diamond set in a bow shaped band of tapering diamonds.

"Hurray," Kanoa shouted, scrambled onto the bed, threw himself on his papa's chest, and kissed him.

Sky groaned under the impact of his son's exuberance.

Jessie laughed and the sound sang through Sky. She wiped the blood off his chin with a towel, and took her own turn kissing him.

"So how soon can I get out of here," Sky asked after enjoying his fiancée's first kiss. "We need to get to Hawaii as soon as I can travel. I won't be able to rest easy until you two belong to me for time and all eternity."

"Well I'm afraid right now you're down for the count, champ," Jessie said gently. "You took a lot of shrapnel to your leg, and you lost the first digit of your little finger, not to mention the concussion that's kept you unconscious for the past two days."

Sky groaned. "Well there goes my basketball career." His brows came together, thoughtfully. "I guess I'll just have to go into the family business. Even with part of my finger missing and a bum leg I can still fly a plane."

"Just not for a while," Jessie said. "Paul says you need one more surgery to remove the rest of the shrapnel."

Something in her voice made Sky ask, "What aren't you telling me?"

"That you're out of the game, love—indefinitely. Paul assured me that after the surgery, and with some physical therapy, you'll be able to walk normally again. Although you might have to live with some reoccurring pain if we decide to live in a cold climate." She ran her fingers through his short-cropped hair and brushed his lips with a soft kiss.

Inexplicably, he found he didn't regret that he wasn't going to see any more military action. He sighed and found himself smiling again. "I can live with that. As long I have you two, I can deal with anything," he said, and gathered his family into his arms.

TENA TOOK HER EYE FROM THE CRACK and quietly shut the hospital room door. She'd stopped short of following Kanoa into the room when he'd escaped her—*the little rascal.* At least she'd managed to give Sky and Jessie some time alone before Kanoa outmaneuvered her, and as it turned out, his escape hadn't been a bad thing. She leaned her head against the door, happy for Jessie and Kanoa.

"I take it things are going to be all right for Jayling and Sky," Takoa said to her back.

She whirled around. His bandaged hands made her heart hurt, and, at the same time, beat with pride. "I'm very happy to say, they are."

He took a step toward her. "I'm glad, but what about us? Are things going to end with happily ever after for us too?" he asked, his voice soft with pleading. He took another step, and opened his arms.

She came into them with a new understanding. "The one thing I've learned from Sky and Jessie is that my past only has the power to destroy the life we choose to have together and the eternity we want to share—if I let it." Tears filled her eyes and she drew a ragged breath. "I'm not going to let it. Not as long as you're sure you want to spend it with me."

"I am," he said, and kissed her.

42

ANN BRANNIGAN SET DOWN HER DUSTER and went to open the front door. The man on the other side handed her a telegram. She took it reluctantly, found some change in her pocket, paid the man, and shut the door.

Dread churned in her stomach as she looked down at the envelope. The last telegram she'd received had turned her hair completely white.

She wandered into the living room, staring at the envelope, not wanting to open it, but tormented by not knowing what it contained.

The silent house pressed in around her. Her husband, Bill, was still at work. So was their daughter in-law, Lynda. Jenny, her granddaughter, was napping, and her grandson, Eric, was at school.

Dropping the telegram on the lamp table, she sat down on the sofa and decided to wait until Bill came home so they could open it together. It stared at her, taunting her. She glared back at it unable to keep her fingers from creeping toward it. They stopped just short of touching it. Could she bare it, if what it contained was terrible news?

After losing Jed in the war, she hated telegrams. They always brought tragic news about people's sons. Well, most of them did. She leaned back against the sofa cushions and hugged herself. It was no use. She couldn't bear not knowing what the telegram contained, even if the news it contained devastated her.

She snatched it up, tore it open, and read the message. A strangled sob choked her. Tears blurred her vision until she couldn't see the words on the telegraph. She fumbled in the pocket of her housedress until she found her handkerchief, but no matter how fast she mopped them, the tears still came.

Ten minutes later, her husband came through the door. Her blotchy complexion and sniffling immediately made Bill rush to her side.

He dropped down beside her on the sofa. "What is it, dear," he asked, folding her into his arms.

"They're married," she said, handing him the crinkled and slightly damp telegram.

"Who," he asked, taking it from her.

"Sky and Jessie."

"What?"

"Five days ago, in the Hawaiian temple."

As though he didn't believe her, Bill unwrinkled the telegram and read the news for himself. "It's true, and they have a son too! What do you make of that?"

"I haven't got a—"

The phone rang.

Ann jumped up and headed for the kitchen phone, surprised she was so steady on her feet.

Bill trailed her, stopping in the kitchen doorway, still holding the telegram.

She picked up the receiver. "Hello."

"Ann, can you believe it?"

"Kedra, I'm still reeling. Having a new daughter and grandson, all at the same time, is a lot to take in."

"I'm sure it is."

"But how, and *where*, did it happen?"

"It must have been on Toolowa. That's where Jessie has been for the past four years."

"Where in the world is Toolowa, I've never even heard of it before."

"I hope you're sitting down. This could take a while," Kedra said.

"Just a minute, I want Bill to hear this too." Ann covered the receiver. "Go into the study, its Kedra Garrison, she is going to tell us how all this happened."

Bill crossed the kitchen and disappeared down the back hall. Ann and Kedra waited in silence until he picked up the receiver and said, "I'm on.""

Kedra launched into her daughter's move to Toolowa, her adoption of a child, what Jessie's telegram told her about Sky's arrival, and the subsequent events.

After almost an hour, Ann asked hesitantly, "So how do you feel about this, considering the pain Sky put Jessie through and all the years they've been apart?"

With no hesitation, Kedra replied, "Jack and I think it's wonderful. We've always known, although Jessie wouldn't admit it even to herself, that she would never love anyone but Sky. In fact, she told us just after she adopted Kanoa that she didn't intend to marry. Kanoa became her life, and she was happy. Not the way parents want their daughter to be happy, but with Kanoa in her life, she was content."

"And we've known for the past few years that Sky wasn't going to stop searching for Jessie. He told us he would always love her, and he wasn't going to settle for anyone else."

"Although, I think he needed to grow up, before they found each other again," Bill said.

Ann sighed, "I'm glad she waited for him to do that, but I wish they would have come home so we could have been with them when they got married."

"So do I." Kedra sniffed, and whispered in a teary voice, "Our babies got married without us." She hiccupped on a little sob before her voice steadied, "But I understand why they didn't come home to get married."

"Yes, they've lost enough years," Bill said. "I don't blame them for not wanting to wait a day longer than it took to get Sky back on his feet, and to the nearest temple."

Ann switched the receiver to her other ear. "Oh Kedra, I hope they took pictures."

"They better have," Kedra said in a threatening tone, and then laughed, "But even if they didn't, at least now we can all finally be at peace."

"Yes, that's exactly how I feel—at peace," Ann said.

"Amen," Bill said heartily.

Epilogue

June, 1946

SKY SLAMMED THE CARGO PLANE DOWN on the runway above the bay, letting the plane speed down it as fast and as far as he dared before applying the brakes. He brought the plane to a screeching halt just outside the hanger with Brannigan/Zenderly Airfreight emblazoned over the wide double doors. Cutting the engine, he jumped down from the plane and hit the tarmac at a dead run.

Takoa met him at the hanger door. "It's about time," he said as Sky tossed the plane's log and cargo ledger into his hands.

"Headwind," Sky said. "There must be a cyclone brewing out there somewhere."

"'Tis the season, and that means I'll be out rescuing Toolowa's newest refugees, but right now you better move it—and fast."

"How long?"

"Over four hours ago."

Sky sucked in a sharp breath. "Where's my scooter?" he asked, just as he spotted it inside the hanger. He dashed for it with no trace of the limp that had plagued him for nearly a year.

Deciding to live permanently on Toolowa had sped his leg's recovery and kept him from the aching pain a winter visit to Salt Lake City had brought on.

Swinging his leg over the motor scooter, he started it up and sped off down the newly paved lane that led through the town square to the hospital.

The scooter had been a necessity at first, one the grateful people of Toolowa had provided for him—as one of their national heroes—so he could get around more easily while he recovered. Now he didn't really need it, or use it much. Most of the time it lived in the hanger, to be used only if he or Takoa were in a hurry or if there was an emergency. It was noisy, and neither of them liked disrupting the tranquilly of the island unless there was an emergency. Sky decided being present for the birth of his baby was definitely an emergency.

Tena met him at the door of the hospital, directing him to Jessie's room. He rushed down the corridor wondering why Tena was working, and thinking she should be in labor too. *She looks like she's ready to pop*, he grinned to himself, opening Jessie's door.

"Finally," Jessie moaned, panting through the last of a contraction. "I was afraid you weren't going to make it in time."

"I got held up by a stiff headwind, besides you weren't supposed to have this baby until next week," he said taking her hand and kissing her.

"This baby, as you well know, has a mind of her own."

It was true. The baby had a habit of coming alive and kicking as soon as Jessie got into bed at night, keeping her from sleeping.

"I hope you're right about the 'her' part. Having a pint sized replica of you would be terrific."

"That's what Kanoa wants too, but how will he feel if his pint sized sister ends up being taller than he is?"

"I think our son is going to top out at a very respectable height, if the way he's growing right now is any indication. Where is he, by the way?"

"Triny is trying to keep him corralled." Jessie groaned as another contraction started. She gripped Sky's hand, beads of perspiration forming on her brow, and together they rode out her pain.

Sky grabbed a towel, mopped the perspiration from her forehead, and tried to distract her. "If Triny's in charge of keeping Kanoa at home, I'm sure we'll be seeing him shortly." He grinned. "I have no doubt he'll escape and weasel his way in here."

Jessie's grip on his hand intensified to painful proportions. "I think this baby is going to come sooner than Paul expects."

"Should I go get him?" Sky asked, alarmed.

"Yes," Jessie said through gritted teeth.

Sky was out the door in a flash and nearly tripped over Kanoa. He managed to side step him before they collided. "You're supposed to be home with Triny," he said sternly.

Kanoa hung his head.

"Well"—Sky lifted his son's chin—"since you're here, you better go in and hold Mama's hand while I get the doctor."

"You mean I can stay?"

"Yes, but don't be surprised if Mama scolds you."

"I don't care, as long as I get to be here when the baby comes."

An anguished moan from the room sent Sky down the corridor and Kanoa through the door.

When Sky returned with Dr. Paul, Tena, and a couple of orderlies, Jessie was in the midst of another hard contraction. Kanoa was mopping her forehead, his face as pained as hers.

Paul put a gentle hand on Kanoa's arm "I think it's time for you to leave," he said.

"Sit down in the hall and wait for me," Sky said, ruffling Kanoa's hair.

Kanoa kissed his mama's cheek and left the room.

Paul checked Jessie and hastily issued orders. "Let's get her on the gurney and to the delivery room—stat, before this baby decides to come while we're on our way." He clapped Sky's back. "Do you want to come and watch the birth or wait with Kanoa?"

"Watch the birth?" Sky asked as the orderlies transferred Jessie onto the gurney and Tena covered her with a blanket.

"Yes," Paul said. "You're welcome to hold Jessie's hand while she delivers or even help with the delivery."

"Here on Toolowa, many fathers choose to be present at the birth of their children," Tena said. "It helps them bond with the baby and support their wives."

Jessie's gasped as another contraction began.

"Honey, I want to be with you for the birth of our baby—if that's all right with you," Sky said, taking her hand and brushing back a long strand of hair that clung to her damp forehead.

Blowing out a breath as the pain eased, Jessie said, "I want you with me."

"Let's go then." Paul waved the orderlies on and they rolled the gurney out the door.

Kanoa jumped up and joined the parade down the corridor. "Is the baby coming?" he asked, running alongside the gurney, his fingers holding tightly to his mama's hand.

"Yes." Jessie squeezed his hand, giving him a flickering smile.

"This is as far as you go, little man," Sky said as they hit the door to the delivery room.

Kanoa squeezed his mama's hand one last time and stopped. "Have me a sister, please!"

Sky ruffled his curly hair and went through the door.

Watching Jessie suffer with the increasingly hard contractions was the most painful thing Sky had ever endured. He held her hand, bathed her brow, and felt more helpless than helpful.

With one last moaning push, Jessie delivered their daughter. As soon as she took her first squawking breath, Sky kissed his wife, while Tena washed, diapered, and wrapped his daughter in a soft blanket.

He took her from Tena, drinking her in. A wispy mop of curly, strawberry blond hair covered her head. She had a little button nose, and her eyes were tightly shut as she continued to squawk.

"She's dazzling"—Sky placed his daughter into the arms of her mother—"just like you, my darling Amazon."

Jessie tisked, gave him the Amazon's spectacular smile, and cooed to their daughter. "She is beautiful, isn't she?"

"Yes." Sky dropped into the bedside chair. He slid his arms around his wife and baby daughter, fell into the emerald eyes that held forever for him, and managed to get out the only words that mattered through his constricted throat. "I love you, Mrs. Brannigan, forever, and ever, and ever."

She replied in a trembling whisper, "And I'll love you for even longer than that."

He kissed her tenderly as their daughter continued to cry.

"Well, you wanted to see her before we named her. So, now that she's here, what's it going to be?" Jessie asked.

"I don't think any of the names we talked about are right for her."

"I agree."

Sky ran his big fingers over the velvet skin of his daughter's arm and held on to her tiny fist. "There's only one name I can think of that will do her justice and describe how I feel about her."

"Jayling," they said in unison, as Kanoa burst through the door.

"Come meet your sister, Jayling," Jessie said.

Kanoa scrambled onto his papa's lap and leaned over his sister, taking hold of her tiny hand. "Hi, Jayling," he said, and kissed her.

Jayling quit crying and opened her big aquamarine eyes.

Her family sighed.

Books by Janelle Clawson

Trilogy: FOR ALL TIME

Part 1 - ABOVE THE CLOUDS
Part 2 - BENEATH THE MOON
Part 3 - THROUGH THE MIST

www.ingramcontent.com/pod-product-compliance
Lightning Source LLC
Chambersburg PA
CBHW022142170626
46807CB00005B/2041